Stanley Swanson – Breed (

This is a work of fiction. All of the characters, organizations and events portrayed in this novel/book are either products of the author's imagination or are used fictitiously.

Stanley Swanson
Breed of a Werewolf

Copyright © 2015 by, S.K. Ballinger

All rights reserved. No part of this book may be reproduced, stored, or transmitted by any means— whether auditory, graphic, mechanical, or electronic— without written permission of both publisher and author. Unauthorized reproduction of any part of this work is illegal and is punishable by law.

Ballinger, S.K.

Stanley Swanson-Breed of a Werewolf, 3rd Edition

ISBN - 9798650939047

Third Edition
(Properly Edited)

S.K. Ballinger

ACKNOWLEDGMENTS

My family first and foremost.

Tawni Rae, Daniel Haynes, Marina O'Brix and the many authors and friends I have.

My father Stephen Ballinger, Grandfather Dewey Fadler and my Grandmother Nina

My children and their patience.
and Amy K.

SPECIAL THANKS

My mother Janet Ballinger. Love you more than you will ever know. Thank you for being who you are and for making me the man I have grown up to be.

Stanley Swanson
Breed of A Werewolf

My journey into the extraordinary began in 1974 in the small town of Stull, KS. Little did I know that this unassuming start would lead me to an eventful career in journalism and eventually, a life-altering encounter with the paranormal.

Working for one of the largest newspaper distributions, the Kansas City Star, I spent my early years immersed in reporting and storytelling. However, my true passion lay in the realm of the supernatural—paranormal existence, sightings, vampires, and werewolves. My name is Kain Edward, and my fascination with mythical creatures traces back to my childhood, fueled by movies that portrayed vampires and werewolves with special powers.

As my career unfolded, I found myself increasingly drawn to the enigma of werewolves. The lack of detailed information on these creatures fueled my curiosity. "Surely there has to be more to werewolves than just being some hideous beast that kills humans at the sight of a full moon?" I often pondered.

My journalistic pursuits took me around the world, interviewing people claiming to have encountered paranormal entities. Despite the numerous stories, my quest for tangible evidence hit dead ends, leading to skepticism and mockery from colleagues. The constant derision, coupled with an unfortunate accident that left me paralyzed from the waist down, eventually led to my early retirement at the age of almost forty.

In the solitude of my home, I returned to my roots, seeking proof of the supernatural. Endless hours were spent in front of my computer, posting inquiries about the existence of werewolves and vampires. The responses were typically brief, leaving me frustrated and despondent. Even the distribution of thousands of business cards worldwide yielded no substantial leads.

Depression and a sense of worthlessness took hold, leading me down a path of addiction to alcohol and cigarettes. The turning point came in 2010, with an unexpected phone call from a young man named Stanley Swanson. He claimed to be a werewolf and offered proof of the existence of supernatural beings.

Though skeptical, the sincerity in Stanley's voice compelled me to meet him in Sacramento, CA. As we conversed for thirty minutes, he shared details that seemed more genuine than any encounter I had experienced before. This marked the beginning of a life-altering chapter.

Stanley Swanson and I delved into discussions that would reshape my perspective on the supernatural. In a long-lost and forgotten personal journal, I chronicled our conversations and the revelations that unfolded, providing a glimpse into a world where myth and reality intersect.

All THAT CAN BE DREAMED OF CAN BECOME REAL

    Kain Edward's anticipation reached a crescendo on the early, cold, and eerie morning he was scheduled to meet Mr. Swanson. The nervous energy surged through him, manifesting in the upper extremities of the only part of his body he could feel. Despite the cold, the excitement was a warm rush that fueled his actions.

    Unable to contain the thrill, Kain rose early, motivated by the knowledge that this day would hold answers to questions that had fueled his passion for the supernatural. Cleaning his house became a meticulous task, driven by the desire to create a welcoming space for the guest he had always dreamed of meeting. As he worked, thoughts of the questions he would pose to Stanley Swanson flooded his mind, adding to the overwhelming anticipation.

    In the solitude of his home, Kain's happiness was palpable, a rare emotion for him in recent times. The prospect of having proof to silence those who had labeled him a freak and dismissed his pursuits as a waste of time filled him with a sense of vindication.

    The financial inability to assist Mr. Swanson on his journey weighed on Kain's mind, but he tried to compensate by making his living space as comfortable as possible. Mixed emotions swirled within him, contemplating the impending arrival of someone claiming to be a werewolf. Questions about Stanley's appearance, judgments, and even the unsettling notion of personal safety played on a loop in Kain's mind.

Noon approached, and with a knock on the door, Kain wheeled himself to the front, overwhelmed with anticipation. Stanley, the supposed werewolf, stood before him— a young twenty-six-year-old who defied Kain's preconceived notions. The shock rendered Kain momentarily speechless as he took in the unexpected reality. Stanley, picking up on Kain's surprise, kindly initiated the conversation, breaking the silence that enveloped the room.

"I presume you are Kain Edward?"

Stanley Swanson, a handsome young man impeccably dressed, exuded a warmth and kindness that quickly dispelled many of the apprehensions Kain had harbored. The meticulously groomed appearance and genuine demeanor of Stanley shifted Kain's perspective, eroding the lingering doubts that had plagued him.

As Kain swung the door fully open, Stanley wasted no time in extending a handshake, his friendly gesture breaking any residual tension. Expressing gratitude for the offer of assistance, Kain wheeled himself, with Stanley gracefully following.

Finding themselves at the front table in the kitchen, the ambiance was chosen for its pleasant view, providing a comfortable setting for discussions that held profound significance. However, Kain couldn't help but notice a curious absence—Stanley had no luggage or bags in tow. This realization sparked a question in Kain's mind about the whereabouts of the much-anticipated 'proof.'

The conversation between them started to unfold, and Kain delicately broached the subject, "Stanley, I've been exploring these topics for quite some time on my own, and I truly appreciate your willingness to share. But, I can't help but wonder, where's the evidence you mentioned? I expected you to have brought something with you."

The curiosity in Kain's voice was palpable, and he eagerly awaited Stanley's response, hoping for clarity on the mysterious proof that had brought them together.

The absence of any tangible evidence for the existence of werewolves weighed on Kain's mind as he couldn't help but express his curiosity. With a respectful tone, he inquired, "Mr. Swanson, if you don't mind me asking, I am assuming this is a short visit as you have brought nothing with you and yet have traveled a long distance?"

Stanley's response was concise but enigmatic, "I travel lightly, Mr. Edward."

Seated at the table, Stanley directly across from Kain, a certain tension lingered in the air. The atmosphere demanded clarification, and Kain, eager for answers, ventured into his second line of questioning.

"Would you like something to drink?" he asked, extending a welcoming gesture to his enigmatic guest.

"I would love to have some ice water," Stanley replied with a warm smile, a stark contrast to the mysteries that surrounded him.

As Kain prepared the drinks, he couldn't shake the feeling that the real revelations of the day were yet to unfold, and the enigma of Stanley Swanson persisted.

Relief swept over Kain as he observed Stanley's demeanor at the table. The young man appeared entirely human, a stark contrast to the fantastical claims he had made on the phone about being a werewolf. Despite the apparent normalcy, Kain found himself standing firm in skepticism. It was challenging to reconcile the mundane presence before him with the extraordinary narrative he had been presented.

Inwardly, Kain grappled with conflicting thoughts. A part of him resisted accepting Stanley's claims, chalking it up to stubbornness ingrained from past experiences. However, the financial commitment made by Stanley to travel for this meeting nudged Kain to give him the benefit of the doubt. Perhaps there was more to the story, and Kain felt compelled to navigate the conversation cautiously, treading the fine line between skepticism and openness. The meeting had just begun, and the mysteries surrounding Stanley Swanson remained intact, waiting to unravel.

Stanley's courteous offer to fetch his own glass of ice water and even prepare a drink for Kain added a layer of normalcy to the situation.

"If you do not mind, Mr. Edward, I will be happy to grab my own glass of ice water. Just tell me where you keep your cups at. If you would like, while I am up, I will gladly fix you a drink as well."

Kain, amused by Stanley's proactive demeanor, responded with a large smirk. "I am fine, thanks, and the cups you can find in the cabinet on your right.

The easy exchange between them hinted at a camaraderie that was starting to develop, but the underlying questions about Stanley's claims still lingered, casting a subtle tension over their interaction. As Stanley rose to fetch his own drink, Kain couldn't help but wonder if this seemingly mundane action would lead to the unveiling of the proof he had been desperately seeking.

As Kain observed Stanley gracefully navigating his kitchen, an air of admiration overcame him. The simple act of Stanley grabbing a cup and walking to the faucet of Kain's old ceramic kitchen sink became a moment of fascination. Stanley moved with a classy style that caught Kain's attention – his footsteps light against the hardwood floor, his suit impeccably ironed, and an odd yet captivating touch as he moved his right hand from the base of the faucet to the tip, observing the water flow into his cup.

Every detail Kain witnessed only served to reinforce the notion that Stanley was something special, even if not the werewolf he claimed to be. The walk back to the table, cup of water in hand, was as inspiring as the initial approach. The ordinary act of fetching water took on a certain elegance, leaving Kain intrigued by the aura of uniqueness that surrounded Stanley Swanson. The meeting was becoming more than just a discussion about the supernatural; it was a study of the enigmatic character seated before him.

As Stanley settled back into his seat, cup of water in hand, he posed a question that cut through the lingering tension, "So, Mr. Edward, what is it that you wish to know about silly vampires and werewolves or even aliens for that matter?"

A warmth spread across Kain as he caught Stanley's gaze, appreciating the informal shift in address.

"Please, call me Kain," he responded, feeling a sense of camaraderie building between them.

The loaded question hung in the air, inviting Kain to articulate the deep-seated inquiries that had fueled his decades-long pursuit of the supernatural. The table was set for a conversation that promised to unravel the mysteries and perhaps provide the answers that had eluded Kain for so long.

As Kain settled into the conversation, explaining his long-standing fascination with vampires, werewolves, and aliens, he must have inadvertently chosen the wrong words in his response. The atmosphere shifted, and a subtle tension replaced the camaraderie that had begun to build between them. Stanley's expression changed ever so slightly, and the room seemed to hold its breath as if awaiting a response that could either bridge the gap or deepen the divide. The unintended misstep hung in the air, leaving the trajectory of their discussion momentarily uncertain.

In an attempt to navigate the unexpected shift in the atmosphere, Kain swiftly adjusted his words, seeking common ground.

"Well, vampires and werewolves seem so intriguing, and they also are of the same nature in some ways to start with."

The words flowed with an air of diplomacy, an effort to course-correct the conversation and maintain a sense of shared curiosity.

Stanley's reaction remained enigmatic, leaving Kain to wonder if the unintentional misstep had been successfully smoothed over or if it lingered beneath the surface, awaiting further clarification. The delicate dance of conversation continued, with the mysteries of vampires and werewolves at the forefront of their discussion, waiting to be unraveled.

Stanley Swanson – Breed of a Werewolf

Stanley's immediate reaction was unexpected as he swiftly stood up, leaning in towards Kain at the midpoint of the table. The atmosphere crackled with tension as Stanley's right hand lay flat on the surface, palm down. The sudden shift in proximity and the assertive gesture heightened the intensity of the moment, leaving Kain momentarily taken aback.

The enigmatic nature of Stanley Swanson was brought to the forefront, leaving Kain to decipher the significance of this abrupt change in demeanor. The table, once a symbol of shared exploration, now seemed to mark a line between them, emphasizing the complexities of the conversation they were delving into. The room held its breath, awaiting the next move in this unfolding interaction between a journalist seeking answers and a young man claiming to be something beyond the ordinary.

Stanley's words, delivered with an intensity that cut through the air, shattered the fragile equilibrium of the conversation.

"You know nothing of vampires or werewolves, Kain!"

The statement, laden with an air of authority, echoed in the room, emphasizing a divide between Kain's knowledge and Stanley's claimed understanding of these mythical creatures.

Kain, stunned by the sudden assertiveness, felt a mix of confusion and curiosity. The atmosphere had shifted yet again, and the mysteries surrounding Stanley Swanson deepened. The encounter had evolved into more than a mere discussion about the supernatural; it had become a confrontation of beliefs, challenging Kain's convictions and laying bare the complexities of the enigma before him. The table that had once symbolized shared exploration now stood as a metaphorical battleground where the clash between skepticism and extraordinary claims played out.

Stung by the unexpected anger in Stanley's words, Kain quickly recognized the need to diffuse the tension that had gripped the room.

"I apologize if I misspoke or if I've offended you, Stanley. I'm genuinely here to learn and understand," Kain offered, attempting to mend the fracture that had emerged in their conversation.

Stanley, though visibly upset, seemed to accept the apology with a subtle nod. The air remained charged, but as Kain awaited Stanley's next words, the young man took a deep breath and continued, revealing a layer of vulnerability beneath the initial anger. The meeting had veered into uncharted territory, delving into the complexities of belief and disbelief, challenging both the skeptic and the one who claimed to embody the supernatural.

Stanley's words cut through the charged atmosphere, his voice carrying a mix of frustration and a sense of revelation.

"You think that werewolves and vampires share certain characteristics or that we are somewhat alike?" he queried, his tone probing as he continued.

"You humans are created with a mind of fantasy, folklore, and lust. You all read, watch movies, and shows in the desire to believe we are what other humans merely write about. This is all your kind knows of us. Let me make it clear to you, Kain, by stating that werewolves were or are nothing more to this day but slaves to vampires!"

Stanley Swanson – Breed of a Werewolf

The revelation hung in the air, a stark departure from the romanticized notions often associated with these mythical beings. Kain, grappling with the sudden shift in perspective, listened intently as Stanley sought to dismantle the fantastical facade that surrounded vampires and werewolves. The encounter had transcended the boundaries of a mere discussion, delving into the complexities of myth, reality, and the enigmatic nature of Stanley Swanson.

Stanley's clenched fist on the table revealed the depth of his emotional response to the assumptions Kain had unwittingly made. Recognizing the gravity of his error, Kain offered another apology, explaining that his beliefs were based on misconceptions. It was in that moment, as the tension lingered in the air, that Kain began to consider the possibility that Stanley might indeed be revealing a truth he had never before contemplated.

Acknowledging his mistake, Kain implored Stanley to elaborate further, eager to understand the perspective that had elicited such a visceral reaction. Still standing, Stanley's fist relaxed, but his gaze remained intense as he stared deep into Kain's eyes. In this charged atmosphere, Stanley posed a serious question, one that demanded Kain's attention and consideration. The meeting had evolved into a crucible of conflicting beliefs, challenging Kain's worldview and prompting him to reevaluate everything he thought he knew about vampires, werewolves, and the enigmatic man standing before him.

"Do you, Mr. Edward, truly believe in what you write about or hope to believe exist?" Stanley's question hung in the air, carrying a weight that extended beyond the immediate context of their conversation.

"I do firmly," Kain responded, a note of conviction in his voice.

The exchange marked a pivotal moment in their discussion, as Kain openly affirmed his belief in the supernatural. The clash of perspectives — one grounded in skepticism and journalistic inquiry, the other rooted in a claimed existence beyond the ordinary — intensified. The unfolding dialogue between Kain and Stanley delved into the complexities of belief, challenging each other's convictions in a collision of worlds where the supernatural and the mundane intersected. The meeting had become a crucible for the clash between the skeptic and the one who claimed to embody the very mysteries Kain had spent a lifetime exploring.

Stanley, in response to Kain's affirmation of belief, sat back down with a soft "Good." Sensing a need to ease the tension, Kain made a somewhat joking remark, suggesting that maybe Stanley should have been a vampire, given the assumptions about their charming and decent-looking nature. Aware of the frustration caused by his previous comparisons, Kain attempted to inject a light-hearted tone into the conversation.

To his surprise, Stanley burst into laughter at the comment. As the laughter subsided, Stanley, with a hint of irony, declared that vampires are more worthless and cruel to the human race than any werewolf could ever be or imagine to be. Despite the serious undertones of the statement, Kain, still in a joking manner, responded in kind, maintaining the attempt to lighten the mood amid the complexities of their discussion. The dynamics between the two had once again shifted, showcasing the intricate dance between serious revelations and moments of levity in their exploration of the supernatural.

Stanley Swanson – Breed of a Werewolf

Kain, following the banter, quipped back with a playful tone, "So you must be the werewolf then, as you suggested?" The exchange, though lighthearted, underscored the lingering ambiguity and complexity surrounding Stanley's claims.

The interplay between seriousness and humor persisted, creating a unique atmosphere where the supernatural and mundane coexisted in a delicate balance. The meeting, initially fraught with tension, now exhibited moments of levity, revealing the multifaceted nature of the encounter between a skeptic seeking answers and a man claiming to embody the mysteries of werewolves and vampires.

Stanley's sudden quietness and the return of that intense stare conveyed a seriousness that brought a hush over the room. He spoke with a sincerity that cut through the light banter, the atmosphere shifting once again. In this charged moment, Stanley addressed Kain with a genuine gesture, leaving the room steeped in anticipation for the next revelation or insight into the mysteries that surrounded the enigmatic man before him. The meeting had ventured into unpredictable territory, navigating the intricate dance between belief and skepticism, truth and fiction, and the elusive nature of the supernatural.

Stanley's question hung in the air, a profound inquiry that seemed to suspend time in the room.

"What if I really were Kain?" he asked, his words carrying a weight that transcended the playful banter.

The atmosphere became charged with an air of mystery, and Kain found himself caught in the gravity of Stanley's words.

The question, laden with possibilities and implications,

opened a door to a realm of uncertainty. In that moment, the meeting transcended its origins as a discussion about the supernatural, delving into the realm of identity, truth, and the enigmatic nature of the man who claimed to be Stanley Swanson. The line between reality and the fantastical blurred, leaving Kain to grapple with the ambiguity of the situation and the potential revelations that lay ahead.

The weight of Stanley's question, with its potential implications, seemed to momentarily shatter the serious atmosphere. Finding it hard to believe, Kain started to laugh in an almost hysterical way, a mixture of surprise and incredulity. With a light chuckle, he replied to Stanley, the tension momentarily diffused by the unexpected turn in the conversation.

The room echoed with a complex symphony of emotions — laughter overlaying a lingering sense of curiosity and uncertainty. The encounter between Kain and Stanley had evolved into a surreal dance, where reality and the supernatural intertwined, leaving both men on the precipice of discovery or revelation. The meeting, initially rooted in the pursuit of answers, had taken on a life of its own, challenging preconceptions and plunging the participants into uncharted territory.

Kain, still caught in a moment of laughter, managed to interject with a humorous response, "Well, I hope if you were, that you would spare my life."

The levity continued, with Kain attempting to navigate the fine line between skepticism and amusement.

However, Stanley, unmoved by the humor, responded with a statement that cut through the laughter, bringing a sudden gravity to the room.

Stanley Swanson – Breed of a Werewolf

"I am a werewolf," he declared.

The revelation, devoid of any trace of jest, left Kain grappling with the unexpected truth that had just been unveiled. The room hung in a suspended moment, the weight of Stanley's assertion settling over the encounter, marking a significant turning point in the surreal meeting between a journalist seeking answers and a man who claimed to embody the supernatural.

Kain, caught in a mix of disbelief and amusement, began to laugh even harder. Despite the seriousness in Stanley's tone, Kain, with a sincerity fueled by curiosity, asked, "Are you serious? A werewolf?"

The laughter persisted, but now tinged with a sense of incredulity as Kain navigated the delicate balance between skepticism and the uncharted territory of the supernatural that seemed to unfold before him. The meeting, already a complex dance of belief and disbelief, took yet another unexpected turn as the mysteries surrounding Stanley Swanson deepened.

Kain, amidst his laughter, managed to compose himself and asked, "Is this the proof you are bringing to the table, Stanley?" The question hung in the air, a pivotal moment where the line between reality and the fantastical blurred.

A calm silence enveloped the room for only a brief moment before Stanley spoke, his voice carrying a forceful weight.

"I did not come here to meet with hopes of trying to amuse you, Kain; I came here to share with you what I know. Is that not what you have wanted?"

The words resonated in the room, bringing a solemnity that cut through the levity that had characterized their earlier banter. The meeting, now steeped in a complex interplay of belief, sincerity, and revelation, had reached a crossroads where the pursuit of truth took center stage.

The intensity of the moment lingered as Stanley, now serious, addressed Kain with a solemnity that shifted the tone of their meeting. Joking seemed inappropriate in the face of Stanley's earnestness, and Kain felt the weight of the conversation pressing down on them.

Suddenly, Stanley's phone rang, interrupting the gravity of the moment. He walked away from the table, his back turned to Kain as he engaged in a brief, private conversation. Kain, left in the room, couldn't discern the content of the call but respected Stanley's need for privacy.

Upon his return, Stanley apologized, explaining that it was his wife who had called. Suppressing any urge to laugh, Kain responded with a hint of humor, attempting to lighten the atmosphere, "I hope it wasn't about me being lunch for a werewolf." The attempt at levity masked the lingering intensity, as both men navigated the complexities of the surreal encounter that had unfolded in Kain's home.

Kain, trying to maintain a balance between humor and seriousness, asked, "So, werewolves get married as well?" The question, though lighthearted, carried an undercurrent of curiosity about the personal life of the man claiming to be a werewolf.

Stanley, while still embodying an air of seriousness, responded with a subtle smile, "Yes, we do, just like anyone else." The revelation added another layer to the complexities of

Stanley Swanson – Breed of a Werewolf

Stanley's existence, intertwining the supernatural with the mundane. The encounter, now a tapestry of belief, revelation, and unexpected humor, continued to unfold in unexpected ways, revealing the enigmatic nature of the man who claimed to be Stanley Swanson.

Stanley, acknowledging the lightheartedness in Kain's question and perhaps recognizing the humanity in the moment, responded with a subtle smile. It seemed as if he took a moment to reflect on the fact that he was conversing with a mortal, a human who was reacting to the existence of creatures from the realm of night and folklore. Despite his claimed identity as a werewolf, Stanley embraced the conversation with a certain openness.

He furthered the dialogue, delving into the intricacies of his existence, "Yes, we do, just like anyone else. The supernatural doesn't erase the everyday aspects of life." The statement held a paradoxical truth, blending the extraordinary with the ordinary in a way that only deepened the mystery surrounding Stanley Swanson. The encounter, a dance between the supernatural and the mundane, continued to unfold, leaving both men to navigate the uncharted waters of belief and understanding.

Stanley, perhaps recognizing the potential isolation that Kain's pursuit of the supernatural might have led to, asked in a more introspective tone, "Do you like to be lonely, Mr. Edward?" The question delved into the personal, inviting Kain to reflect on the impact of his chosen path and the potential isolation that might have accompanied his relentless quest for the mysterious and the supernatural. The encounter, now exploring not just the realms of folklore and creatures of the night but also the inner dimensions of the individuals involved, continued to evolve into a deeply introspective exploration."

S.K. Ballinger

Kain, reflecting on his own life, admitted to the loneliness that had accompanied him for many years. He shared with Stanley that he had never married or had children, relying solely on a disability check that served as a stark reminder of his existence. The vulnerability in Kain's response added a layer of depth to the conversation, emphasizing the personal sacrifices and challenges he had faced.

Sensing the weight of the moment, Stanley, in an attempt to lighten Kain's mood, continued the conversation. The encounter, now touching on the personal struggles and triumphs of both men, became a shared exploration of the human experience, transcending the boundaries of the supernatural and the ordinary.

Stanley, in a surprising and candid revelation, shared, "My wife and I also have two children, which I know, Mr. Edward, would suggest that we also have sex." The statement, though straightforward, carried an element of humor, as Stanley seemed to acknowledge the natural assumptions and reactions that might arise when discussing the personal aspects of his life as a werewolf.

The revelation not only added a touch of levity to the conversation but also humanized Stanley in a way that transcended the supernatural. The encounter, now weaving through the threads of belief, personal experiences, and shared moments of humor, continued to evolve into a unique exploration of the intersection between the extraordinary and the mundane in the lives of those who claimed to embody the mysteries of folklore.

It seems there might be a bit of humor in Stanley's response before he finished with a slight smile, stating to Kain,

Stanley Swanson – Breed of a Werewolf

"Well, we do try to keep things interesting." The remark, delivered in a jokingly manner, added another layer of complexity to the encounter, balancing the seriousness of the supernatural with the shared experiences of everyday life.

The subtle smile and the playful tone suggested a camaraderie between the two men, bridging the gap between their differing perspectives. The meeting, now a tapestry of belief, revelation, humor, and shared experiences, continued to unfold, offering glimpses into the multifaceted nature of the encounter between a journalist seeking answers and a man who claimed to embody the supernatural.

Stanley, with a blend of candidness and humor, addressed the unspoken assumptions that might arise from his earlier revelation. He clarified, "I would assume that when I said sex, that you immediately had pictured the sexual position of doggy style perhaps. To let you know, we do make love the same as you humans do. We are not dogs, just to remind you of that, Kain."

The statement, delivered with a touch of playfulness, sought to dispel any preconceived notions and emphasize the shared humanity in the midst of discussions about werewolves and the supernatural. The encounter, now navigating through the intricacies of belief, personal experiences, and humorous moments, continued to challenge expectations and offer a nuanced exploration of the intersection between the extraordinary and the ordinary in the lives of those who claimed to embody the mysteries of folklore.

Feeling a sense of comfort in Stanley's tone and mannerisms, Kain opened up about the challenge of believing such extraordinary claims. He expressed to Stanley that accepting this information as true would take time to digest, especially without any tangible proof being presented. Despite Kain's desire for confirmation, Stanley remained steadfast in his decision not to reveal any conclusive evidence.

Recognizing that he might not receive the proof he sought, Kain decided to shift the focus back to his original purpose – asking more questions for his journal. The encounter, now a delicate dance between skepticism, belief, and the pursuit of knowledge, evolved into an ongoing exploration of the mysteries surrounding werewolves, vampires, and the enigmatic Stanley Swanson.

Choosing to shift the focus to a more personal note, Kain asked, "So, how did you and your wife meet?" The question aimed to unravel the human side of Stanley's life, providing an opportunity for him to share a story that transcended the supernatural and delved into the realm of personal connections.

As Stanley began to unfold the narrative of his relationship, the encounter continued its nuanced exploration, weaving through the tapestry of belief, personal experiences, and the shared aspects of human connection. The meeting, initially grounded in the pursuit of proof and revelations, had transformed into a multifaceted exchange, revealing the intricacies of the lives of those who claimed to be touched by the supernatural.

Stanley, prompted by Kain's question about how he and his wife met, flashed a big smile — the first genuine one Kain had observed throughout their initial meeting. This smile, radiant and genuine, conveyed the depth of Stanley's affection for his wife. The shift in demeanor offered a glimpse into the emotional connection that transcended the supernatural aspects of Stanley's life.

Stanley Swanson – Breed of a Werewolf

The encounter, now touching on matters of the heart and personal relationships, provided a rare moment of warmth and authenticity. The shared understanding of love and connection became a common ground that connected the two men, fostering a unique bond in the midst of their exploration of the mysterious and otherworldly.

Stanley's revelation carried a weight of time and history. He shared, "We met sixty-two years ago in a little cottage just outside of London." The statement painted a vivid picture of a long and enduring love story that spanned decades.

The revelation added a layer of depth to Stanley's character, transcending the immediate encounter and offering a glimpse into the richness of his personal history. The meeting, now an intricate tapestry of belief, personal experiences, and shared moments, continued to evolve into a rare exploration of the human side of those who claimed to embody the mysteries of folklore.

Kain, recalling the iconic American Werewolf in London, chuckled lightly as he connected Stanley's real-life meeting with his wife to the familiar scenes depicted in movies.

"I see, the American Werewolf in London, I have watched that numerous times over," he remarked, finding a humorous link between Stanley's story and the cinematic portrayals of werewolves.

To Kain's surprise, Stanley also laughed, sharing in the enjoyment of the very same movie that had captured the imaginations of many. The shared laughter, referencing a piece of popular culture, added a touch of camaraderie to the encounter, bridging the gap between the supernatural and the familiar narratives that permeated everyday life. The meeting, now a blend of belief, shared experiences, and humor, continued to unfold in unexpected and enriching ways.

Stanley, while acknowledging his enjoyment of American Werewolf in London, made a distinction, noting, "I have watched that a few times, but that really does not portray anything about our breed." His statement emphasized the divergence between cinematic portrayals of werewolves and the reality, as per Stanley's claims.

The clarification added a layer of authenticity to Stanley's narrative, highlighting the disparity between fictional representations and the nuanced reality of his own experiences. The encounter, now delving into the discrepancies between folklore and personal accounts, continued to unravel the intricacies of the supernatural as perceived by one who claimed to be intimately connected with it.

Feeling a growing sense of camaraderie between them, Kain couldn't help but address the apparent discrepancy in Stanley's age. With a mix of curiosity and genuine interest, Kain questioned the incongruity of being twenty-six years old while claiming to have met his wife sixty-two years ago.

Stanley, perhaps anticipating the question, began to unravel the complexities of his existence. He explained, in great detail, the unique aspects of a werewolf's life, emphasizing the marked differences from the immortal existence often attributed to vampires. The conversation, now delving into the intricacies of the supernatural, became an opportunity for Kain to gain further insights into the mysteries surrounding Stanley's claimed identity and experiences.

Stanley Swanson – Breed of a Werewolf

Stanley's revelation about the ability of werewolves to choose their apparent age shed light on the intricacies of their existence. He explained, "This is a significant difference in our respective beings, Kain. When you are born a werewolf, you essentially choose what age to slow down your growth and age at. I assure you it is not as good a time as one might think. We do not have a fountain of youth or a higher being which you humans call your GOD; we only have one another."

Kain, intrigued by this unique aspect of werewolf life, asked, "So if you get to choose your own age, then why did you choose twenty-six years old?"

With a large smile on Stanley's face, he answered with ease, "Simple. I am old enough to know a lot about this world we live in, old enough to get married, have kids, and so much more. Know that we still age, but it is taken to a factor level that I will not turn another year older or show any signs of age for twenty-six more years, which is the age I chose. We are not what you humans refer to as immortal just as the Drakulis may appear to be; they too are not. Both of our respective beings can be killed."

Stanley's explanation delved into the nuanced aspects of werewolf life, challenging preconceived notions and adding depth to the understanding of his claimed identity. The encounter, now exploring the intricacies of supernatural existence, continued to unravel the mysteries surrounding Stanley and the world of werewolves.

Kain, intrigued by the concept of choosing one's apparent age as a werewolf, sought further clarification.

"So... the age you chose is the next year of your life, which would mean if you would have opted to stay a young child of eleven years old, then you would not age again for another eleven years, is that correct?"

Stanley, perhaps accustomed to explaining this unique aspect of werewolf life, responded with a patient explanation. He clarified, "That's correct. The age we choose determines the span of years before we age again. If I had chosen to remain eleven years old, then I wouldn't show any signs of aging for another eleven years. It's a choice that each werewolf makes, taking into consideration the experiences and knowledge they wish to accumulate during that particular age span."

The conversation, now navigating the intricacies of werewolf existence, provided Kain with a deeper understanding of the choices and considerations involved in the unique aging process of Stanley and his kind. The encounter, enriched with these revelations, continued to weave through the mysteries and complexities of the supernatural.

Stanley, continuing to unravel the complexities of werewolf existence, added a crucial detail. He explained, "Exactly, Kain, except for one bit of information you should learn or write down if you wish. That would be that we, our breed of werewolves that are born into, are not mature enough to make such decisions until age twelve. Why anyone would want to stay that age is beyond me, as I know I sure as hell would not. Some choose to do so at the age of twelve or later because they simply do not wish to live longer and have a better connection of sorts, a comfort level if you will."

As Kain delved deeper into this supernatural realm, he couldn't help but express the complexity of the information.

"So what of your wife of sixty-two years ago? What was

Stanley Swanson – Breed of a Werewolf

she like or what was her age?"

Stanley, always smiling when speaking of Julie, responded, "She, which her name is Julie, was young and beautiful at twenty-three years of age when we married."

Feeling the weight of the intricacies unfolding, Kain remarked, "This is so complicated, Mr. Swanson."

"Please call me Stanley; we are beyond calling one another by our last names," Stanley insisted, making the conversation more personal.

Stanley's ease in conversation and Kain's growing intrigue led to more questions. Kain inquired, "So did your wife know you were a werewolf, or was she already a werewolf; how did all that work out?"

"She was not a werewolf; she chose to be a werewolf. And yes, if I had not saved her from harm, she would have never known me to be the breed I am to this day."

The unfolding narrative, now intertwining personal choices, relationships, and the supernatural, painted a picture of Stanley's life that transcended the boundaries of mere folklore. The encounter, enriched with personal anecdotes and shared stories, continued its journey into the mysteries surrounding werewolves and the enigmatic Stanley Swanson.

As the conversation deepened, Kain, determined to capture every detail of Stanley's narrative, continued to ask a barrage of questions. Balancing the delicate dance of skepticism and belief, Kain was meticulous in piecing together the intricate details of Stanley's life as a werewolf. The encounter had evolved into a shared exploration, where Kain sought to unravel the mysteries of the supernatural, armed with the firsthand account of someone who claimed to be intimately connected with it.

In these moments of inquiry and revelation, the encounter became a tapestry of belief, shared experiences, and the insatiable quest for understanding. Kain, once a journalist chasing tales of vampires and werewolves, now found himself in the midst of a firsthand account that blurred the lines between fiction and reality. The unfolding narrative, rich with personal anecdotes and supernatural revelations, continued to captivate Kain's imagination and challenge the boundaries of what he thought possible.

"So you did not tell her you were a werewolf?" Kain inquired, seeking to understand the dynamics of Stanley's revelation to his wife.

"No," Stanley replied, and his once happy smile faded away. There was a subtle shift in the atmosphere, hinting at a more serious turn in the conversation.

"Would you like me to show you something, Kain?" Stanley proposed, prompting a surge of anticipation in Kain.

This could be the moment where he would witness undeniable proof or, perhaps, even witness Stanley transform into a werewolf. The prospect intrigued Kain, and the conversation had reached a point where tangible evidence was eagerly awaited.

"Is this the part where you turn into your other self or do you have to wait for the full moon?" Kain playfully added, a smile on his face.

Stanley Swanson – Breed of a Werewolf

Stanley, finding humor in Kain's remark, laughed while taking a drink of the water Kain had offered. Leaning inward toward the table, Stanley prepared for what might be a pivotal moment in the encounter, leaving Kain on the edge of anticipation and curiosity.

"The full moon you all have grown up to believe changes my breed is merely a myth. We can turn at any time we wish to. The full moon is when we try to protect our young from harm, as they can change easily by the glow, and it is a good time for us to hunt. It can, for the young or newly transitioned, seem as though they may not have any control at times. How that myth became, I, myself would love to know. The full moon provides much light, and you should know, Kain, that we like to keep as hidden from your kind... humans. It is rare for us to be out late on a full moon. So your moon theory that most believe in is actually opposite from the stories," Stanley explained, demystifying the common belief about werewolves transforming during a full moon.

Kain, still intrigued by Stanley's revelations, continued to press for the proof he had hoped for.

"Interesting, then why will you not show me that you are a werewolf? You seem to have so much knowledge, and I want to believe you, Stanley, but you have to know that I have been guided to false hopes for so long."

Stanley, placing both hands together into a fist on the table, reiterated, "That is not what I came here for, as I mentioned earlier, Kain. I am here to share with you insight, explain to you of my breed, and let you be aware that we are not hideous monsters that change at the mere sight of moonlight and ravage towns while we kill humans. There is so much you need to know, and then perhaps I will show you myself in what it is you have longed to see."

The unfolding narrative, now touching on the dispelling of myths and the desire for genuine understanding, continued to draw Kain into the enigmatic world that Stanley claimed to belong to. The encounter, rich with revelations and unanswered questions, hung in the balance between skepticism and the tantalizing promise of a deeper truth.

Realizing that persuading Stanley to reveal his werewolf form might be an uphill battle, Kain decided to inject some humor into the situation.

"So you can show me yourself without being in person?" Kain chuckled lightly, trying to lighten the mood.

After a brief laugh, Stanley stood up from his seat. His once resting hands, now interlocked, relaxed with his palms placed down on the table, mirroring his earlier gesture.

"We have unique abilities like that of what most vampires can do, though slightly different, which is to seduce the mind of individuals. While a Drakulis can see the future, the breed of werewolves can see the past and can do so with humans as well," Stanley revealed, unveiling another layer of the mysterious capabilities of his kind.

The encounter, now navigating between humor and revelations, painted a portrait of supernatural intricacies that challenged Kain's preconceived notions. As Stanley continued to share the unique attributes of werewolves, the conversation swirled around the complexities of their existence, leaving Kain in a state of both wonder and skepticism.

Stanley Swanson – Breed of a Werewolf

It took everything in Kain's power to suppress the frustration bubbling within him. The fantastical claims Stanley made, especially about the ability to see the past and manipulate minds, seemed to collide with Kain's understanding of reality. The line between what he had longed to believe and the skepticism bred by a lifetime of disappointment was becoming increasingly blurry.

Expressing his growing unease, Kain told Stanley that he had heard enough of these seemingly implausible tales. The concept of vampires possessing the ability to glimpse the future or manipulate minds to traverse time was pushing the boundaries of Kain's willingness to suspend disbelief. The realization that he might be falling into a narrative spun for the sake of amusement or some obscure motive began to weigh heavily on Kain's mind.

As Stanley continued to delve into the supernatural attributes of his kind, Kain grappled with the internal conflict between the desire to believe and the ever-present specter of doubt. Was Stanley genuinely sharing the truth, or was this an elaborate charade meant to exploit the curiosity of a disabled man who had been the subject of mockery? The tangled web of questions and uncertainty persisted, and Kain found himself caught in the crossroads of belief and skepticism.

"Interesting, Stanley, so if you wanted to then, you are telling me that you can take me to certain times of your life then?" Kain posed the question, hoping for a response that would provide the evidence he sought, even without witnessing Stanley transform into a werewolf.

Stanley's reply held the promise of the proof Kain had been yearning for.

"Yes, not only certain parts of my life, but at any moment of my life as long as I was born or alive during that time."

Kain found it challenging to accept such a remarkable claim. The notion of being able to witness any moment of someone's life seemed implausible, even for someone with an affinity for the supernatural. Deep in thought and somewhat skeptical, Kain struggled to reconcile the fantastical tales he was being told with the realities of his own experiences.

"Just let me show you something to prove I am not just making this all up, Kain," Stanley proposed, sensing Kain's skepticism.

"Show me what then?" Kain responded, his curiosity piqued, yet guarded against the possibility of further disappointment.

The moment held the potential to either solidify the extraordinary claims or cast them further into the realm of skepticism.

Kain, captivated by the unfolding events, found himself unable to contain his intrigue with Mr. Swanson. As Stanley stood up from his chair with a certain majestic posture, he requested Kain's cooperation in a peculiar demonstration. Stanley asked if he could move to the other side of the table, emphasizing that he wouldn't need to get too close. Intrigued but cautious, Kain made room for Stanley to navigate around the table.

Once in position, Stanley made a simple yet enigmatic request – for Kain to look into his eyes. Stanley's eyes, at first glance, appeared no different from Kain's own reflection in the mirror. However, as Kain fixated on Stanley's gaze, he noticed an unusual phenomenon unfolding around him. The room seemed to darken, the natural light fading away, leaving an eerie gloom. The window, which moments ago revealed a lack of external light, now contributed to the illusion that the surroundings had succumbed to almost complete darkness.

Emotions and questions flooded Kain's mind as he sat there, silently absorbing the mysterious experience. The room had transformed, and Kain couldn't quite comprehend what was happening. The atmosphere hung heavy with an otherworldly aura, leaving him in a state of both wonder and confusion.

Suddenly, with a snap of Stanley's fingers, Kain felt as though he had been abruptly awakened from a deep slumber. The room reverted to its original state, as if the strange occurrence had never transpired. Kain, now wide awake, couldn't contain his inquiries. He questioned Stanley about the peculiar event, expressing his suspicion that he might have been hypnotized or subjected to some form of manipulation. The air was thick with curiosity and uncertainty, and Kain sought answers to unravel the mystery that had just unfolded before his eyes.

""I merely took you to a moment in my life, Kain. Did you not enjoy the experience?" Stanley chuckled, seemingly amused by Kain's reaction to the unusual demonstration.

Struggling to maintain his composure, Kain conveyed his earnest desire to be taken seriously, emphasizing the disappointment he had endured from past letdowns. He probed Stanley about the peculiar trick he had just performed, seeking an explanation for the unexplained phenomenon.

"You only want to show me but never tell me how you did it?" Kain inquired, his skepticism still lingering.

With a chuckle, Stanley attempted to shed light on the inexplicable event. "It is just one of our abilities, Mr. Edward. I only wanted you to see that there is so much you do not know about the real world of our kind."

Feeling a sense of frustration that this encounter might be following the familiar pattern of unfulfilled promises, Kain started to sense a dead end. Sensing Kain's mood shift, Stanley swiftly redirected the conversation, introducing a lighter topic.

"Tell me, Kain, have you ever been to New Orleans?" he asked, catching Kain off guard.

Expressing his limited travel experiences, Kain admitted to never leaving his home state of California, prompting him to question Stanley's sudden interest in New Orleans.

"I would like to take you there," Stanley proposed, injecting a new layer of intrigue into their conversation.

Kain was utterly astonished as Stanley clarified that he didn't mean turning him into a werewolf but wanted to give him an unforgettable experience in the French Quarter of New Orleans. Excitement surged through Kain as the prospect of visiting the enchanting city had always been a dream, one he had only explored through readings and images.

However, Stanley had more surprises in store. He explained that he would take Kain to the French Quarter when he was twenty-six years old. Bursting into laughter, Kain playfully countered, claiming he was no longer young, and those times had passed.

With a warm smile, Stanley gently revealed, "That's just

one of my abilities, Kain. I, too, will be twenty-six again." The revelations continued to unfold, and as their conversation progressed, Kain found himself growing more at ease, although a certain level of skepticism lingered regarding Stanley's true purpose in being there.

Stanley's revelation left Kain in another fit of laughter, thinking it was another facet of their peculiar conversation. Yet, Stanley was serious and insisted that he would show Kain everything about his kind, on the condition that Kain would continue writing and sharing the information. It felt like a somewhat forced agreement, leaving Kain uncertain about the extent of his commitment.

Expressing his reservations, Kain questioned, "I do not know what all you want me to write about as you have given me much detail about you and your kind and vampires as well. What is left?"

Stanley, with a mysterious smile, assured Kain that there was much more to unveil. He explained that the world of werewolves and vampires was intricate, with secrets and complexities yet to be explored. Intrigued and cautiously optimistic, Kain agreed to continue documenting their encounters and the revelations Stanley promised to share. The journey into the supernatural continued, and Kain found himself on the brink of discoveries that surpassed the realm of his wildest imagination.

Kain, still processing the unexpected turn of events, nodded in agreement. The offer to explore the realms of the supernatural was enticing, and the chance to document his experiences further fueled his curiosity. Shaking Stanley's hand firmly, Kain responded, "I suppose if you're willing to show me the extraordinary, I'll do my best to capture it in words. But why me? Why reveal all this to a simple writer?"

    Stanley, with a cryptic yet reassuring expression, replied, "Your curiosity, Kain, your persistent pursuit of the unknown. We've been watching you for a while. You are unique, and your words have the power to shape perceptions. It's time for the world to know what lies beyond their understanding."

    The gravity of Stanley's words sunk in as Kain realized the magnitude of what he was getting himself into. The prospect of unraveling the mysteries of the supernatural world and sharing them with the public was both thrilling and daunting. It marked the beginning of a partnership that would transcend the boundaries of reality, leading Kain into uncharted territories of the extraordinary.

    As Stanley bid farewell, Kain couldn't help but feel a mix of excitement and trepidation about the journey that lay ahead. As he watched Stanley leave, the echoes of their conversation lingered in his mind. The promise of encounters with creatures of the night, supernatural abilities, and the secrets hidden from the human realm had stirred something within Kain.

    Days turned into weeks, and the anticipation grew. Stanley kept his word, and their subsequent meetings delved deeper into the intricacies of the supernatural. Kain found himself engrossed in a world that transcended the boundaries of his imagination. Each revelation, whether about werewolves, vampires, or other mystical beings, became a new chapter in Kain's extraordinary journey.

    As Kain documented his experiences, his writings took on a life of their own. The once skeptic writer had become a chronicler of the supernatural, weaving tales that blurred the lines between reality and fantasy. His encounters with creatures of the night, mysterious realms, and the enigmatic hierarchy that governed these beings unfolded like a gripping novel.

Through it all, Kain's skepticism wavered, replaced by a growing acceptance of the extraordinary. His interactions with Stanley and the supernatural beings opened his eyes to a reality he never thought possible. The more he learned, the more questions arose, propelling Kain further into the depths of the unknown.

The bond between Kain and Stanley deepened, evolving into a partnership that extended beyond the realm of mere documentation. They shared moments of camaraderie, laughter, and even heated debates about the nature of their discoveries. Stanley, once a mysterious visitor, became a mentor and friend to Kain, guiding him through the intricate tapestry of the supernatural.

As Kain's writings gained recognition, the world began to take notice. The tales of creatures that existed beyond the shadows captured the imagination of readers worldwide. Kain's once solitary life transformed into a journey that connected him to a larger, more mysterious universe.

Yet, amidst the wonders and revelations, Kain couldn't shake the nagging question – why had Stanley chosen him? The answer, it seemed, lay shrouded in the secrets of the supernatural, waiting to be unveiled in the chapters yet to be written in Kain's extraordinary tale.

S.K. Ballinger

TRUST IS TRUST

Thrilled to be home and anxious to have met Kain, Stanley was quick with excitement to share the details of his encounter. The sprawling almond orchard, bathed in the soft glow of the setting sun, seemed to welcome him back with a soothing serenity.

Julie's eyes flickered with curiosity as Stanley shared the story of his encounter with Kain Edward, a seemingly ordinary writer who had been thrust into their extraordinary world. The words flowed between them, weaving a narrative that transcended the realms of human understanding.

"So, why did you show him a part of your past?" Julie asked, her gaze penetrating the layers of Stanley's thoughts.

Stanley pondered for a moment before responding, "There's something about Kain, something that made me believe he could be the one to bridge the gap between our kind and humans. He's different, Julie, not like the others who stumbled upon our existence."

Julie nodded in understanding, her mind delving into the complexities of fate and choice. The idea of entrusting a human with their secrets was unprecedented, yet Stanley's intuition held a weight that resonated with her own instincts.

"I just hope we made the right decision," Stanley added, his voice tinged with a hint of uncertainty.

Julie placed a reassuring hand on his, her touch conveying a silent solidarity.

Stanley Swanson – Breed of a Werewolf

"If it feels right, Stan, then it probably is. We've navigated through centuries, adapting to the changes. Perhaps Kain is the missing piece, the one who can tell our story without the fear of persecution."

As the night unfolded, the couple continued their conversation, discussing the intricacies of their lives and the potential impact of this newfound alliance. In the quietude of their home, surrounded by the timeless whisper of almond trees, they contemplated the dawn of a new chapter—one that held the promise of understanding, acceptance, and a connection that transcended the boundaries of their supernatural existence.

His longing for his wife and children underscored the duality of his existence—one foot in the mysterious world of werewolves and the other firmly grounded in the familial bonds of a loving home.

"How have the kids behaved?" he asked, a mixture of curiosity and paternal responsibility evident in his voice.

"Jade has been doing well today, and our son Sabe, who takes after you, has been on the computer all day," Julie replied.

In that simple nod of acknowledgment, Stanley recognized the challenges of raising children in an era dominated by technology—a universal struggle that transcended the supernatural nuances of his own life. The familiar scene of a concerned father navigating the nuances of his son's interests underscored the generational gap that persisted, even within a family touched by the extraordinary.

As the Swanson family reconvened in the warmth of their cozy home, the ordinary and extraordinary seamlessly merged, creating a delicate harmony. The love and connection shared by the Swansons became the anchor in their lives, a reassuring constant that provided solace amidst the enigmatic uncertainties that defined their extraordinary existence.

In this domestic tableau, the echoes of both the mystical and mundane coexisted, weaving a narrative that hinted at the intricate tapestry of their lives. The Swansons, with their unique blend of supernatural secrets and familial bonds, stood as a testament to the resilience of love in the face of the unknown.

Stanley, with a slight grin of happiness on his face and both hands on his hips, relished in the wonders of being a parent. Standing at the base of the staircase, he pulled out the card he had found in an old, run-down gas station restroom—the card that belonged to Kain Edward. As he glanced over it, contemplating the prospect of making a new friend who was willing to listen, the love of his life descended the stairs.

Stanley's eyes gleamed at the sight of the astonishing lady he had saved and married. Julie, in her beautiful red velvet dress, with long, wavering brunette hair and a glowing skin tone, radiated beauty. As Stanley admired his wife, the card in his hand slipped from his grasp and fluttered to the floor. Though Julie's presence brought him immense joy, Stanley was still fixated on sharing the details of his visit with Kain, looking into her eyes as he prepared to recount the encounter.

Excitement sparkled in Stanley's eyes as he eagerly shared his thoughts with Julie.

"I am going to make a breakthrough with this Kain Edward guy. I shared with him just a little bit about who we are and what we are capable of."

Stanley Swanson – Breed of a Werewolf

Julie, intrigued and supportive, responded, "That's wonderful, Stan! What did he think about it? Is he convinced?"

Julie listened, conflicted by the potential risks but understanding the weight of Stanley's intentions. As the conversation unfolded, she couldn't help but reminisce about the struggles they faced as a supernatural family hiding in plain sight. The secrecy and fear that had surrounded them for centuries.

The room resonated with the tension between their desire for connection and the necessity of maintaining their hidden existence. Julie, ever the protective force in their relationship, couldn't shake off the worry.

Stanley, sensing her concerns, continued, "Julie, it's not just about Kain. It's about changing perceptions, breaking stereotypes. If we keep hiding forever, the misunderstandings will persist. Maybe, just maybe, Kain can be a bridge between our worlds."

Her gaze softened, torn between caution and hope.

"I just don't want anything bad to happen to us, Stan. We've been living peacefully for so long."

Stanley, gently taking her hands in his, replied, "I know, Julie. That's why I'm being cautious. I won't jeopardize us. But if we can show Kain a different side of our kind, it might be worth it."

The air in the room held a delicate balance between the mystical and the mundane, echoing the intricate dance the Swansons performed in their lives. The allure of connection and understanding, shadowed by the persistent fear of exposure.

As the conversation unfolded, Stanley found himself explaining his motives and intentions, seeking not just acceptance from Julie but also her understanding. They were navigating uncharted waters, torn between the desire for a genuine connection with Kain and the ever-present need to safeguard the secrets that defined their existence.

Julie sighed, acknowledging the complexity of their situation.

"Just promise me you'll be careful, Stan. We've come too far to risk it all."

Stanley nodded, affirming his commitment, "I promise, Julie. This could be a step towards a new era for our kind."

The room, once filled with uncertainty, now held a sense of unity as the Swansons faced the challenges that lay ahead. The delicate dance between secrecy and connection continued, and only time would reveal the true consequences of their choices.

The tension in the room on the first day back with his family became palpable. Late at night, with their kids sleeping, Julie attempted to broach a sensitive topic in a calm voice. Over the years, Stanley, the very Lycan who saved her life, had tirelessly spoken of an impending war between vampires, werewolves, and humans.

"What is wrong with letting it be? We do not know if there will be a war or not. We do not sense the future, but only the past, Stanley."

Stanley's face shifted from happiness to frustration, confused by Julie's lack of enthusiasm.

Stanley Swanson – Breed of a Werewolf

"Julie, you know that a war is in the making of the future, and you also know it is going to bring mankind into the mix. There will be much death and many changes. We need the humans to know they can trust us and not the Drakulis."

The mood in the room grew more strained as Julie thought to herself about the futility of dressing up for a conversation that seemed never-ending.

"Humans are afraid of both our breed and the Drakulis, Stanley. When are you going to realize this?"

In a snapping and bitter tone, Stanley shouted before attempting to calm his nerves.

"I will not realize it, Julie! I am simply trying to justify us. We have lived a long time and have a family of our own. These stories and movies are not going to end that portray our breed as monsters that just go out and kill humans on the night of a full moon. Last time I checked, more people think that the Drakulis are just amazing creatures of their own right. Screw the movies. Look at what they have done to us, which is never seen on the screen or read in the books. We were slaves, Jules! They, the humans, do not know this, and I feel it is only right to get the message out."

The tension in the room on the first day back to his family was growing irritable with Julie in an unenlightened way. Late at night, with their kids sleeping, she tried to speak with him in a calm voice, even though she was growing old of Stanley's belief in this war he always claimed would one day happen. Julie, over the many years, hearing Stanley, the very Lycan who saved her life, became tired of his discussions about the notion that a war between vampires, werewolves, and humans would happen.

"What is wrong with letting it be? We do not know if there will be a war or not; we do not sense the future, but only the past, Stanley."

Confused by his excitement and Julie not sharing in his moment, Stanley's face then shifted from happy to frustration.

"Julie, you know that a war is in the making of the future, and you also know it is going to bring mankind into the mix. There will be much death and many changes. We need the humans to know they can trust us and not the Drakulis."

The mood in the room had quickly become to a point that Julie would think to herself that she had dressed up for him, which was pointless as the conversations between both her and him would continue.

Julie with only a look of sympathy and concern for her husband would follow with her own plea to him.

"Stanley, I love you, and I believe in you and your journey, but this is not the time. You have not even mentioned why I am dressed up or why Sabe is spending his time killing on the computer or why Jade is shuttered in her own world. Do you know that while you were gone meeting with this Edward guy that you have consumed yourself with, to share what should not be shared, I had to go feed for the kids while they stayed home alone?"

Just as typical life can be when your partner is gone on travel or business. The same would hold true with them as well. Stanley, as he tried to take in what she was saying to him, would respond with the fact that their kids are growing up and should be able in sorts to take care of themselves for a short period if need be.

"Sabe is getting old enough to feed himself; he may be fourteen years old, but he has learned a lot from me. Jade though eleven years old, she is a young girl, and I am grateful she is shunning herself from the dangers of this putrid world we live in. Remember this love, we are not hiding just to hide; we are and have always been the hunted from not only the Drakulis but the humans as well. I just do not understand why you are not willing to trust me in the decision of what it is I am trying to do."

While the argument could stand firm on both sides, Julie holding back her tears of this yelling match by giving him the thought of what had happened with Jade while he was gone was eager to give insight into what Stanley has missed in the short days he was not present.

"It is like missing the first steps of your baby, Stanley, and you have missed that with Jade."

Confused by her comment, he would ask while shaking his head.

"What could I have missed? She is safe, she is fed, and she is loved, Julie, what more?"

Again, this was not the response she was wanting to hear from him.

"You really have no clue, do you, Stanley? Jade has transitioned almost fully to our breed and has done so without much pain. I would have thought of our entire breed that you might find that interesting. Our son Sabe does so without a single crackling of his bones, and he goes about at times doing so with ease. I find it hard to manage him as he tries to replicate you. The kids need their father, Stanley!"

Stanley trying to avoid the situation and conversation as feeling a bit ashamed of himself calmly would say to her in an uneasy voice.

"I know my children, our children, Julie."

As he falls to one knee weak with the thought of their daughter at such a young age transitioning, Stanley does his best to reassure Julie that he will figure something out in time.

"I have never heard of a breed able to do what you suggest our daughter has done. While this grows concerns for me, Jules, I will contact a friend of mine to see if he might know of such a possibility as what might be happening with our daughter. I will not allow this to intervene with the journal that Kain has begun to write nonetheless, and I only ask you for your blessing."

Julie on the other hand was growing weak of the conversation as Stanley was still adamant of finishing what he had already begun with Kain and this written journal. It would be then that she would finish stating to him before walking back up the very staircase she had come down from in hopes to surprise her husband.

I'n the wake of the extensive discourse I've just articulated, Stanley, it becomes apparent that your resolute pursuit of a forthcoming war persists, despite my impassioned expressions elucidating the potential repercussions for our progeny and their transformative experiences. Even in the face of such consequences, you tenaciously cling to this insatiable desire. Have my words fallen on deaf ears, Stanley?'

Stanley Swanson – Breed of a Werewolf

Julie, grappling with overwhelming emotions, ascends the staircase, suppressing tears but pauses to cast a disheartened gaze back at Stanley, vividly conveying her upset demeanor.

"Stan, this wasn't the life I envisaged, wherein you'd go to such lengths to engage with a human, potentially exposing us to peril. Can you not fathom the danger looming over us? Have you contemplated the implications within our community, the very code we hold dear?"

The discordant exchange persists, neither party yielding ground. In a sotto voce exclamation, Stanley retorts, "This was the life you envisioned when you implored me to turn you into one of us, damn it!"

As emotions escalate, akin to how individuals vent during moments of distress, Stanley's remark to Julie attains a certain intensity.

"This evening was not intended for such turmoil, Stanley. I merely yearned for a pleasant time together, rejoicing in your return home," laments Julie, attempting to stem the rising tide of tears.

Attempting to justify his imminent departure, Stanley elucidates to Julie that their plans for relaxation or a pleasant evening must be postponed, as he is scheduled to fly out to meet Kain the next morning. This revelation crushes Julie.

"To hell with Kain, Stan! What about your own damn family?" she vehemently exclaims.

Stanley contends that he is presently present with her, emphasizing the futility of their current argument, and questions,

"When will you recognize its importance?"

Remaining on the staircase, Julie, tears now streaming down her face, expresses her concern, "I can't endure this tonight, Stanley. I simply wanted to enjoy your presence and plan a nice evening together."

The tension intensifies as Stanley defends his impending departure, leaving Julie emotionally distraught.

"Why you though? I do not hear of any others of our breed seeking help from a human, why you, why all of a sudden are you wanting to carry through with sharing of who we are?"

At this juncture, Stanley's emotions were a tempest of fury and distress. He found himself exasperated by Julie's failure to comprehend his perspective, her seeming reluctance to entertain the notion of altering his course, or abandoning what he perceived as the utmost importance to their very existence.

"First of all, you were brought in as a breed, not born as one. As I stated to you, I saved your life, and for this one instance, you cannot see my reasoning for wanting to warn humans of what will eventually happen. You were not there when my father had to send my mother, his wife, off to a Drakulis to be a damn hell hound, while my father, brother, and I watched them take her. The burning of our breed, as we were outnumbered by them, the hate, the fog, the rage we had but could not do anything much about, or the damn fact my father told my brother and me to run as fast as we could through the woods as a battle was waging. I promise you, Julie, it is going to happen again but it will be much worse with humans involved if they do not trust our breed. That was the last time my brother and I would ever see our father again and I will not allow the same to happen to our kids."

Stanley Swanson – Breed of a Werewolf

Julie, swift to counter Stanley's account with her own sentiments, retorted, "This is what you think of at nights when we are together? You are so drawn up in the past that you cannot let go, and then you take me as though I am not a breed of yours? I am ashamed of you, Stanley. Regardless of a possible war you think will happen in the future, you disrespect me in such a manner that I am only glad that Jade and Sabe are sleeping right now. You go ahead and visit this Kain human and share everything you want to with him if that helps you rest better at night, but perhaps you will do it in a better manner than you have done so with me this evening."

As she began walking upstairs, where the night was supposed to be great and relaxing, Stanley attempted to call her back, his voice carrying an almost pleading tone.

"Julie, I am sorry, can we please talk calmly?"

The damage had been done, but amid the tense aftermath, a subtle voice, that of their son Sabe, emerged from around the corner at the top of the stairs. He descended the very steps that his mother had just ascended, becoming an inadvertent witness to the turmoil that unfolded.

"Dad, I am ready for a war as I have heard over many years now you speak of the Drakulis."

"Son, this war is not a place for you as we have to maintain our breed, which is why a person such as Kain is so important to me. One day you will understand of what it is that I am doing."

As this conversation unfolded, Sabe, fueled by a desire to prove his readiness, decided to transition into a werewolf. He believed this transformation would symbolize his readiness for the challenges his father was preparing for.

"I can take care of myself, father, and I even fed myself the other night while you were gone. Just don't tell Mom as she too went to gather food for us."

"Son, I am proud of you, but this is not about strength, intelligence, or even the war; it is about sustaining our livelihood. We have hidden for a long time now, and we may very well do so for another couple of hundred years, but why not share some glory to teach those that do not know that we can be trusted, unlike the Drakulis?"

Sabe had no concrete response to his father's statement, but he silently hoped that his father would trust them and heed what his mother was trying to convey, even though he only caught a fragment of their conversation. The atmosphere gradually shifted to a more relaxed one as the night grew later.

"Son, I do trust you all, and tell me that you did not hunt near a farm?"

"Not too close..."

"Tell me you did not approach a farm, son!"

Sabe finally admitted that he was on a farm the night he caught his own food and apologized to his father for not being honest initially.

"Dammit son, what have I told you about that?"

Tired from his recent argument with his wife, Stanley

redirected the conversation to a more positive note.

"So what did you get for dinner then, tell me at least a baby goat, son?"

"Six chickens, dad."

While rubbing Sabe's head in a gesture of approval, Stanley, looking up at the ceiling, beamed with pride. He went on to explain the importance of not venturing out late at night to feed, cautioning that both the Drakulis and fellow werewolves were omnipresent. Stanley emphasized the need to avoid starting a war prematurely, highlighting that farmers often reported missing livestock and had been known to shoot at those who took from them. Proud of Sabe's initiative, Stanley instructed him to watch after his mother and sister as he would continue his flight back to Stull, KS in the morning.

"Will do, dad, and with what mother had said, I hope she is wrong."

"Get to bed, son. I will see you soon."

The night concluded with a mix of pride, caution, and a tinge of apprehension for what the future might hold.

STULL, KANSAS

Waiting for Stanley's arrival felt like an eternity for Kain, each passing moment filled with a mix of anticipation and eagerness. The next day couldn't come soon enough, and Kain was anxious to continue their conversations. He had more questions to ask, and the desire for another past experience lingered in his mind like a tantalizing possibility just out of reach.

As the hours crawled by, Kain found himself growing increasingly restless, the obnoxious ticking of the clock serving as a constant reminder of the time that separated him from the enlightening discussions with Stanley. But finally, the moment he had been waiting for arrived, marked by a hopeful knock at the door.

Kain's face lit up with the biggest grin as he wheeled himself towards the entrance. A whole day had passed since their last meeting, during which Kain meticulously documented every detail of their conversation. The notes allowed him to reflect on the wisdom shared by Stanley, giving him a chance to critique and absorb the valuable insights.

This encounter was more than just a dream coming true for Kain; it was a realization of a deep longing and desire. He was determined not to let this opportunity slip away, recognizing that these conversations with Stanley made him feel whole again. The door swung open, and there stood Stanley, a semi-smile on his face that spoke volumes.

"May I come in?" Stanley asked.

"Absolutely, you may," Kain replied, his excitement

palpable.

The room became a haven for the exchange of knowledge and experiences, a space where questions flowed freely, and wisdom was eagerly shared. The atmosphere was charged with the energy of two minds hungry for learning and understanding.

As the conversation progressed, Kain found himself captivated by the stories and insights that Stanley generously shared. The semi-smile on Stanley's face transformed into a genuine expression of joy as he witnessed Kain's enthusiasm and thirst for knowledge. The mentor-student dynamic was evolving into a true friendship, built on a foundation of shared experiences and a mutual passion for growth.

Hours turned into a timeless flow of dialogue, and Kain couldn't help but marvel at the depth of wisdom he was gaining.

As Kain eagerly settled into the conversation, a palpable excitement filled the room. He was ready to continue learning, to absorb the wisdom that Stanley generously shared and to meticulously document every detail in his journal. However, there was a subtle hint that Stanley might not be in the greatest of moods, a nuance discerned by Kain from the expressions on Stanley's face. Yet, Stanley remained true to the commitment of the meeting, and the learning continued.

"So where did we leave off, Kain?" Stanley inquired, breaking the momentary silence.

"Well, you took me through that intriguing past life experience," Kain began, his eyes gleaming with curiosity.

"I realized you're nothing like a vampire or a Drakulis, as

you put it, and that your kind ages in a magnificent way. I might have left out a few details in my recollection, but I'm all ears and ready to listen."

Stanley, with a thoughtful look, briefly scanned his rental house, as if searching for something that lingered just beyond his immediate awareness. Breaking the silence, he suddenly asked,

"I might have asked before, do you not have any family?"

"I do have some family," Kain replied, his tone reflective.

"But no children, no wife, and unfortunately, both my parents are deceased."

The atmosphere in the room shifted subtly as the conversation delved into more personal territory. Kain sensed that Stanley's question had opened a door to a deeper understanding of each other's lives. Despite the potential heaviness of the topic, the exchange felt natural and unforced, a testament to the bond that was forming between the two.

Stanley nodded, acknowledging Kain's response. "

Family plays a significant role in shaping who we are," he remarked, his semi-smile momentarily returning. "But sometimes, our chosen paths lead us on unique journeys. It's a part of the human experience, wouldn't you agree?"

Kain nodded in understanding, appreciating the depth Stanley brought to the conversation. The mentorship extended beyond the realms of supernatural tales into the intricacies of life, loss, and the pursuit of knowledge. As the dialogue continued, Kain found himself not only learning about the supernatural but also gaining insights into the complexities of human existence.

With a smile on his face, Stanley continued to share his unique perspective with Kain, unveiling the intricacies of his supernatural existence. However, there was a detectable shadow in Stanley's expression, suggesting a possible inner turmoil. Undeterred, Stanley pressed on, his commitment to the meeting unwavering.

"So, are you content with being alone, Kain?" Stanley inquired, his curiosity evident.

He observed the absence of pictures on Kain's walls, a detail that sparked his interest and led him to contemplate the potential solitude that had marked Kain's life for an extended period. Stanley couldn't fathom the concept of loneliness, and he candidly expressed his thoughts.

Kain, with a mix of frustration and resignation in his voice, responded, "Stanley, I don't have the luxuries you do. I can't heal like you, I don't have the financial means, and I certainly haven't been around as long as you have. Being a goddamn cripple, living in Stull, KS, surviving on a disability check – it's not a choice I made happily. You, Stanley, you're my only something to look forward to, something I've been waiting for a long time."

Stanley, understanding the gravity of Kain's situation, offered a nod of acknowledgment.

"Then let's continue our discussions. I'll share more about my breed and the impending war," he stated, steering the conversation back to the supernatural realm.

But Kain, ever observant, couldn't help but notice Stanley's apparent melancholy. With genuine concern, he asked, "Stanley, I couldn't help but notice that you seem a bit depressed. I hope everything is well at home, and your family is doing fine."

Stanley, with a sigh, shared a glimpse of the struggles he faced.

"My wife is not thrilled about me sharing information and my interest in you. What should have been a nice return home turned into arguing. It's not common for our breed to engage in debates, so yes, it's been a bit depressing."

Feeling responsible for the disruption, Kain apologized, "I didn't mean to create trouble for you and your family. If you want to cancel our sessions, I'll respect that. I'm grateful for what you've shared with me so far."

Stanley, regaining his composure, reassured Kain, "No need to apologize. This is my decision, and it carries importance few would understand. My wife and I will move past the other night. Let's continue, shall we?"

Relieved that Stanley was willing to continue, Kain wheeled himself to the table, pen and paper in hand, ready to absorb more knowledge. Stanley delved into the topic of feeding, explaining the unique dietary requirements of his breed.

As Stanley spoke of consuming live food and warm blood, Kain, in awe, interrupted, "So you basically kill people and share them over dinner with your family?"

Stanley clarified, "Not all werewolves do that. Times have changed. I, for instance, no longer kill humans. We are all different. Unlike vampires who leave corpses to decay, we consume what we prey on in full."

Kain challenged Stanley's perspective, asking, "So that makes it right to hunt and kill humans? What gives you the right to do that?"

Stanley defended, "We have to live just like you, Kain. Perhaps you should think differently the next time you eat meat. Wasn't that once a living creature?"

The conversation delved into the ethical considerations of their dietary choices, with Kain questioning the morality of hunting humans. Stanley revealed that his breed had shifted to consuming young animals for sustenance.

As Stanley disclosed details about the lifestyle of his breed, including their dietary habits, Kain couldn't help but feel a mixture of disgust and intrigue. He questioned the number of humans Stanley's breed consumed on average.

Stanley, with a playful smile, remarked, "You look a bit nervous, Kain."

"Not nervous, just pointing out that you've been around for over sixty years, and that's a lot of people, not to mention your family to provide for," Kain replied, probing deeper into the complexities of werewolf existence.

Stanley laughed, sharing that his family, like many others of their breed, also contributed to providing for themselves. He revealed that he and his family primarily consumed young animals and had refrained from killing humans for the past nine years.

Relieved by Stanley's assurance, Kain acknowledged, "It's a bit disgusting, but I understand you're different from us."

Stanley concluded with a poignant reflection, "Eat what you can consume, let the others prosper, and don't let it go to waste. Unlike vampires, we don't leave corpses behind."

The conversation then took a turn as Stanley shifted to a more lighthearted topic, expressing his amusement at how humans portrayed werewolves in movies and books. He mentioned the Twilight series and how it failed to capture the true essence of their breed.

While Kain pointed out that it was just a movie, Stanley emphasized the misrepresentation, highlighting the agility and versatility of werewolves in reality. He explained their ability to stand on hind legs, walk on all fours, and manipulate their bone structure.

Stanley chuckled, "The only downfall is that when we transition from werewolf to human presentation, we're naked. That's why you'll find clothes near the front doors of a werewolf's home."

As the evening unfolded, Kain continued to absorb the fascinating revelations about Stanley's breed, finding himself intrigued by the complexities and similarities between humans and werewolves. The mentorship continued, transcending the supernatural into the realms of shared experiences and mutual understanding.

Still writing and jotting everything down that Stanley has put forth, Kain is picturing in his mind of how incredible it would be to see a werewolf crawling for its prey on a dark night like that of what a wild cat would do in shallow grass sneaking upon its prey. High shoulders alternating with each bend, quietly moving closer and closer before striking. The imagery projecting through his brain had made Kain wanting even more to see Stanley transition; forget seeing the past again as it was no longer a proven need or proof of their existence.

"I know you're not here to reveal your true self, your true being, but I do hope that in time you will, Stanley," Kain expressed, his curiosity lingering beneath the surface.

"I'm sure in time you might, Kain, but you stand correct. For one, I don't feel you're ready to see me as I really am. Just as the saying goes, 'seeing is believing,' and the eyes don't always accept. It's no different than witnessing a Drakulis transform into fog. In real life, a human has a hard time comprehending such acts of myth. What do you think differentiates our breed from them, the vampires?" Stanley inquired, delving into the intriguing comparisons between werewolves and vampires.

"I'm not sure, Stanley, but that's why I want to know more about your kind—to share with others what you speak of your breed," Kain replied, his thirst for knowledge evident.

Before continuing, Stanley, with a tinge of disdain in his voice, expressed his hatred towards the Drakulis, focusing momentarily on movies and books. He brought up the movie 'Interview with a Vampire' and shared his appreciation for the poignant moment involving a little girl bitten and forever trapped in a youthful existence.

"That is one advantage our breed has over them," Stanley noted.

"If there was ever a true telling of their lost souls, it was that moment in that movie. The little girl who played that role was extraordinary. I truly hope you can share a story that can make others as telling of us as the author Anne Rice did for them, Mr. Edward."

"I'm going to try and do the best that I can, Stanley, though I'm not writing a story. Just a written journal," Kain clarified.

"Regardless of a story or a journal, I believe that what you continue to write down will make a difference, Kain, and I appreciate that," Stanley acknowledged, the weight of their exchange lingering in the air.

The mood shifted from discussing movies to a more serious tone, and Kain couldn't help but notice Stanley's lingering irritation. He wondered if it stemmed from the recent argument Stanley had with his wife, Julie.

"You seem a little on edge. Would you like something to drink, or would you prefer I wheel myself out and try to catch you some dinner—perhaps a deer or some other animal?" Kain offered, attempting to ease the tension.

Stanley, appreciating the gesture, replied, "No need, Kain. I'm fine. Let's continue with our discussions."

As the evening unfolded, the conversations oscillated between the supernatural and mundane, creating a unique tapestry of shared experiences and insights. Kain remained committed to absorbing the wisdom Stanley shared, recognizing the significance of their interactions. Stanley, in turn, appreciated Kain's dedication to documenting their encounters, understanding the potential impact on others. The mentor-student dynamic continued to evolve, transcending the boundaries of their supernatural existences.

The evening progressed with a mix of laughter and more serious conversations, as Kain continued to delve into the world of werewolves through Stanley's experiences. Yet, despite the attempts at humor and bonding, a lingering tension persisted in Stanley's demeanor.

Kain couldn't ignore the undercurrent of distress and asked sincerely, "Are you okay, Stanley?"

"I am fine," Stanley responded, his tone not entirely convincing.

"Just not going to make my flight back home. My wife is going to be really pissed off at me now, as the night before was not good, as you know."

Sensing Stanley's frustration, Kain offered a solution, "I'm sure there's another flight. Maybe we should continue our discussions over the phone, so you won't have to deal with the repercussions with your family."

Stanley considered the suggestion, acknowledging the importance of being present for his family.

"Your suggestion is not a bad idea. I have to respect my wife and family. It's also important that we see one another in person, as that is the genuine purpose of this, I feel. Let me ask you, Kain, would you be interested in traveling to Sacramento to my home and meeting my family?"

While Kain felt honored by the invitation, his hesitancy

surfaced.

"It would be a great privilege, and it's not like I have something better to do, Stanley. It's just kind of sudden. Also, I really don't have the funds to do so; remember, I am on disability."

The unspoken apprehension in Kain's words revealed his underlying nervousness about staying with a breed of werewolves, particularly given the strained relationship with Stanley's wife, Julie. The potential risks loomed in his thoughts, and the idea of Julie's displeasure added to his concerns.

Stanley, sensing Kain's reservations, offered reassurance.

"I will gladly assist you in any payment. I only suggest this, as our time with note-taking and discussions will soon be diminished rather quickly at some point in time. It's your call, but I will be leaving in the morning and cannot promise you when I may return."

As Kain weighed the pros and cons of the unexpected invitation, he realized the unique opportunity it presented. Despite the uncertainties and the financial constraints, the prospect of delving deeper into the world of werewolves, meeting Stanley's family, and continuing their discussions in a different setting sparked a curiosity that outweighed his concerns. The decision lingered, hanging in the air, as the two continued their conversation into the late hours of the night.

With a slight contemplation reflected in Kain's expression, he finally agreed to embark on the journey to Sacramento, deciding to meet Stanley's family and continue documenting their encounters in the journal. The decision, though made with a degree of trepidation, marked a pivotal moment in Kain's pursuit of knowledge about werewolves, pushing him beyond the boundaries of his comfort zone.

As the two conversed about the upcoming visit, events were unfolding in Sacramento, taking an unforeseen and ominous turn. Unbeknownst to Stanley and Kain, the information shared between the human and the werewolf had potentially reached unintended ears, ears belonging to beings who would not appreciate the divulgence of supernatural secrets.

The cloak of secrecy that shrouded the werewolf community was a fundamental code, a code never to be breached, especially when it came to involving outsiders like humans. The consequences of such breaches were swift and severe. The Drackulis, ancient and elusive vampires, were not known for their leniency. Any whiff of betrayal or information leakage could ignite a series of events leading to a confrontation, the consequences of which were unpredictable.

As night fell, casting a shadow over the quiet surroundings, Kain and Stanley continued their discussions, unaware of the unseen forces that might be gathering in the darkness. The living room, where they shared their knowledge and stories, became a temporary haven before the dawn of a new day.

Morning approached, and with it, the beginning of a journey that Stanley believed might unfold into a certain war. The anticipation hung in the air as both Stanley and Kain, bound by an unusual camaraderie, prepared to face the unknown challenges that awaited them in Sacramento. Little did they know that the consequences of their interactions, the information shared, and the journey they were about to embark upon, would ripple across the supernatural realm, setting in motion events that could alter the delicate balance between werewolves and vampires.

In the dim light of the living room, the two unlikely companions found a brief respite in sleep, unaware of the complexities that awaited them in the waking world. The air was thick with uncertainty, and as the first rays of dawn broke through the night, illuminating the room, they would set forth on a path that had the potential to reshape their destinies and plunge them into a world teetering on the brink of war.

GRAVAKUS TO BE KNOWN

The night unfolded over the Swanson plantation like a velvet curtain, with only a faint glow from the moon casting gentle shadows across the landscape. The tranquility of the Swanson household was seemingly undisturbed, with the children, Sabe and Jade, nestled into their beds, their dreams undisturbed by the world outside. Meanwhile, Stanley, the head of the family, was away, his absence keenly felt in the sprawling plantation house.

Julie, the matriarch of the Swanson family, moved quietly through the halls of the mansion, attending to the various tasks that demanded her attention. She couldn't help but feel a sense of anticipation and anxiety as she waited for her husband's return. Each passing moment fueled her hope that this reunion would bring a positive change, perhaps even surpassing the challenges of previous encounters.

Stepping outside the grandeur of their ancestral home, a legacy left behind by Stanley's father, Julie found solace in the routine of tidying up the front porch. Despite her efforts to maintain composure, her mind couldn't help but race with thoughts of Stanley's return and the uncertainty that awaited him.

The Swanson plantation, a testament to the family's legacy, stood as a pristine symbol of opulence. The house, meticulously cared for over the years, remained a stunning reflection of their wealth and taste. Three grand pillars adorned the entrance, and through the towering French doors, one could catch glimpses of intricately designed staircases leading to the upper levels.

However, the splendor of the house did not shield it from

potential threats. As Julie worked diligently on the porch, a sudden panic gripped her. The realization that danger was lurking nearby settled in her soul, and her movements became more urgent. The house, no matter how magnificent, could not guarantee safety.

Suddenly, a change in the night air caught Julie's attention. A slight fog began to roll in, and her heightened werewolf senses immediately detected an ominous presence – the scent of a Drakulis. Panic surged through her, and with a quick, instinctual response, she abandoned her sweeping and rushed inside. The broom clattered to the ground as she locked the door behind her, her heart racing.

Julie's focus shifted to her children, who slept peacefully, oblivious to the impending danger. In a determined but calm manner, she woke Sabe first, his shoulders receiving an almost vigorous pat. The urgency in her eyes conveyed a silent message – trouble was at their doorstep, and swift action was required to ensure the safety of her family. The night, once serene, had transformed into a tense struggle against the unknown forces that threatened the Swanson household.

The urgency in Julie's voice cut through the peaceful silence of the Swanson household as she gently woke her son, Sabe.

"Son, wake up now," she whispered, her voice barely audible. As Sabe's eyes fluttered open, Julie placed a delicate finger to her lips, signaling him to maintain silence.

"Shh..." she cautioned, her tone carrying a weight of concern.

Stanley Swanson – Breed of a Werewolf

Julie wasted no time and began to brief Sabe about the imminent danger that had encroached upon their home. In hushed tones, she instructed him to be cautious and, if the need arose, to protect his younger sister, Jade. Their family, like any other living under the constant threat of supernatural dangers, had a contingency plan—a secret underground passage designed to ensure their escape in times of peril.

Still groggy from sleep, Sabe struggled to fully comprehend the gravity of his mother's words. He rubbed the remnants of sleep from his eyes, watching as Julie moved stealthily towards Jade's room. The air hung heavy with tension as the weight of responsibility settled on Sabe's shoulders.

As Julie reached the other end of the hallway, a sudden and forceful knocking echoed through the house, emanating from the front door. The unexpected disturbance caused Julie to momentarily divert from her path toward Jade's room. Her senses heightened, she moved slowly towards the source of the disturbance, her mind preparing for the confrontation she was almost certain awaited her—a Drakulis, a creature of the night.

The knocks persisted, loud and rhythmic, demanding attention. Julie steadied herself, attempting to maintain composure, and hoped that Sabe had absorbed the gravity of the situation she had just conveyed to him.

"One moment," she responded, her voice projecting a façade of normalcy while her mind raced with apprehension.

The knocks continued, each one intensifying the ominous atmosphere that hung in the air. Julie steeled herself for what lay beyond the door, her instincts warning her of the impending danger. All she could do was trust that Sabe, awakened by his mother's words, was prepared for the unexpected challenge that awaited them. The night, once quiet and peaceful, had transformed into a battleground where the Swanson family's fate hung in the balance.

With her hand poised on the doorknob, Julie took one final deep breath, attempting to gather her composure amidst the turmoil of emotions swirling within her. As the door swung open fully, an unexpected sight awaited her – a man, handsome and impeccably dressed, standing on the threshold. The unmistakable scent that emanated from him revealed his true nature; he was a Drakulis. Julie's instincts tingled with a mix of fear and uncertainty, especially as encounters with Drakulis had been rare and never so spontaneous.

"Sorry to bother you, madam, at this time of evening, but I would really appreciate letting me have a word with your husband, Stanley Swanson, and please do tell him my name is Gravakus," the man spoke politely.

"Sorry, kind sir, but my husband is not here at the moment. Can I ask what this may be about?" Julie replied, her heart pounding, attempting to conceal her nervousness.

As the rapid beats of her heart echoed in her ears, Gravakus continued, seemingly unperturbed by the tension he caused, "It would appear, madam, or would you prefer me to call you Julie, that your husband is trying to do something very uncommon of your breed, which is why I am here."

Julie, trying to mask her anxiety, took another silent deep breath. She realized the gravity of the situation but played along, hoping to buy time for her children to escape the impending danger.

Stanley Swanson – Breed of a Werewolf

"You can call me Julie, that is fine. My husband is not here, and he's not expected to return until tomorrow morning. He has been traveling. I will not lie to you, Gravakus, as I know that you are not alone. What concerns do you have with my husband and what he is trying to do?" Julie inquired, her eyes locked with Gravakus's, both aware of the power play at hand.

Gravakus, enjoying the verbal dance, shared a knowing smirk. He was well aware that the scent of their breed was easily detectable, and he understood the unacceptability of the uncommon attraction between werewolves and humans in his own kind.

"I am not here to be mind-played any further, Mrs. Swanson!" Gravakus exclaimed, his frustration evident.

"We are very aware of what your husband has been doing with this stupid and old crippled man in Kansas. Here is what you are going to do for us, and you will do it. You are going to let this worthless man of yours bring Mr. Edward home, and you will have him turned over to me personally."

Julie, despite her nervous facade, stood her ground.

"I cannot guarantee you anything, Gravakus. If it makes you feel any better, I am not fond of the idea of what my husband is doing. Nonetheless, he is my husband, and I will respect him along with his wishes."

Gravakus, growing more serious, issued a stark warning, "I am going to only say this, Mrs. Swanson, if you do not comply with me, as time is not on our side with this sharing of information your husband has begun, then you will have left me little choice and have collateral. Do you not understand the severity of what he is doing to not only us but your breed as well?"

"I understand you perfectly clear, but I do not control my husband the way that your kind is controlled perhaps. I would only say to you, Gravakus, that you are more than welcome to make a visit tomorrow when he is to arrive. Now, if you do not mind, I must tend to my kids as it is late and they are sleeping."

Unknown to both Julie and Gravakus, Sabe watched from his bedroom window upstairs, barely discerning the events unfolding beneath the porch covering. Julie remained resolute, willing to do anything to protect her family. She understood the potential for this situation to turn tragic but refused to yield.

Following his mother's instructions, Sabe briefly left the window to wake up his little sister, Jade, and inform her of the ongoing situation. The heated conversation on the front porch escalated, each word carrying the weight of an impending conflict.

"Well, if it is your wish to be silly or equivalent to a human, then perhaps I shall treat you just as that. I really had no intentions of having to hurt you, but you seem to leave me with little choice as you support your husband who shares such secrets or knowledge. This war that Stanley has long believed to one day happen is going to be, and will be, done so by his own doing." Gravakus declared ominously, leaving a palpable tension hanging in the air. The night, once peaceful, had become a battleground for the Swanson family's future.

As Gravakus tightened his grip on Julie, his right hand forcefully under her chin, she found herself unable to break free. Tears welled up in her eyes as she attempted to pry his hand loose, her struggles proving futile. Gravakus, unmoved by her distress, slowly walked backward from the front porch, dragging her into the yard while maintaining his tight hold.

"I hope your children witness this, you disgusting, ignorant beast, and your ignorance in what could have easily been ignored," Gravakus sneered, relishing in the torment he was inflicting upon Julie.

In that desperate moment, Julie contemplated fighting back, but the overwhelming scent revealed that six vampires, Gravakus's followers, emerged from the woods. She understood that taking on such a formidable force was beyond her capabilities. Julie was prepared to sacrifice herself if it meant buying more time for her children to escape.

Unbeknownst to Julie and Gravakus, Sabe watched the harrowing scene unfold from above, witnessing his mother's near-death experience. With his sister awake, he couldn't stand idly by, defying the lessons his father had instilled in him about protecting family. In her fleeting moments of life, Julie softly spoke to Sabe while still in the grasp of Gravakus.

"I have told you all I know. My husband will be arriving again tomorrow, that is all, Gravakus. Please let me go?" she pleaded, her voice strained.

Gravakus, with a sadistic smile, tightened his grip further, his nails piercing the skin of Julie's neck. Sabe, witnessing his mother's agony, realized the urgency of the situation. He swiftly instructed Jade to leave the house through the hideaway basement and run to their uncle Stephen, eight miles away. Jade, initially hesitant, finally let go of her brother's hand and tearfully made her way to safety, trusting that Sabe would protect their family.

S.K. Ballinger

Gravakus sensed the awakening of the Swanson children and the anticipation of two of his followers rushing to the house. However, he commanded them to hold back, recognizing that the young breeds posed no immediate threat. Even as he continued to slowly take Julie's life, Gravakus had no interest in harming the children.

"This is cute, Julie, and I give you great comfort in letting you know, as you take your last few breaths, that your kids are free and unharmed. You, on the other hand, will die tonight as your foolish boy, whom I see at the window upstairs, insists on watching your fate," Gravakus declared callously, reveling in the anguish he had unleashed upon the Swanson family.

The night, once filled with the tranquility of a plantation, had transformed into a nightmare of despair.

Tears streamed down Julie's face as she reluctantly made the decision to transition into her werewolf form. Sabe, against her instructions, had not left the house and had transformed as well. Gravakus struggled to maintain his grip on Julie's now much stronger neck as she shifted into her natural state.

Once on the ground, Sabe swiftly joined his mother's side, attacking Gravakus. With a powerful claw to the face, Sabe split open Gravakus's left cheek and viciously bit at him, causing Gravakus to lose his grip on Julie's throat. The mother-son werewolf duo communicated through their minds, and Julie instructed Sabe to find his sister and not to return. Reluctantly, Sabe leaped off Gravakus, darting away into the woods without looking back.

As Sabe made good ground, he eventually glanced back to check if his mother was following him. It became apparent that

Julie had no intention of abandoning their threatened home. Sabe, torn between protecting his mother and following her wishes, decided to turn back to defend her.

Upon his return, he found his mother surrounded by four vampires. Two of them already lay defeated at Julie's hands, their once-human souls burnt into the ground. Fueled by adrenaline and confidence, Sabe joined Julie in the fight. The remaining vampires fled to rejoin Gravakus, their maker.

Julie and Sabe, side by side, growling with claws out, made their way back to the house. Gravakus, sensing the threat, had disappeared after Sabe slashed his face. Once inside, Julie told Sabe to gather nothing, anticipating the possibility of their enemies returning. In werewolf form, Sabe shed a tear, apologizing to his mother for not leaving her in danger.

"Sorry, mother, but I could not leave you in danger like that," Sabe expressed.

"You are every bit your father. I am very proud of you, but we must go quickly to Stephen's. No time to discuss, Sabe, now let us make our way," Julie responded.

Leaving the house, both Julie and Sabe dropped to all fours, running at an incredible speed, convinced that danger still loomed close by. On the run, Julie contemplated how to confide in Stephen about Stanley's actions. She understood the importance of keeping the secret within their own breed to preserve the sacred code they had obeyed since the first Lycan lived.

Thoughts raced through Julie's mind during the eight-mile run, including concerns about what might happen to Stanley if other breeds learned of his actions, just as the Drackulis had that very night. The night, which began with a threat to their peaceful plantation, had spiraled into a chaotic battle for survival, leaving Julie and Sabe to grapple with the consequences of the secrets that had been unveiled.

Stanley Swanson – Breed of a Werewolf

THE COMFORT OF AN UNCLE

Jade, with the urgency of her brother's instructions, sprinted through the woods to reach her Uncle Stephen's house, seeking the comfort she always found in his presence. The moonlight guided her path, casting shadows from the tall trees that whispered secrets of the night. When she arrived at Stephen's doorstep, her knocks were filled with desperation until he answered, embracing her with the warmth of familial love.

"Jade, what are you doing out this late, honey?" Stephen inquired, his werewolf features emanating both strength and beauty.

Before Jade could respond, Stephen, with his heightened senses, detected an unsettling disturbance at the plantation miles away.

"Get inside now, Jade!" he commanded, closing the door behind her.

Concern etched on his face, Stephen asked her to recount what she had seen, urging her to be honest. Still frightened, Jade explained that she had seen nothing but had followed Sabe's instructions to use the hidden basement path and seek protection at Stephen's house.

"I am glad you listened to your brother. You are safe with me. Were they in danger, Jade? How many exactly?" Stephen questioned, trying to gauge the severity of the situation.

"I do not know, Uncle. I never saw our mother again after she put me in bed, and Sabe woke me with such seriousness," Jade replied tearfully, her confusion mirroring her fear.

Sympathetic to her distress, Stephen attempted to comfort her.

"I am sorry, young one, but it appears that there were vampires at your home from what I can sense. Go to the kitchen area and wait for me."

Frustrated with himself for letting his guard down, Stephen contemplated his next steps. Attempting to call Stanley's house yielded no answer, deepening his concern for his brother's safety. He questioned Jade about Stanley's whereabouts, knowing that his brother would have contacted him if there was trouble. Jade explained that her father wouldn't be home until tomorrow morning, as he was in Kansas visiting someone her mother disapproved of.

"Kansas?" Stephen responded with a disgruntled tone.

"What guy do you speak of, and for what purpose?"

Jade quickly shared what she overheard the previous night.

"From what I understand, Uncle, he is human and has something to do with trying to find out what we are. I'm not sure, but it sounds like he writes or takes notes of us." The revelation hung in the air, leaving both uncle and niece grappling with the implications of Stanley's actions and the potential threats that lurked in the shadows of the night.

Stephen realized that now was not the time to inquire further, especially not from a young child like Jade. His primary concern was the well-being of Julie and Sabe. He told Jade that they were going to get in the car and head back to her home to check on her mother and brother. Though Jade was hesitant, Stephen assured her that nothing would happen to her and asked for her trust.

Just as they prepared to make their way to the car, Stephen had another sense, prompting him to change his plans. He quickly instructed Jade to get back inside the house and stay close to his side. Inside the den, Jade, in an unsettled voice, questioned why they were not leaving and expressed her fear that something bad had happened to her family.

"I believe they are fine, Jade. We shall wait a few moments. One day, young lady, you will have abilities you are not aware of yet. You seem to have been practicing your senses to suggest that you feared something might have happened?" Stephen reassured her, trying to alleviate her anxiety.

To calm her further, Stephen inquired if she had been practicing her transitioning as well. Jade admitted to her efforts, describing that it didn't hurt much when she transitioned and felt she could fully do so if needed. Encouraging her progress, Stephen asked her to demonstrate her abilities. Jade swiftly transitioned her upper extremities, revealing a remarkable and painless transformation that left Stephen astonished and proud.

He provided Jade with clothes, and shortly after she had dressed, Stephen sensed someone at the door. Before he could address it, Jade informed him of people outside, unable to identify them. Impressed with her keen senses, Stephen applauded her new-found ability, explaining that the individuals approaching were her mother and brother. They quickly went to the door, where Julie and Sabe, now clothed, stood. Julie's concern was evident as she softly asked if Jade had made it safely.

"Yes, she is standing behind me, Julie. She was safe with me and impressed me like never before as she transitioned. Please make yourself at home as we have much to discuss," Stephen reassured Julie.

Filled with relief, Jade joyfully shouted, "MOM!" Julie, overwhelmed with emotion, knelt down to hug her daughter, expressing her pride in Jade's progression and promising a discussion soon.

After the heartfelt reunion, all four of them went back to Stephen's den, seeking safety. Here, Stephen was eager to know the details of the attack, Stanley's involvement, and the role of the mysterious human. Sabe, grateful for his sister's safety, began explaining what had happened, but Stephen interrupted, asking Julie to show him the past so he could witness it himself.

Julie gently placed her hands on Stephen's head, and through their shared gaze, she took him back to the incident. The past-travel lasted only a few minutes, and upon returning to the present, Stephen started to laugh in a non-humorous tone. He could only articulate what he saw, "Gravakus... what would make this old Drakulis do such a thing as to attack a breed?" The question hung in the air, setting the stage for a night filled with revelations and discussions about the unfolding events in the supernatural world.

Before he would continue on with questions, he would first share his gratitude towards Sabe for doing what he did which more than likely saved his mother's life. He would go on to explain to Julie that Gravakus is worthless, which is why he always has more followers than others of his kind do. He also explained to Julie and the kids that this is something that he will settle with Gravakus in time, then politely told the kids to go to the living room as he wished to speak to Julie alone for a moment. Sabe did not want to leave as he wanted to hear what his uncle had to say.

"I am old enough, Uncle. Did you not see in full of what I did?"

"I know you are, Sabe, but there is more that your mother needs to know or that I wish to share with her that I do not feel you need to be a part of. You are still my nephew, still young, and have plenty of room to mature. Now do as I asked and go to the living room. Your days of fighting for us will near, I assure you."

Disgruntled as a young kid could be, Julie follows up with what Stephen said.

"Go now, Sabe, and you as well, Jade. We will be staying the night here this evening, so make yourselves ready for bed as morning will soon come."

Stephen goes on to tell Julie more about Gravakus and reassures her that he will handle him. His concern was more about what his brother Stanley was doing with this human.

"I despise what Stanley is doing with this garbage, Stephen. Why so sudden and out of no rationing of reason would my husband and the man I dedicate my life to decide to discuss our breed?" She said in a frustrated manner before continuing.

"Stanley keeps talking about a war that is going to happen and that this man is writing about us to share with humans in hopes that their race will side with us when and if a war does, in fact, occur."

Stephen, as well as his sister-in-law, was not happy that his brother was doing this. There is a reason why werewolves are in constant hiding. They are feared by both Drakulis and humans alike. To make things worse is that it is a code that their breed does not share secrets of all that they are, as mentioned previously. He would agree in his mind with Stanley of the war he has spoken of to Julie over the years but was not willing to debate with her about his opinions as he kept it to himself.

Nonetheless, he was left to give reason for a plan to her for what took place the very night that Gravakus had created friction between their respective beings. The actions that took place are not tolerable as over the last few decades both Drakulis and Lycans would avoid one another to keep peace maintained as it was crucial to their survival in the long term. There was, in fact, a time long past of an agreed treaty of terms had been settled between the two to salvage their respective interests.

"As for Gravakus, he has broken a document of trust of ours, Julie. While I will not share or go into great detail about my brother and his wrongdoings by breaking our code of conduct, the focus shall be on your attackers. I wish for you not to speak of the war that Stanley believes in is all I ask."

"Why is that, Stephen? Is this war my husband speaks of for many years going to happen?"

"There are many fights that have taken place and still do to this day between our breed and vampires which will never stop. As far as a war is concerned, there was only one, Julie, which was that when our breed were slaves to the Drakulis. A future war is not a possibility as long as we can retain this document from Stanley or this human who writes down the words to which my brother shares. If we can do that before many hear about this behavior, then all can still be kept at peace. Gravakus, nonetheless, has to be dealt with regardless."

Stephen eventually calms Julie down in his own brilliant and wise way. Doing his best, he assures Julie that she should rest her mind as in the morning will be a busy one, as that is when his brother Stanley is supposed to be arriving back at their home. With his senses taking control of him, he believed that Gravakus was already on his way back to Coney Island, NY, which is the place that he lived. Stephen did not mention this to her based on his senses but more on his own wisdom. It was also obvious that this is a common thing from the past for both Drakulis and vampires to do.

He tells Julie that these lost souls will strike a fight, win or lose, and always return from the scene back to their place of stay in a timely fashion. All Drakulis have many followers that protect the one that changed them to be. If to try and strike on a Drakulis home, it is not wise as many of his/hers that they have changed will easily sacrifice their own lives to defend them. Not an easy task to do, to say the least; of picking a fight, but the breed of werewolves simply does not tolerate attacks upon them lightly.

Julie was taking all this information in deeply that Stephen was sharing with her. Confused by the suggestive thought of Stephen or Stanley taking care of Gravakus would grow concern in her thoughts. If this is true of the followers, then how could it be possible for a werewolf or a pack could penetrate a single Drakulis? Stephen furthered the insight to Julie by letting her know that these followers of a Drakulis are by the many and there is never a sure way to determine the numbers of just how large of a group they may consist of.

While she was mesmerized by the mere thought of what

she has been listening to, she simply had to know why Stanley would wish to share such information about their breed and even that of Drakulis to a mortal. She only wished for some other explanation that did not involve what she had already heard, which is that Stanley believes that humans will join the breed's side in case of a war. Julie would look to Stephen, as he was so wise, for a better reasoning and once more asked Stephen for the possible answer.

"Let me ask you what my brother has shared with you, Julie?"

"He has not shared anything with me, Stephen; that is just it. Life seemed normal until one morning he told me he had a business trip he had to make. Next thing I knew is that he was meeting this man named Kain Edward, who was once a journalist. Stanley arrived back home, and we had an argument; then he left again the next morning to visit Kain yet again. None of his behavior seems reasonable, Stephen. He put his family in harm's way when Gravakus arrived at my door because he had caught wind of what it was that Stanley was doing. All I want is our hidden and normal life back. I wish for my husband to let this human be forgotten."

"I promise you, Julie, that I will do all that I can to return your life as it was back the way it should be. For now, and with all that you and the kids have been through as of late, get your rest. While you seek an answer to what has happened, even I cannot fully respond with an assuring answer at this moment."

Julie complied with Stephen and made her way to the guest room where her kids were fast asleep. Stephen, not thrilled by his little brother's actions, would try mightily to keep his own self calm until he visits with his brother when he returns. Nothing should ever be so important to put your family at risk in such a way that Stanley did. Even the breed of werewolves themselves would be furious about what he is trying to prove or accomplish, and to the least of all sources of life, that of a mortal.

S.K. Ballinger

THE RETURN HOME WITH A GUEST

Next morning, as was planned, Stanley and Kain would fly to California as scheduled. As they landed, not having much conversation on the flight, Kain was extremely nervous and not feeling very well. Stanley, quick to notice, would reassure him that while he is with him, no harm will happen.

After a few hours of driving from the airport, they had made their way further from civilization, and Kain noticed they were more deeply in the areas of surrounding orchards. His eyes marveled as they neared the gated driveway. Stanley was extremely thrilled to be home, smiling with great anticipation to see his family. As the gate opened with a push of a button, they continued driving down this nice and winding road. Kain could only take in the scenery with a small smile of his own before they came to a stop at the circle drive.

"Nice fountain, Stanley, and what an incredible home you have. Must be tough to keep clean, I would think."

"Not really difficult actually, as my breed happens to be very well kept and tidy if you will. This house belonged to my father and has been in the family for hundreds of years. We have done a lot of work to keep it maintained, but it is well worth it."

"I would say so, it is beautiful," Kain marveled.

"Well, perhaps it is time to get out of the car so I can show you around some. Besides, I am anxiously waiting to see my wife and kids," Stanley suggested.

Stanley would leave Kain sitting while he went to the trunk to pull his wheelchair out. Stanley would shout to the front of the car to Kain, explaining to him that his wife might be a little pissed off for not telling her that he was bringing a guest back. Stanley also cautioned Kain that Julie not being aware of this might make things a little complex at first.

It was then that Stanley noticed something was not right at his home. He quickly slammed the trunk of his car down and told Kain that he would be right back and to remain seated in the vehicle. Stanley quickly ran inside his home with a sense of urgency. Once inside, he began to shout for anyone who would listen.

"Julie??....Kids??"

As Stanley called out, an eerie silence greeted him. The usual bustling sound of his family seemed absent, replaced by an unsettling stillness that hung in the air. Anxiety began to tighten its grip on Stanley's chest as he navigated through the familiar corridors of his ancestral home.

He rushed to the living room, where the fireplace usually crackled with warmth and laughter echoed. Instead, the room felt cold, and an uneasy feeling settled in Stanley's gut. His eyes scanned the room, searching for any sign of his family, but all he found was an unsettling emptiness.

"Julie? Kids?" Stanley's voice carried a tinge of desperation as he continued his search, moving from room to room. The silence seemed to echo back, amplifying the worry that crept into his thoughts.

Back at the car, Kain sat with a growing sense of unease. The picturesque surroundings now felt haunting as he watched Stanley's hurried actions. The beautiful home that moments ago exuded charm now felt like a quiet witness to an unfolding mystery.

Minutes felt like hours as Stanley reemerged from the house, his face etched with concern. He approached the car, his gaze locking onto Kain's curious eyes.

"They're not here, Kain. Julie, the kids—they're not here," Stanley uttered with a mixture of disbelief and fear.

A heavy silence hung between them, punctuated only by the distant rustling of leaves. The vibrant home that had promised warmth and reunion now stood as an empty shell, casting shadows on the uncertainties that awaited them. Stanley, torn between anxiety and the need for answers, turned to Kain, searching for some form of reassurance or guidance in this unexpected turn of events.

Unfortunately for him, there was not a response as he ravished from the lower level to the upstairs, panicking as he checked every room and corner of his house.

While Kain was still sitting in the car, waiting as told to do, he could not help but notice what looked like the shadow of two bodies on the ground. He hesitated for a short moment while studying these images in his mind under the clear blue sky and sunshine. Even himself had a feeling that something terrible had taken place. Kain shouted as loud as he could from the car.

"Stanley, you might want to come see this!"

Hearing the shout, he quickly ran out of his house, slamming his front door to only look at Kain who was pointing in the direction of what he thought were human shadows. Stanley went directly to that area and was not happy with what his discovery was, knowing it was the remains of perished vampires. With a soft voice in his vocals, he would explain to Kain.

"A Drakulis and a few vampires were here!"

With his head hanging low, kneeling down and with his hand on the ground where the few shadows would lay, Stanley immediately calls his wife's phone in hopes to hear something, but little good did it do. Kain was confused and worried that it was by him, perhaps all has unfolded. Feeling it was him to blame for what may have taken place while Stanley was visiting with him in Kansas.

"I am so sorry, Stanley."

Stanley, in a mixture of grief and anger, shook his head and replied, "This is not your fault, Kain. There's something more sinister at play here." He stood up, his eyes scanning the surroundings, trying to piece together the puzzle of what had transpired in his absence.

As Stanley continued his investigation, he noticed signs of struggle near the shadows. Broken branches, disturbed soil, and the faint scent of blood lingered in the air. His instincts kicked in as he realized that his family had faced an attack.

"They were ambushed," Stanley muttered, clenching his fists in frustration. "I should have been here to protect them."

Kain, grappling with guilt, tried to offer comfort. "Stanley, there's no way you could have known. It's not your fault."

But Stanley's mind was racing, fueled by a mixture of

grief and determination. He needed to find his family, and he needed answers. The home that had once felt like a sanctuary now stood as a grim reminder of the dangers that lurked in the shadows.

"I need to track them down. We need to find who did this," Stanley declared, his gaze piercing into the distance.

Kain, though overwhelmed by the sudden turn of events, nodded in agreement. Together, they began to assess the scene, searching for any clues that might lead them to the perpetrators. The once picturesque orchards and winding roads now became a backdrop to a desperate search for answers, as Stanley and Kain delved into a world where the line between human and supernatural blurred, and the consequences of their actions echoed in the ominous quiet of the surroundings.

Kain said to Stanley, not knowing how to truly express himself but sensing the frustration on Stanley's face. The only place Stanley could think of calling next was that of his brother Stephen. It was the closest to them and also the safest place to go, as he had preached to his kids that if danger ever came their way at the plantation, they should seek their Uncle Stephen.

Stanley then looked up at the upper level of the house where Sabe's bedroom was and noticed the glass from his window had been shattered. He then did something that Kain had not yet seen: witnessed Stanley, while in human form, showing his amazing strength and ability. Stanley leaped from the ground to the top of the roof next to his son's window with the greatest of ease. That would be all Kain needed to see with his own eyes to know for a fact that Stanley was telling the truth about everything he claimed to be. Still sad at what had taken place, he was still astonished from being able to see what just happened.

Stanley Swanson – Breed of a Werewolf

Knowing it was not a time to ask questions of Stanley, Kain kept quiet and in disbelief. He was also just as concerned about his family while still feeling at fault. Kain, in his mind, knew that if Stanley was not with him, then perhaps these shadows that lay on the ground would not have ever taken place.

It was at this point in time, with luck, that Stanley's family and brother were coming towards the plantation from the orchard woods. Kain's heart began to race as he was not certain who it was coming down the driveway but trusted that Stanley was there and would not allow harm to him, as he suggested.

As the car came to a stop just behind Stanley's, Kain rolled his window up and locked the doors just to be safe while watching the rearview mirror. He was suddenly at ease once he noticed a little girl step out of the car, assuming it was Stanley's daughter. It, in fact, was her as he continued to watch.

Thrilled by Jade to see her father's car and standing at Sabe's window, Jade took off running while shouting 'Dad!' While Kain watched this little girl running past the car, Sabe was just as fast to join her side. Stanley, emotional as he was, lit up with joy and jumped down from the rooftop. Julie would soon follow behind her overjoyed children but would pause by the passenger window where Kain remained seated.

Looking at him eye to eye, she semi-transitioned to express to this crippled man in her werewolf form by giving him an angry growl of displeasure. Julie, in disapproval of Kain being there at the house, could only say a quick word to him which was Human with a nasty but quiet grumble of her vocal chords. Kain did not do anything as he moved his body a bit further from the window as he was feeling in much trouble and still plenty of guilt. Julie then continued past him to rejoin her husband.

While in a bit of shock from seeing an almost full werewolf that he had long awaited for, there was soon a tapping on his window, which was from Stephen.

"She means you no harm; she, as most of our breed, simply do not like humans."

It was a momentary relief for Kain as he watched Stephen continue to follow Julie. It was all surreal to Kain as he watched a family bonding with concern for one another. He realized at that very moment that werewolves were indeed breeds with emotions, feelings, and thoughts. The only time this afternoon that Kain would smile was when he watched Stanley jump from the rooftop and to the ground to give his family many hugs and kisses.

As Kain sat in the passenger seat of the car and not really able to hear from the distance, he could only watch as Julie was pointing in his direction and assume she was not happy with him. Then Kain knew for a fact she was not happy with Stanley as she slapped him across his face.

Kain began to get nervous for his life as Stephen turned from his brother and his family and started to head back towards the car. For whatever reason, Kain quickly re-locked the door while making sure the window was rolled up tightly. Stephen, though, gently squatted down to the window with his hands on his knees.

"Really, Kain? You think a window rolled up would save you from us, our kind?"

This was followed by a humorous laugh from Stephen. Then Stephen walked to the driver-side door and sat in next to Kain.

Stanley Swanson – Breed of a Werewolf

"You mortal man have stirred up a lot of problems for us. I am Stephen, Stanley's brother, and what he has shared with you must stop, I believe. Now is not the time, so I apologize, but do know that Julie will more than likely request your written journal. It will be her decision nonetheless."

"I have not even written much down, and most of all remains back at my house. I apologize for any wrongdoings. I am not even certain what all has taken place."

"Well, I can assure you that you will find out in time, Kain. Shall we take you inside the house now, or would you prefer to sit in this miserable heat?"

"That would be fine as it is a bit muggy out here."

"I am supposing that wheelchair is for you?" Stephen said, in a joking manner.

Kain was relieved with the humor and told Stephen it was. Stephen then removed the wheelchair and kindly helped Kain into his unwanted seat.

"Well, Kain, this should be an interesting night, and I have some questions for you myself. As for the lady, my sister-in-law, as I said a bit earlier to you, she means you no harm but she is highly sick with you."

"I had no idea this was happening, sir."

"Please call me Stephen, as the term sir is what we often had to refer to the Drakulis when we were slaves."

Kain apologized to Stephen, as that is something he knew

Stanley had mentioned to him in the past, about their breed being slaves, often referred to as hell hounds.

"I am aware that Stanley has shared that with you and a lot more, Kain. We do not break code or give an advantage to those of our breed, which is why we are not thrilled with what Stanley has done with meeting you."

"Do not blame Stanley, as this is something I have wanted for years to know; he just happened to find me. Your brother is a good person."

"Why? Because he shares our secrets with you, has taken you back in past time or this fulfills you in a way I do not understand?"

While still wheeling Kain toward the house, while Stanley and his family have already made it inside, Stephen slows down the pushing so he can have a few more choice words with Kain.

"No, because I believe in your breed."

"Kain, you have no idea of our secrecy, our breed, what we have been through or such. What I do know is this, Kain, what my brother has shared with you and if it were to get in the wrong hands, could easily kill our breed out and this is why I am not willing to agree with you or my brother. I will further have you know, that his wife and kids nearly died last night which would suggest it was because of your quest for answers."

"I am sorry, it was not my intentions to cause harm."

"Which is why I have not taken your life as we speak, Kain, but rather helping you inside. Besides, I cannot wait to hear what my brother's wife has to say to you."

Being nervous has not left for a second with Kain as he is wheeled into the house for the first time. Stephen settles Kain down in the front room of this magnificent home, where Stephen then sits down, and both Sabe and Jade join by his side.

"Well, this is such a nice home you all have here, kids," Kain would say as he tried to relax his body.

It did not take long while it was an awkward moment; Sabe starts to get a bit irritated while looking at Kain as he knows perhaps none of this would have happened if not for him. Sabe then gets up from the comfort of his cushion on the couch and begins to approach Kain. As he becomes very close to his face would say.

"Do I scare you, Mr.?"

"No," Kain replied with a look of confusion on his face.

As fast as he had told him he was not scared, Sabe transitioned in full form of their breed. With a bit of drool/saliva dripping from his teeth and an inch from Kain's face, he stared deep into his eyes while growling. Kain only budged a bit as he moved his head back slightly, hands gripping the wheels of his wheelchair.

"Sabe, stop scaring the poor human," Stephen demanded while the youngest Jade laughed hysterically.

Just as fast as Stephen said that, Sabe grabbed some clothes before transitioning back to human form. Then there was just silence as a single tear ran down from Sabe's right eye. Kain again blamed himself without saying so, as his head just dropped from chin to chest.

"I am so sorry for what had happened the other night, I deeply apologize to you all. I should not be here and will ask Stanley to return me to my home."

Stephen quickly acknowledged his emotions and in a soft voice told Sabe to be seated. Then it was Jade's turn to take a stab at Kain to show her young frustration to the fact that they almost lost their mother the night before. As she became close to Kain in his wheelchair, she would say in her innocent young voice.

"Do you know why we are mad at you, human?"

"Yes, because I have put you in harm's way. I have said this many times over and admit I am in the wrong."

"It is not that alone or a single reason; it is because we are few. We are not like you humans that have many friends, lose one only to make another, have family galore, or share lives. Once we lose just one of our family or friends that are all breeds, they will never be replaced as easily as it is for you humans. Do you have family?"

"I do, but not close as I have told your father Stanley."

"Do you talk with them?"

"No, not really."

"But you have the option to, yes?"

"I do have the option, but I choose not to."

"Why is that?"

"Because I am not that close to them. My parents have both passed away, I have no kids and I have given up on life as I sit in this wheelchair and have been known as a freak because of my desire to find those like you. I have no job and I live off disability, so I choose not to communicate with the few family members I have nor do they with me."

"That is truly sad, but we all have a choice that sometimes is hard to make. I lose my mother, father, brother, or even my Uncle; I will not have a choice to make. We do not have the ability or freedom to go out and express ourselves as you do; we are limited in our choices, Mr."

"Which is what makes us wise in time," Stephen interrupted while stating that Jade is very wise.

Kain is fast to agree with Stephen, just based on what Jade had just said to him.

"You are a very bright young lady and have taught me something. Sorry, to not get off subject a bit, but I hope your mom and dad are doing good as I have not heard from them. Also, if you do not mind, I was wondering if I could have a drink of water," Kain would ask in a still nervous voice.

Stephen gladly decides to show Kain around the house a bit with the exceptions of taking him upstairs, of course, due to him being in a wheelchair. Stephen would only say to Kain as both kids left the area.

"As far as my brother returning you home, I do not believe that is going to happen. Your place of stay has been compromised now. I have a feeling that you are going to be witnessing a lot of our breed over the next few days, so take mental notes if you wish, but I would not recommend seeing you write anything more down," Stephen warned.

As the sun would soon fall, while the glimpse of the moon you could see of the purple haze just before night came. It was time for the late evening to soon begin.

THE FINEST OF FEASTS

From the upstairs comes a shout from Stanley.

"Please, Stephen, gather all around the table as we must soon eat."

With that said, Stephen guides all the others of the house to the dinner table. There they would sit with not much to say to one another as Kain patiently watched each of them. It would not be long before Kain would almost be as an outsider and as though he was not even there as Sabe, Jade, and Stephen would carry on many conversations among themselves, just as most families would do.

He would listen to them talk about everything from the typical 'How have you both been doing with your education, what games Sabe has been playing, Jade and her stretching, etc. were discussed.' Kain had a fine moment with nothing but a smile on his face as he thought to himself. This is what he has not had in a very long time, and to witness such between this breed was a light hope that one day he too could find that happiness. While he knew they were not human, they acted just as though. Kain smiles even larger.

While the discussions between Uncle and his niece and nephew continued, Stanley and Julie finally made their way from the upstairs and soon arrived at the table. As usual, as werewolves are while in human form, they were dressed very classy. Julie sits at one end of the table next to her kids while Stanley sits opposite from her next to his brother and Kain. Kain asks the obvious questions.

S.K. Ballinger

"So what are we having for dinner?"

While forgetting that they do not eat human food, he suggests a simple and common form of food, which was that of a local nearby place to order some pizza. All at the table nearly lost their appetite with the mere suggestion. Stanley was steadfast in correcting Kain by telling him not to bring up human food at their table, for this is his first night back with his family and they will feast on lamb tonight.

Remembering that the breed only eats that of something recently killed, he was apologetic as he needed to remind himself he is with werewolves.

"Perhaps there is a place around here not too far from these orchards that I may call in an order for myself?" Kain suggested in a polite manner.

To his dismay, as Stanley told him there is not any place nearby for what it is that he would prefer to eat. Kain would do his best to try and fit in with them; after all, he was their guest, which is what he had accepted by agreeing with Stanley to visit his family. It was now their lifestyle, not his.

"I was kidding of my suggestion, so lamb it is." Kain smiled.

Even though he was not joking, as there is no way he would eat something freshly killed or uncooked if it was not in the form of sushi. After a short moment of what he had mentioned, it brought back memories to Julie when she once was a mortal.

"I once used to love pizza before I became what I am,

Kain."

Immediately her kids both looked at her in a disgusting manner and in almost shock, as that is something they did not know about their mother. She continues.

"You have to keep in mind, Kain, I was once human before my husband saved my life. While our bodies change, our mind does not. We always have memories to try and forget, share, and so much more."

Kain was very intrigued by her few statements and was quick to ask.

"So, once you changed or transitioned, you had automatically become grossed out with human food?"

"Not that fast, but over time, yes. Keep in mind for us, that once you are transitioned everything changes and does so rapidly. Stanley would, to his dismay, even bring me human food while he cared for me, but my body could not take it after so long and in turn would reject my consumption."

"So with these memories you have then, can you not remember how something as simple as a slice of pizza once tasted to you, Julie?"

"I can, but it is not what I remember as I quickly become sick at the thought of it. My desire is now freshly killed food."

Stanley intervenes for a moment to suggest that the kids need to be fed as it is getting late. Julie apologizes and explains to Kain that she must go and get food for dinner. Stanley gladly stands up from his chair and places his napkin on the table.

"I will go tonight, love, you keep Kain company as I know you have been busy providing while I have been gone recently."

Julie shows a fast smile to her husband in a gratitude gesture and sits back down. Stanley approaches the front door and removes all of his clothes and hangs them up before transitioning. Once he does transition, the hunt to a nearby farm would ensue. He runs fast through the woods and knows of many surrounding cattle ranches within his ten-mile radius that they choose from, which are never the same in any given three-day stretch.

The vision werewolves have is astonishing as it appears of future distance of only seconds with a blur surrounding the focal point or destination.

Once he approaches a farm which was full of lambs and quickly looks for the youngest of them all, just as he had told Kain about how they have eaten in the last nine years it remains true, which was to kill only what they can eat and typically was that of a newborn. There, a baby lamb was off by a feeder and surrounded by a few other adults. It was a fast kill to say the least as Stanley rushed in violently while immediately going for the throat of the baby lamb.

The room fell into an eerie quietude, only interrupted by the distant sounds of the surrounding lambs. The lamb, victim to the ferocity of Stanley's jaws, bore numerous lacerations on its body, its throat already crushed. Swiftly, Stanley returned home, still carrying the lifeless lamb in his mouth.

Entering the house, he dropped the mangled carcass on the floor and transitioned back to human form, donning his clothes once more. Clothed, he picked up the lifeless animal and proceeded to the kitchen where his family awaited, excitement gleaming in their eyes. Kain, however, found himself disturbed, grappling with the urge to avoid vomiting.

"Something wrong, Kain?" Stanley inquired, presenting his night's catch.

"Well, I just am..."

Before Kain could complete his sentence, Julie interjected, "What, it's not in hamburger form?"

Laughter echoed from the kids as Stanley suggested to his wife, "Perhaps, love, if you wouldn't mind, as he is our guest and we should have manners. Would you kindly take our food to the kitchen and butcher it up some?"

Reluctantly, Julie complied, lifting the calf effortlessly from the table. Stephen, on the other hand, became somewhat agitated.

"I thought you were documenting everything about our breed, Kain. If so, I would have thought you could have stomached a situation like this."

"I certainly was trying to, Stephen. It's not every day that I see a large animal with blood all over the place and then placed in front of me."

"Let him be, Stephen. It's only one night, and he'll have documented this," Stanley intervened.

In the kitchen, Julie ripped portions off the calf using just her hands, stealing a few for herself. She grabbed plates and walked each portion out to the table. Sabe quickly transitioned before Stanley declared to his family, including Sabe, "Tonight, manners we will show to Kain and only use our teeth."

Jade, eager to showcase her full transition, protested, "Awe, but dad, I am still in practice of transitioning and can do so fully, just ask Stephen."

"Not tonight, Jade. We'll discuss this at a later time."

Pouting, they all began to transition only their teeth to eat what Stanley had caught. Kain, still a bit sickened, marveled at their ability to consume the meat. Blood stained their hands, and meat was torn off by their powerful jaws and sharp teeth, all in human form.

"Thanks for the catch, Stanley," Stephen remarked, licking his lips with blood dripping around his mouth.

Jokingly, Stephen offered Kain some, saying, "You sure, Kain? You wish not to try some; you're missing out."

"No thank you, I'm not all that hungry. I am more of a vegetarian these days."

Despite his hunger, witnessing the gruesome feast had completely robbed Kain of his appetite.

The meal concluded after roughly ten minutes, allowing Kain to observe the unusual behavior of his werewolf hosts. Intrigued by the refrigerator and plates, seldom used by the family, he questioned Stanley about their purpose. Stanley explained that they were part of a facade, meant to maintain the appearance of normalcy in case of unexpected visits from law enforcement or nosy neighbors.

Stanley Swanson – Breed of a Werewolf

Stanley elaborated on their encounters with the local police, who investigated complaints from cattle farmers about missing livestock. The family's apparent lack of aging and prosperity had stirred curiosity among the locals, necessitating a well-crafted illusion. Plates and kitchen appliances served as mere props to perpetuate the illusion of a conventional human lifestyle.

"All an illusion, Kain. The very plates we are eating off of have not been used in many years. The stove does not even have gas running to it. The only few real things we have that you humans have are electric, plumbing, and, of course, televisions as well as the internet. We live just as you mortals do, just without the need to stock food, use dishes, or cook, for that matter."

Satisfied with the explanation, the family belched in contentment after the exquisite meal. Stephen then announced their early departure the next morning to visit Gravakus, a revelation that seemed to unsettle Julie, who felt excluded from the decision.

"Stanley! Why are you going to do this when all he wants is this friend of yours that sits at our very table? Do you not think of the safety of your family? Turn Kain over to Gravakus, and let us be as we were before; it is that simple," she exclaimed.

Stanley defended his decision, stating, "Julie, this is why I am going. If these Drakulis dare try to harm my family over my actions, he will know not to do so again."

Concerned for the family's safety, Julie pressed, "What of us, Stanley, that remain here? There were many of them the other night; what makes you think they will not come back?"

"They will not come back any time soon, I assure you,

Julie. But if it gives you some comfort, I have already called some of our close friends over to help watch out in case they were brave enough to try," Stephen intervened.

Still upset, Julie glanced at Kain with disgruntled looks. She questioned the duration of Stanley's absence and the distance to Gravakus' residence in New York. Stephen clarified, "Gravakus lives on the other side of the country, in Coney Island, NY."

Frustrated, Julie expressed her dissatisfaction, realizing her husband was embarking on a perilous journey. She didn't want Stanley to place himself in harm's way and protested, "You have got to be kidding me when you say you are leaving yet again, but this time to place yourself in harm's way."

Stanley reassured her, saying, "Julie, if all goes as planned, we will only be gone for a few days, less than a week, I promise you."

"Screw your promises, Stanley! And what of your friend Kain?" Julie retorted.

"Kain will remain here; it would be far too dangerous to take him with us."

"So you wish for me to watch after a human that I had no part of wanting to have here in the first place?"

Stanley shouted, "Love you, Julie, and this is a matter that has to have action upon!"

The remaining three at the table continued their discussion about their plans. Kain, feeling thirsty, asked for water. Despite the heated mood, Stephen replied, "We have running water and

Stanley Swanson – Breed of a Werewolf

electricity, as you can see. Just because we don't have the grocery items you humans eat, we are still very much like you. Perhaps I was wrong, and you should start writing on paper what it is that we say."

As the night unfolded, Stephen continued sharing concerns about the impending visit of close friends who would be guarding Stanley's family during their trip to meet Gravakus. A notable figure among them was Francais, a dear friend of Stephen, who was set to perform a transition on his niece Natalie.

Intrigued by the prospect, Kain asked, "Is that where you turn her into your breed?" Eager to document this unique process, he awaited Stanley's response.

Stanley clarified that the transition would resemble what he had done to Julie. Turning to his brother, he inquired, "Is this the same Natalie from many years ago who was caught in the fire?"

Stephen affirmed, opening up about Natalie's tragic past. A once innocent girl, Natalie, along with her two brothers and mother, fell victim to a furious mob of vampires. The local community, fueled by prejudice, surrounded their house, demanding eviction based on their secret lives. A Drakulis known as Dritallion fueled the rage, leading to the horrifying act of setting their home ablaze.

Francais, living nearby, sensed the danger too late but managed to rescue Natalie, aged seven, in a courageous transition. Despite suffering burns himself, he carried her to safety in a secluded area near a hospital. Natalie, scarred for life with third-degree burns, barely clung to life, surviving only because her mother was a werewolf. Francais, determined to protect what remained of his family, faced the challenges of caring for her during her extended recovery.

As Natalie grew older, she learned about the werewolf lifestyle from her uncle. At the age of twenty-one, desiring a transformation, Francais granted her wish. This decision served as a redemption for his fallen sister and fulfilled Natalie's longing for a new life free from her painful past.

Stanley's question interrupted the poignant narrative, "Is this something you think you are ready to witness, Kain?"

"Absolutely I am, though a bit nervous about how these close friends of yours will take to me," Kain responded.

Stephen reassured him with a few laughs, explaining that their friends wouldn't bother him much, respecting his space.

"Besides," he added, "they will know that there is not much a cripple human could do to them."

"Thanks," Kain replied with a half-smile, appreciating the humor amid the intense discussions.

As Stanley retired upstairs to speak with his wife and kids, Kain couldn't help but entertain the fleeting thought of being transitioned into the werewolf breed. Stephen, perceptive to Kain's contemplation, addressed the unspoken desire promptly.

"It is not going to happen, Kain. I am sorry," Stephen asserted, sensing the unspoken wish in Kain's demeanor.

Perplexed, Kain queried, "What do you mean, Stephen?"

Stephen, with a sense of regret, explained, "I know that you may wonder what it would be like to be a werewolf, to walk again, heal, and age slowly. You are human, and that is how it will remain."

"Julie was human as well, but Stanley changed her," Kain pointed out, hoping for a different outcome.

"While this is true, Stanley should not have done so. He was not as wise as he is currently when he made the decision to do so back then. I am sorry again, Kain, but you will never be one of our breed," Stephen clarified, closing the door on the possibility for Kain.

Stephen's words, though disappointing, were a necessary reality check to curb any unrealistic expectations. He understood the implications of raising hopes for a human to experience the extraordinary benefits of being a werewolf.

"You should get your rest as we all will be having a busy day tomorrow," Stephen advised Kain before heading off to bed. As a parting gesture, he dropped off a glass of water for Kain, offering a light pat on his shoulders.

Alone with his thoughts, Kain continued documenting the events he had witnessed. Engrossed in his writing, he was interrupted by Julie's entrance into the dining room.

"Could not sleep, I see, Kain?" she observed.

"No, not at all, Julie, just figured I would correct some of my writing," Kain replied, maintaining his focus on the task at hand.

Curiosity brimming, Julie questioned his motivation, "Why is it you are doing this, and I know it is something that you have been fascinated with for many years, as Stanley has told me. But really why?"

Kain responded, "How many people who believe you to be just a mythological being are out there, and how often is a person able to witness the truth of such beings?"

Julie, with a hint of skepticism, offered her perspective, "Perhaps we wish to be known as only a mythological being, Kain, which is why we remain hidden from the real world."

Pushing the conversation further, Kain pondered, "What happens if this war that your husband so truly believes were to be true? Shouldn't people know that you exist so that they can have a better understanding of your breed?"

"Most humans will never understand us, and many fall to the realm of jealousy, just look at yourself, Kain," Julie remarked.

"What of me, Julie?" Kain inquired.

"You are old and cannot walk, but I am sure you would love to walk again, no?" she retorted.

"Well, who would not want to walk again? Why, of course, I would love to. Just like this Natalie girl that will be transitioned tomorrow, why not me as well?" Kain questioned, voicing his hidden desires.

"First of all, Natalie is of a breed family, so we shall not discuss that, Kain," Julie stated firmly. She continued, emphasizing the boundaries, "Your hopes and desires need only to be that of your original purpose, which is to document, even though I do not agree with it. Know that if you step outside of those boundaries, you will not have a promising end."

"Is that a threat, Julie, as I had no intentions of doing otherwise?" Kain challenged.

"Not a threat, Kain, rather a promise. You know I do not agree with my husband and what you two are doing and the danger you have caused," Julie concluded, leaving Kain to absorb her words.

Feeling like an outsider, Kain continued writing, processing the complex dynamics within the Swanson household. Despite the internal conflict, he looked forward to witnessing the upcoming transition. The hope of becoming a werewolf may have been dashed, but the kindness shown to him was something he could still appreciate.

As the night waned, Julie left to retire, content with one last conversation with Kain, knowing she would be keeping a close eye on him for the next week. Alone, Kain wheeled himself to the couch, his makeshift bed for the duration of his stay at the Swanson's plantation. The night came to an end, leaving Kain alone with his thoughts and the anticipation of the events to unfold.

S.K. Ballinger

ARRIVAL OF THE SWANSON CLAN

Morning unfolded swiftly, promising a day filled with activity for Kain as he anticipated meeting the friends who would be keeping a watchful eye on the Swanson family during their visit to Gravakus. Nervous yet intrigued, Kain prepared himself for the unique experience that awaited him – witnessing a live transition, a phenomenon he had recently yearned for himself.

Around seven in the morning, the first of the friends arrived in a sleek escalade. Stanley's longest and dearest friend, Jeremia, stepped out, greeted by a warm hug from Stanley.

"It has been a while, old friend. So glad to see you. Of all, I trust it is you," Stanley exclaimed, his enthusiasm evident.

As more friends arrived, the atmosphere became lively with laughter and camaraderie. The arrangements made to safeguard Stanley's family and Kain were apparent, and the gathering felt like a small family reunion. The reactions to Kain varied among the friends; some were indifferent, while others didn't mind his presence and were even willing to share information with him, echoing Stanley's openness.

"Julie, how have you been? You look astonishing!" Jeremia happily commented upon seeing Stanley's wife.

"Oh, you know Jeremia, the same as about forty-three years ago," she replied with a light laughter, sharing in the joy of seeing an old friend.

Sabe and Jade, the Swanson children, echoed the excitement with big smiles, shouting, "Jeremia!" as they received warm hugs from him.

Stanley Swanson – Breed of a Werewolf

Amidst the celebrations and shared memories, the morning unfolded like a relaxed family gathering. The friends, familiar with each other, engaged in lively discussions that continued until the late afternoon. Kain found comfort in the scene, a semblance of normalcy in the lives of these extraordinary beings.

However, amidst the festivities, Stanley and his wife, Julie, stood off to the side against a white wall in the hallway. Stanley, with his head resting on Julie's forehead, gently brushed his right hand down her cheek, a tender moment that spoke volumes of their connection. It was a brief pause in the festivities, a silent acknowledgment of the strength they drew from each other in the midst of their unique existence.

"I am so sorry for what I have started, Julie, and know that I love you."

Julie's emotions, weakened by the fast-paced events of the past few days, betrayed her as a single tear ran down her face.

"I know you do, Stan. I am just worried for you now."

From the other room, Stephen observed the tender moment between his brother and sister-in-law. He walked towards them and reassured Julie.

"He will be fine, Julie. He is, after all, my little brother, and I will not let harm be done to him, just as I would not allow with all of you."

Stephen's comforting voice and sincere gesture provided a measure of ease for Julie.

"Stanley, we should get going before long," Stephen suggested.

With a soft kiss to his wife, Stanley said his goodbyes to his kids and expressed gratitude to their friends. As he walked away, he left Julie with a heartfelt reassurance.

"You are in safe hands, love, and after we meet with Gravakus, I will be home as a changed husband. You are my everything, my world, and my life."

Despite the reassurance, Julie let her head fall against the wall while Stanley walked away. Stanley proceeded with his goodbyes, and as he did, Sabe, his son, tried to plead to go with them. Stanley firmly rejected the idea.

"Son, this is going to be a visit with a very bad outcome at the end, not for me, but for the Drakulis who caused unwanted trouble. You will have to sit this one out."

Understanding, Sabe expressed his love for his father and wished for his safe return. Jade, Stanley's daughter, clung to her father, tearfully asking him to stay and let Kain leave.

"The damage, my amazing and wonderful daughter, has already been done, and now your father has to correct it, hon."

As Stanley and Stephen made their way to the front door, their friends silently observed, knowing that challenges awaited them. Kain stood by the door, offering his good wishes.

"Be safe, Stanley, and you as well, Stephen. I only wish that I could help correct all that has been unfolded."

Stanley Swanson – Breed of a Werewolf

Stephen, aware that Kain's presence played a role in the unfolding events, patted Kain's shoulder, silently conveying reassurance.

Kain wheeled himself to find Julie, seeking some form of forgiveness. She genuinely accepted his approach, acknowledging the challenging days ahead.

"Well, as if the last few days have not been interesting enough, then the following days shall be," Julie remarked.

Happy that Julie seemed to have softened towards him, Kain hoped for a budding friendship. Julie informed Kain about Natalie's upcoming transition that night and advised him to prepare for an unimaginable spectacle. She mentioned that it would be loud and difficult to watch but would culminate in a display of beauty.

Julie, sensing Kain's curiosity, shared a proposal.

"If you would like to see that night, I will show you?"

Eager for a glimpse into the past, Kain accepted her offer.

"Yes, I would love for you to show me, Julie."

She wheeled Kain to the living room, instructing Jeremia, Stanley's closest friend, to ensure privacy. Jeremia gladly complied, standing back as Julie initiated the past travel experience.

S.K. Ballinger

DEATH CAN COME FAST, BUT SO CAN LIFE

In the cozy confines of the living room, Julie found herself seated directly across from Kain, a palpable tension lingering in the air. A sense of secrecy enveloped the room as Jeremia, ever vigilant, stood guard to ensure the sanctity of the moment. His eyes darted around the perimeter, ensuring that no unwelcome intruders would disturb the delicate proceedings about to unfold.

Julie, tasked with the solemn responsibility of sharing a revelation that carried the weight of altering Kain's very existence, assumed a posture of both trepidation and resolve. The gravity of the impending revelation was evident in the furrowed lines on her forehead and the subtle hesitance in her movements. This was no ordinary disclosure; it was a revelation that had the potential to truncate nearly three days from the tapestry of Kain's life.

As Julie began to articulate the profound information, Kain's countenance shifted, mirroring a blend of curiosity, anticipation, and a latent anxiety. The knowledge of this temporal sacrifice, imparted to him by Julie beforehand, had left a lingering unease in the pit of his stomach. He understood that what was to transpire in the next moments would be a journey into the intricate folds of time itself, a path fraught with uncertainties and consequences.

In an effort to prepare both herself and Kain for the impending temporal voyage, Julie locked eyes with him, seeking a connection that transcended the physical realm. The intensity of her gaze mirrored the way Stanley, back in the familiar landscapes of Kansas, had peered into the depths of Kain's soul.

Stanley Swanson – Breed of a Werewolf

This shared gaze was more than a simple exchange of glances; it was a silent pact, a mutual understanding that transcended the spoken word.

The living room, once bathed in the warm glow of ambient light, now began to dim gradually, casting an ethereal atmosphere upon the scene. The fading luminosity mirrored the fading boundaries between the present and the impending temporal excursion. Shadows danced on the walls as the room itself seemed to hold its breath, poised on the precipice of an extraordinary journey through time.

As the dimness deepened, the past and the present intertwined, creating a seamless continuum that defied the conventional constraints of time. The living room became a vessel, propelling Kain and Julie into an enigmatic landscape where the echoes of bygone days resonated alongside the palpable anticipation of days yet to unfold. In this twilight zone, the duo braved the enigma of temporal manipulation, the air pregnant with the weight of an imminent temporal shift.

And so, with a room now shrouded in the mysteries of temporal travel, Julie, Kain, and Jeremia stood at the nexus of past and present, ready to unravel the secrets that lay hidden within the folds of time itself. The journey had begun, and the living room, once a mundane space, had transformed into the staging ground for an extraordinary odyssey through the annals of temporal existence.

In the quiet and seemingly unremarkable town of Fresno, CA, the clock of fate ticked resolutely in the direction of heart-wrenching tragedy. The time placement for our narrative harks back to a period when Julie, engulfed by the warmth of her own family, had yet to fathom the impending tempest that would

S.K. Ballinger

irrevocably alter the course of her existence.

The canvas of this sorrowful tale unfolds on a mundane evening, a time when Julie, accompanied by her then-husband and their two cherubic boys, embarked on a routine trip to a local store to procure the essentials of life – groceries. Little did they know that this ordinary outing would unravel swiftly and mercilessly, leaving behind a trail of fatality, sorrow, and heartache that would resonate through the corridors of time.

As the family traversed the roads of Fresno, blissfully unaware of the imminent tragedy that awaited them, the hands of destiny orchestrated a collision of profound consequence. It was late evening, and a fateful encounter with a drunken man would thrust them into a maelstrom of calamity. The inebriated stranger, navigating the labyrinth of life in a reckless stupor, careened across the center lane with a cruel indifference to the lives in his wake.

The impact was merciless, as the drunken man's vehicle clipped the driver's side of Julie's family car with devastating force. The repercussions of this collision were immediate and catastrophic. The entire left side of their vehicle crumpled, a visceral testament to the unrelenting force that had descended upon them. In the blink of an eye, Julie's once vibrant husband, aged only twenty-eight, met his untimely demise upon impact, leaving behind a void that echoed with the cruel finality of life's capricious whims.

With their car spiraling into a chaotic dance of destruction, the harrowing journey was far from over. The vehicle flipped and tumbled, an unbridled force of physics propelling it into a series of somersaults before it mercifully came to a rest. Amidst the twisted wreckage, tragedy had claimed another soul. One of

Julie's precious children, aged a tender five years, was ejected from the mangled car, meeting an abrupt and heartrending end on the cold pavement.

In this small town, where lives were interconnected like the intricate threads of a fragile tapestry, the echo of that night lingered on – a haunting reminder of the fragility of life and the inexorable cruelty that time could unleash. Julie, now burdened with the weight of unimaginable loss, stood at the crossroads of a shattered existence, grappling with the unfathomable grief that would become the backdrop of her journey through time and the depths of her own resilience.

Trapped in the twisted wreckage of the once-ordinary family car, Julie's world had descended into a nightmarish abyss. With pain coursing through her battered body and blood obscuring her vision, she strained to survey the grim tableau through the shattered rearview mirror. There, amidst the wreckage, lay her three-year-old son, his life extinguished in the merciless throes of the calamity that had befallen them.

As Julie wept, her anguished gaze shifted to the young man emerging from his overturned car, seemingly unscathed in stark contrast to the devastation surrounding him. Blood-streaked eyes clouded her vision, but she could discern his stumbling approach towards her. His voice, bearing the weight of realization and remorse, echoed through the chaos.

"Is anyone hurt?"

Julie, a symphony of agony, managed to scream for help, her heartrending cry intertwined with the desperate plea for her lost children. The young man, sickened by the scene of tragedy he had unwittingly wrought, continued towards the mangled car, tears streaming down his face.

Amidst the cacophony of approaching sirens, an officer arrived, swiftly assessing the catastrophic scene. His first concern, however, was Julie's safety. Promising to return shortly, he urged her to remain calm. Meanwhile, the intoxicated young man, overwhelmed by guilt, was met with the authoritative commands of the law.

"Stop where you are at and put your hands on your head!"

In a state of remorseful distress, the man complied, falling to his knees, his pleas for forgiveness intermingled with tears. The officer, stern and resolute, warned him to keep his hands raised, emphasizing his right to defend himself later.

As the officer knelt beside the remorseful man, intending to restrain him with handcuffs, a sinister twist unfolded. In a sudden revelation, the seemingly human officer transformed into something otherworldly – a vampire. With predatory glee evident on his face, the vampire unleashed his insatiable hunger on the hapless man, whose fate was sealed in a macabre dance of feeding and despair.

The ghastly scene unfolded with an eerie swiftness, a grotesque tableau against the backdrop of tragedy. The vampire, posing as an officer, indulged in a feeding session, exploiting the precious moments before the arrival of genuine help. As the scene bore witness to both mortal suffering and supernatural malevolence, the intersection of two worlds unveiled itself in a nightmarish spectacle of blood, death, and the inescapable grip of the paranormal.

This is what a Drakulis and vampires alike call easy feed.

Stanley Swanson – Breed of a Werewolf

In the aftermath of the gruesome spectacle, Julie, ensnared in the wreckage of the mangled car, found herself in a surreal nightmare, forced to bear witness to a horrifying scene that defied reason. As she screamed desperately for help, the cacophony of sirens drew nearer, promising the arrival of salvation amidst the desolation.

The vampire, sated from his ghastly feast, turned his attention toward Julie, his lips licked in sinister satisfaction. Despite her own critical condition and the traumatic loss of her family, Julie continued her anguished pleas for assistance, her cries echoing on the desolate road.

As the vampire advanced toward Julie, reveling in the impending chaos, a sudden interruption shattered the eerie scene. Stanley Swanson, in his werewolf form and fresh from his own nocturnal hunt, halted abruptly upon hearing Julie's desperate screams. Uncharacteristically intrigued by the human's distress, he sprinted through the woods with the agility and speed characteristic of his lupine form.

Upon arriving at the scene, Stanley, guided by his acute sense of smell, identified the vampire posing as a police officer. Witnessing the imminent threat to Julie's life, Stanley dropped his prey and grappled with a decision. Despite harboring an intense loathing for Drakulis and their kin, he felt compelled to intervene, moved by the profound grief emanating from the distraught human.

As the vampire closed in on the wrecked vehicle, Stanley, with a glint of determination in his eyes, readied himself for action. Ignoring the impending arrival of law enforcement, Stanley, equipped with powerful claws, emerged from the shadows, landing between the vampire and Julie.

S.K. Ballinger

In a futile attempt to repel the werewolf threat, the vampire drew his gun, firing rounds that, though painful, proved ineffective against Stanley's resilient hide. A primal growl emanated from Stanley as the vampire discarded his firearm, charging at the werewolf with a malicious smile. Julie, hanging on the precipice of consciousness, bore witness to the surreal clash between these mythological creatures.

Claws clashed, and fangs bared as the nocturnal battle unfolded before Julie's fading eyes. In a surprising turn of events, the werewolf proved dominant, driven by an unusual connection to the human's grief. Stanley, assured of the vampire's demise, shifted his focus to Julie, who hung between life and death.

With a display of formidable strength, Stanley ripped the car door off its hinges and effortlessly severed the seatbelt that bound Julie. Cradling her limp form in his powerful arms, he darted into the woods, leaving behind the aftermath of the supernatural confrontation.

The next morning's news would recount the tragic events, reporting the deaths of Julie's husband and children. An officer's disappearance would be noted, and investigations would unfold in the mortal realm. The police, unaware of the supernatural intervention, would search the woods for Julie, suspecting a wild animal attack.

In the shadowy realms of Drakulis and werewolves, the truth would remain hidden, locked within the lore of the supernatural. The media, oblivious to the extraordinary forces at play, would eventually move on, forgetting the bizarre incident that unfolded on that fateful night, buried in the annals of time without the scrutiny of modern surveillance.

Stanley Swanson – Breed of a Werewolf

In the sanctuary of Stanley's secluded abode, the passage of time unfolded like a slow, lingering melody. He dedicated an entire week to the meticulous care of Julie, a survivor marked by tragedy, nursing her back to a semblance of health. Sacrificing his own needs, Stanley tirelessly attended to her every wound, ensuring her comfort within the confines of his inexplicably luxurious dwelling.

As the days passed, Julie, oscillating between consciousness and the realm of dreams, found solace in her surroundings. Stanley's silent vigil by her bedside became a reassuring constant in her hazy reality. The stately home, a stark contrast to the chaos that had unfolded outside, provided an unexpected haven.

When Julie finally summoned the strength to speak, her voice, though feeble, echoed a profound ache. "

I want my babies back and my husband John," she murmured, her words carrying the weight of a shattered life.

Stanley, his stoic demeanor masking the turbulent emotions within, offered no immediate solace. From a distance, he sought to soothe her questions as Julie grappled with the surreal circumstances that now enveloped her.

"I am not naive to what I saw with my eyes and whatever you may be, why would you not have just let me die?" she implored, her eyes reflecting a mix of despair and curiosity.

Stanley, the enigmatic werewolf, struggled to provide satisfactory answers.

"I felt you had lost so much in such a small amount of

time. I could not watch this evil take your life at the end of what you had just endured."

Her dissatisfaction with his response grew, as she insisted that her existence had become devoid of purpose. Julie questioned why Stanley had intervened instead of allowing the conventional forces of officers and medical teams to handle her fate.

Undeterred by her frustration and the unwelcome moniker of "beast" assigned to him, Stanley calmly explained, "Do you not remember what had happened, what did you see at the last moment before I intervened?"

Julie, recounting the gruesome scene with the vampiric officer, grappled with the newfound knowledge of the supernatural entities that lurked in the shadows. The reality of werewolves and vampires clashed with the boundaries of her comprehension.

Stanley, navigating the delicate terrain of justification, asked, "Should I have let that officer do the same to you?"

"I would have preferred to die," she replied, her defense fueled by a mix of desperation and internal turmoil.

In a tense exchange, Julie expressed her physical agony, enumerating the injuries she knew plagued her. The makeshift room, filled with medication to alleviate her suffering, served as a painful reminder of the wreck's aftermath.

"How do you even know my damn name!" she erupted in frustration, demanding an explanation for the intimate details that now bound her to this enigmatic savior.

Stanley Swanson – Breed of a Werewolf

"News," Stanley replied succinctly, confirming her status as the lone survivor of the calamitous event.

As the weight of her losses pressed down on her, Julie, in an emotional outpour, reiterated her desire for death, questioning Stanley's motives in saving her.

"I wish you would have just let me die as I have nothing now. I do not even know what the hell you are for certain. You are agreeing to what I said I had seen, which was that of a werewolf and vampire. So you are the beast that saved my life to be miserable?" she exclaimed, frustration etched across her tear-stained face.

With an air of patience wearing thin, Stanley delved deeper into the complexities of their respective breeds. He introduced the existence of Drakulis, vampires of a higher order, and contemplated the consequences of a different fate for Julie.

Julie, captivated by the supernatural revelations, questioned Stanley's intentions.

"What is your plan with me, you beast?" she demanded, her voice a mix of fear and curiosity.

Growing weary of the persistent name-calling, Stanley offered her an unexpected choice – freedom. He jokingly suggested, "It is your call, and you are welcomed to stay here as long as you stop calling me a beast."

Yet, sensing an unrest within Julie, Stanley's demeanor softened as she contemplated her future. He approached her with empathy, acknowledging her lingering pain and the importance of her connection with her family.

S.K. Ballinger

"Julie, know what I did was not to put you in entrapment with me. I am sorry for what you have been through and endured. If it is to seek your relationship with your parents, I fully understand that. I only wish you the best."

As Stanley reached for the phone to call paramedics, Julie interrupted, seeking clarity on the man behind the werewolf facade.

"What are you exactly, and what is your name as I have not even asked you?"

With a touch of humor, Stanley revealed, "My name is Stanley Swanson, and I am what your kind refers to as werewolves or our proper defined breed term, which is that of a Lycan."

Amidst her injuries, Julie found herself intrigued by the revelation.

"What makes you different from them, like the very one who was going to kill or change me that was dressed as an officer?" she queried.

Stanley, ready to dispel the myths surrounding his kind, shared the intricacies of their existence, highlighting the strengths and weaknesses that set them apart. As the night wore on, Julie found comfort in the conversation, gradually softening towards the being she once perceived as a threat.

"I saw him, the officer, shoot you several times. Did it hurt at all, and I have noticed that you have healed," Julie inquired, curiosity overcoming her pain.

Stanley Swanson – Breed of a Werewolf

Stanley, ever willing to demystify his existence, explained the nuances of werewolf resilience. Their exchange continued, touching on silver bullets, vulnerabilities, and the fundamental disparities between vampires and werewolves.

Julie, captivated by the unfolding narrative, sought details about the bullets that had wounded Stanley. With a touch of humor, Stanley recounted the uncomfortable process of removing non-silver bullets and underscored the challenges unique to his breed.

"Another reason we are much different than those blackhearted and relentless life-takers that you can stab over and over, which has no ill effect on them," Stanley remarked, guiding Julie through the intricacies of vampire weaknesses.

As the night progressed, Julie found herself immersed in the fantastical lore spun by Stanley. His willingness to share the intricacies of their supernatural world unveiled a tapestry of truths, challenging her preconceptions.

Aware of Julie's limited time, Stanley gently urged her to make decisions about her fate. He emphasized that her symptoms indicated a dwindling timeframe, underscoring the urgency of her choice. Stanley assured her that, whether she chose to stay or leave, she would be okay.

The night wore on, and as the clock struck three in the morning, Julie, grappling with both physical and emotional pain, took a deep breath. Her heart, a wounded vessel, signaled the impending crossroads where fate and choice collided.

In a moment of predestined clarity, Stanley, asleep but attuned to something amiss, stirred. With an intuitive sense of urgency, he sprung into action, rushing to Julie's side. His right hand gently rested on her chest as she met his gaze with a grateful smile, tears cascading down her face.

With the other hand, Stanley instinctively reached for the phone, poised to summon paramedics once more. However, in a surprising twist, Julie, soft touch guiding his hand, redirected the phone back to its base.

"What is your emergency, and how can we assist you?" echoed through the phone.

With a serene smile, Julie replied, "Sorry, nothing, and I apologize, as my kids were playing with the phone." Her hand, resting on Stanley's, steered the phone back to its resting place.

Confusion etched across Stanley's features, Julie, still smiling through her tears, uttered words that would alter her destiny.

"Make me you, your kind, your breed that you have spoken of."

Stanley, with a somber shake of his head, expressed the impossibility of such a transformation, bound by the laws of the Lycan. Julie, undeterred and accepting of her fate, implored him to let her rest forever, free from the torment of her mortal wounds.

"I am not afraid anymore, Stanley. I am hurting so badly inside, and you have done all that you can. I am only grateful that in my last moments, I will leave this world seeing your face."

As the delicate moment unfolded, the gravity of the choice Stanley faced loomed over him. Time slipped away like sand through his fingers, and the urgency of the situation pressed him to decide swiftly. Julie, the mortal he had saved, teetered on the precipice of life and death. The options were stark - passively witness her demise or defy the code, biting her and ushering her into the enigmatic realm of werewolves.

With her injuries, the outcome of turning her into a werewolf was uncertain, but Stanley couldn't bear the thought of idly watching her perish. A call to paramedics, in his wisdom, seemed futile at this critical juncture, given the severity of her condition. Thus, he had to make a rapid decision, to bite her or not.

Despite having explained the transitioning process to Julie, Stanley had omitted the excruciating pain integral to the transformation. His right hand, still on her chest, felt the heartbeat dwindling. In the final moments, as her last heartbeat approached, Stanley, driven by an innate impulse, transitioned himself, sinking his teeth into her neck.

The werewolf transition from human involved a bite lengthwise across the neck, a unique method designed to penetrate vital organs without risking a snapped neck. The precision of the process, witnessing the werewolf's massive jaws clamping down while holding steady, was, in its own way, a mesmerizing spectacle. There was an observable healing aspect during this transformation, an intricate dance between the supernatural and the physical realm.

Pain became the fulcrum of this process. Julie, gasping for breath, her eyes wide open in a final acknowledgment of the werewolf before her, was undergoing her last moments as a human. The agonizing part was yet to unfold. Her bones crackled, crunched, and changed, preparing for the metamorphosis into a werewolf at will. Fast flashes of forming intermingled with the pain, accompanied by loud screams, signifying the inevitable.

Stanley, fraught with concern, released her neck, transitioning back to his human form. Kneeling beside her, he could only wait, hoping that Julie would survive the bite he had just administered. The room held a heavy silence as her body became still, the once-beating heart now stilled by the trauma of the transition. Stanley, with a mix of trepidation and guilt, placed his hand back on her chest, observing her now perfect body, devoid of recent injuries. The anxious wait for the restart of her heart intensified, and Stanley grappled with the realization that he may have erred in his decision.

In what seemed like an eternity, a sudden beat pierced the stillness, marking Julie's rebirth into a new life. Panic seized her as her back arched, a deep breath ushering her into this uncharted existence. Laying flat on the bed, her eyes shut momentarily, she grappled with the aftermath of the trauma. Stanley, a complex swirl of emotions within him, watched with amazement as the transition succeeded. Balancing the dichotomy of sorrow and joy, he uttered to her in brief, "My lady."

As Stanley uttered those words with his head respectfully bowed down, Julie, in her newfound existence, took a moment to acclimate herself to the sensations of her revitalized being. The surge of energy coursing through her surpassed anything she had ever experienced as a mortal. Her hands traced along the contours of her naked body, a conscious exploration of the strength and vitality that now pulsed within her. With her head turned towards Stanley, she gracefully leaned to the side, planting her feet on the floor and sitting upright.

The transformative process had endowed her with

Stanley Swanson – Breed of a Werewolf

newfound strength, yet the adjustment was not seamless. Her balance, momentarily disrupted by the weight of her enhanced abilities, required a brief pause to regain equilibrium. In the midst of this silent exchange, devoid of spoken words, Julie extended her right hand, placing it gently on top of Stanley's head. The juxtaposition of her strength and his humble posture created a poignant tableau.

Breaking the silence with a light, grateful smile, Julie finally spoke, "Thank you for giving me this new life." The sincerity in her words resonated with a mixture of awe and gratitude. The weight of her acknowledgment hung in the air, a poignant moment between two beings connected by a supernatural twist of fate. The room held a palpable energy, laden with the significance of the transformation that had just occurred.

With her rebirth into a new existence, Julie found herself harboring an immediate bitterness towards the Drakulis and vampires, her memory retaining the trauma of that harrowing night. Yet, what struck Stanley as somewhat shocking was her apparent disdain for humans as well.

The desire to feed overpowered any lingering connection she might have had with her previous mortal life. Stanley, sensing the urgency and potential danger, stood up from where he had been kneeling, retrieving the sheet that had slipped off Julie during her transformation and modestly draping it around her naked form.

In a reciprocal gesture, Julie leaned over and placed a sheet over Stanley, embodying a newfound camaraderie in their shared, supernatural journey. Concerned for her well-being, Stanley suggested that Julie acquaint herself with her enhanced self before embarking on the primal quest for sustenance.

S.K. Ballinger

In an attempt to ease her transition, Stanley presented the limited human food he had gathered since rescuing her from the nightmarish wreck. However, the ferocity of her hunger overwhelmed any semblance of restraint. Julie, with a swift and seemingly instinctive shift, transformed into a werewolf for the first time, displaying no signs of the pain one might expect from such a transformative process.

Faced with an uncontrollable urge to feed, Julie knocked away every offered item, dismissing the notion of human sustenance. Stanley, realizing the futility of reasoning with her in human form, reluctantly transitioned into a werewolf as well. The air was charged with tension as they stood, werewolf to werewolf, engaging in a primal standoff.

In an attempt to communicate through the silent language of their kind, Stanley repeatedly sought to calm Julie and guide her back to her human form. However, the hunger that gripped her seemed insatiable, as if she had been starved for an eternity. The struggle escalated as she quickly moved past Stanley, charging out of the front door.

To his surprise, Julie demonstrated a degree of cunning, purposefully heading away from populated areas. Stanley, swift to follow, struggled to keep pace with her heightened senses. Within moments, she led them to a local farm, located just two miles from their starting point.

With astonishing strength, Julie took down two full-grown cows. The first, struck with a powerful blow, collapsed to the ground. The other met a similar fate, succumbing to Julie's relentless assault. Despite the agony emanating from the still-living cow, Julie reveled in her meal.

Stanley Swanson – Breed of a Werewolf

Recognizing the brutality of the scene and the consequences of his actions, Stanley intervened by swiftly ending the suffering of the remaining cow. In the aftermath, as they stood amidst the remnants of their impromptu hunt, Stanley, with a tone of wisdom shaped by experience, implored Julie, "We feed on the young, as you cannot consume all this yourself nor I." The words echoed with a reminder of the complexities and responsibilities that came with their supernatural existence.

The bucolic scene, shattered by the grisly symphony of death, prompted an old farmer to emerge from his homestead, clutching a shotgun in anticipation of marauding wolves. However, what met his eyes was far more surreal and terrifying – two werewolves, Stanley and Julie, kneeling amidst the aftermath of their ruthless hunt. The moonlit night bore witness to Julie's unbridled savagery, marking her first encounter with a human victim.

The unfortunate farmer, gripped by fear, reacted with the only defense he had: he raised his shotgun, firing rapidly at the werewolf duo desecrating his pasture. Julie, seemingly unfazed by the barrage of bullets, moved with supernatural agility. In a heartbeat, she abandoned her prey, leaving the mutilated cow behind, and charged towards the farmer.

In a swift and merciless stroke, Julie's claw slashed across the old man's throat, ending his life in an instant. The farmer's body crumpled to the ground, his eyes reflecting the terror of his final moments. The night bore witness to Julie's first kill of a human, a gruesome initiation into her newfound existence.

As the lifeblood of the farmer stained the soil, Julie turned her attention towards Stanley. He stood at a short distance, an unwilling witness to the brutality that unfolded. With a mixture of awe and concern, he addressed Julie, attempting to guide her away from the aftermath.

"We need to go back home, Julie. Please listen to me; you've fed now," Stanley implored, hoping to redirect her newfound hunger for blood.

The gravity of the situation settled upon him as he realized the potential consequences of their actions. It was a stark reminder that their supernatural existence came with a heavy burden, a balance they had to strike to coexist with the human world.

To his relief, Julie, her predatory instincts momentarily sated, acquiesced to Stanley's plea. She nodded, acknowledging the guidance he offered. The events of that fateful night became a haunting memory, a tale of survival and hunger, and Julie, with newfound clarity, heeded Stanley's advice. The echoes of the farmer's final moments lingered in the air as they retreated from the farm, leaving the moonlit pasture behind. It was a chilling reminder that their lives, now intertwined in the delicate dance between humanity and savagery, would be forever shaped by the choices they made under the pale glow of the moon.

ENLIGHTENED

As Julie recounted her harrowing experiences to Kain, the transition from the supernatural world to the harsh reality of their existence unfolded. Kain, visibly moved by the tragedy that had befallen Julie's family, couldn't contain the mixture of emotions evident on his tear-streaked face. His joy at her return from the past was overshadowed by the grim reality of the officer's vampiric nature and the insidious ubiquity of vampires in their world.

"So these vampires are everywhere?" Kain inquired, his voice tinged with disbelief and a hint of fear.

Julie, having braved the horrors of that night, took a moment to compose herself before delving into an explanation that would unravel the hidden tapestry of their existence.

"They are teachers, doctors, kids at a park, all places that you humans work at and worse. It is how both our kinds survive. The only place, to our breeds' knowledge, as an agreement was made long ago between the Drakulis and Lycans, is that we will never be a part of the human military."

Kain's eyes widened, grappling with the realization that the ordinary facets of human life were infiltrated by these supernatural entities. The mundane surroundings now became potential hiding places for creatures that thrived in the shadows. The revelation sparked a storm of questions within him, his curiosity overriding the lingering fear.

"How can this be, as you all do not age, well, your breed does, but so slowly. How is it you are able to not be noticed from the lack of aging?" Kain's voice betrayed a sense of incredulity as

S.K. Ballinger

he sought understanding.

Julie, with an air of seasoned wisdom, replied matter-of-factly, "Very simple." She paused for a moment, gauging Kain's attention before elaborating on their covert survival techniques.

"We never stay in one place for a long period of time, and we have those that help with changing locations, identification cards, and so much more. The Drakulis will actually find a higher-up human they put the fear into so that they will do whatever they ask of them, which is really common in most jobs and law enforcement. It has been this way for many decades and will never change, but instead continues to be a controlling factor."

As Julie demystified the intricacies of their clandestine coexistence with humans, Kain's perspective shifted, grasping the complexities of their existence in a world where the supernatural hid in plain sight. The veil of secrecy lifted, revealing a delicate dance between survival and subterfuge, a dance in which their lives were irrevocably entwined.

In the wake of Julie's revelations, Kain found himself grappling with the intensity of the newfound information. The gravity of her willingness to share her story, especially the darker aspects of her past, resonated with Kain's appreciation for the trust she bestowed upon him. Realizing the opportunity to document this unique narrative, he seized the moment to delve deeper into the complex intricacies of her life.

Curiosity led Kain to inquire about Julie's first conscious act of taking a human life, a question that seemed to carry a weight only she could provide context to. Julie, with a nonchalant laugh, began recounting the tale.

Stanley Swanson – Breed of a Werewolf

"My first kill of a human was when the officer showed up at Stanley's apartment the night just after my transition," she disclosed, her tone devoid of remorse. She continued, elucidating the physiological aftermath of her transformation.

"When a transition happens, Kain, it takes a lot out of your body, and when you come to, your senses are the first to be enhanced and then followed by hunger," she explained, offering a glimpse into the instinctual drives that guided her actions.

"It was never my intent to kill him that night, as I am sure that he had a family, just as I once did," she added, a detached acknowledgment of the collateral damage her kind often left in their wake.

Kain, driven by a thirst for understanding, sought to unravel the intricacies of that fateful night.

"My GOD, so this poor cop shows up, which I would assume was a follow-up from the call that was made the first time by Stanley?"

"You are correct, Kain," she affirmed.

"He was simply doing his job and was completely innocent." She detailed the elaborate charade played out that night to deflect suspicion, revealing her strategic thinking.

"I remember as my wedding band had busted off my finger during my transition, that I told Stanley to act as though we were just dating," she continued.

"I panicked once more in my mind as this cop would not find any kids, which was the excuse I used when I hung the phone up on them. With his back towards me, before the cop could ask any more nosy questions, I let go of Stanley's hand, and that was it."

The abrupt transition from deception to brutality fascinated Kain, who probed further.

"What was it like, when you killed him, the cop?"

"Yep, and it felt good as well, not killing him and eating portions of him, but rather the transitioning part of it all," she admitted unapologetically.

The macabre revelation was delivered with a calm demeanor that belied the grisly reality.

As Julie laughed recounting the events, she shared the aftermath, describing the urgency to relocate.

"Awe Stan, I remember him so vividly that night yelling at me to stop as I was shredding this poor man apart before transitioning back to human form. He told me to start helping him pack as fast as we could, which is how we ended up in the plantation his and Stephen's father owned. Oh, those were the days."

In the midst of their conversation, Jeremia, the vigilant member of their group, interjected with crucial information.

"Natalie is near ready for her transition by Francais."

Julie's attention turned to the impending event, inquiring about the location of the transformation. Francais revealed it would take place in the farthest guest room of their house. Julie, addressing Kain, conveyed the significance of the impending ritual.

"It is time, Kain, and I hope you are prepared, and so you know, you will be blocked from most of the view."

"Why is that?" Kain queried.

"Unless you want to risk being attacked just like I had done to the cop, then it would be in your best interest. Just as we can sense the smell, that of Drakulis; we have a keen sense of a human. It would be wise to take my advice," Julie warned, emphasizing the gravity of the situation that awaited them.

S.K. Ballinger
PATIENCE MAKES BEAUTY TO A NEW BREED

Amid the anticipation and excitement that permeated the air, Francais, with tears of joy streaming down his face, beckoned everyone to gather before ascending the stairs. His voice quivered with emotion as he shared the poignant tale of his niece's tragic past, a victim of a deliberate fire orchestrated by a Drakulis.

The nefarious act claimed not only her entire family but also Francais' own kin. Having lived with Francais for years, marked by the scars of that fateful night, Natalie sought the transformation willingly, casting aside the usual code governing their kind. Francais, determined to grant her wish, sought the blessings of those present.

"My niece, as some of you may know, fell victim to a house fire, which was a planned attack from a Drakulis. In this act of crime, the fire killed her entire family and mine as well. She has lived with me for many years now as I attended to her wounds. It was per her request for me to transition her, and I will gladly throw out the code to grant her this. She knows of all our breed and what we can do and what we should not. I ask of everyone who is here for their blessings is all."

Amid smiles and congratulations, Zea, holding a mug of beer and appearing much older than he let on, expressed his unconventional toast to Natalie's future. The rest, unfamiliar with Zea's casual demeanor, exchanged puzzled glances. Kain, intrigued, approached Zea and inquired about the beer, puzzled by the contradiction of werewolves consuming human food.

Zea, with a sly smile, offered Kain a beer, assuring him it

had no effect. The banter continued as Kain humorously referred to the beer as "liquid bread." The camaraderie, though fleeting, lightened the atmosphere before the impending transition.

As Francais led the group upstairs, dimming the lights, Kain, left at the bottom, engaged in a conversation with Drennan, a werewolf with a notorious disdain for humans. Drennan, living up to his reputation, refused to assist Kain, leaving him struggling in his wheelchair. Determined, Kain managed to hoist himself onto the first step, prompting Julie to intervene. Her command to Drennan showcased the pack's loyalty and their expectations of mutual respect.

With Kain now among them, albeit with some reluctance from Drennan, they all reached the guest room. Natalie's live transition was imminent.

"Natalie honey?" Francais softly called through the door, his voice filled with a mix of concern and anticipation.

In her mumbled voice, reflective of both fear and excitement, Natalie replied, "Yes, I am ready, Uncle." The stage was set for the transformative moment that would reshape Natalie's destiny.

Francais gently opened the door to Natalie's room, and a hushed air of anticipation settled in the room. He entered, explaining that he had brought a few friends to help protect her during the transition, honoring Stanley's request. Natalie, despite the gravity of the situation, nodded in agreement, a silent acknowledgment that she trusted her uncle's judgment and welcomed the company.

As they all entered, Kain couldn't help but feel a deep

sense of empathy for this young lady, whose disfigurement bore the scars of a painful past. Determined to provide support and respect her wishes, he chose to witness the transformation in person, eschewing the past experiences Julie had shared with him.

The room bore a different atmosphere from Julie's transition, and the group took measures to ensure Natalie's safety by restraining her to the bed. Wanting to offer her some comfort during this challenging moment, they presented options, but Natalie, in a gesture that spoke volumes, declined.

"I have you, and that is all I need," she reassured her uncle with a serene conviction. In the midst of her impending transformation, Natalie found solace in the presence of family and trusted friends, a testament to the strength of their bond. The room echoed with a mixture of tension and familial support as the stage was set for Natalie's journey into the next chapter of her existence.

Francais, with a calm yet solemn tone, instructed Natalie to close her eyes and assured her that the process would be swift. As her eyes shut, the room dimmed, and Francais swiftly transitioned, clamping down on her throat with calculated precision, holding his position for what felt like an eternity. Natalie's body went into shock, her limbs kicking in a visceral response to the bite, reminiscent of the throes of death. Her final breath escaped her, and as Francais released his grip, her limbs fell lifeless.

In the aftermath, Natalie's scars, remnants of a tragic fire, began to vanish. The sounds of bones cracking and crunching accompanied the transformation, as her body morphed from disfigured to that of a part-werewolf in flashes of pain and marvel. The completion of the process brought about an endless perfection, leaving Kain in awe of the incredible metamorphosis, a reward despite the screams of pain.

Her Uncle handed Natalie a mirror, and as he removed the restraints, she gazed upon her transformed self for the first time. Tears streamed down her face as she beheld her natural, twenty-one-year-old body, free from pain and suffering. The room, filled with happiness and smiles, erupted in applause, celebrating Natalie's newfound joy.

Amidst the claps of success, Natalie, overwhelmed with gratitude, stared into the mirror, her hands tracing her tear-stained face. Her moment of self-discovery was interrupted as hunger, a characteristic of her new werewolf nature, consumed her senses. The mirror dropped, forgotten, as she transitioned into her new form and charged towards Kain, who stood at the back of the room.

Drennan, sporting a smile, watched the spectacle unfold, while the others moved quickly to slow Natalie down, preventing her from reaching Kain. Though terrified, Kain found solace in the protective barrier formed around him, witnessing the consequences of Natalie's newfound werewolf instincts.

"Restrain yourself, Natalie!" Francais yelled urgently as everyone remained in their human forms.

Francais, while looking into Natalie's newly transformed dark eyes, spoke to her calmly, "It's okay, Natalie. Please transition to human form, and we will provide you with food. Please." He begged her to regain control of herself.

Responding to her uncle's calming voice, Natalie obediently transitioned back to her human form. Embracing her uncle tightly, tears streaming down her face, she glanced over his shoulder to catch sight of Kain. His nod and a slight smile conveyed happiness for her newfound state.

Francais swiftly fetched some clothes for Natalie, and with great excitement, he announced to everyone, "Tonight, we celebrate a new breed among us. Let her feed tonight, everyone, and welcome my niece."

The group descended, and even Drennan carried Kain down without being asked. They gathered in the kitchen, where a pack member had prepared Natalie's first meal – a younger goat. Francais encouraged Natalie to eat however she wished, whether in human or werewolf form.

Seated with a huge smile on her beautiful new face, Natalie began to help herself, choosing to eat in her human form. Kain found it challenging to watch, as the memories of the lamb from the previous day flashed before him. The celebration continued with the sharing of stories, explanations, and teachings about their breed for Natalie.

In the den, as Kain diligently chronicled his observations in his journal, Zea approached him.

"Fun facts you must be writing down there, friend."

"Just recording what I've learned, Zea, nothing more," Kain responded, focused on capturing the extraordinary events he had witnessed.

WANTED ANSWERS

Zea, the oldest and wisest among the friends gathered to watch over Stanley's family, harbored intentions beyond the immediate protection duties. During Stanley and Stephen's absence to meet Gravakus, Zea discerned that Julie had shared a past travel experience with Kain. Intrigued by Kain's meticulous questioning of Julie, Zea recognized an opportunity to leverage Kain's newfound knowledge.

He sought to enlist Kain's assistance in uncovering the details surrounding the death of a friend during a historical battle between werewolves and vampires that occurred several hundred years ago. The timing had to be precise to avoid interference from the others.

Waiting patiently until after Natalie's transition, as the celebration ensued, Zea deemed it an appropriate moment to approach Kain. Julie left the room momentarily to prepare for the evening's events, providing Zea with the opportunity to speak with Kain privately.

Upon her departure, Zea swiftly entered the room, seeking Kain's cooperation in unraveling the mystery of his friend's demise in the fierce 1897 battle between werewolves and vampires. Kain, initially hesitant, inquired about the nature of his involvement and the potential impact on his aging. In his kind, old tone, Zea responded reassuringly.

"You have a keen eye for detail, given your time as a journalist, do you not, Kain?" Zea remarked, addressing Kain's observational skills.

"Yes, you could say that I do," Kain responded quickly.

S.K. Ballinger

However, concerns lingered about the potential toll on his lifespan, contemplating the significant time travel back to witness an event from centuries ago.

Zea, sensing Kain's reservations, reassured him with a slight grin on his face.

"It will be a fast journey, my friend, in and out. At best, maybe three days for having to go back so far, but it should only take less than five minutes. I beg of you, as I have to know what killed one of my dearest friends."

Although hesitant, Kain was curious about witnessing an actual battle between the age-old creatures of the night. Zea, aware that time was of the essence before the interference of others, pressed on.

"Please, Kain. I will not beg any more to a mortal. I need to know why my friend turned into a ball of fire that night. It is crucial to our breed. We do not have much time before the others here will stop this from happening, as this is not my place of stay. You have traveled with Stanley and Julie; please do so with me."

Kain eventually agreed, hoping Zea's assurances about the timeline were accurate. Already weakened and aged from his previous experiences with Julie, Kain cautiously gave his consent, seeking confirmation on the duration of the journey.

"Only five minutes, right?"

With a simple nod, Zea grabbed both of Kain's arms and then his shoulders, expressing gratitude.

"Let us begin, Kain."

Stanley Swanson – Breed of a Werewolf

The transition into the past was accompanied by a dazzling display of lights that enveloped Kain's senses. As the brightness subsided, the gruesome reality of the promised battle unfolded before him. Amidst the chaos, Kain found himself surrounded by thrills and a profound sense of sadness as vampires mercilessly tore apart and murdered many werewolves.

The battlefield was a nightmarish tableau, with the ground stained crimson and echoes of anguished cries filling the air. Dark shadows hinted at the presence of Drakulis, mysterious creatures lurking in the periphery of the conflict. The sheer scale of the war was overwhelming, leaving Kain uncertain about what exactly he was supposed to observe.

Vampires, clad in dark attire, shredded and ripped apart werewolves with terrifying efficiency. The brutality of the scenes unfolding before him left Kain with mixed emotions—excitement at witnessing the supernatural battle and profound sadness at the loss of life on both sides. The struggle continued as the combatants fought fiercely, and the battlefield echoed with the sounds of death and chaos.

Amidst the carnage, Kain observed dark shadows morphing into Drakulis, some meeting their demise in the midst of the conflict. The battle, reminiscent of ancient wars, unfolded on a grand scale as the numbers of both vampires and werewolves diminished. Some fled from the relentless violence, seeking refuge, while others met their demise in the fierce struggle for survival.

As the dust settled, only a few combatants remained, bearing the scars of the brutal confrontation. Some lay lifeless on the blood-soaked ground, while others continued to suffer. The scene was a stark reminder of the harsh realities of the supernatural world, where ancient beings clashed in a struggle for dominance.

The passage of time seemed distorted in this nightmarish tableau, and Kain continued to observe the dwindling numbers on both sides. Shadows danced in the moonlight as the survivors dealt with the aftermath of the relentless battle. Some vampires and werewolves, weakened and battered, sought refuge, while others faced the inevitable fate of perishing in the unforgiving conflict.

Caught in the maelstrom of supernatural warfare, Kain wished for more specific guidance from Zea, desperately trying to discern the significance of the scenes unfolding before him. The unintended immersion into this chaotic past left him grappling with the complexities of the battle, uncertain about how the events he witnessed would impact the present and the future.

As Kain continued to observe the supernatural battlefield, his keen eyes discerned a lone werewolf that had managed to escape the brutal conflict. Positioned on a hilltop, far removed from the war-torn grounds, this werewolf seemed to survey the chaos from a safe vantage point. Kain's thoughts raced as he considered the identity of this observant creature. He surmised that the werewolf perched on the hilltop could only be Zea, the wise and aged companion who had initiated this mysterious journey through time.

The werewolf on the hill stood as a silent sentinel, overseeing the tumultuous events with a watchful eye. Kain marveled at the creature's ability to navigate the perilous landscape and find refuge on the elevated terrain. From his distant position, Kain felt a connection to the lone werewolf, recognizing its significance in the unfolding narrative of the ancient battle.

Stanley Swanson – Breed of a Werewolf

Taking mental notes, Kain pondered the details he observed, intending to share them with Zea upon his return to the present. The hilltop werewolf, presumed to be Zea, became a focal point in Kain's observations. He marveled at the creature's strategic choice to distance itself from the brutal confrontation, opting for a position that offered both safety and a comprehensive view of the unfolding events.

As the battle raged on, the hilltop werewolf remained a constant presence, a silent witness to the ebb and flow of supernatural warfare. Kain's curiosity intensified, prompting him to question the werewolf's motivations and role in the broader conflict. In the midst of chaos, this lone figure on the hill became a symbol of resilience and strategic insight.

With each passing moment, Kain's desire to uncover the identity and purpose of the hilltop werewolf grew stronger. The creature stood as a mysterious sentinel, embodying the enigmatic nature of the supernatural world. As the battle unfolded beneath its watchful gaze, Kain couldn't shake the feeling that the werewolf on the hill held the key to unraveling the secrets of the past and understanding the intricate dynamics at play in the ancient struggle between vampires and werewolves.

The village, enveloped in an eerie ambiance, bore witness to the aftermath of the supernatural battle. In the dim light of the evening, remnants of the conflict lingered as the once vibrant community now stood in desolation. The haunting presence of Drakulis permeated the air, casting shadows upon the few remaining werewolves who valiantly clung to survival.

Kain's attention was drawn to a specific direction, guided by the assumption that Zea, the watchful werewolf atop the hill, maintained a vigilant gaze. As his eyes followed the line of Zea's

S.K. Ballinger

unwavering stare, they landed upon a dilapidated home with a front porch in ruins. It was within this somber tableau that Kain sensed the focal point of his quest—a scene that held the key to unraveling the mysteries of the past.

In the cold silence of the village, Kain discerned a werewolf sprawled on its back, locked in a dire struggle against a formidable adversary—a vampire adorned in a silver-colored suit, an image that resonated with a sense of ominous authority. The vampire's top hat lay casually beside him, adding an air of theatricality to the grim tableau. It was evident that this particular Drakulis was no ordinary foe; his attire suggested a certain sophistication that belied the brutality of the ongoing conflict.

Kain's keen observational skills allowed him to discern the unfolding drama with finer detail. The vampire, still pinning the struggling werewolf beneath him, extracted something minuscule from the inner recesses of his suit pocket. The weakened werewolf, ensnared in the clutches of the powerful vampire, writhed in agony, battling against the impending doom that loomed overhead.

As Kain continued to watch, a sense of foreboding gripped him—an awareness that the unfolding events carried profound significance. The tiny object retrieved by the vampire held an air of malevolence, and its purpose remained shrouded in mystery. The tableau of the struggling werewolf and the sinister vampire painted a macabre picture, emblematic of the relentless conflict between two ancient races.

In the stillness of the village, where the echoes of battle still reverberated, Kain found himself ensnared in the unfolding drama. The stage was set, and the enigmatic confrontation between the werewolf and the Drakulis unfolded, each moment

Stanley Swanson – Breed of a Werewolf

etching itself into the annals of a history that transcended time and held the key to secrets yet to be unveiled.

As Kain continued to bear witness to the tragic tableau of the past, the vampire's cruel act unfolded before him with chilling clarity. The small object placed in the werewolf's mouth became the catalyst for a rapid descent into unimaginable agony. The werewolf convulsed, grasping at his chest, while the victorious vampire casually retrieved his top hat from the porch. A macabre flourish followed, as a red rose, plucked from the very pocket that held the enigmatic object, was cast down to rest beside the suffering werewolf.

In the blink of an eye, the vampire, having secured his dark prize, leaped from the porch and rejoined the ongoing battle, leaving behind the once defiant werewolf. The inferno that consumed him from the inside out marked the tragic end of a life, witnessed by Kain with a profound sense of sorrow. The flames, relentless and unforgiving, devoured the werewolf's form, leaving nothing but ashes in their wake. It was a swift, merciless death, and Kain felt the weight of the tragedy pressing upon him.

As Kain turned his gaze away from the engulfing flames to search for the werewolf who had managed to escape earlier, he discovered the hilltop to be empty. The once vigilant sentinel, possibly Zea, had vanished, leaving Kain alone amidst the lingering echoes of the fierce battle and the stench of death that permeated the air. Stranded in the past, Kain observed the remaining chaos, unable to intervene or alter the course of events.

Meanwhile, in the present, Jeremia entered the room and discovered Zea desperately trying to pull Kain back from the temporal abyss. Shocked by Kain's visibly accelerated aging, Jeremia demanded an explanation.

"What are you doing?" Jeremia shouted.

"I have no idea what has happened. It is as though he must have seen something very tragic that has caused his mind to be locked in or he blacked out as I am trying to pull him back," Zea replied urgently.

Jeremia wasted no time and called for Julie and the rest to assess the situation. Panic set in as they witnessed Kain's rapid aging. Julie, fearing the worst, accused Zea of causing the predicament.

"What have you done, Zea?"

"I wanted to see how my dear friend had died, and if Kain might have been able to see something that I had missed. It could be a secret way of a fast death to our breed, Julie," Zea explained.

In a race against time, Julie urged Zea to find a solution, recognizing the dire consequences of Kain's accelerated transformation. Drennan, alarmed by the situation, questioned the duration of Kain's journey into the past.

"What was the amount of time did you have him in the past?" Drennan asked.

Zea, still attempting to pull Kain back from the temporal rift, shouted in response, "It only lasted ten minutes!"

"Please tell me not from the battle you had escaped from, Zea. You know that alone was much too far ago and would take much life from him," Jeremia scolded.

Amidst the chaos, Kain's weakened voice struggled to

convey a crucial piece of information.

"It was a red rose petal that killed your friend, Zea." The revelation hung in the air, a cryptic key to understanding the tragic events of the past.

The room, once filled with panic and urgency, now brimmed with a sense of relief as Kain returned from his involuntary journey through time. However, the toll on his physical form was undeniable. His once-vibrant demeanor had been replaced by the weariness of accelerated aging, transforming him into a man who appeared to be a decade older than before.

Kain, struggling with the pain and disorientation caused by his rapid aging, received some solace from Julie who rushed to provide him with water. The others, equally concerned, gathered around him, their expressions a mix of curiosity and worry. While the celebration for Natalie's successful transformation had taken a brief pause, the focus shifted to Kain and the cryptic revelation he had brought back.

"What of this rose petal you speak of?" Jeremia inquired, his eyes fixed on Kain.

"It is what killed Zea's friend," Kain responded, his voice strained but resolute.

"Are you certain of what you saw?" Zea questioned, a furrowed brow betraying his concern.

"Yes, they will kill any of your breed if consumed in the mouth or digested, it would seem," Kain insisted, emphasizing the gravity of his discovery.

S.K. Ballinger

The revelation hung in the air, casting a somber shadow over the room. The werewolves exchanged glances, contemplating the implications of this newfound knowledge. The once joyous atmosphere had shifted, replaced by an undercurrent of uncertainty and dread.

Julie, her concern evident, asked Kain, "How did you discover this? What happened during your time in the past?"

Kain, still catching his breath, recounted the vivid scenes he had witnessed – the battle, the werewolf on the hilltop, and the tragic demise of Zea's friend. He described the vampire, the red rose petal, and the swift, merciless death that befell the werewolf. The details unfolded like a grim narrative, leaving the werewolves in a state of shock.

Zea, grappling with the weight of Kain's words, spoke with a mixture of grief and determination, "If this rose petal poses a threat to our kind, we must investigate further. We cannot allow such a method to be used against us."

Drennan, absorbing the severity of the situation, nodded in agreement.

"We need to gather information, understand the extent of this threat, and find a way to protect our kind from such a deadly weapon."

As the gravity of the situation settled upon them, the werewolves knew they had a new challenge to face. The mysterious red rose petal, once an innocent symbol of beauty, had become a harbinger of danger, and the pack was compelled to uncover its secrets to ensure the survival of their kind.

Stanley Swanson – Breed of a Werewolf

Amidst the confusion that enveloped the room, the werewolves found themselves grappling with a revelation that carried grave implications. Questions echoed through the air as each member of the pack pondered the significance of red roses in their lives.

Had any of them been near a rose garden? Encountered red roses in any form? The collective answer was a resounding no. It became evident that, perhaps unknowingly, they had been avoiding these flowers for reasons deeply ingrained within their supernatural instincts.

Kain, drawing on his knowledge of lore and cultural symbols, recalled the imagery associated with vampires, particularly the iconic use of the color red. In tales of old, vampires were often depicted wearing red, or crimson-lined capes as a warning to werewolves.

This association, though not a direct parallel, hinted at a primal aversion shared by Lycans toward the color red. Kain mused over the possibility that this instinctual reaction was akin to the way a bull reacts to the color red in a matador's cape—an ancient defense mechanism deeply embedded within their supernatural existence.

The tension within the Swanson house escalated as the werewolves grappled with the 'red rose' theory. The revelation had injected an air of uncertainty into their lives, challenging the assumptions they had held about their interactions with the world. It was a moment of collective realization, and each werewolf pondered their past encounters with roses, wondering if they had unknowingly skirted danger.

In the midst of the chaos, Zea, the sage of the group,

seized the opportunity to alleviate the growing tension. With a sagacious nod, he announced his intention to fetch human food for Kain, subtly slipping away from the animated discussions. Though the pack was preoccupied with the 'red rose' revelation, Zea's departure did not go unnoticed by Kain, who harbored a deep appreciation for the wise elder.

As Zea made his way to the door, he turned to Kain with a knowing look.

"Rest assured, my friend. We'll get to the bottom of this mystery," he reassured Kain before exiting the house.

Meanwhile, the lively chatter continued among the remaining werewolves. Julie, in a determined tone, addressed the group, "We need to find out more about this red rose threat. Knowledge is our greatest weapon. Let's pool our insights and investigate further."

With a renewed sense of purpose, the pack set out on a collective quest for understanding, determined to unravel the secrets behind the ominous red rose that now loomed over their supernatural existence.

The revelation about the potential threat posed by red roses sent shockwaves through the werewolf pack, prompting a flurry of phone calls and messages to other Lycan communities. Concerned for the safety of their brethren, the werewolves reached out to family, friends, and allies, urgently sharing the newfound information and seeking confirmation from other packs.

As the calls echoed through the night, the Swanson house became a hub of communication, with werewolves speaking in hushed tones, sharing details of the 'red rose' revelation. Anxiety permeated the air as they awaited responses, hoping to receive assurances that this was not an isolated concern within their own pack.

In the midst of this chaos, Zea's departure to procure food for Kain went unnoticed by most, overshadowed by the urgency of unraveling the mystery of the red rose. Julie, in her role as a pack leader, took charge, coordinating the outreach efforts and maintaining a semblance of order.

Back on the road, Stanley and Stephen continued their journey to the other side of the country to meet with Gravakus. The road stretched before them, and the hum of the engine provided a rhythmic backdrop to their thoughts.

As the miles rolled by, the anticipation of meeting Gravakus heightened with every passing mile, as the Swansons sought guidance in the face of a threat that seemed to transcend their understanding of Lycan lore.

Back at the Swanson house, the atmosphere remained charged with a sense of urgency and uncertainty. The phones continued to buzz with incoming calls and messages, the pack awaiting responses that would shed light on the veracity of the 'red rose' threat. In the interconnected web of Lycan communities, information flowed like a lifeline, binding them together in their shared quest for knowledge and protection.

S.K. Ballinger

THE TRAVEL THAT HAD TO BE

As Stanley and Stephen traveled down the rain-soaked U.S. Route 40, the windshield wipers intermittently slashing away the droplets, the mood in the car shifted from anticipation to reflection. The weather mirrored the uncertainty that had settled in their hearts. The rhythmic hum of the engine provided a somber backdrop to their conversation.

Stanley, hands firmly gripping the steering wheel, navigated the highway with a sense of purpose. The passing landscape, shrouded in mist, seemed to echo the mysteries that awaited them. They discussed their plan with Gravakus, the ancient and revered figure who held the potential answers they sought in the face of the 'red rose' revelation.

Amidst the discussion of strategy and history, stories of shared battles, victories, and moments of camaraderie served as a testament to the bond they had forged.

As they drove down a particularly long and monotonous stretch of the highway, the rain intensified, adding a layer of challenge to their journey. The sparse traffic and the drab surroundings seemed to amplify the tension that lingered within the vehicle. The passing miles, marked by faded road signs and the occasional flicker of distant headlights, stretched before them.

Suddenly, a car overtook them on the passenger side. Stanley, glancing down instinctively, was met with an unexpected sight. In the backseat of the passing car, a little boy looked at him. At first, the child wore a seemingly innocent smile, but in the blink of an eye, that expression transformed into one of pure disgust.

Stanley Swanson – Breed of a Werewolf

In that fleeting moment, Stanley recognized the telltale signs – the child in the passing car had identified him as a werewolf. It was a revelation that sent a shiver down his spine. The encounter with a Drakulis, a vampire, served as a stark reminder of the clandestine world they inhabited, where recognition could happen in an instant, even on a desolate highway in the pouring rain.

The passing car vanished into the distance, leaving Stanley and Stephen with a shared sense of unease. The encounter with the Drakulis child added an unsettling layer to their journey, amplifying the stakes of their mission to consult Gravakus. The road ahead, obscured by rain and shadows, seemed to hold secrets that awaited their discovery.

As the rain continued to cascade down, Stephen's grip tightened on the wheel, the car slicing through the wet darkness. Stanley's urgent command cut through the drumming of rain on the roof.

"Stephen, slow down!"

Stephen, without a moment's hesitation, slammed on the brakes. The car skidded on the slick, rain-soaked road, windshield wipers working frantically to clear their vision. The vehicle slowed, but a thick fog advanced towards them with unsettling speed. Stephen, his instincts sharp, recognized the imminent threat and prepared for an unknown confrontation.

"Brace yourself, brother!"

Just as the car and the fog were on the verge of a collision, the ancient Drakulis responsible for the death of Zea's friend in 1897 materialized in front of them. Adorned in a suit, complete

S.K. Ballinger

with a top hat, and wearing a malevolent grin, he transformed from the advancing fog and positioned himself slightly sideways to ensure a direct impact with their vehicle. The force of the collision caved in the entire front of the car, propelling both Stanley and Stephen through the shattered windshield.

In a simultaneous and graceful transition, both brothers transformed mid-air as they crashed onto the rain-soaked pavement. The screech of brakes echoed from the few other travelers on the highway, their curiosity piqued by the unexpected spectacle. Stanley and Stephen, now in their werewolf forms, rolled on the road before coming to a halt, their claws embedded in the asphalt. Raindrops continued their descent, creating a surreal atmosphere around the two formidable creatures.

Acknowledging the possibility that their secret might be exposed to unsuspecting humans, Stanley and Stephen stood up, their instincts on high alert. In unison, they prepared for the adversary who orchestrated this unsettling encounter. Stephen, aware of the Drakulis's ability to transform into fog, cautioned Stanley about the unique strengths of their opponent. The ancient Drakulis, untouched by the impact that crumpled their car, stood before them, an eerie figure emerging from the mist.

"Hello hell hounds," he greeted, his voice a haunting echo through the rain-soaked night. The encounter set the stage for a confrontation that transcended time and tested the limits of their supernatural abilities.

The lunatic Drakulis, Dimitris, picked up his top hat from the rain-soaked ground as the two werewolf brothers, Stanley and Stephen, faced off against him amidst the wreckage of their car. Another vehicle rammed into the already wrecked car, intensifying the chaotic scene. Dimitris addressed them with a mocking tone.

"For you nasty and pathetic once-slaves, let me introduce myself. My name is Dimitris, and I hear you are traveling to meet Gravakus, while you, Stanley, I presume, are sharing secrets with a human?" he humbled them.

With a fellow bow and a wave of his top hat, Dimitris provoked Stanley, who charged at him. Effortlessly, Dimitris leaped above Stanley, colliding with Stephen in mid-air. The fight ensued between the werewolf brothers and the sadistic Drakulis. Stanley ran toward Dimitris, aiming to end the psychotic encounter. However, Dimitris displayed unparalleled speed and strength, kicking Stephen into Stanley.

Getting up without apparent effort, Dimitris walked toward the brothers as if they were innocent newcomers. In an act of brutality, he ripped off the front panel of a wrecked vehicle and smashed it over Stanley and Stephen. Without warning, he leaped onto Stephen, producing a red rose petal from his coat pocket, attempting to force it into Stephen's mouth.

Stanley quickly pushed the rubble aside, lunging at Dimitris, biting into his right shoulder. Stephen joined the fray, overpowering Dimitris. The intense struggle unfolded, leaving the brothers and Dimitris in a tangled heap.

As the conflict raged, a highway patrol car pulled up, its flashing lights slicing through the falling rain. The patrol officer, witnessing the chaotic scene, pulled out his gun in fear. Unaware of the supernatural entities before him, he began shooting at the beasts he believed were attacking a person.

In response to the gunfire, Stanley and Stephen rolled

away, dodging the rounds while hunkering down to heal. Dimitris quickly regenerated from the werewolves' bite marks, approaching the officer with a sinister smile, popping his neck. The frightened officer shouted at him to stop and raised his taser gun, giving Dimitris a final warning.

"Stop and put your god damn hands in the air!" the officer shouted, unaware of the supernatural nightmare unfolding before him.

The situation escalated as Dimitris continued walking towards the officer, ignoring the threat of the taser. The officer, desperate to defend himself, fired the taser gun, but Dimitris effortlessly caught both lines and pulled them, disarming the officer and dropping the prongs to the ground.

Panicking, the officer reloaded his gun and warned Dimitris to stop or face deadly force, slowly backing towards the driver's side of his patrol car. Unfazed, Dimitris adjusted his blazer with a nonchalant shake, demonstrating his lack of fear. Aware that the officer might resort to using his firearm, Dimitris hoped to avoid any damage to his favorite suit.

The officer, realizing deadly force might be his only option, began shooting at Dimitris as he continued to approach. Bullets penetrated Dimitris, who exhibited no signs of pain, maintaining a half-smile on his face. In the absence of any visible wounds, the officer, now gripped with extreme fear, shouted his bewilderment.

"What in the hell are you?"

"I am nothing but a myth to you humans, and I can promise you that I am far worse than any hell you could ever imagine," Dimitris grinned menacingly, revealing the dark truth behind his supernatural existence.

As the officer tried to retreat to the safety of his patrol car, Dimitris swiftly closed the distance. The officer's attempt to escape was futile, and with a quick, lethal bite to the neck, he succumbed to Dimitris's vampiric influence. The transformation from mortal to vampire was rapid, and the newly turned officer stood alongside his new master, ready to serve Dimitris in the unfolding chaos.

Observing the turn of events, Stephen knew that the pursuit of Gravakus could not be delayed. Despite the recent battle and the presence of a newly created vampire ally, Stephen urged Stanley to continue the mission, emphasizing that he would be fine.

Stanley, torn between loyalty to his brother and the urgency of the task at hand, struggled with the decision. However, the memory of the betrayal and harm inflicted on their family by Gravakus strengthened his resolve. It was his duty to confront the evil that had shattered the trust between their kind and Gravakus.

With a heavy heart, Stanley reluctantly agreed to Stephen's request. He cast a final glance at his brother, head bowed in determination, and sprinted toward the nearby tree lines. As Stanley disappeared into the shadows, Stephen turned his attention to the newly turned vampire and prepared for the challenges that lay ahead. The pursuit of Gravakus continued, fueled by a determination to bring justice and restore the balance that had been disrupted by the malevolent vampire lord.

As Dimitris sent his newly turned follower after Stephen, the eager vampire moved swiftly, driven by the newfound bloodlust that often consumed those recently turned. Dimitris remained close behind, guiding his loyal understudy with an air of malevolence. Stephen, recognizing the impending threat, prepared to face the challenge alone, his back arched and his mouth open in a powerful howl.

The echoing howl cut through the night, a cry for help that carried for miles. Stephen, the older and wiser of the two brothers, knew the power of his vocal cords and strategically used the sound to alert other supernatural beings in the vicinity. Meanwhile, deep in the woods, Stanley, though tempted to return after hearing the call, trusted his brother's judgment and continued on, hoping that help would arrive for Stephen.

The battle unfolded as Stephen faced off against Dimitris and his newfound follower. Stephen, aware of the formidable opponent he confronted, braced himself for the onslaught. He understood the gravity of the situation – a Drakulis, skilled in turning others to bolster his ranks, and a recently turned vampire, driven by the primal urges of a newborn. Stephen knew that defeating these two adversaries would require everything he had, and failure would likely mean the end of his existence.

The confrontation escalated into a fierce struggle, with Stephen defending himself against the relentless attacks of the two bloodthirsty foes. Each move was a calculated effort to outmaneuver and counter the relentless assaults, as Stephen fought for his survival and the chance to continue the pursuit of Gravakus. The outcome of this battle would shape the course of their ongoing quest for justice and revenge against the malevolent vampire lord.

The unfolding circumstances played into the enemy's favor as the follower, driven by instinct, prioritized attending to the injured humans near the wreckage. The newly turned vampire quickly sought out the beating hearts, biting them and turning them into vampires in the process. As Stephen, desperate for aid, hoped other supernatural beings might have heard his howl, he knew that ending the fight quickly by taking out Dimitris was crucial. If successful, the remaining vampires could easily be subdued or forced into submission.

As Stephen charged toward Gravakus and the vampires still in the process of transforming, the loyal follower leaped between him and Dimitris. With hand cuffs removed from his belt, the follower revealed the pointed ends, aiming to strike Stephen. In a daring move, the follower lunged towards Stephen, but the plan backfired. The opened handcuff lodged deeply into Stephen's back, causing momentary pain, but Stephen, unfazed, retaliated swiftly. He dug his claws into the side of the follower and threw him with great strength towards the side of a victim's car.

Dimitris, observing the skirmish, expressed satisfaction with his follower's attempt, seemingly unaware of the follower's predicament. However, the situation escalated as three more vampires swiftly joined Dimitris's side, ready to reinforce their leader. The odds were stacking against Stephen, and the fight took an even more perilous turn. The outcome of this struggle would not only determine Stephen's fate but also influence the trajectory of the ongoing quest to confront the malevolent Gravakus and seek retribution for the atrocities committed against the Swanson family.

Stephen, nursing his injuries, reached around to his back and pulled the handcuffs out, deciding to wield them as a makeshift weapon. With a display of his brute strength, he threw the cuffs with precision towards Dimitris. The fast-moving objects neared their target, but one of the vampires attempted to deflect them, only managing to slow them down and cutting through their hand in the process. This gave Dimitris just enough time to elegantly slide to the side, avoiding the potentially dangerous projectiles.

As the thrown cuffs failed to reach their intended target, Dimitris acknowledged that his follower and the other vampires were clearly outmatched by Stephen. Intrigued by the challenge, Dimitris decided that the confrontation would be a duel between himself and the formidable hellhound. He casually walked towards Stephen, a sick smile of enjoyment playing on his lips.

Stephen accepted the challenge, noticing that the few vampires and the injured follower had stayed back, showing a mutual desire to witness the climax of this deadly encounter. Both adversaries signaled their intent to end the fight as they closed the distance between them. Dimitris popped his neck with unnaturally long nails growing, and Stephen flexed his upper body, extending his razor-sharp claws to their full length.

Halfway to Stephen, Dimitris came to a sudden stop, standing in the rain amidst the wreckage. He observed a few tree tops in the distance moving, prompting him to whistle sharply between his fangs, calling his follower and the three vampires to join the fight. Dimitris, though a maniac, was also a cunning Drakulis, anticipating that something unexpected might be approaching.

Within seconds, Dimitris's expression shifted from the sick smile of amusement to one of concern. He continued to stare at the tree tops, which abruptly ceased their movement. A strange silence enveloped the scene, broken only by the falling rain and the faint growl emanating from Stephen in the distance. The unexpected pause left Dimitris unsettled, sensing that a formidable force might be lurking in the shadows, ready to reveal itself. The impending confrontation held an air of anticipation, and the outcome remained uncertain in the midst of this supernatural battleground.

With a horrible sound emanating from all directions, the unmistakable crack of pavement echoed through the area, and Dimitris knew that they were now surrounded by werewolves. It was a rare and unusual scenario, as Drakulis and vampires typically held the upper hand over hellhounds. The supernatural battleground had shifted dramatically.

Dimitris, with his follower positioned behind him and the three vampires standing to the side, realized that the fight was about to come to a swift and decisive end. From behind the follower, a massive werewolf emerged, towering over him. In a quick, brutal motion, the werewolf bit down on the upper half of the follower's head, effortlessly ripping it off before tossing it into the distance. The werewolf, with a light-colored fur indicating its advanced age, left the now headless body to fall limply to the road.

In a series of rapid movements, each vampire was swiftly dispatched from the rain and mist. Emerging from the gray of the late evening were eight werewolves, converging on the scene. Among them, walking confidently towards Dimitris, was Stephen, the smile on his face reflecting gratitude that his call for help had been answered by werewolves from another pack.

Dimitris, now facing a dire situation, couldn't contain his frustration and anger. Yelling in a manner that everyone could hear, he taunted the werewolves, questioning their ability to kill what they couldn't catch.

"How can you kill what you cannot catch, you stupid and pathetic hellhounds?" Dimitris shouted, his words revealing his growing irritation and resentment at being outnumbered and outmatched.

The werewolves, however, remained silent, poised for the final confrontation that would decide the fate of this supernatural showdown.

Within moments, Dimitris found himself surrounded by all the werewolves, their imposing figures closing in on him. However, just as the pressure was mounting, Dimitris demonstrated the swiftness he was known for. True to his word about not being caught, he transformed rapidly into a thick fog that enveloped the space where he stood, and in an instant, he was gone, leaving only the lingering mist.

With Dimitris vanished, the werewolf pack turned their attention to Stephen, suggesting that he follow them into the woods for safety and a place to undergo the transformation. Stephen, grateful for their assistance, nodded in agreement, and together, they sprinted off through a side road and deep into the woods.

Unbeknownst to both the werewolf pack and Stephen, a little boy who had been in the back seat of a passing car during the battle witnessed the supernatural conflict. Revealing himself as a vampire, the boy and his father observed the events from a distance, acting as trackers with a singular purpose. They refrained from intervening when Dimitris whistled, instead meticulously keeping track of the direction the werewolf pack had taken into the woods.

After an exhaustive run through hills, rain, and mud, the

pack and Stephen reached a cabin many miles away from the highway battle.

Upon entering, they were greeted by an elderly individual who had prepared an assortment of clothes for them to change into. Among the eight members, three were women, and the rest men. Once everyone was settled, they gathered around a coffee table, basking in the warmth of a crackling fireplace.

While most of the werewolves continued with their routine, three of them sat near Stephen, bearing news that weighed heavy on their minds. The first to introduce himself was the werewolf who had offered them shelter during their time of need.

"My name is Emery, and this is my cabin – your place of safety," Emery introduced himself, radiating an air of authority and hospitality.

Stephen, grateful for the refuge, expressed his appreciation not only to Emery but also to those gathered around him. In an attempt to provide context, Stephen explained that he had no prior knowledge of the Drakulis who had attacked him and his brother, except for the name Dimitris. He further delved into their intentions, detailing their quest to confront the notorious Gravakus. The werewolves surrounding him were already acquainted with these activities through their extensive tracking network.

Emery, with the wisdom of age and the experience of a past war involving the breeds' enslavement, admired the bravery displayed by Stanley in seeking out and confronting the elusive Drakulis, Gravakus. Stephen, discerning Emery's knowledge and insight, was open to sharing more details. However, before they could delve into further discussions, Emery felt it necessary to address a somber topic – the fate of Stephen's family.

Before much else could transpire, Emery spoke with genuine sympathy, "Stephen, we have some very troubled news we need to make you aware of."

Stephen, sensing the gravity of Emery's words, listened intently as he warmed his hands by the comforting fireplace. The anticipation in the room hung heavy.

Emery, now a bearer of unsettling news, continued, "Your sister-in-law, Julie, is no longer..." The words lingered in the air, and a palpable tension settled over the room.

Stephen's hopeful inquiry about his brother's safety loomed in the background, awaiting an answer that could potentially shatter or sustain his fragile hope.

"Tell me my brother is fine and made his way from harm?" Stephen's anxious inquiry hung in the air as Emery prepared to deliver more details about Julie.

The room fell silent, aware of the weight of the impending revelation.

"As I had mentioned, your sister-in-law, Julie, is no longer..." Emery began, attempting to share more about her loss of life.

However, Stephen erupted in disbelief and outrage before Emery could complete his sentence. Standing up, tears streaming down his face, Stephen vehemently rejected the notion that Julie could be gone.

Stanley Swanson – Breed of a Werewolf

"How dare you suggest such things as we had left her in the safety of well-trusted breed members. Do not tell me of this news as I will not accept. Julie and their son Sabe took on a Drakulis and vampires not long ago, so this assumption you bring before me is pure shit!" Stephen's raw emotions poured out, and those in the room sat down, giving him space to vent.

The atmosphere was heavy with sadness, but Emery remained calm, attempting to guide Stephen through the difficult revelation.

Emery continued to speak, offering further explanations and details until another werewolf named Sheree stepped forward. Tearfully, she took Stephen's left hand, confirming the truth of Emery's words. Despite Stephen's initial resistance, the harsh reality was sinking in.

"It is true of what Emery speaks of, Stephen. I should have you know that a good friend of yours by the name of Jeremia has contacted us himself." Sheree's sorrowful admission added another layer of confirmation.

Stephen, still grappling with his emotions, released Sheree's grip, wiping away tears, and offered an apology to Emery for his earlier outburst.

Desiring more information, Stephen questioned the circumstances surrounding Julie's death, the well-being of the children, and the state of his pack members. Sheree, in her soft Scottish accent, explained that Julie had been engulfed in flames and surrounded by red rose petals. This information came from a mortal named Kain, who had witnessed the tragic event while trying to free Stephen's pack. Sabe and Jade were reported to be in the care of Kain and were alive.

S.K. Ballinger

Determined to understand the significance of the red rose petals, Stephen pressed for more details.

"What of these red rose petals? What is the purpose of them, and how is it possible they were the cause of her death or a threat to our breed?" The room awaited answers to these perplexing questions.

Stephen, taking a brief moment to gather himself, recalled the chilling encounter with Dimitris on the highway, realizing that this very Drakulis must have been responsible for Julie's demise. The memories of the night of their fight flooded back, specifically the instance when Dimitris had attempted to force a rose petal into Stephen's mouth. Sheree, sensing the weight of the situation, instinctively backed away, allowing Emery to provide further clarification.

"We do not know for sure, Stephen; we just know the entire house of your brothers was surrounded with red rose petals. From what Jeremia had told us, all of your pack members were extremely weakened and sick. They were not even able to transition," Emery explained, his voice tinged with both empathy and concern.

Stephen, his mind racing with thoughts of vengeance and justice, was eager to understand more about the circumstances surrounding Julie's death. The symbolism of the red rose petals and their deadly impact on werewolves perplexed and angered him. Sheree, sensing the gravity of the situation, approached Stephen cautiously.

"We've heard that Kain, a mortal who witnessed the incident, claimed that Julie became a ball of flame surrounded by those red rose petals. As for Sabe and Jade, they are still alive and under the care of others," Sheree gently conveyed, her Scottish accent adding a touch of solemnity to the words.

The revelation that a simple rose petal could be used as a weapon against werewolves left Stephen grappling with a sense of vulnerability he had never experienced before. The unknown nature of this threat fueled his desire for revenge and justice against those who had orchestrated such a tragic end for Julie.

Stephen, growing weary of the heartbreaking details surrounding Julie's death, felt an urgent need for swift justice against those responsible. Without further deliberation, he expressed his gratitude to Emery and the others for their assistance and information. As he made his way towards the cabin door, he issued an open invitation for anyone willing to join him on his quest for vengeance.

"If any would like to join with me, feel free to, as I know exactly where to go and will be doing so with or without. This is a good pack I will be heading to, as I know them well," Stephen declared with determination, his eyes reflecting a burning desire for retribution.

Emery, recognizing the gravity of Stephen's mission, chose to sit this one out, acknowledging the strength and capability of his trusted pack members. However, the seasoned elder offered support in a different way by arranging for three skilled individuals to accompany Stephen on his perilous journey.

"Sheree is extremely smart, Stephen, and very agile. I send with you, as well, the two strongest members of my pack, Drake and Issac," Emery suggested, emphasizing the physical prowess and resilience of the companions chosen to assist Stephen.

S.K. Ballinger

Sheree, Drake, and Issac, honored by Emery's trust, expressed their readiness to stand by Stephen's side. Sheree, with her intelligence and agility, Drake, known for his sheer strength, and Issac, demonstrating exceptional resilience, were a formidable trio prepared to aid Stephen in his pursuit of justice.

Stephen, grateful for the support offered, shook hands with each of his newfound allies, acknowledging the weight of the task ahead. The air in the room grew tense with determination, as Stephen, Sheree, Drake, and Issac prepared to embark on a journey fraught with danger, fueled by the desire to end the killing spree of the Drakulis and avenge the tragic loss of Julie.

"I thank all of you for helping me and that you heard my call for help. Sheree, Drake, and Issac, I am grateful that you have accepted the challenge that our breed faces. Emery, stay wise and know that you will not be forgotten for what you have done for me and my family. I will do all in my power to keep your pack safe," Stephen expressed his gratitude sincerely, his eyes reflecting determination and a profound sense of purpose.

Emery responded with words of encouragement, acknowledging the gravity of the situation. "I trust that you will do so, Stephen, and again, I am sorry to have had to share such news of tragedy. You seem wise; use that to your advantage. Perhaps we have a werewolf who has joined forces with the Drakulis. There would be no other way for the sudden and simple weaponry of a rose to be spread about otherwise. Now, make your way and keep our breed strong. Do so safely, friend."

Before Stephen could depart, he inquired about his brother Stanley. Emery's stern response conveyed the urgency of the situation.

Stanley Swanson – Breed of a Werewolf

"We have tried to call, as I am sure others have, but to no avail. We have sent word out; that is all we have been able to do. While we wait to hear something in return, it is best you act quickly."

Stephen, driven by a mix of sadness over Julie's tragic fate and determination for justice, embraced the challenge that lay ahead. Uncertain of whether his brother was aware of the events, he attempted to call Stanley before losing reception in the high hilltops. With no answer, he could only assume that Stanley hadn't retrieved his phone from the wrecked vehicle.

Acknowledging the need to move forward, Stephen, Sheree, Drake, and Issac bid their farewells to Emery and the pack, setting out on their journey to regroup with Jeremia. The weight of the recent events hung in the air, propelling the companions forward with a shared mission and the hope of unraveling the mysteries surrounding the rise of the Drakulis.

S.K. Ballinger

LIFE LOST AND TO NEVER BE FORGOTTEN

Julie, consumed by worry and curiosity, decided to investigate Zea's prolonged absence. She quietly excused herself from the group and ventured into the woods where Zea had gone. As she neared the location, she noticed a peculiar trail of red rose petals scattered on the ground. This sight immediately raised her suspicions, and a feeling of unease settled in her gut.

Following the trail cautiously, Julie arrived at a clearing where she witnessed a scene that would forever alter the course of her life. Zea, once perceived as a trusted ally, stood there with Kain, surrounded by red rose petals. The sight was haunting – a macabre display of power and betrayal. The red petals seemed to pulse with an otherworldly energy.

As Julie comprehended the gravity of the situation, a sinister figure emerged from the shadows – Dimitris, the Drakulis with a penchant for chaos. The realization struck her like a bolt of lightning – the red rose petals were a deadly weapon wielded by the Drakulis. Their potency against werewolves became horrifyingly evident as Zea, once a cherished friend, succumbed to their fatal influence.

Dimitris, reveling in the unfolding tragedy, gloated over the success of his plan. He explained with malevolent pleasure how he had manipulated Zea into betraying the werewolf pack. The Drakulis had carefully orchestrated this act of treachery to sow discord and confusion among the werewolves.

Julie, overwhelmed by shock and grief, confronted Dimitris, demanding an explanation for this heinous act. The

Drakulis, relishing the chaos he had caused, revealed that the knowledge of the red rose's lethal potential was a closely guarded secret among the Drakulis. It was a means to assert dominance and control over the werewolf breed.

Dimitris, seizing the opportunity to further his own agenda, taunted Julie about the impending doom that awaited her family. He hinted at the broader conspiracy involving Gravakus and the Drakulis, leaving Julie grappling with a sense of helplessness and desperation.

As the night unfolded into a tapestry of despair, the news of Julie's confrontation with Dimitris reached the werewolf pack. The revelation about the deadly secret of the red rose sent shockwaves through the community. Werewolves everywhere questioned their safety, and trust among the pack members shattered.

The repercussions of this betrayal rippled through the supernatural world, sowing seeds of doubt, fear, and a thirst for vengeance. The red rose, once a symbol of love and beauty, had become an instrument of terror and tragedy, leaving the werewolves grappling with a new reality – one where even the most sacred bonds could be shattered by the sinister machinations of their adversaries.

At the Swanson's plantation the real tragedy unfolds.

As the unsettling atmosphere permeated the house, Kain watched the events unfold, feeling a mixture of sorrow and guilt for the turmoil he inadvertently brought upon the werewolf pack. Julie's apology echoed in his ears, and he acknowledged her words with a solemn nod.

"Do not apologize to me as it is what I have chosen to do. My concerns rest with your family, and I can rest easy when my day comes to an end to have met such incredible beings. I thank you and your family, Julie," Kain responded, his eyes reflecting a sense of gratitude amidst the impending chaos.

Julie, still reeling from the revelations, offered assistance to Kain, displaying a sense of compassion even in the face of betrayal. However, Jeremia's urgent warning interrupted their conversation, compelling Julie to focus on the imminent danger.

"Julie, lock the doors as we may need to plan for an attack," Jeremia's voice echoed through the house, urgency lacing every word.

Julie, fueled by a protective instinct, rushed to secure the entrances, determined to shield her family from the impending threat.

The celebratory atmosphere disintegrated into panic as the werewolves, weakened and unable to transition, felt an unfamiliar sickness taking hold. Natalie, newly transitioned, voiced her concern, seeking answers from her uncle.

"What is happening, Uncle?" she pleaded, her eyes reflecting a mix of fear and confusion.

Francais, the voice of reason in the chaos, issued orders to gather the children and seek refuge in the kitchen. Drennan, struggling with his inability to transition, warned Julie of the severity of the situation and proposed an immediate escape.

"Julie, this damn human is what they must be following. I cannot transition and am weak. Whatever is happening, we must use the escape route now," Drennan urged, desperation evident in his voice.

Julie, torn between her determination to protect her home and the safety of her family, faced a difficult decision. Francais, entering the room, pleaded with her to prioritize the well-being of their weakened pack members.

"This is not about standing up to a Drakulis or vampires, Julie. Do you wish to have this house burnt down as what took place with my niece Natalie long ago? We are weak and cannot transition. Whatever happens to be outside this house is restricting us from being able to. We have no time, Julie, and we must move quickly. If not for us, then do so for your kids," Francais implored.

Reluctantly, Julie conceded, accepting the harsh reality that they needed to abandon their home for the sake of their lives. The scent of fear lingered in the air as the pack prepared to face an unknown adversary, their collective strength compromised by an unseen force.

Julie stood near the locked door, her senses heightened, and her heart pulsating with a mix of fear and determination. The voice from the other side revealed itself as Siluk, the son of the oldest known Drakulis, claiming to have the house surrounded. Siluk's menacing tone echoed through the walls, emphasizing that he was not Gravakus, and he demanded the Swanson family to show themselves.

"You have limited choices Swanson family as I have your house surrounded. I assure you that I am not the weak-minded Gravakus who should have killed you when he had the chance. No, nothing like that fool at all. I am Siluk, the son of the oldest known Drakulis, and I do not give options. Show yourself to make this easy, and I will only ask once," Siluk's voice persisted.

Facing the locked door, Julie remained steadfast, her gaze unwavering. Jeremia rushed into the room, urging her not to unlock the door, pleading with her to prioritize the safety of her family.

"Do not unlock that door, Mrs. Swanson, I beg of you. Please, while you can, think not of who is behind that door, but instead think of your family," Jeremia implored.

"Jeremia, my friend, I thank you for having known you as long as I have. Do not tell me what to do with my family, as you have stated, my kids are to safety. I will confront whoever tries to control me," Julie asserted with a resolute tone.

Glancing back at Jeremia, who had tears forming in his eyes, Julie continued to approach the door. Her hand neared the lock, and she spoke with unwavering conviction.

"I trust that whatever may happen, you will long protect Sabe and Jade. If a war is what they wish to happen, as my husband has suggested might, then I will give our breed a reason to win. Sometimes, in war, the gentle come out strong. Do what must be done, live for our breed as I do."

Jeremia pleaded once more, expressing the unknown influence affecting their behavior, their weakness, and distorted senses. But Julie, with a finality in her decision, remained undeterred, ready to face the looming threat for the sake of her family and their werewolf breed.

Siluk, true to her commitment, remained steadfast and

resolute, refusing to entertain any alternatives as she keenly caught the sound of approaching footsteps on the front porch. Unperturbed by Jeremia's presence, she took charge and swiftly unlocked the door. As the door swung open, a surreal scene unfolded before her eyes – the ominous silhouette of the Drakulis set against a backdrop of ethereal light red powder cascading from the sky like a delicate snowfall.

In a rapid and determined advance, Siluk closed the distance between herself and the otherworldly creature. Jeremia, driven by a surge of protective instinct, attempted to rush forward despite the limitations of his frail body. However, Siluk, in a deft move, seized Julie and slammed the door shut, effectively barricading Jeremia from intervening.

As the door shut with a decisive thud, Jeremia wasted no time in reopening it, only to be greeted by a scene that defied explanation. Julie lay on her back, Siluk atop her, surrounded by a bed of red rose petals. The moonlit sky, once serene and calm, transformed into an otherworldly canvas, as every inch of the atmosphere and the ground below was bathed in a haunting red glow, courtesy of the falling red ash.

In a surreal tableau, Jeremia, compelled by concern and disbelief, struggled to navigate his way out of the confines of the house. As he emerged, Julie locked eyes with him, and her lips parted to convey a message, a communication that transcended the bizarre circumstances enveloping them. With an intensity that matched the crimson ambiance, she uttered words that echoed in the eerie stillness, making them audible to Jeremia's ears, providing a strange sense of clarity amidst the unfolding chaos.

Kain, having wheeled himself back to the front room, found Jeremia standing just outside the front door. The others had successfully sought safety underground, leaving the two men to face the impending danger. Julie, casting one last meaningful glance towards Jeremia, whispered once more under her breath.

"Let this be known and give my husband strength and much knowledge of what it is that we, our breed die of."

With tears streaming down his face, Jeremia, fully aware of the danger but unable to transition, respected her final wish. "Now go," Julie commanded, a solemn directive that resonated with the weight of impending tragedy. Turning his back on their kind, a rare act, Jeremia vowed to watch over Julie and Stanley's children, ensuring their safety.

As Jeremia made his way back to the escape route, he seized Kain, determined to spare him from witnessing the inevitable tragedy. However, Kain resisted, uttering in a subtle tone, "Leave me be, Jeremia."

"Julie would not have wanted this, Kain, even though she does not like mortals, especially you," Jeremia argued.

"Julie would not want what is happening to be unnoticed either. This, in part, is my doing, and I will stay behind to deal with my own fate, just as she is dealing with hers. I am going to do all that I can to correct my actions," Kain explained, revealing a resolve to face the consequences of his choices.

"Be as you will, then," Jeremia responded, his tone filled with a mixture of sadness and warning.

"Know that if her loss is in vain, I myself will seek you. When I find you, your death will not come easy. Be well and document with great detail and make sure it will remain in

Stanley's hands."

Jeremia descended into the escape route to join the others underground, leaving Kain near the door entrance. Meanwhile, Siluk's attention shifted, momentarily easing off Julie as he responded to Kain's offer.

"It is me that you want, and I am here. I will give all that it is that you wish to have, my written journal if you show no harm to her," Kain pleaded.

"Your written journal, you say?" Siluk replied, considering the proposition with a sinister curiosity.

"Yes, just please do not harm her as she is innocent in all of this," Kain implored.

"Oh, yes she is," Siluk responded cryptically, leaving the fate of Julie and the unfolding events hanging in the balance.

With a subtle nod from Siluk, a vampire emerged from the shadows of the house, positioning itself before Kain. Staring down at the helpless mortal, the vampire meticulously searched every pocket, meticulously inspecting even the recesses of Kain's wheelchair. Finding nothing, he communicated his findings to Siluk with a gesture of empty hands raised in the air.

"Here is what I am going to do, Kain," Siluk declared, his voice carrying an ominous weight.

"First, I am going to let you witness Julie's death so that you can document that. Then, I will take you back to your place of stay, which I believe is somewhere in Kansas, where I will search for this journal that you write. I will not make you one of our kind, as I am sure you have desired to be transitioned to our breed so you can walk once again. Instead, I will have you bleed out and die slowly, allowing you time to relive the foolish actions you have taken." A sinister grin played on Siluk's lips.

"She is innocent, and do you forget the agreement your kind have made with theirs?" Kain interjected, a desperate plea for reason.

"That agreement was broken when Stanley met you!" Siluk shouted, his tone revealing a deep-seated resentment.

Reclaiming his position on top of Julie's lifeless body, Siluk seemed eager to sample a rose petal that had caught his attention. Placing his left hand on her lower jaw and reaching for a rose petal lying beside her on the ground, Kain couldn't contain his desperation, yelling for Siluk to stop. Ignoring the desperate plea, Siluk locked eyes with Julie, his gaze filled with a malevolent intensity, as if relishing the impending agony he was about to inflict.

"You, your breed have and remain to be ignorant. I do not understand why we even had you as our watchers or slaves as you might prefer. I take great pleasure in trying this new discovery my twin brother has used in the past to a true test. Your husband will know of this, which is my intent. He will weep for what you have given while he himself will soon follow. As for the human that can only sit and watch at your front door, he will soon die himself. His journal, written to share with humans, these ridiculous mortals, will be found by us and destroyed. We, not your breed, will save the next wave of wars that your Stanley Swanson so believes in from happening. We were meant to rule the world, not have it intervened with!" Siluk declared with a sense of conviction and superiority.

Stanley Swanson – Breed of a Werewolf

Julie, her jaw still tightly gripped by Siluk's hand, could only shed tears. Despite her vulnerable position, she persisted in defending not just herself, but the honor of their breed.

"Forget that Stanley is my husband. He is more than just that and not even that of a father. He is a breed of werewolf and will not stop from his belief. You killing me as you plan will not sway him but only make Stanley complete the war he has envisioned by conquering all of your lifeless souls," Julie boldly stated, emphasizing the indomitable spirit within her.

"That is really cute and well said, Mrs. Swanson, and I suppose we shall see if this is true. For you, though, you will never know. I take a most fulfilling joy in watching you suffer. Make this easy for yourself and open your mouth so that I can place this rose petal upon your tongue and watch you swallow it. Fight, then I will crush your jaw, making it much easier for me to do so," Siluk sneered, reveling in the sadistic pleasure of the impending torment he planned to inflict on Julie.

The tension hung heavy in the air as Julie faced a decision that could impact not only her fate but also the destiny of her husband and their entire breed.

As Kain watched the horrifying spectacle unfold before him, the weight of helplessness became unbearable. Siluk's words echoed in his ears, detailing the grim fate awaiting not only Julie but also Stanley and himself. Overwhelmed by a surge of desperation, Kain lunged from his wheelchair, propelling himself towards the steps of the porch.

Tears streamed down Kain's face as he cried out to Julie, pleading for forgiveness. Julie, her spirit broken, surrendered to the inevitable. Siluk, reveling in his sadistic victory, placed the rose petal in her mouth, and a sinister laughter erupted from him, resonating with a contented malevolence. The final tears of Julie traced paths down her beautiful face, her glowing blue eyes, a distinct trait of their werewolf breed, reflecting both pain and resignation. In those haunting moments, the inevitability of a swift yet agonizing death for their breed hung heavily in the air.

Siluk, removing himself from Julie's lifeless form, stood a few feet back, an embodiment of malevolent satisfaction. Julie, grappling with the pain that seized her, reached for her abdomen with both hands. Amidst the torment, a single word escaped her lips, a desperate plea directed towards Kain.

"Salvation."

The utterance lingered in the air, carrying with it a sense of urgency and a cryptic message that hung unanswered in the chilling night. The implications of Julie's final word reverberated through the silent darkness, leaving Kain to grapple with the aftermath of the gruesome scene, haunted by the knowledge that the salvation she sought might remain forever elusive.

As the chilling echo of Julie's final word, "Salvation," hung in the air, a dreadful transformation unfolded. Julie, lying on the ground, began convulsing violently, and in an instant, a burst of fire erupted from within her, consuming her form until only ashes remained. Siluk, wiping his hands on the side of his pants, reveled in sadistic satisfaction at the horrifying spectacle he had orchestrated.

In the aftermath, Kain lay helplessly on his stomach, his world shattered by the grotesque demise of Julie. Siluk, eager to continue his reign of terror, ordered one of his vampires to restrain Kain, who was nearly lifeless from the trauma he had just witnessed. A follower of Siluk approached, easily lifting Kain by the back of his shirt, dragging him towards their waiting vehicle, leaving the abandoned wheelchair behind.

During the involuntary journey, Kain, with one last glimpse, surveyed the area where Julie once lay, only to find her reduced to ashes. Siluk followed, his malevolent presence lingering over the grim aftermath.

Siluk, contemplating further atrocities, expressed a desire to burn down the house but refrained from doing so to avoid unnecessary attention. Instead, he left the scene unchanged, a haunting memorial of rose petals for Stanley to confront when he returned. Siluk smirked, reveling in the psychological torment he intended for Stanley.

"You will die for what you have broken, and I will find happiness in knowing you will live the rest of your new immortal life in hell!" Kain cried out, defiance burning in his eyes.

"Hell, you say? The Devil you humans believe in or the God that you humble yourselves over have no control over me. You, however, should begin to pray to this said God of yours as you will be seeing him soon," Siluk retorted with a chilling confidence.

Kain, tossed unceremoniously into the back seat of Siluk's vehicle, could say no more. Siluk, undeterred, commanded two of his followers to search the house for other members of the werewolf breed, knowing they couldn't have gone far. As his minions rushed into the house, Siluk returned to his vehicle, setting course for Kansas, the home of Kain, leaving behind a scene of unspeakable horror and despair. The night had witnessed the ruthlessness of Siluk, setting the stage for an impending confrontation with Stanley Swanson and the relentless pursuit of his warped vision.

FINDING WAYS TO DO WHAT MUST BE DONE

Stanley, still grappling with the sorrow of leaving his brother behind, navigated through the woods in relentless pursuit of Gravakus. The moonlit night, with its cold air, enveloped him, and despite the grim circumstances, he never allowed fear to infiltrate his lifeblood. Pausing momentarily, he inhaled the crisp night air, determined to press on. The realization dawned upon him that he needed clothes and a means of transportation to continue his journey to Coney Island.

As Stanley traversed the woods and covered miles with occasional breaks for a breather, the scent of a campfire wafted through the air. A distant glow indicated a gathering, and the prospect of encountering humans piqued his interest. Unaware of the tragic events that transpired in his absence, Stanley, devoid of a phone left behind at the highway battle, remained oblivious to the brutality inflicted upon his wife.

Approaching the campsite, the sounds of bottles smashing and boisterous voices reached Stanley's ears. Deciding to blend in, he shifted into human form, taking cover behind a large tree while surveying the area for potential clothing sources. The campers, young and immature in his discerning eyes, engaged in their nocturnal revelry. Among them, a cocky and intoxicated individual stood out to Stanley.

Spotting a backpack close to a tent, Stanley cautiously approached, aiming to retrieve some much-needed clothing. As he reached for the backpack, positioned to the right of him, he noticed a pair of jeans peeking out. Moving stealthily, he attempted to avoid detection, but a misstep on a twig alerted the

S.K. Ballinger

campers to his presence.

Caught in the act, with the backpack in his hands and poised to extract the jeans for modesty, Stanley became the center of attention. One of the young ladies in the group spotted him, her eyes widening in surprise and perhaps a hint of fear. The unexpected encounter set the stage for an unforeseen interaction with the campers, adding a layer of complexity to Stanley's already tumultuous night.

"What the hell are you doing!" she yelled in a startled voice.

With his back towards the campers, Stanley, realizing he had attracted attention, stopped in his tracks. A man from the group, likely under the influence, shouted at him.

"Hey man, what the fuck are you doing with our shit?" the man exclaimed, a note of hostility in his voice. He continued, "You just walked into the wrong campsite, dude. To think that you are going to just take our things and be gone is a huge mistake."

Stanley, with a huge grin on his face and a slight shake of his head in a 'here we go' motion, heard a gun click behind him. Undeterred, he returned a comment of his own in a calm voice, "You do not want to pull that trigger, I promise you, kid. I just need some clothes, and I will be on my way as I am in a hurry."

"You're going to put that backpack down, or things are going to get really bad for you," the other guy chimed in, backing his friend's threat with the presence of a gun.

In the midst of the tense confrontation, a shocked lady among the campers couldn't contain her panic and shouted, "Who

Stanley Swanson – Breed of a Werewolf

in the hell comes roaming around in these parts naked and in the cold? Shoot him already, John!"

The situation escalated, with Stanley standing defiantly, the threat of violence hanging in the air. The campers, caught off guard by the unexpected intrusion, faced an enigmatic stranger who seemed unperturbed by the danger that surrounded him.

Before John could even consider pulling the trigger, Stanley initiated a swift transition, revealing his transformed backside to the group of young adults. In a matter of seconds, his physique, hair, and sheer brawn conveyed to them that he was no ordinary human. John, astonished, turned to the rest of the group.

"Did you see that shit?" he exclaimed, the group nodding in agreement, momentarily left speechless by the supernatural display.

With the backpack still in his hands, Stanley positioned it strategically in front of his exposed areas as he turned to face them slowly, covering himself as best he could.

"I am not here to hurt any of you, and trust me, it would not take much to do so if your friend were to pull that trigger. I am going to need some of your clothes, and I will be on my way," Stanley asserted, addressing the group while maintaining eye contact with the man holding the gun.

In his haste and without paying attention to the backpack he grabbed, Stanley had unwittingly taken one belonging to a lady in the group. John, still pointing the gun, issued a threat with a tense undertone, "Dude, I don't know what you are, but man....I will pull this trigger, I swear to God."

Stanley, determined to defuse the situation, elaborated, "If you pull that trigger, you will not like the outcome that will follow. Just let me be, and all will be well, with the exception that I need your vehicle. You all can go about your fun night, get laid, or whatever your intentions might be, but I need to be on my way."

John's friend advised him to put the gun down as he began removing his own pants. Stanley, with a bemused look on his face, tried to suppress a laugh.

"Um, you do not have any other pants here with you?"

"Dude, I don't have any other pants, but if you wish to take the girls that are in the backpack, then that is just as fine for me," John's friend responded.

With John lowering the gun and Stanley realizing the mix-up with the backpack's contents, he couldn't help but express a light laughter.

"Continue on with removing your pants then, and keep your under layer on, please. I hope that you are not left in embarrassment, kid, but thanks," Stanley remarked, adding a touch of levity to the unusual exchange.

The young man complied with Stanley's request and removed his pants, leaving them on the ground before him. Growing impatient with the delay and eager to continue his journey, Stanley, now lacking the simplicity of having clothes, slowly advanced towards the group. Despite the evident fear, none of them dared to move, their eyes fixated on the approaching supernatural entity. The gun in John's trembling hand hinted at his unease.

Stanley Swanson – Breed of a Werewolf

Within inches of John and his friends, Stanley knelt down, exchanging the ladies' backpack for the pants. As he stood up, preparing to leave and offering a simple thanks, one of the young ladies, seemingly enlightened by his presence, kindly offered assistance.

"Would you like some food, a flashlight, or something else to help you?" she asked.

Stanley, still walking away toward the tree where he had initially hidden, replied to the generous offer, "I am fine, and thank you, but as I said, I am going to need this vehicle as well. So, who does this jeep belong to?"

"Shit... it is mine," John admitted, dangling his keys in front of him, offering the means for Stanley to take control of the situation.

Stanley, now partially clothed, approached John peacefully, accepting the keys from him. He reassured John that his jeep would be returned in fine shape, emphasizing the importance of keeping the night's events a secret. As Stanley sat in the driver's seat, he warned the group with a scare tactic, showcasing another fast transition into his werewolf form.

"If I hear of anything of this night, I will come back to find each one of you individually and make sure that it ends there, wherever you might be," Stanley declared from the distance of the jeep, instilling a sense of fear in the group. Just before driving off, he made one last request.

"May I please borrow one of your phones to make a quick call to my wife?"

S.K. Ballinger

The kind lady who had offered assistance gladly walked over, smiling with a bite on her lower lip. Stanley thanked her, dialed Julie's number, and left a brief message assuring her of his safety, concluding with a heartfelt "you are my world." Returning the phone to the young lady, Stanley faced John's eager inquiry.

"If you don't mind me asking, whoever or whatever you are, how am I going to get my jeep back, man?"

Aware of the eight-hour drive ahead of him, Stanley suggested to John to watch the news after their camping trip.

"Give me one day is all I ask of you, and if you do not see it on the news, then feel free to file it missing," Stanley replied, leaving John with a sense of anticipation.

Still in shock from witnessing Stanley's rapid transformations, John's friend asked with genuine curiosity, "Mister, are you a werewolf or something like that?"

"You do not seriously believe in that type of myth, do you?" Stanley chuckled, leaving the group to ponder the surreal encounter they had just experienced.

As Stanley drove away into the night, the campers remained in awe, grappling with the unbelievable events that unfolded in the moonlit woods.

"If you don't mind me asking you, whoever or whatever you are, how am I going to get my jeep back, man?" John inquired, seeking assurance about the fate of his vehicle.

Aware of the lengthy journey ahead, Stanley suggested to John to monitor the news after they returned from their camping

Stanley Swanson – Breed of a Werewolf

trip.

"Give me one day is all I ask of you, and if you do not see it on the news, then feel free to file it missing," Stanley reassured him.

Still reeling from the shock of witnessing Stanley's rapid transformations, John's friend couldn't contain his curiosity.

"Mister, are you a werewolf or something like that?"

"You do not seriously believe in that type of myth, do you?" Stanley chuckled, dismissing the notion with a laugh.

With a large smile on his face, Stanley began to leave. John and the rest of the campers, despite witnessing the unbelievable, hesitated to admit to themselves what they had seen. Instead, they extinguished the fire and retreated to their separate tents, engaging in hushed conversations about their surreal night experience. The lingering words of Stanley echoed in their minds, a strange memory that defied rational explanation.

Stanley, grateful for the campers' unexpected kindness, resumed his journey on the road, en route to his confrontation with Gravakus. Thoughts of his brother lingered, a haunting concern overshadowing his quest. He reflected on the fortunate turn of events with the campers, acknowledging that the situation could have taken a horrific turn if the young man with the gun had pulled the trigger. Despite the unusual encounter, Stanley pressed on, determined to fulfill his mission while grappling with the complexities of his supernatural existence.

S.K. Ballinger

THE HOME THAT ONCE WAS

Back at Stanley's plantation, now a desolate area with the exception of those fortunate enough to escape the encroaching threat of the 'red rose petals' surrounding the house, survivors sought refuge in the underground trails designed by Stanley's father for such dire scenarios. The two vampires, followers of Siluk, soon discovered the hatch leading to the tunnels, sparking their curiosity and determination to locate the remaining pack of werewolves.

"Get down there now, you fool! I can smell their filth, and they are not far," one vampire commanded the other.

The underground trail, illuminated by flickering lights along the way, presented a labyrinthine network. The survivors, unaware of the distance separating them from the pursuers or the two left behind, raced through the tunnels, attempting to transition into werewolves. The transition would not only grant them increased speed but also serve as a gauge of their proximity to the ominous red rose petals above ground.

After a swift transformation, all three survivors—Drennan, Francais, and Jeremia—caught up to Natalie and the kids. Amidst the flickering lights, they saw Natalie with Sabe and Jade under her protection. Relief washed over Natalie as the three approached. Francais, the wisest among them, reverted to human form and urged the others to transition quickly, sensing that the danger was far from over. He ordered his niece, Natalie, to watch over Jade, who was not fully capable of transitioning.

Just before they could proceed with transitioning, Sabe urgently yelled to Francais, his voice echoing through the tunnels, "Francais, be vigilant, they're still on our tail!" The urgency in

Sabe's voice heightened the tension, and the group understood that their escape was far from guaranteed.

"Where is my mother?" Sabe asked, his face etched with concern.

"Now is not the time, young one, but I will explain when we get to safety from these tunnels. Now do as I say and transition, Sabe," Francais ordered, sensing the urgency of the situation.

The scent of the two vampires chasing them down in the tunnels grew stronger, indicating they were gaining quickly. Sabe transitioned, and the entire pack ran as fast as they could, hoping to reach the exit hatch at the end of the tunnel and evade the pursuing vampires. Despite being able to pick up the scent, they couldn't determine the number of vampires on their tail.

The vampires, reveling in the pursuit, taunted the werewolf pack with threatening words echoing through the tunnels.

"We know you are down here, you hell hounds!" they shouted. "You are going to love what we have discovered with these red roses."

Excitement coursed through the vampires in the confined space of the tunnels, bolstering their confidence in facing the werewolves. Their overconfidence led to a critical mistake, as one vampire, fueled by the thrill, shouted with laughter, the sound reverberating through the tunnel.

"You all should have stayed for the show of what happened to the lady when a red rose petal was shoved in her mouth!"

Sabe came to a slow stop, a tear rolling down his face, causing the others to pass him before they halted and turned back to him.

"Sabe, come on, boy, right now!" Francais shouted, the urgency in his voice matching the gravity of the revelation. The pack now faced not only the immediate danger of the vampires but also the haunting reality of the fate that befell one of their own.

Sabe, unable to ignore the vampires' echoing voices, realized they spoke of his mother. In a brief moment of silent realization, an emptiness filled him, signaling the tragic fate of his mother. Enraged, Sabe charged in the opposite direction from the pack, heading towards the vampires, who continued to taunt and mock them.

Drennan, recognizing the danger in Sabe's actions, instructed the remaining pack to continue forward, assuring them that he would go after Sabe. Francais, with a sense of urgency, implored Drennan not to lose another member of their pack that night.

"Do not let us lose another tonight, please, I beg of you," Francais pleaded.

Drennan, displaying his agreement with a powerful flex of his body and a wicked grin, watched as the rest of the pack moved on. He then set off after Sabe, navigating the tunnel with the intermittent flickering of lights. The darkness might be an advantage for werewolves, whose heightened senses and powerful night vision made the pursuit more manageable.

Stanley Swanson – Breed of a Werewolf

As Drennan drew closer to Sabe, he began to hear growls of pleasure emanating from him. The scene that unfolded before Drennan was beyond comprehension. Sabe, fueled by grief and rage, had unleashed his fury upon the vampires who had pursued them. The details remained obscured, known only through Drennan's eyes. Sabe, in a frenzied state, had brutally attacked the vampires, leaving one shredded and torn apart, and the other reduced to a mere shadow forever imprinted on the dirt path of the tunnel. The aftermath painted a grim picture of the intensity of Sabe's vengeance and the visceral brutality that unfolded in the dark confines of the tunnel.

"We need to regroup with the others and do so now, for others may be coming," Drennan pleaded, recognizing the urgency of their situation.

Impressed by Sabe's fierce display, Drennan shouted to him, encouraging him to finish off the mangled vampire before catching up with the rest of the pack.

"I am proud of you, boy, and perhaps one day you will be as strong as me. Now, finish that mangled vampire off so we can catch up with the others," Drennan urged.

Sabe, standing up from the vampire he had subdued, took the last of his anger out on the already near-dead creature. With a fatal blow to the vampire's neck, Sabe severed its head, ensuring its demise. As the burning shadow next to the other vampire indicated their deaths, Sabe couldn't help but face the direction of what was once his home, aching to see his mother running towards him.

Drennan, understanding the depth of Sabe's grief, assured him there was nothing left to do. He also promised to share Sabe's mother's last wish before she left the breed. Sabe complied with Drennan's request, and just before running back through the flickering light ways of the tunnel, he cast one last look at the shadows. This glance served as a reminder of his capabilities and a solemn vow to forever seek the destruction of any vampire he might encounter.

The weight of the loss sank in for Sabe, a young child who, in a fleeting moment, comprehended the extent of the vampires' evil intentions and hatred toward their breed. Though difficult to process, Sabe forged ahead, determined to honor the memory of those he had lost by defending his kind against the looming threat of vampires.

Drennan and Sabe swiftly rejoined the rest of the pack at the exit hatch, where their fellow werewolves patiently awaited their return. With a renewed sense of unity, they pulled each other up from the tunnel, forming a formidable pack once again. However, the familiar orchards and woods that were once a sanctuary were now devoid of safety.

Lacking clothes, campers, or any means of transportation, the pack agreed on a plan to create a distraction to secure a vehicle. The strategy involved killing something sizable and placing it in the road to stop an oncoming vehicle.

The night air grew colder as they embarked on a hunt in the woods, and it wasn't long before Natalie proposed a bet, asserting that she would find the distraction first. Jade, not fully ready to transition, voiced her dissatisfaction, but Jeremia reassured her, offering to accompany her to keep a watchful eye.

The pack dispersed in various directions, each on the lookout for the perfect distraction. Bragging and playful banter echoed through the woods as the mental communication between pack members began. In the distance, Natalie's voice carried, shouting in triumph as she believed she had found the ideal distraction.

The woods echoed with the triumphant cry of victory as Natalie claimed her win in the distraction hunt.

"I win!" she exclaimed.

Excitement spurred the rest of the pack to rush towards her, but their enthusiasm waned as they discovered Natalie feasting on a buck.

"You are eating the distraction Natalie!" her Uncle admonished.

"Damn, that is a nice buck though Natalie, I will give you credit for that," Drennan remarked with a grudging acknowledgment.

Francais intervened, reminding them that all bets were off, and the priority was to secure a vehicle immediately. He instructed Natalie to wound any subsequent animals to make the distraction more convincing. Francais, known for his seriousness and commitment to survival, stressed the urgency of finding a new safe haven to share the events that had unfolded.

As they attempted to regroup after the unexpected feast, another shout echoed through the woods.

"Will this one do?"

Jeremia, seemingly not cut out for babysitting duty,

realized he had lost track of Jade. The pack hurried towards her, only to discover that Jade, using her heightened senses, had successfully wounded another deer in human form.

"Excellent job done!" Francais commended her.

The pack, now more determined than ever, refocused on their mission to create a convincing distraction for securing a vehicle and ensuring their survival in the wake of the recent threats.

As they waited for a car to approach on the nearby highway, Jeremia, still feeling a bit careless after momentarily losing track of Jade, jokingly admonished her not to run off again. The pack was thoroughly impressed with Jade's maturity and capabilities, with Francais expressing his admiration.

"You possess such maturity than I have ever seen from our breed," Francais remarked, indicating that Jade might be a breed worth watching closely, potentially signaling the emergence of a new kind within the Swanson bloodline.

Drennan, not missing a beat, took charge by picking up the wounded deer. The group moved towards the highway, staying a safe distance away, waiting for the opportune moment to create their distraction without causing any accidents.

As they observed the limited traffic on the late-night highway, they noticed Natalie's growing impatience. The injured deer, moaning in pain and kicking its legs, proved to be a tempting target for her hunger, intensified by the recent transition.

Despite the celebratory lamb feast, it was evident that the meal hadn't satisfied Natalie's hunger. She eyed the wounded deer, desiring to put it out of its misery and consume it to satiate her lingering hunger.

With a few cars approaching, the need for action became apparent.

"Who is going to throw the bait?" Francais inquired, prompting the pack to decide on the execution of their distraction plan.

As Drennan descended the hill with the wounded deer under his arm, the others watched with expressions of disinterest, especially considering Natalie's untrustworthiness at the moment. Unfazed by Jeremia's urging, Drennan took charge, determined to execute the plan his way.

Reaching the highway's edge on this moonless night, Drennan patiently waited for the right moment. Jeremia's impatience got the better of him, and he shouted, "Just throw it, Drennan!"

Ignoring Jeremia's directive, Drennan opted for what he thought would be a more humane approach. Placing the injured deer on its hooves, he gave it a gentle slap on the rear, hoping it would run across the road. However, the plan backfired when the deer, instead of serving as a distraction, ran down the side of the road and back into the woods. The others watched in disbelief, and Drennan had to face the consequences of his unexpected blunder.

Returning to the group, he was met with a mix of laughter and disbelief from the kids and Natalie. Jeremia, losing patience, chided him, "Way to go, Drennan. Now we will have to find another distraction. Why is this having to be so difficult?"

Drennan defended himself, stating, "I did not see you offer to throw the damn deer, Jeremia."

"I would have had I known you were going to just set it free," Jeremia retorted.

"It was not what I thought was going to happen, as most deer run to the other side having to cross the road," Drennan explained.

Before the tension could escalate further between the two, Francais intervened, calling for silence. Concerned, he asked, "Any of you see Sabe?"

The group scanned the surroundings, hoping to locate their missing pack member.

As the group frantically searched for Sabe and the mood grew tense, little did they know that Sabe had taken the initiative to become the much-needed distraction. Swiftly transitioning back to human form, he sprinted to the highway, strategically positioning himself in the path of an oncoming vehicle. The others, unaware of his plan, watched in concern as Sabe, now naked, ran in front of the approaching car.

The plan unfolded perfectly as the driver slammed on the brakes in panic, swerving before coming to a halt. To the driver and passenger, it seemed they had hit a young boy who lay motionless on the ground. Without prior discussion of Sabe's intent with the pack, they gathered to decide their next move, uncertain of Sabe's condition or whether the car had struck him.

Natalie, quick to assess the situation, recognized this as an attempt to minimize harm to humans while securing the vehicle.

Stanley Swanson – Breed of a Werewolf

She sprinted to the car, transitioning back to human form just before entering. With a swift getaway, she floored the stolen vehicle, creating a considerable distance between them and the bewildered owners, who were still focused on the seemingly injured boy.

The timing of the car theft was impeccable. The owners, grappling with the confusion of encountering a lone boy in the dead of night, managed to maintain their composure. The lady, taking charge, quickly dialed for help while the man assured Sabe, "Stay still and don't move, son. Help will be here soon."

Meanwhile, Sabe continued his convincing act, moaning as if in pain, allowing the distraction to unfold seamlessly.

The man and woman, focused on the injured Sabe, remained unaware of the stolen vehicle. Sabe, committed to his act, continued to moan, buying precious time for the pack to make their move. The couple, concerned for the boy's well-being, had numerous questions swirling in their minds but were willing to wait for a sign of life.

In the woods, Jeremia took charge, instructing the others to head down the side of the highway to rendezvous with Natalie, who had successfully driven off with the stolen car. He assured them that he would watch over Sabe until their return, ensuring both of them would be retrieved safely. The stolen vehicle soon returned, blending in with the passing traffic, and a few other vehicles stopped to offer assistance to the seemingly injured Sabe.

Natalie and the pack, now naked except for Jade, who remained clothed, stopped at a distance to observe the unfolding events. Sabe, aware of their presence, noticed the stolen vehicle. Jeremia, transitioning to human form as he ran towards the car, aimed to access it through the open doors. The pack anxiously awaited Sabe's cue, uncertain of how he would navigate the situation surrounded by humans. Natalie, behind the wheel, kept her patience, seeking guidance from Sabe, as the rest of the pack remained clueless.

Finally, Sabe rolled over, pointing towards the opposite direction of Natalie's position with the car, mumbling, "My little sister is over there; she was behind me in the woods, not far." The pack now had a lead to follow and a purpose as they considered their next moves to secure their members and continue their journey.

As the men desperately searched for the imaginary girl in the woods, shouting in vain for a response, Sabe seized the opportunity to execute his escape plan. The stolen car sped away, leaving behind the chaos of the search. The woman who had stayed with Sabe turned back to find him gone, a testament to the speed and agility of the young werewolf.

Inside the car, a wave of smiles and nods followed Sabe's successful escape. Francais, expressing genuine pride, commended him, stating, "Very well done. Your father will be proud of what you have done." The acknowledgment of his father's approval brought a sense of reassurance to Sabe.

With the stolen vehicle heading in the farthest direction from its rightful owners, Natalie, now at ease, inquired about their destination. Francais, considering their options, replied, "We will head east and as far away from this area as we can get. I have a few friends on the coast of Delaware and many in New York."

Acknowledging that their current stolen vehicle wouldn't be their last, the pack began to make plans to abandon it at a rest area and secure another. As the crowded car continued on its journey, with Sabe and Jade seated between Drennan and Jeremia, Jade succumbed to the weight of her emotions, breaking down at the thought of their mother. Sabe, anxious for answers, turned to Drennan, reminding him of his promise to explain.

"What of our mother and our home?" Sabe queried, desperate for clarity and understanding. The air in the car became heavy with anticipation as they awaited Drennan's response.

As the weight of the news settled in, what had started as a moment of courage and laughter quickly turned into a somber situation. The smiles and enthusiasm that had filled the car now gave way to frowns and heavy hearts. Jeremia took on the responsibility of explaining the fate of their mother and the vampire raid that had devastated their home.

"I know Drennan was going to tell you, Sabe, of what took place, but I will do so as I was the last, other than Kain, to see your mother."

Sabe, with a quiver in his voice, questioned the heartbreaking truth, "So it is true then that our mother is no longer?"

Jeremia, meeting Sabe's gaze, responded with sorrow in his eyes, "I am sorry to have to tell you, but you, young one, stand correct. She gave her life that night so that we all may still have ours."

Jade, unable to contain her grief, broke down further upon hearing the news. Sabe, holding his sister tightly, fought back tears, knowing he had to be strong for her. Amidst his grief, hatred for Kain, the one responsible for their mother's demise, surfaced.

"What of Kain, Jeremia? I hope that human dies a horrible death for what he has caused to our mother and breed."

"Kain himself, with guilty feelings, stayed behind, Sabe. I am sure that he himself is, in fact, dead, if not than more than likely will be soon."

The remainder of the drive was marked by a heavy silence. The uncertainty of Stanley's well-being loomed over them, and the unanswered calls to his phone heightened their concern. The group prepared for the worst, all the while shielding Sabe and Jade from the grim reality. As Jade found solace in sleep within her brother's arms, Jeremia, addressing Sabe, acknowledged the responsibility he now bore.

"Until we meet with your father or uncle, the two of you are under my strict care. I will do all that I can to keep you informed, Sabe. Now would be a good time to rest as we have many hours of driving ahead of us." The night pressed on, filled with grief, loss, and the unknown.

DESTINATION STULL

The journey from the now abandoned plantation continued, with Kain in the back seat of Siluk's car, flanked by two uneasy followers who were visibly struggling to resist their primal urges to end the life of the human in their midst. Siluk, sitting in the passenger seat, wore a frustrated expression. He hadn't received any updates from the followers he had sent after the remaining werewolf breeds, and the uncertainty of their success troubled him. Kain, astute in sensing Siluk's agitation as he repeatedly checked his phone, decided to break the tense silence.

"Does it bother you to think that the breed of werewolves have made it to safety while perhaps the two worthless vampires you sent after them might be nothing more than shadows now?" Kain's words were carefully chosen to provoke a reaction from the vampire leader.

Siluk, unsettled by Kain's remark, chose to ignore the comment about the werewolves. Instead, he turned his head from the passenger seat to look directly towards Kain, his expression hardening.

"So you know, I am going to have much fun with you as I watch you die slowly, mortal," Siluk declared in a harsh tone, his threat hanging in the air like an ominous cloud.

Kain, undeterred by the looming danger, decided to speak his mind openly. "You know what I have learned. It is really simple if you don't mind me being honest with you. I have learned that you, Drackulis or Vampire, are just as sick-minded as you are in the movies or books that have been read. What I know now, I only wish could have been known to the world much sooner of the truth of your kind," Kain bravely commented, challenging Siluk's perception of himself and his kind.

Amused by Kain's audacity, Siluk replied with a sinister smile, "What you have gathered in the form of paper or otherwise, I soon will have. Know that all those that you have listened to, seen, and written in this journal of yours will have been done so for nothing. Once we arrive at this home of yours, you will provide me with the journal and share with me everything you claim to have witnessed that I may be unaware of. I will give you only a few choices, which are to die without pain or die with pain before your life comes to an end." Siluk's words echoed through the confined space, foretelling the dark fate awaiting Kain.

Beyond himself with great excitement as he found it funny that Kain would have the nerve to say such to him, Siluk replies with a smile.

"What you have gathered in the form of paper or otherwise, I soon will have. Know that all those that you have listened to, seen, and written in this journal of yours will have been done so for nothing. Once we arrive at this home of yours, you will provide me with the journal and share with me everything you claim to have witnessed that I may be unaware of. I will give you only a few choices, which is to die without pain or die with pain before your life comes to an end."

Kain, feeling a newfound courage after witnessing the death of Julie, smiled in the face of Siluk, undeterred by the impending danger. He continued the conversation, unafraid.

"Death to me, then, so be it, or are you going to wait until my last beat of my heart to make me a slave to you like your followers have become?"

"To change you to a vampire would be an insult to what we are, and that should be the least of your worries. As I said before, the woman I took great pleasure in killing, you are not going to become a vampire. Why would I give you the privilege to be healed, walk again, and enjoy the everyday of living as I do? You will suffer slowly, and I will continue on as you bleed out from your legs that you apparently do not feel from your events that took place."

"Then do what it is you are going to do to me, you worthless Drakulis, who is so fast to take a weak and defenseless being as you did to Julie. Might as well pull over now and end my life. I am not going to share with you anything that I know or give you the journal that seems to have started this war Stanley believes in. You're a pathetic disgrace to your own kind in what you do. I am honored that I will not walk again if it were to mean me being changed to a slave of yours. You truly are nothing more than a creature of the night."

Kain's words, filled with defiance and disdain, echoed in the confined space of the car, challenging Siluk's perceived power and authority over him.

In frustration by Kain's rant and slightly offended, Siluk struggled to contain the desire to end Kain's life right then and there. He believed himself to be the smarter of the two and hesitated to succumb to Kain's taunts.

"Creature? You, of all mortals, dare call my kind a creature when it is the beasts that you humans shy away from, which is that of hellhounds. The humans are the mere creatures more so than us or even that of the beasts you claim to share information with. Look at yourself as a prime example, as you, just like other humans, live for nothing but fantasy, not knowing if we are real or not or, as you put it, mythology. The human race is as pathetic as they come. I was blessed to be what I am today. You all are worthless, helpless for one another, and blind. It is no wonder that your minds are so easily seduced by us. In time, while some of my own kind feel the need to have a balance, I will see that it will never happen. We are made to rule, and that is what the outcome will be."

Kain, still smiling at Siluk, responded in a few words, not out of fear but to provoke further agitation.

"Let you yourself not forget that once you were a human, as you suggested to me. Also, let us not forget about the breed you hate so much and once enslaved. One breed in particular strikes my mind that will see that balance is kept, and you will die by his very hands. This breed of a werewolf happens to be a friend of mine, and you likely know him to be Stanley Swanson. I only wish that I would be alive to see what it is that he will do to you before carrying on in determination with great vengeance."

Siluk, laughing at the seemingly futile attempts of this handicapped human, assured Kain that what he said was not something the breed could achieve, especially someone like Stanley.

"There is so much you have not heard, Kain. I am not going to share with you what I know, as there is no need for that. Stanley, this so-called friend of yours, will die just as I had the pleasure of doing so to his all-so-willing and stupid wife Julie."

The conversations between the two continued to grow more impatient with one another as they drove through the night.

Stanley Swanson – Breed of a Werewolf

Kain's mouth was eventually bound shut, silencing him temporarily. The talking would only resume when they arrived the next day at Stull, Kansas. The early morning light began to reveal itself on the eastern horizon, casting an eerie glow over the landscape. Kain, feeling uneasy, knew that his time of living was about to end. Still, he refused to share information with Siluk, determined to keep his knowledge from falling into the wrong hands.

"If you think that the hellhounds, which they are, would be the only mythological beings to have traveling experiences with others, you are highly mistaken. These movies and books you mortals watch or read should have let you know one truth of a Drakulis. Damn you are so ignorant to not follow through with your eye for detail or research. While the breed can past travel, my kind have the option of doing either past or future. So, I will have what I need from you regardless."

Siluk, though intrigued by Kain's comments, remained skeptical. The tension in the car continued to build as they approached Stull, both unsure of what awaited them in the darkness of the coming night.

Siluk continued to divulge unintentional details about the capabilities of Drakulis as they drove toward Kain's home. He spoke of the unique traits possessed by the strongest and longest-lived Drakulis, highlighting their ability to vanish in fog, turn humans into vampires, and become nearly invisible, just as depicted in movies. Kain absorbed this information, silently acknowledging the potential danger such creatures posed.

As they arrived at Kain's house, Siluk expressed disdain for the humble abode, deeming it unworthy of their presence. He demanded information on the location of Kain's journal, eager to expedite their journey to Kansas.

"What a nasty place of living you have. Nonetheless, I really wish to begin that of our long trip to Kansas and need to know where all of your files are...this written journal. Please make this fast for both you and us."

"As I have said, you will not find my journal, and it is something that I will not share with you of where it might be, but will only say that it is not in my home."

"Looks as though we will destroy your house to be sure. Enjoy watching what was once your place of comfort, as it will be the last projection in your mind."

"Comfort? I haven't had that feeling in a long time until now."

"I am not sure how you interpret the word comfort in knowing you are going to die. I am, however, going to end this endless search for the journal with you rest assured."

"Very simple to interpret, by me finding comfort in knowing Stanley is going to find you, and when he does, you will be the one caught off guard as he makes you become nothing more than a fallen shadow."

The exchange between Kain and Siluk was filled with tension, each holding their ground with their own convictions as they approached Kain's house.

Siluk's sadistic satisfaction was evident as he grinned

while inflicting severe wounds upon Kain's legs, rendering him paralyzed and bleeding profusely. The malicious act was intended to cause Kain to bleed to death slowly, ensuring a painful demise. As Kain helplessly looked on, Siluk, keeping his promise, ordered his followers to search the house for any evidence of the supposed journal.

"Enjoy your last moments of life, you sickening and pitiful human. Say what you want, and it would be wise of you to start speaking to this GOD of yours. So choose your words in desperation before your eyes start to close, and your heart becomes nothing more than a few beats apart. Watch the last few moments of your house being destroyed, and know that this soon-to-be war was created by you. While you take notice of that, I want you to remember how easy it was to take Julie Swanson's life and that all other breeds of werewolves will suffer the same fate as her. We will keep only the few as they once were that of slaves. Humans will panic, and those that try to get in the way, such as the military, will stand no chance. This world is meant for only one type of breed, and that is of my kind. Your vanquished soul will only be able to look on in despair and because of you!" Siluk declared before standing up and giving orders to his followers."

"Tear this place apart now!" Siluk commanded, prompting his followers to ransack Kain's house. As Kain, unable to intervene, succumbed to the slow embrace of death, the followers executed Siluk's orders, destroying everything in their search for the elusive journal. Despite their efforts, the journal remained undiscovered, leaving Siluk frustrated.

"Take this near-dead body to his basement and leave him in the dark. Not a one of you are to bite this crippled piece of shit of a mortal."

Only one follower adhered to Siluk's directive, while the others continued the futile search. Minutes later, the three followers reconvened under Siluk's lead, and they swiftly exited the house, leaving Kain alone in the dark basement. Siluk's focus now shifted to the Drakulis temple in Santa Cruz, CA, a significant location that held importance in their dark plans.

WELCOME CONEY ISLAND

Stanley, having successfully reached Coney Island in the camper's jeep, left it behind to navigate the bustling city on foot. True to his word, he kept the vehicle safe, a testament to his integrity even amidst the looming confrontation with Gravakus. As he moved through the city, Stanley's heightened senses led him to detect the unmistakable scent of a Drakulis nearby, signaling his proximity to the vampire he sought.

Despite the numerous vampires inhabiting Coney Island, Stanley was undeterred. The bustling city, filled with lost souls and vampires alike, was unlike any environment he had encountered before. The overpowering scent of Drakulis was prevalent, making it clear that this location served as a hub for these dark creatures. However, Stanley's determination overshadowed any concerns about being outnumbered.

As the sun began to set, casting an ethereal glow over the late evening, humans and the rare members of Stanley's own breed retreated while vampires roamed freely. The moon ascended, bathing the city in its silvery light. Stanley closed in on an enormous house near the beach, sensing that Gravakus rested on its deck.

With every step, the desire for vengeance fueled Stanley's pace. His family's suffering at the hands of Gravakus spurred him forward, but he resisted the urge to transition and attack prematurely. As he neared the house, the tension in the air heightened. It took immense willpower for Stanley to refrain from unleashing his fury.

Within striking distance and no immediate intervention from Gravakus's followers, the Drakulis turned his attention toward Stanley. A silent yet unmistakable gesture, Gravakus wagged his pointer finger in a 'no' motion, signaling a warning to Stanley, who braced himself for the impending confrontation..

Stanley, his rage barely contained, came to an abrupt halt just a few feet away from Gravakus, who, with a seemingly calm demeanor, urged restraint.

"I would not recommend making a scene unless you wish to have this war you speak of happen now when it can still be easily avoided. No sense in showing all that are around us that we exist. Even I am smart enough to admit that," Gravakus advised, attempting to diffuse the tension.

Stanley, however, was done with secrecy and retorted, "I no longer care of being hidden and will gladly start this war for all to see as I kill you for what you did."

Gravakus, still composed, responded, "If I had truly wanted to kill your family or your wife that I had in my grips, I would have done so as it was frankly an easy task. I should mention as well, that boy of yours is going to turn out to be trouble for our kind by the way."

In a surprising move, Gravakus slightly turned his cheek, revealing claw marks inflicted by Stanley's son as he defended his mother. The Drakulis swiftly covered the marks, but the gesture served as a reminder and perhaps an attempt to invoke understanding from Stanley. It worked, prompting a reflective moment for Stanley as he contemplated his family's well-being and felt pride in his son's bravery.

Gravakus then proposed a more peaceful approach, "Please, if you wish, Stanley, follow me down to one of my

Stanley Swanson – Breed of a Werewolf

favorite sitting areas by the beach, and let us talk. Let us both make this easy, and I only ask for you to give me a chance to fill you in on what is happening."

As both Stanley and Gravakus made their way to the sitting area, the air was thick with tension, and Stanley's internal struggle was palpable. Gravakus, however, seemed to radiate confidence, waving off his followers with a simple gesture that conveyed a level of trust not lost on Stanley.

Seated across from each other at a table, Gravakus took out a flask filled with blood and took a quick swig, a casual display of his otherworldly nature. The timing couldn't have been better, as a waitress approached, inquiring if they would like to order from the menu.

"No, I am good thanks, but perhaps my friend here would like something that is a bit undercooked," Gravakus remarked in a polite tone, acknowledging Stanley.

"I am fine, thank you, ma'am," Stanley replied promptly, determined to keep the conversation on track.

The waitress left them to their devices, and the two adversaries locked eyes, both keenly aware of the significance of their meeting.

"Get to the point, Gravakus, and let me make this clear that we are not friends. You wanted to talk, so speak now before I lose interest in what it is that you wish to say," Stanley demanded, his impatience evident.

Gravakus, unfazed by Stanley's directness, decided to delve into the heart of the matter.

S.K. Ballinger

"Do you even know much of the war that took place hundreds of years ago, Stanley?"

"I know enough that we were slaves to your kind. What is your point?" Stanley retorted, his eyes narrowing with suspicion.

"Oh, young Swanson, so much more that you need to know, and yes, your women and even children were slaves to us. Nonetheless, times have clearly changed, no?" Gravakus responded cryptically, laying the groundwork for what promised to be a revelation of significant proportions.

The evening unfolded, pregnant with the weight of their shared history and uncertain future, as Gravakus prepared to unveil the untold truths of the ancient conflict that had shaped the destinies of their respective breeds.

Stanley, though skeptical of Gravakus's motives, felt an overwhelming curiosity about his family's history and the origins of the war that had defined their existence. Gravakus offered him a unique opportunity – a past travel, a chance to witness firsthand the events that had shaped their destinies. However, the warning about the grim nature of those historical moments hung heavily in the air.

"I can appreciate you willing to do this, but your kind only see the future," Stanley pointed out, his suspicion lingering.

"Exactly, which is why I have to trust you, Stanley, as you will be the one doing it," Gravakus explained, a peculiar glint in his dark eyes.

The notion of trust between enemies seemed paradoxical, yet the gravity of the situation compelled them to find common

Stanley Swanson – Breed of a Werewolf

ground.

As both locked eyes, the ambient noise of Coney Island seemed to fade away. Stanley's piercing light blue eyes, indicative of his werewolf nature, bore into Gravakus's dark pupils, tinged with a hint of blood red. The tension in the air was palpable as the ancient vampire and the werewolf, bound by a shared history of conflict, prepared for a journey through time.

The world around them blurred, and the present yielded to the past as Stanley felt an indescribable force pulling him backward through the corridors of time. The scenes shifted rapidly, and he found himself immersed in a world that was both familiar and alien.

Gravakus observed the unfolding events with a detached curiosity, knowing that the revelations awaiting Stanley could reshape his understanding of their shared legacy. The past, with all its complexities and secrets, was about to unravel before Stanley's eyes. The journey to the roots of their bitter enmity had begun, and only time would tell what truths it held.

In the mid-1700s, a turbulent era marked by ignorance and prejudice, the scenes that unfolded before Stanley during his journey into the past were nothing short of tragic. The quaint town, a microcosm of the time, bore witness to a harrowing conflict that would shape the destinies of vampires, werewolves, and humans alike.

The images revealed a chaotic tableau of destruction and suffering. Humans, blinded by their ignorance, unknowingly fought alongside vampires, casting aside their humanity in a wave of violence. Homes were torched, and females of all ages were cruelly seized and confined in cages. The air was thick with the

S.K. Ballinger

acrid scent of burning structures and the anguished cries of the innocent.

Amidst the chaos, a handful of werewolves, desperate to protect their kind, revealed themselves to the humans. This misguided alliance only fueled the myth that would persist through the centuries – the belief that werewolves were savage beasts in league with the supernatural.

The town became a battleground, with the few surviving mortals caught in a maelstrom of violence. The vampires, veiled in secrecy until that moment, unveiled their true nature, as did the sinister Drakulis. The werewolves, once concealed among the humans, fought fiercely to defend their kin.

The turmoil reached its zenith as the werewolves, outnumbered and outmatched, faced a relentless onslaught. From every corner, foes emerged – vampires, humans, and the feared Drakulis. The clash of civilizations unfolded in a tragic symphony, with lives lost to fangs and blades alike.

The werewolves, unable to withstand the combined forces aligned against them, met their demise one by one. Beheading became the grim method of execution, severing the supernatural beings from their mortal coil. The once-hidden truth of their existence was exposed in the most brutal fashion.

As Stanley watched these events unfold, the weight of history bore down on him. The past, with its horrors and miseries, revealed the genesis of the age-old conflict that had plagued his family and the supernatural world. The mid-1700s stood as a testament to the consequences of ignorance, fear, and the destructive power of prejudice.

Stanley Swanson – Breed of a Werewolf

In the spectral echoes of the past, the vision of a tumultuous time in the mid-1700s played out before Stanley's eyes like a tragic drama. He observed with an intensity that bordered on painful nostalgia, catching glimpses of his father, Sebastian Swanson, as a younger man. There, beside him, were the younger versions of Stanley and his brother, Stephen, innocent witnesses to the unfolding chaos.

Amidst the chaos and destruction, a figure emerged from the throng, an aged werewolf with fur as white as snow. Stanley recognized him as his grandfather, though the distance and the tumultuous events made it challenging to hear the exact words exchanged. It was evident, however, that the elderly werewolf urgently communicated something of grave importance to Sebastian.

In the midst of the fray, Sebastian, torn between familial duty and the impending danger, knelt down to address his two boys. The weight of the moment hung heavily in the air, and the urgency in Sebastian's eyes conveyed the severity of the situation.

"Boys, I need you to listen closely," Sebastian implored, his voice carrying the weight of responsibility.

"You both will run and seek shelter far from here and never look back. Continue to run until you meet another breed of a werewolf. Stephen, I expect you to watch closely over your brother Stanley. With that, I leave you this key as you should seek California, where you should learn from there."

The gravity of the situation hung heavily in the air, and the urgency in Sebastian's eyes conveyed the severity of the situation. Stephen, the elder of the two brothers, sought clarity, asking the poignant question that echoed in the air.

S.K. Ballinger

"What of you, Father?"

Sebastian's response was swift, delivered with a tone of determination forged in the crucible of war.

"No time to answer questions; just know that I am staying behind with your grandfather as I will do all to find my wife and your mother they have taken. Now go!"

The brothers, entrusted with a key and a directive to seek California, became reluctant participants in a fateful escape, their father's words echoing in their ears as they sprinted away from the chaos, leaving behind the battlefield and their family.

Stanley emerged from the haunting tapestry of the past, grateful for the fleeting glimpse into the tumultuous events that shaped his family's destiny. The scenes from the mid-1700s unfolded like a tragic opera, with Sebastian Swanson at the center, leading his brethren against the encroaching forces of vampires and the ever-looming threat of the Drakulis.

As Sebastian ordered his sons to flee, the battle raged on, a relentless symphony of chaos and bloodshed. The aged werewolf, Stanley's grandfather, declared a rallying cry for his kin, a proclamation that resonated with the few remaining werewolves.

"Brothers and Sisters surrounding this battle, we shall no longer submit to any more of this as we have watched them take our wives, kids, and family. Tonight we take back what was once ours. We will seek all who look human and kill...let these humans see us for who we are, and let our lives be known!"

United by the elder's impassioned words, the werewolves fought valiantly, determined to reclaim their lives and loved ones.

However, despite their unwavering spirit, the war concluded in tragedy. The vampires, swift in their conversion of humans, overwhelmed the werewolves, claiming victory in this brutal conflict.

Sebastian, too, succumbed to the relentless onslaught, leaving a legacy of courage but also the bitter taste of defeat. The fate of those taken as slaves, including Sebastian's wife, remained shrouded in mystery, an unanswered question echoing through the ages.

Stanley, having witnessed the sacrifices and struggles of his forebears, emerged from the past with a profound appreciation for the resilience of his breed. The unfairness of the war, the imbalance between vampires and werewolves, was starkly evident. Grateful for the revelation but burdened by the weight of history, Stanley pulled away from the past, a silent acknowledgment of the sacrifices made for his existence. Gravakus, attuned to Stanley's emotions, awaited his response, recognizing the impact of the shared past on the present and the future.

Gravakus, with a calm demeanor despite Stanley's outburst, began to reveal the intricate web of motivations and complexities that had led to the historical conflict. Stanley's anger and sorrow simmered beneath the surface as he listened to the Drakulis speak of a war he himself had ignited.

"You know who started that war, Stanley? It was me."

Stanley, unable to contain his rage, lunged across the table, grabbing Gravakus by the shirt, and bared his teeth in a primal snarl. The air was charged with tension, and just as Stanley was on the verge of unleashing his werewolf form, Gravakus stood up, hands still held captive by Stanley's grip.

"I started the war to try and keep balance. I am sorry that you had to witness some of your family being killed, but in the process, many of us had died as well. I once had the hard reality of seeing my parents grow old and die. It is not easy, and I am sorry, Mr. Swanson," Gravakus explained, a mixture of sincerity and remorse in his eyes.

"Balance is key to both our respective kinds. While you look at us as night stalkers, it is true that many are. You look at my followers; they only feed off of those that hate or do crime. Not all of us that are a Drakulis hope to end your breed, I certainly do not," he continued. "This war of yours will happen one day, but will not happen as soon as it might if I have anything to do about it. Believe it or not, Stanley, we need your breed as you will need help from us. Now, if you do not mind, as you are creating a scene here, please let go of my shirt."

Stanley, begrudgingly, released his grip, prompting Gravakus to continue with his revelation.

"Drakulis are few, but vampires are of many strong. I myself have thirty faithful followers, minus the two that became shadows at your home. I say faithful as I know they are while being very loyal to me. However, I cannot say that other followers to their masters are. Many vampires are careless and change so many mortals that they easily can become the size of a small army."

The layers of truth, deception, and the intricate dance between the different breeds unfolded before Stanley, creating a tapestry of complexity that went beyond his initial perceptions. Gravakus, with a tone of both camaraderie and warning,

Stanley Swanson – Breed of a Werewolf

continued to unravel the story that would inevitably shape the destinies of both werewolves and vampires.

As Gravakus continued to explain the intricate threads of past events and future consequences, Stanley wrestled with conflicting emotions, trying to reconcile the horrors of the past with the complexities of the present.

"This planet we walk and at this pace will eventually be overrun by our kind, not your breed or the humans that highly occupy it. Which is why we need the balance to survive," Gravakus declared, his tone revealing a hint of desperation.

"While I understand some of what you are telling me, I am having a hard time adjusting and believing in you. To have bloodshed on even your own is something I cannot comprehend," Stanley commented, voicing the conflict within.

"That war was an attempt to eliminate many of my kind with purpose, as I have mentioned, and in time, I had hoped that it would have worked, but it has been clear to me for many years that it was and will never be such," Gravakus explained, trying to justify the actions of the past.

Stanley, though intrigued by Gravakus's revelations, couldn't shake off the memory of the night his family was attacked.

"What of my wife and the threat you had put towards her and my kids? I am confused why you did the attack. I understand the importance of the balance you seek and wanting to get my attention for the journal my friend Kain is writing, but breaking the treaty of both our kinds has forever been prohibited. You should have waited for my return and talked civil with me as you are now. I believe things might have been much different that night had you done so," Stanley pressed, seeking answers that would ease his skepticism.

"I was one of a few Drakulis that heard of this information of you sharing with a human of our identity and secrets. It was my immediate reaction, and I knew if I could not find you fast enough that night, then threatening her seemed a way for any other Drakulis to know that some action was being taken by us. Look at it as a way of buying your family time as that was my purpose. I will admit, though, had I stayed and found your friend Kain that night at your house, I would have killed him quickly. I ask that you can understand this while I was basing it all off first instinct, which is what I live with on a daily basis. Just as your breed is able to see the past, we can see the future to a certain point, as you know, and this journal that Kain writes is the very thing that starts the war, Stanley. This war that is going to happen will be more than any of our respective beings have yet seen. While we are able to see the future, it is a bit blurry; I can promise you of what I saw is the truth," Gravakus explained, providing context to his past actions.

"Why would you not take advantage of my past travel and see where the journal is or what I have shared with Kain?" Stanley inquired, seeking clarity.

"Because time has already served its course, and I only wish to make amends with your breed and instill trust. As I may have mentioned before, we need you, and you will need us," Gravakus replied, emphasizing the importance of unity in the face of an impending war.

The table was set for a delicate dance between trust and suspicion, as Gravakus laid bare the intricate web that connected

Stanley Swanson – Breed of a Werewolf

their fates. Stanley, torn between his desire for vengeance and the harsh realities of an impending war, began to see the shades of gray that colored the world he thought he knew.

As the evening unfolded, the table by the beach became a stage for an unusual connection between Stanley and Gravakus. Despite the looming war and past grievances, they engaged in a conversation that seemed almost casual to the onlookers. However, beneath the surface, a complex web of emotions and motivations weaved itself into their discourse.

"Might I ask why you take self-punishment of sitting so close to the ocean?" Stanley inquired, curious about Gravakus's peculiar choice of seating.

"Look around you for a moment, Stanley. Why I choose to be here or sit this close to the beach is so that I can somewhat remember what it was like to once be human. We do not have the luxury of life that your breed has, which is very familiar to these humans. While there are very few of you here right now, they are down there at the beach, swimming, sitting in front of a fire, and having fun with friends or family. We do not have the ability to do such things, and while we have a black heart with no emotions, for some reason or another, I have feelings you could say," Gravakus explained, his face occasionally touched by the ocean mist that elicited a rapid burning and healing process.

"Our kind of being a Drackulis and vampires can get a little bored in life because of the fact we are limited in what we can do in simple human form. It has taken a very long time for us to even be able to adapt to daylight. Some things over evolution or time, we are still very vulnerable and weak to the truth of a stake to the heart and saltwater. While the burning of my face every so often from just the ocean spray of this night hurts, it gives me comfort that perhaps I am not just a completely dead soul after all. It is a reminder to me that this is as close to the enjoyment I will ever get to have as I once did before becoming what sits before you."

Gravakus's revelation exposed a side of his existence that mirrored a longing for the human experiences he once had. The vulnerability he displayed, both physical and emotional, painted a picture of a creature wrestling with the limitations of his immortal existence.

However, Gravakus quickly shifted the conversation back to the pressing matters at hand, particularly Stanley's decision to share the werewolves' secrets with a human, Kain.

"While I have been a bit open to you, Stanley, I hope you can do the same with me. Do you not realize that giving your breed's secrecy to this human is harmful to your existence? If any Drakulis finds this journal, it will give us leverage over all breeds of werewolves. From what I have seen thus far, you are going to be the key to end this war and help me in keeping the balance I speak of."

"What of your kind? How does it affect you personally?" Stanley asked, probing into the consequences for Gravakus's kind.

"Very simple, Stanley. If this journal lands in the wrong hands, then the balance I have sought will have been for nothing. There are only a few Drakulis that agree with me in seeing that vampires are gradually taking over us. It is only a matter of time before I myself will be tracked down and punished for doing what it is that I have done and continue to do with talking with you."

The revelations unfolded against the backdrop of the

Stanley Swanson – Breed of a Werewolf

crashing waves, creating a surreal atmosphere that blended the supernatural with the deeply human aspects of their existence. As the night wore on, the intricate dance between predator and prey continued, the stakes escalating with every passing moment.

As the moon hung low in the night sky, casting an ethereal glow upon the beach, the meeting between Stanley and Gravakus reached a pivotal point. The air was heavy with the weight of their decisions, and the crashing waves served as a backdrop to their complex negotiations.

"Are you suggesting that we join sides?" Stanley questioned, grappling with the notion of aligning with a creature he once deemed an enemy.

"While I am suggesting that, Stanley, I am not thrilled with the idea, just as many of your breed will not be either. In uniting our respective beings, there will be many who will disagree. I am not even sure that I can persuade any help from my kind, but I can guarantee that I will be loyal to you," Gravakus replied with a smile.

The prospect of two ancient species, werewolves, and Drakulis, joining forces seemed both unprecedented and uneasy. Their collaboration, however, was born out of necessity, a fragile alliance in the face of an impending war.

Stanley, now aware of the potential consequences of his actions with Kain, sought clarity on Gravakus's intentions. "My intentions? Simple, join you as I agreed and work together to ensure the journal does not reach another being's hand, either of our kind or a human. Take what you have or know of and destroy it. You need to know that if the Committee in Santa Cruz even has the slightest idea of what I am doing, I will only have you to rely

S.K. Ballinger

on to help me."

Gravakus's straightforward response laid bare the gravity of their collaboration. Trust, a rare commodity between their kinds, was a fragile bridge upon which they now stood. Stanley, grappling with the enormity of his decisions, began to explain the events of his journey, the highway incident, and his concerns about trust, particularly given the involvement of a Drakulis.

Gravakus, with an extensive network of followers spread across states, was well-versed in the ongoing events. His ability to gather information from his loyal subjects made him privy to the recent highway incident, and he was prepared to share his insights with Stanley.

"It seems trust is a fleeting concept, even among our own kind. The incident on the highway was orchestrated by one of my followers. A necessary test, if you will, to gauge your reactions and responses. Trust is earned, Stanley, and in this dark world, it is a currency more valuable than gold," Gravakus explained, revealing the calculated nature of the events.

As the night unfolded, the collaboration between Stanley and Gravakus began to solidify, though the road ahead was fraught with challenges. The complexities of their intertwining fates unfolded against the timeless backdrop of the moonlit beach, setting the stage for a formidable partnership between werewolf and Drakulis.

As the moon continued its silent watch over the beach, Gravakus unfolded more layers of the intricate web that connected their destinies. The revelations poured forth, each word adding weight to the burden Stanley carried.

Stanley Swanson – Breed of a Werewolf

"I am aware of what took place that night, Stanley, and you should find comfort in knowing that your brother Stephen, if I recall his name correctly, escaped. He was lucky to have done so with the help of another pack. As for the Drakulis that caused your wreck and appeared in the form of fog, he is a twin brother of Siluk known to me as Emroff, who goes by Dimitris. He happens to be the more psychotic of the two and is very much older than even I. They also happen to be on the council, sitting on each side of the highest known as Sirtimi, claimed to be their father," Gravakus revealed, unraveling the intricate hierarchy of the Drakulis.

With each piece of information shared, the bond of trust between Stanley and Gravakus solidified. The intricate politics and familial ties within the Drakulis were laid bare, offering Stanley a glimpse into the complexity of his newfound ally's world.

Stanley, grateful for the news that his brother had survived that fateful night, felt a renewed sense of purpose. However, their conversation took an unexpected turn when Gravakus's phone rang, disrupting the serene atmosphere of their moonlit meeting place. The gravity of the call etched worry lines on Gravakus's face, and Stanley watched as the Drakulis received news that shattered the semblance of tranquility.

The abrupt end to the call and the distress evident on Gravakus's face foretold troubling news. Urgency tinged his voice as he spoke to Stanley, "Stanley, you need to go back to your home immediately and seek answers!"

Perplexed and alarmed by the urgency, Stanley demanded an explanation.

S.K. Ballinger

"What has happened? Tell me now!"

Gravakus's response was cryptic, hinting at a tragedy unfolding.

"It is not my place to speak of this news I have been informed of. Just know that your rage is only about to begin, Stanley."

"This conversation between the two of us is far from over. If more tragedy has happened while my search for you has occurred, then I will have no more words with you again, as you will not have time to sputter a single breath," Stanley declared, his resolve firm and his eyes reflecting the storm brewing within him.

Their meeting, once a tentative alliance, now took on a new urgency. The threads of fate intertwined, pulling them deeper into the shadows of a world where alliances were fragile, and tragedies awaited in the darkness. The journey back home for Stanley promised answers, but also the ominous prelude to an approaching storm.

The night air carried with it an aura of uncertainty, and as the moon hung low over the beach, Stanley and Gravakus stood at the crossroads of a tentative alliance. Gravakus, feeling a newfound confidence in their understanding, was determined to prevent any further tragedy brought about by his own kind.

"I will go with you, Stanley," Gravakus offered, genuinely concerned for the unfolding situation.

But Stanley, his resilience shining through, declined the Drakulis's offer with a hint of sarcasm.

Stanley Swanson – Breed of a Werewolf

"Sorry, but I have big boy pants and will leave on my own. If there is something you wish to tell me, now would be the time."

Gravakus, standing from the table, remained guarded about the details but stressed the urgency of Stanley's mission. "Your family is in trouble, is all I can say for sure, Stanley. It seems as though both Dimitris and Siluk are taking active actions towards your breed. Let me go with you; I insist, as I may be able to help."

The Drakulis was persistent, knowing that Stanley might not be adequately prepared for the challenges that awaited him. Gravakus was aware that their fragile trust might be shattered in the face of impending danger, but he was determined to offer his assistance and bridge the gap between their worlds. Tired of the endless cycles of his existence, Gravakus saw an opportunity to make a difference, to change the narrative between his kind and werewolves.

Faced with the urgency of the situation, Stanley reluctantly agreed to Gravakus joining him. The pact formed between them was fragile but necessary. The past was set aside, and the present dangers took precedence. The beachside conversation, once filled with revelations, now turned into a preparation for the impending storm.

As they began their journey back to confront the shadows that encroached upon Stanley's family, the air crackled with tension. Stanley, burdened by the weight of uncertainty, couldn't help but pose a question to Gravakus, seeking reassurance and understanding in the face of the looming threat. The moonlit night bore witness to their alliance, an uneasy pact formed against a common enemy, transcending the boundaries of their respective realms.

"What can you tell me, Gravakus? What are we up against, and how can you help?"

Gravakus, persistent and determined, insisted on accompanying Stanley to face the impending danger, understanding that the situation required a united front. He was well aware that the looming threat could potentially strain the newfound bond of trust between them, but he saw it as an opportunity to redefine his existence, tired as he was of the centuries-long existence of shadows and secrets.

In this moment of vulnerability, Gravakus was ready to shed his fears and face whatever consequences awaited him. No longer afraid of his own fate, he sought to build a bridge of trust with the werewolf, a creature with whom his kind had a long and tumultuous history. It was a chance for redemption, a desire to prove that creatures of the night could come together for a greater purpose.

However, Gravakus's motivations went beyond the immediate crisis. He needed to gather more information and verify the urgency conveyed by his follower during the brief phone call. The desire to understand the gravity of the situation and perhaps find a way to prevent further chaos fueled Gravakus's resolve.

With a surprising show of camaraderie, Stanley, recognizing the potential benefits of Gravakus's company and assistance, swiftly agreed to the alliance. The mention of a fast and reliable car to take him home was met with an unexpected revelation from Gravakus – a private jet, a symbol of his extravagant lifestyle.

Luxuries like a private jet, reserved for the wealthiest and most powerful, hinted at the extraordinary nature of Gravakus's existence. Stanley, though momentarily taken aback by this revelation, realized that such conveniences were not uncommon for beings with ancient origins. It was a stark reminder of the vast differences in their worlds, yet a shared goal and the urgency of the situation overshadowed any reservations Stanley might have had.

As they prepared to board the private jet, the night held the promise of uncertainty and danger, but also the potential for an alliance that could shape the course of their intertwined destinies. Gravakus, looking beyond his vampiric nature, aimed to prove that even creatures of the night could strive for unity when faced with a common enemy. The journey ahead would test the strength of their newfound alliance and reveal whether trust could truly overcome the shadows of the past.

The night unfolded as Gravakus and Stanley, with a shared sense of urgency, embarked on a journey through the skies. The choice of air travel, a mode of transportation typically unsettling for werewolves, underscored the gravity of the situation. Stanley, however, pushed aside his inherent discomfort, compelled by the pressing need to confront the looming threat that awaited them.

Seated within Gravakus's opulent private jet, Stanley couldn't help but marvel at the wealth surrounding him. The interior exuded luxury, adorned with items that surpassed the wildest dreams of most humans. This extravagant setting stood as a testament to the age and affluence of Gravakus, a being who had navigated the centuries and accumulated treasures beyond mortal imagination. The opulence served as a stark reminder of the stark contrast between the worlds of humans and supernatural beings.

S.K. Ballinger

Hours passed in relative silence, with Gravakus engrossed in conversation with his driver, a loyal follower who adhered to the importance of discretion regarding the events unfolding at Stanley's home. The subdued atmosphere in the jet hinted at the seriousness of the situation, keeping any unnecessary discussions at bay.

As they approached the airport in Wilmington, DE, the urgency of their mission was palpable. Gravakus, before the plane left the runway on short notice, informed Stanley that he would be accompanied by a couple of his well-trusted followers. The revelation added a layer of complexity to their journey, with the involvement of vampires in a mission typically associated with werewolves.

Stanley, though disgruntled by the unusual conditions and the prospect of sharing the sky with vampires, chose to trust the alliance that had been forged between him and Gravakus. The thousands of feet above ground provided a unique perspective, offering a mix of discomfort and reassurance. The knowledge that even the formidable Drakulis, with their ability to transform into fog, would be vulnerable to the elements at such altitudes provided Stanley with a semblance of comfort.

As the private jet soared through the night sky, the tension in the cabin mirrored the uncertainties of the impending confrontation. The alliance between werewolf and vampire faced its first significant test, high above the world where their fates would soon intertwine with the challenges awaiting them on the ground. The journey held the promise of revelations, alliances, and confrontations that would shape the course of their intertwined destinies.

The air inside Gravakus's private jet grew heavy with

anticipation and sorrow as Stanley, desperate for answers, used Gravakus's phone to make a series of heart-wrenching calls. Gravakus, silent yet empathetic, watched as Stanley navigated through the emotional turmoil.

Stanley's trembling fingers dialed Julie's number, longing to hear her voice. The call went unanswered, and her voicemail played, capturing the essence of her absence. Despite the dire situation, the sound of Julie's voice brought a fleeting smile to Stanley's face.

Compelled to ensure the safety of his children, Stanley then tried calling his brother, Stephen. The silence on the other end of the line heightened the tension within the cabin. The jet's engines roared as it taxied down the runway, leaving no room for delay.

With a growing sense of urgency, Stanley knew he needed to reach someone from his pack before losing signal. The first choice was Jeremia, a trusted friend and confidant. As the phone rang, Stanley's eyes were filled with a mix of fear and determination.

Jeremia's voice broke through the connection, offering a brief moment of solace. Stanley, in a rush of words, informed Jeremia of his encounter with Gravakus and the dire circumstances that led to his impromptu flight. His plea for information about Julie and the safety of his children hung heavily in the air.

Jeremia, grappling with the weight of the devastating news, urged Stanley not to return home. The revelation of another attack and the assurance that the children were safe hinted at the impending tragedy. Stanley's desperation grew as he pressed for

S.K. Ballinger

details about Julie, his love, and life partner.

The emotional toll on Jeremia was evident as his voice cracked, unable to shield Stanley from the truth any longer. As the connection faltered, Jeremia's final words lingered in the air, revealing the heartbreaking fate that had befallen Julie.

"Please, I beg of you, Stanley, do not return to your home as your wife, Julie, has lost her life. She was..."

The signal abruptly cut off, leaving Stanley in a vortex of anguish. Shockwaves of grief surged through him, and the air in the jet became charged with the weight of tragedy. Stanley, crushed by the revelation, turned his gaze toward Gravakus, eyes ablaze with a mix of sorrow and rage. The painful truth had shattered his world, and the journey ahead promised not only revenge but a reckoning with the demons that now haunted him.

The jet, now soaring through the night sky, carried the weight of Stanley's shattered world. The abrupt loss of signal and the devastating news from Jeremia had pushed him to the brink of despair. In a fit of anguish, Stanley clenched Gravakus's phone in his hand, the werewolf within him surfacing with glowing eyes and a heart consumed by grief.

Desperation and rage radiated from Stanley's gaze as he confronted Gravakus. The ancient Drakulis, recognizing the volatile nature of the situation, met Stanley's eyes with a somber honesty. He spoke with a calm assurance, urging Stanley to channel his emotions toward redemption rather than succumbing to the darkness that threatened to consume him.

"I did not want to tell you, Stanley, but your friend spoke the truth. You must not rage here. Focus on redemption, and I will help you find it. I know the Drakulis responsible for this tragedy – it was Siluk."

Stanley, overwhelmed by a flood of memories with his wife, struggled to hold back tears. The glowing intensity of his eyes began to fade as the realization of Julie's loss settled in. In his brokenness, he questioned Gravakus about the omission of such a crucial detail.

"Why would you not have told me this? You speak of trust between our kinds, yet you kept silent about the most important thing – my wife's death. Why should I not kill you, as I feel more empty than ever before?" Stanley cried out.

Gravakus, maintaining a steady gaze and extending a comforting hand, implored Stanley to think of the family he still had – his children and brother. Despite the tragedy, Gravakus spoke of the revenge that awaited Stanley, assuring him that their paths would converge with those responsible for the pain inflicted upon him.

"Trust in me, Stanley, and you will have your revenge. Perhaps we should change the course to another place of comfort rather than your house."

Stanley, however, resolute in facing the harsh truth, insisted on maintaining the course toward his home.

"Keep the course to my home. I wish to see with my own eyes. I will have my revenge upon your kind, and it will not end thereafter."

Gravakus, expressing sympathy for Stanley's loss, conveyed his deep sorrow. As the jet continued its journey, the followers on board sought brief respite, resting while Stanley remained seated, his hands on his forehead, tears streaming down his face. Gravakus, beyond the pilots, maintained a vigilant watch over the grieving werewolf. A single tear traced a path down Gravakus's cheek, a silent acknowledgment of the shared sorrow that bound them in that moment of profound loss and impending vengeance.

THE LANDING TO THAT OF ONCE WAS

The plane descended, landing with a profound sense of foreboding. As reception became available once more, a follower's phone rang, bearing news that Gravakus received with a cautious demeanor. The urgency in the caller's voice compelled Gravakus to listen intently, prompting him to ask everyone to maintain a hushed silence.

The news from the trusted follower unfolded, revealing details about the red rose that had taken Julie's life and shedding light on the events surrounding that tragic night. As Gravakus processed the information, he handed the phone back, a thoughtful expression etched on his face. The tension in the air was palpable, intensified by the continuing footage on the television inside the jet.

"This is not good," Gravakus remarked, his voice carrying a weight of concern. "It appears that the patrol car has caught video of you and your brother's night. We may not be as hidden as we once were. Dimitris has played a fool, and your breed is vividly exposed."

Stanley, absorbing the revelation, responded with a measured skepticism, challenging the significance of the footage.

"This is not how the war I believe to be begins, Gravakus. This is only video caught on a fuzzy camera during a downpour. It's hard to make out what my breed looks like – we resemble bears. It should not be a cause for concern, nor should Dimitris' disappearing act."

S.K. Ballinger

Gravakus, despite Stanley's attempt to downplay the situation, maintained a furrowed brow, recognizing the potential implications of their exposure. The delicate balance they had tried to maintain between the supernatural world and the oblivious human society seemed to be teetering on the edge of collapse. As they disembarked from the jet, the news on the television screen continued to play, each frame unraveling the events that had transpired on the highway, casting an uncertain shadow over their clandestine existence.

As the footage played on the television screen inside the jet, it became evident that, despite the obscured visibility caused by the rain, the events captured would now be exposed to a broader audience through various media outlets. The very existence of werewolves, once relegated to myth and legend, was on the verge of being revealed. The camera, hindered by rain and lacking crystal-clear visibility, hinted at the truth, leaving room for skepticism among those who viewed the footage – a skepticism that could serve as a thin veil of protection for the supernatural beings.

Gravakus, accustomed to navigating the intricacies of the supernatural world, recognized the limitations of mortal technology and the potential repercussions of this revelation. He and Stanley, standing side by side, watched the footage closely. The raindrops splashing off an almost imperceptible blur revealed a figure resembling a man walking, complete with a top hat and discernible shoulders.

"See right there, if you look closely, Stanley," Gravakus pointed out, "watch the raindrops splashing off an almost clear blur which nearly shows a figure of a man walking. You can see the top hat and the shoulders from where the drops become horizontal."

Stanley Swanson – Breed of a Werewolf

Stanley, keenly observant, added, "Not only that, Gravakus, but also you can see the footsteps being made in the puddles."

Gravakus nodded in agreement, acknowledging the finer details that remained hidden to the untrained human eye.

"That is what humans are blind to see, friend. Not many pay attention anymore to the finer details of what is before them, and it makes these mortals so easy to judge what they do not understand."

The revelation on the screen underscored the delicate balance between the supernatural and human worlds, exposing the vulnerabilities that came with their existence. The unfolding events hinted at an impending struggle to maintain secrecy in a society that had long dismissed the fantastical. Gravakus and Stanley, united by circumstance, faced the challenge of navigating a world that now teetered on the edge of acknowledging the supernatural.

As the news clip continued, it revealed a shocking sequence: a lone werewolf in the distance, standing behind what appeared to be a trooper. The footage took a grim turn as the werewolf bit down on the trooper's head, prompting the news to blur the image and abruptly end the video. Speculation and fear would inevitably ripple across the world, painting the werewolves as monsters, creatures of the night, and threats to innocent lives. This exposure, far from the ideal unveiling of their existence, cast the werewolf breed in a menacing light, threatening to disrupt the fragile balance between the supernatural and human worlds.

Concern etched across Stanley's face as he processed the implications of this revelation. The war he had sought to delay and the potential conflict he and Gravakus had discussed seemed imminent. Gravakus, however, met the unfolding events with a certain amusement.

"Looks like that war I have tried to put off and the one you believe to happen may not be far off after all," Gravakus remarked, a smile playing on his lips as they both observed the television screen.

Stanley, relieved to see his brother's distant figure in the background, acknowledged the urgency of their situation. Time pressed against them, and with the need to return home, he signaled to Gravakus that they must proceed as discussed.

Exiting the private jet, they made their way to Gravakus's waiting vehicle nearby. Before departing, Gravakus made one final mention of the recent developments.

"I hope you are prepared, as I warned you earlier of what you might see, Stanley. I was told that there is perhaps a new type of weakness for your breed in the form of a red rose. What that means, I have not a clue, but it is what your wife died from. I wish that you do not hold me accountable, as I am the one who killed her."

Stanley, grappling with grief and anger, responded firmly, "All I ask of you, Gravakus, is that once we arrive at my home, you let me be. While I will mourn for the love I lost and the mother of our children, it would be wise for you to not be close."

"I understand, and rightfully so. Now, point my driver in the direction we need to go," Gravakus agreed, acknowledging the sensitivity of the upcoming moments. The vehicle set forth, carrying the weight of sorrow and uncertainty as they headed

Stanley Swanson – Breed of a Werewolf

towards the Swanson residence.

As the journey continued, several hours passed before Gravakus's car reached Sacramento, CA. As they ventured deeper from the city, the air grew heavy with the unspoken grief that Stanley carried. In an attempt to distract themselves from the impending tragedy, they resumed their discussions about Kain, the journal, and the looming war. The weight of anticipation hung in the air, and with every mile that drew them closer to the Swanson residence, the atmosphere inside the vehicle became increasingly somber.

Upon arriving at the plantation, a desolate scene greeted them. There was an eerie silence, and the absence of any signs of life only amplified the gravity of the situation. Stanley, feeling a sickness in the pit of his stomach, urged the car forward, only for it to come to a halt before reaching the house.

"Why are you stopping here as we are not yet close?" Stanley's voice carried a mix of impatience and anguish.

"I have stopped here because you are already weak, and it is not just from the hurt you feel at having lost, but more so because there are red rose petals still scattered across your lawn," Gravakus explained, a solemn expression etched on his face.

"I do not care what you say about these red roses. What I care about is seeing what may remain of my wife, who lost her life at the one place I assured her safety, our home."

"Stanley, neither you nor I know exactly what these roses might do to you. Take caution, and we will pull up slowly, is all I am asking."

S.K. Ballinger

Frustrated with the cautious approach and weary of the ongoing conversation with Gravakus, Stanley removed himself from the halted vehicle. Two followers began to step out as well, but Gravakus signaled them to stay back with a wave of his pointer finger.

"Let him be, as it will be me who follows him. Stay at the car, you two, as Stanley is not going to hold back his anger after seeing what remains of his home while he was gone in search of me." Gravakus's stern tone left no room for argument, and he emerged from the vehicle to accompany Stanley on the heartbreaking journey towards his once-secure haven.

The atmosphere inside the car was tense as the two followers followed their master's instructions, taking their seats and watching in silence as Stanley, their leader, began the journey down the remainder of his driveway. His physical condition seemed to deteriorate with every step, a palpable unease settling over the trio. The weight of impending dread hung in the air, casting a shadow on the otherwise mundane act of traversing the familiar path home.

As Stanley approached his house, the source of his discomfort became increasingly evident. A single rose petal lay on his path, a stark contrast to the dark surroundings. Intrigued, Stanley halted, his gaze fixated on this seemingly innocuous petal. The contradiction of its beauty against the ominous atmosphere made him ponder the inherent danger it posed to their enigmatic breed.

Contemplating the delicate nature of the rose petal, Stanley gingerly picked it up, cradling it between his pointer and thumb fingers. He marveled at its softness, the richness of its color, and couldn't help but draw parallels to the symbolism a rose

Stanley Swanson – Breed of a Werewolf

typically held for humans – a symbol of love and beauty. This momentary pause allowed him to reflect on the fragility of their existence and the potential menace hidden beneath the alluring exterior.

As Stanley brought the rose petal close to his nose to inhale its fragrance, Gravakus, his loyal follower, caught up to him. Recognizing Stanley's contemplative state, Gravakus stood back, offering him a moment of solitude to engage with the petal. However, the experience took an unexpected turn. Stanley's internal turmoil escalated rapidly, manifesting in physical distress.

The softness of the petal and its symbolic connotations clashed violently with the harsh reality of their existence. A sudden surge of instability overwhelmed Stanley, culminating in a bout of vomiting. He clutched his stomach in agony, the rose petal slipping from his grasp and fluttering to the ground, now tainted by the turmoil within him.

Despite the setback, Stanley pressed on with determination, each step heavier than the last. The path before him became adorned with an increasing number of rose petals, an unsettling sign of impending doom. Dragging his feet, he soldiered on until he reached the fountain in front of his house, a beacon marking the culmination of his journey.

Collapsed to his knees, Stanley was a picture of suffering – nauseated, sick, and weak. Tears mingled with the gravel beneath his hands as he cried out to Gravakus, who remained a stoic presence behind him.

"Why would this or any Drakulis do this, what purpose does this serve?" Stanley's anguished question echoed in the air, a plea for understanding in the face of an inexplicable and ominous

S.K. Ballinger

event. Gravakus, standing firm, had no immediate answers, leaving Stanley to grapple with the uncertainty that shrouded their reality.

As Stanley lay flat on the ground, the weight of his emotions pressing down on him, Gravakus, his loyal companion, stood close by. The pallor of shock and sorrow painted Stanley's face as he shouted for Julie, fully aware that his plea would be met with silence. He assumed the posture of anguish, with only his toes, knees, and palms supporting him on the cold gravel. The haunting echo of his own voice lingered in the air, the unanswered question 'why' hanging heavy over the scene.

Gravakus, despite his seemingly lifeless heart, responded to Stanley's silent plea with a gesture of compassion. He lowered himself, extending a hand towards Stanley, a symbolic offering of solace in the face of an inexplicable tragedy. Stanley, grappling with the profound grief that enveloped him, managed to gather his emotions enough to accept Gravakus's outstretched hand. It was a moment of shared pain and understanding between master and follower, a connection that transcended the peculiar circumstances that surrounded them.

In a tender attempt to console Stanley, Gravakus spoke, his voice resonating with an unexpected warmth, "Let me walk this yard of yours and check your home to see if I may find anything of importance to you, Stanley. I will do whatever it is that you ask of me to help."

Stanley, still reeling from the shock, responded with a voice laden with sorrow, "I only wish to see that of my wife's remains. If you can help as you say, then point to me the right direction."

Stanley Swanson – Breed of a Werewolf

Gravakus, ever loyal and composed, directed Stanley's attention, "Look to the slight left of your front door and off the deck area. There is almost a perfect circle that has no rose petals in it. I would suggest that is where she remains. Let me carry you there, Stanley."

However, Stanley, fueled by a sense of determination and the desire to confront his grief on his own terms, replied, "I will make my own way to what I had long lived for, which was that of my wife." His words carried a profound weight, a declaration of personal agency in the face of heart-wrenching circumstances.

As Stanley rose to his feet, his movements guided by a mixture of grief and resolve, Gravakus respected his decision. The two figures, master and follower, stood side by side, united by a shared pain, yet divergent in their chosen paths of coping. The air hung heavy with sorrow, uncertainty, and the unspoken bond between them as they navigated the harrowing journey towards the place where Stanley's wife rested in eternal stillness.

Stanley's determined walk soon morphed into a slow crawl as his weakened state intensified. Gravakus, ever attentive, kicked the rose petals aside, creating a makeshift path to facilitate Stanley's precarious journey. The air was thick with the acrid scent of burnt roses, and the ground beneath was a somber canvas, scorched and desolate from the aftermath of an unknown calamity.

Summoning every ounce of strength left in him, Stanley resorted to crawling on his belly, dragging himself forward with hands that bore the weight of anguish. The path was grueling, each inch gained a testament to the relentless will of a grieving soul. Finally, he arrived at the circled area of burnt ground, a desolate canvas marked by the absence of rose petals.

S.K. Ballinger

In this sorrowful place, Stanley began to scour the soil, desperate for any sign of his wife. His hands sifted through the earth, searching for a trace of the one he had loved so dearly. To his heart-wrenching discovery, slightly off to the far left, lay the wedding band she had once worn. The symbolic token of their union lay dormant in the desolation, and Stanley, driven by a surge of life willpower, pushed himself to the limits to reach it.

Inching closer to the elusive band, his outstretched fingers strained against the overpowering presence of the relentless roses. Just as he neared his goal, Gravakus, ever-vigilant, extended his hand, retrieving the wedding band, and placed it gently in Stanley's open palm. The silent exchange spoke volumes of the unspoken bond between master and follower, a poignant moment of understanding in the face of unspeakable loss.

It became evident that Stanley's devotion surpassed the bounds of life and death, extending to the very core of his existence. Gravakus, acknowledging the depth of Stanley's sacrifice, resolved to carry him, now defenseless and weakened, away from the haunting petals that had become harbingers of tragedy. Gravakus kept a watchful eye, ensuring that Stanley did not lose his tenuous grip on the remains of his beloved wife.

Once they reached the safety beyond the perilous petals, with Stanley still grappling with his physical weakness, a follower of Gravakus made a callous remark that cut through the heavy air like a bitter wind. The insensitive comment, uttered with a light chuckle, mocked the tragic fate of Stanley's wife.

"From what I have heard is that she had become a firework show out of control as she more or less blew into a ball of fire from a rose petal placed in her mouth."

Stanley Swanson – Breed of a Werewolf

The words hung in the air, an affront to the mourning atmosphere, and a tense silence settled over the group. Gravakus, with a steely gaze, made it clear that such insensitivity would not go unpunished. The weight of the situation lingered, casting a shadow over the collective grief, and a somber stillness enveloped the tragic scene.

Stanley, fueled by an unrelenting surge of willpower, shoved Gravakus to the side as the offending vampire's callous words echoed in the air. Despite his weakened state and the lingering effects of the rose petal's curse, Stanley underwent a swift and dramatic transformation. In a matter of moments, he shifted from vampire to werewolf, his body pulsating with newfound strength and ferocity.

A deafening roar erupted from Stanley as he pounced on the ill-fated vampire, who had dared to mock the tragedy that befell his wife. Claws extended, he mercilessly shredded the vampire with a series of powerful swipes, the air filled with the sounds of tearing flesh and anguished cries. Gravakus, shoved aside, wisely stood back, recognizing that intervening would be a dire mistake in the face of Stanley's justified rage.

The vampire's existence became a fleeting shadow, extinguished within seconds as Stanley, with a final, lethal bite, crushed the vampire's neck, severing the head from the body. The visceral brutality of the scene unfolded in a blur, leaving no room for mercy.

However, the remaining two followers, now revealed as vampires, showed their true allegiance, and fury simmered in their eyes. Enraged that their master had allowed the demise of one of their own, they advanced toward Stanley, fangs bared and nails poised for attack. Gravakus, understanding the consequences of their actions, conveyed a silent message to Stanley with a bow, essentially saying, 'deal with them.'

Stanley, still in his formidable werewolf form, faced the oncoming vampires without hesitation. With ruthless efficiency, he dispatched both assailants in a manner mirroring the fate of their predecessor. Gravakus, though seasoned in witnessing various battles, couldn't bear to watch as the gruesome spectacle unfolded before him.

The werewolf form gradually subsided, and Stanley transitioned back to his human self, standing near Gravakus. The aftermath of the confrontation was evident in the torn bodies scattered around, a stark reminder of the gravity of their situation.

"So this theory of the rose is, in fact, true?" Stanley inquired, grappling with the grim reality that had unfolded before him.

Gravakus, showing a rare vulnerability, removed his coat and handed it to Stanley to cover up his naked body, a silent gesture of remorse and acknowledgment.

"I truly am sorry, Stanley, but as I mentioned to you not long ago, it is real as it seems," Gravakus admitted, his tone carrying the weight of regret for the tragic events that had transpired.

The air hung heavy with sorrow and the harsh reality of their existence, the repercussions of the rose's curse manifesting in both physical and emotional scars.

Stanley, still holding his wife's wedding band in his palm, gazed at it with a mixture of sadness and determination. Making an unspoken promise in his mind never to forget, he carefully tucked the precious memento into the pocket of the jacket Gravakus had just given him for cover. His gaze then shifted back to his house, still surrounded by the haunting rose petals, and with a heavy heart, he whispered to himself, "I will return one day."

Gravakus, sensing the gravity of the situation, spoke in a subtle voice, breaking the poignant silence.

"We need to leave here and find another place of safety as we are not alone. Like the scent your breed can smell of us, I can sense many vampires lurking not far from here. I know that you would stay not fearing, but there are many, and we will not be able to take on the numbers, especially in your condition."

Stanley, acknowledging the wisdom in Gravakus's words, replied, "We will leave then and make our way to Nevada."

"If that is what you wish, then so be it, friend," Gravakus responded.

Stanley corrected him, "Refrain from referring to me as your friend. I only suggest Nevada as that is a very well-populated State of my breed. Once we arrive, then we will continue on to Vegas, as it is heavily populated, and I happen to like the MGM, which is where we will stay until I make further contact with my brother or the pack that is protecting my kids."

Gravakus, curious about their destination, questioned, "So, no commitment to being friends, and you wish for me to be with you in a heavy population of werewolves?"

Stanley, ever steadfast, explained, "Just as I found you in Coney Island, which appeared to me that my breed was not of many then, yes."

"Fair enough, I suppose. I will make the call to the pilot," Gravakus acquiesced.

But Stanley had different plans, stating, "No, we will be driving."

"You are being complicated, Stanley," Gravakus remarked.

"I need the time to think, is all, and a long drive will give me that," Stanley asserted.

Gravakus, showing a hint of amusement, remarked, "Are all of your breed stubborn like you are?"

Stanley, undeterred, pressed the urgency of their departure, stating, "Are we leaving, or are we waiting for the many vampires to arrive?"

"Okay, point made," Gravakus conceded, realizing the gravity of the situation and the need for prompt action.

The air buzzed with tension and anticipation as they prepared to embark on a journey fraught with uncertainty, leaving behind the haunting memories of rose petals and a tragic past.

The night air hung heavy with an unsettling mix of tension and anticipation as Stanley and Gravakus made their way to the car. Stanley, having chosen driving over flying, believed the long journey would afford him the time needed to reflect on the tumultuous events that had transpired. The shadows cast by the once-threatening vampires now lay dormant, silent witnesses to the brutal confrontation that had unfolded.

Maintaining a proximity to these shadows, the duo navigated the darkness with a watchful eye, cautious not to attract any unwanted attention. Gravakus, walking by the remnants of the vampires that now existed only as shadows, couldn't conceal his disdain for the fallen followers. With a calculated step, he ground his foot deep into the soil, his voice dripping with contempt as he muttered, "Worthless idiotic followers."

Stanley, catching this act of disdain, almost allowed a smile to play across his face. The gesture resonated with him, a shared sentiment toward those who had callously mocked the tragedy of his wife. In that brief moment, there was a flicker of understanding between master and follower, a silent acknowledgment that transcended the chaos around them. Perhaps, Stanley mused, there was potential for a connection between them, a bond that could evolve into something resembling friendship over time.

As they approached the car, a sleek and shadowy vehicle that blended seamlessly with the night, Stanley took a moment to cast a final glance at his house. The rose petals still lingered, but the promise of returning one day provided a distant glimmer of hope. The engine roared to life as Stanley turned the key, and the car, now their sanctuary, surged forward into the darkness.

The road stretched ahead, an uncharted path leading them to Las Vegas, Nevada. The hum of the engine and the rhythmic beat of the tires on the asphalt served as a backdrop to their journey. The landscape shifted outside the car window, the night unfolding in a symphony of shadows and distant city lights. Gravakus, sitting beside Stanley, remained a stoic presence, his eyes scanning the surroundings for any potential threats.

S.K. Ballinger

    The miles passed, and the duo ventured deeper into the heart of the night. The silence within the car spoke volumes, each occupant lost in their own thoughts, contemplating the twists of fate that had brought them together. The road stretched endlessly, a metaphorical path leading toward new beginnings, and perhaps, the forging of an unexpected camaraderie between a werewolf and a Drakulis.

THE PANIC OF WHAT COULD BE

The news of the dead patrol officer spread like wildfire across the globe, creating a ripple of disbelief and fear among the general population. Some dismissed it as a joke, while others, aware of the existence of supernatural beings like werewolves and vampires, prepared for the potential end of the world. Among these mystical communities, the footage was not taken lightly; they knew the harrowing scenes captured were real.

As the world grappled with the shocking events, a sense of urgency permeated the air. The United States Secretary of Defense, Adam Speldere, took the podium for a news conference, addressing the unprecedented situation that had unfolded.

"As most of you may know now, we may not be alone as humans from the footage that has taken place and has been viewed on all forms of broadcasts," Secretary Speldere began, his tone serious and measured.

"We are currently working with every outlet possible on this precautionary and unusual event that has taken place."

He continued, "There has been no proof of any type of evidence that this actually happened, but it would suggest that action be taken by not only us as America but every country as well. We have no evidence suggesting that this is real as no body was found of the officer or those that were in the accident. However, the officer is, in fact, missing, which is why we are not taking this lightly."

Secretary Speldere stressed the importance of caution, acknowledging the gravity of the situation.

S.K. Ballinger

"Again, we are going over every possible aspect and outlet as we have to be certain before taking further action. I ask that during these times as many have questions that we all stay calm."

He assured the public that specialists with technology were diligently working on analyzing the footage from the patrol car.

"We have many people who are specialists with technology that are working diligently with the footage recorded from the patrol car as fast as we can."

The Secretary concluded with a promise to keep everyone informed as new information emerged.

"We will keep all informed as any new information can be released to us, which we will then be able to share with others of this horrific tragedy that seems to have happened."

The world held its breath, caught between disbelief and the eerie realization that the supernatural might not be confined to myths and legends. The fate of the missing patrol officer hung in the balance, and the unfolding events promised to reveal a truth that could reshape the very fabric of reality.

Amidst the press conference, a moment of tension unfolded when a reporter, seizing an opportunity, directed a pointed question at Mr. Speldere.

"Mr. Speldere, would you say that werewolves exist off the footage you saw, and this is a simple yes or no question if you don't mind?"

The gathered crowd awaited his response with bated

breath. Mr. Speldere's expression betrayed a hint of uncertainty as he responded in a non-committal manner, "Mythology of such a creature is something left for the experts to analyze. There have been many reports of a Sasquatch, Bigfoot, or the Loch Ness Monster after all. With today's advanced technology of computer rendering and the many things one professional can do to an image, it takes a true expert to decipher it all."

Persistently, the reporter pressed for a straightforward answer, "It was a yes or no question, sir."

A hint of hesitation lingered as Mr. Speldere reluctantly replied, "No, folklore or mythology does not exist."

The room buzzed with murmurs as the cryptic response left many with lingering doubts. Another reporter, eager to dig deeper, questioned the Secretary of Defense.

"If that is the case, then why is it that you feel to express this conference nationally, as you yourself have seen more in-depth footage, I am sure?"

Mr. Speldere maintained his composure, stating, "We take situations that involve those that protect our citizens very seriously. The fact that we cannot find the officer or those involved in the accidents of that highway have answers needed."

As the queries continued, Mr. Speldere, sensing the need to conclude the conference, prepared to leave the podium. However, before departing, he delivered a final statement that sought to address the uncertainty shrouding the supernatural claims.

"We are prepared for any outcome of what might be a

S.K. Ballinger

possibility and will take all actions necessary to protect not only our country but the world we live in. I think it is too soon to go off assumptions of a video that went viral. What is important is that there are missing people that either staged this, which I do not believe, or, in fact, may have died. Our focus remains the same, and that is to investigate and get answers. We will keep all aware of any further information that we may have on this situation. Thank you for your time and understanding, and as I said, please keep calm in this time of tragedy for those that may have fallen victim and their families."

    With those words, the conference concluded, leaving the world with a mixture of skepticism, fear, and a lingering sense of the unknown. For now, the myth of werewolves and vampires was put on hold, relegated to the realm of uncertainty. Yet, for those who were intimately acquainted with the supernatural, action needed to be taken, for their reality was far more complex and perilous than the world could fathom.

STANLEY & GRAVAKUS ARRIVE AT THE MGM

The journey from California to Nevada had been a tense and calculated endeavor for Stanley and Gravakus. With the news of the dead patrol officer circulating rapidly, they knew they were now under close scrutiny. Arriving safely at their destination, the opulent MGM hotel in Las Vegas, offered them a temporary sanctuary. However, the weight of the unfolding events pressed upon them, and in their room, a palpable silence hung in the air.

As the night unfolded, the glow of the city's lights seeping through the curtains, Gravakus broke the quiet with a mild tone, "The Secretary of Defense sure did put on a short lie."

Stanley, gazing out at the shimmering skyline, responded, "Not here to bullshit with you, Gravakus. And this news you are watching, I only hope that this Speldere has bought time for us, as there are going to be humans and those in the military that will believe that we exist."

The television in the room flickered to life, casting an artificial glow across their faces as the late-night news commenced. The anchor's voice cut through the dimness, providing an update on the mysterious events that had captured the world's attention.

"In a recent press conference, the United States Secretary of Defense, Adam Speldere, addressed the viral footage of the dead patrol officer. While he dismissed claims of supernatural creatures such as werewolves, skepticism remains high. Some experts argue that the government's attempts to downplay the incident might be a tactical move, keeping the public calm amidst growing concerns."

Gravakus, his piercing gaze fixed on the screen, remarked, "They're trying to control the narrative. Keep people in the dark."

Stanley, leaning back in his chair, added, "And for good reason. If the truth gets out, it won't just be humans hunting us. Other supernatural beings will be drawn to the chaos."

The news segment continued, presenting various perspectives on the incident, but the truth remained elusive. The room echoed with the distant sounds of the vibrant city outside, a stark contrast to the weighty atmosphere within.

Gravakus, ever analytical, commented, "Speldere bought us time, but the clock is ticking. We need a plan."

Stanley, his eyes reflecting a mix of weariness and determination, nodded in agreement. "

We can't stay here for long. The longer we linger, the greater the risk of exposure. We need to find out more about what happened on that highway and stay one step ahead."

As the news segment concluded, the room fell into silence once more. The uncertainty of the situation hung thick, like the smoky residue of a clandestine secret. In the heart of the glittering city, two beings, one human and one not, contemplated the complexities of their existence and the challenges that lay ahead.

The room, bathed in the artificial glow of the television, held a heavy silence as both Stanley and Gravakus took a moment to reflect on the whirlwind of events that had unfolded in such a short span of time. The weight of the recent tragedies pressed upon them, creating an air of discomfort that lingered between the two.

They sat at a noticeable distance from each other, the awkwardness of the situation palpable. Stanley, his fingers tightly gripping the wedding band that served as a tangible connection to his lost love, sighed audibly. In the solitude of his thoughts, he questioned, "How did all of this happen?"

Gravakus, keenly aware of the somber atmosphere, attempted to lighten the mood and responded to Stanley's rhetorical question.

"It would go like this. You and this Kain guy shared secret information of both our respective beings and so on. Then twin brothers in Dimitris and Siluk found much information which would be damaging in a major way of slaying your breed. Shall I go on?"

Stanley, not amused by the attempt at levity, replied, "You have said enough, and you should know it was not just Kain, which I also need to get in touch with if he is even still alive. I fear, Gravakus, that a breed of werewolf may have shared information with a Drakulis."

"What makes you think that?" Gravakus inquired.

"Think about it, Gravakus. Why all of a sudden does this new way of killing my breed arise? In order to know would suggest to me that someone has taken another to the past, which can only be done by a breed."

Gravakus contemplated Stanley's words, realizing the gravity of the situation.

S.K. Ballinger

"This could very well be true, and you have a valid point in what you say, but who would that be is the question. Granted, it is obvious that it was either Siluk or Dimitris that has past traveled, as they have used this new weapon of a rose to your breed. I thought I had trust issues with my kind; I now know that the breed of werewolf seems to have the same."

The room fell into a thoughtful silence as the implications of their conversation settled. The enigma surrounding the events deepened, and the bonds of trust between supernatural beings became increasingly fragile. In the heart of the glittering city, two unlikely allies grappled with the complexities of their existence, their fates intertwined by a web of secrets and the looming threat of an unknown adversary.

The conversation in the dimly lit room continued to weave its way between Stanley and Gravakus, a tense exchange as they tried to unravel the mysteries that bound their fates together. Both were in agreement that a werewolf, likely one of their own kind, had betrayed them by revealing the deadly secret that led to the tragedy Stanley now faced.

Stanley's voice, edged with frustration and grief, cut through the air, "Why would a werewolf betray their own kind? What could drive one to share such a lethal method of killing with the Drakulis? It's what ended my wife's life, and I need to understand why."

Gravakus, unable to hide the weight of his own concerns, admitted, "That is why it was very important for me the night I visited your home, Stanley. I needed to find Kain and that journal. Either it has been written now or later, the fact remains that it is now freely available to all of those of my kind. Such damaging ways of killing your breed off the very thing I have tried to

Stanley Swanson – Breed of a Werewolf

maintain. It would only be a matter of time before it would fall into the wrong hands, which is that of Siluk and Dimitris. They will share it at the temple. Never thought a breed would turn, which frustrates me more than you know. My friend, either you like that term or not, you have not a clue of these mercenary Drakulis and what they are capable of, especially that of Siluk. This has become quite the mess because of all this."

The room hung heavy with the weight of the revelations. Stanley absorbed the information, grappling with the betrayal from within his own kind. The trust that had been breached left wounds as deep as those inflicted by the deadly rose petals.

Gravakus, not one to let silence linger, shifted the focus of the conversation.

"Here is some information from my kind to yours, Stanley. What do you get when you spell Siluk backward?"

Stanley, momentarily puzzled, took a moment to think before realization dawned. "Kulis."

A sense of foreboding crept into the room as Stanley questioned, "You have got to be kidding me, right, Grav? I know that you have mentioned to me that they are the sons of a higher Drakulis, but what does that mean of him? Is he more powerful than even his father?"

Gravakus responded with a somber tone, "Not a son of a higher Drakulis, but rather the highest and once most powerful. It is too soon to know truly how powerful Siluk is or his twin brother Dimitris, which you should know as well. They have a way to the throne of the temple. Dimitris, after all, was named after his father Sirtimi, which is no coincidence of the name spelled backward; it shows that Siluk is the heir of the two but still as equal to his brother. I have no more than that to share with you, Stanley. Just know they will never be as light as their father."

The room's atmosphere grew heavier, the revelation of the lineage and potential power of Siluk and Dimitris casting a shadow over their already dire circumstances. The tangled web of betrayal and ancient rivalries threatened to engulf them as they navigated the treacherous path ahead.

The shared knowledge about the Drakulis lineage proved to be a double-edged sword, offering Stanley valuable insight into the formidable adversaries he faced. Though the revelation of Siluk and Dimitris being the sons of the highest and once most powerful Drakulis was disconcerting, it provided a strategic advantage. Stanley, ever the tactician, recognized the importance of understanding the strengths and weaknesses of his foes.

Stanley, with a determined glint in his eye, acknowledged, "This information about the Drakulis lineage is vital. Knowing that Siluk and Dimitris are the heirs to the highest Drakulis gives us a starting point. I'll have to plan strategically for the battles that lie ahead."

Gravakus, his expression serious, added, "With your breed far outnumbered, as you know, and even if the humans joined your breed in such a war, which seemed to be your purpose to begin with, this is a battle that simply is not going to end well for either of you. While our numbers will have taken a fall, we will continue on as Siluk and Dimitris will see to it."

The weight of Gravakus's words hung in the air. It was a stark reality check, a reminder of the challenging road ahead for the werewolves. In theory, Gravakus seemed correct – the

Stanley Swanson – Breed of a Werewolf

werewolves were outnumbered, and the Drakulis had a resilience that surpassed mere mortality. The impending conflict loomed like a dark cloud over both species.

However, Stanley, with a hint of defiance, responded, "Numbers can be deceiving, Gravakus. Werewolves have a unique advantage that your kind lacks – the ability to breed. We can mate with both humans and our own kind. Our numbers might not be as finite as they seem."

Gravakus acknowledged the point with a nod, recognizing the significance of the werewolves' reproductive capabilities. The complexity of the supernatural world continued to unfold, revealing the intricacies of the impending clash.

As the conversation reached a natural pause, the room fell into a contemplative silence. The air was thick with the tension of an uncertain future, where ancient rivalries and newfound betrayals intertwined. Stanley, drawing strength from the knowledge acquired, began to strategize for the battles that lay ahead, aware that the path to victory would be fraught with challenges and sacrifices.

Stanley, now having developed a measure of trust in Gravakus, saw an opportunity to share an insight that could reshape the perception of their seemingly dire situation. With a thoughtful expression, he began to articulate the unique advantage that werewolves possessed in terms of reproduction.

"While both Drakulis and vampires are able to engage in sexual activities among yourselves or with humans, you must be aware that you cannot reproduce with a black and dead heart that defines your existence. All living beings have life pumping through them, regardless of their form, except for your kind. Even plants rely on natural sources for sustenance. It's a somber reality, Gravakus, to never give life as you are unable to experience the essence of living. You are just a walking corpse that can only propagate your kind by biting them. So, while Drakulis have had the numerical advantage over us, my breed has been steadily gaining."

This revelation struck a chord with Gravakus, prompting him to ponder the implications of werewolf reproduction. The intricate dynamics of their respective species became more apparent with each exchange of knowledge.

Stanley, sensing the need for a united front against the impending threat, acknowledged the urgency of their situation.

"We have got some work to do; it starts with me finding my pack and my kids."

He shifted the focus to Gravakus, seeking assurance of their continued alliance.

"What about you, Gravakus? What are your actions moving forward? I'm trusting that you are not going to rally with your kind to plan a war against us, especially now that we understand the power of the rose to my breed."

Gravakus, with a contemplative expression, recognized the gravity of the situation.

"I have no intention of joining any war against your kind, Stanley. Our survival might depend on the collaboration between our species. I will continue to gather information, monitor the movements of Siluk and Dimitris, and ensure that my kind does not act impulsively. Trust, as you said, is essential in times like

Stanley Swanson – Breed of a Werewolf

these."

The room held a weighty atmosphere, a tacit acknowledgment of the delicate balance they now navigated. Two beings, born of different worlds, found themselves bound by a shared fate and a common enemy. As they prepared to face the challenges ahead, the trust between Stanley and Gravakus became a fragile foundation upon which their alliance rested.

Gravakus, feeling a twinge of discomfort at Stanley's earlier comment, sought to remind him of the essential distinction between his motives and those of Siluk and Dimitris. He responded with a measured tone, attempting to clarify his purpose in the first war.

"Remember, friend, my purpose in the first war was to help maintain a balance of all life. Let us not forget that, Stanley. There is a fundamental difference between me and Siluk and Dimitris. Their intent is to eliminate all werewolves over time, aiming to subject humans to slavery under their rule, or, if you prefer, under the rule of my kind. Their vision is a world dominated solely by Drackulis and their followers."

Gravakus, unlike the malevolent twins, understood the perilous consequences of a world without the existence of werewolves. He left Stanley with a crucial reminder that not all Drakulis were alike, emphasizing the importance of discerning individual intentions within his kind.

"As for me," Gravakus continued, "I am going to head back home and meet with those of mine to see if there is any new movement on this traitor within your breed. If I hear of anything, I will let you know. Take my phone, as I have many others."

S.K. Ballinger

The gesture of handing over his phone carried significance – a symbol of the trust he was placing in Stanley. It was a tangible connection that underscored their mutual interest in navigating the looming threats and uncovering the traitor in their midst. As Gravakus prepared to depart, the room lingered with a mix of tension and alliance, a complex interplay of trust and strategy in the face of an uncertain future.

Stanley, with a nod of acknowledgment, accepted the phone, recognizing its potential as a crucial link between their two worlds. The room, now occupied by a solitary figure, echoed with the weight of their shared burden and the intricate dance of allegiances in a world teetering on the brink of supernatural conflict.

The departure of Gravakus and Stanley marked the beginning of their individual journeys, each driven by a unique set of objectives within the unfolding supernatural drama. As they parted ways, the weight of their shared history and the challenges ahead lingered in the air like an unspoken pact.

Stanley, holding Gravakus's phone in hand, felt a renewed sense of purpose. The first crucial step in this complex puzzle was to find his children, knowing they were under the protection of the pack. The bond with his offspring and the werewolf community fueled his determination.

However, amidst the urgency to reunite with his children, Stanley couldn't shake off the nagging concern for his brother, Stephen. The whereabouts and well-being of his sibling were uncertainties that haunted his thoughts. Reuniting with Stephen held a place of equal importance in Stanley's heart, adding layers of complexity to his already intricate mission.

Stanley Swanson – Breed of a Werewolf

Gravakus, on the other hand, departed with a mix of solemnity and regret. His parting words carried sincerity as he wished Stanley success in his endeavors. The short-lived alliance between the werewolf and the Drakulis had left an indelible mark, a testament to the unpredictable nature of their world.

"Feel free to call me anytime you want, Stanley, and I wish you much success in reuniting with your breed. It has been fun in the short time, and again, I am truly sorry for what has taken place a few days ago."

The genuine apology from Gravakus resonated, acknowledging the unexpected turn of events that had altered the course of their lives. Despite the inherent enmity between their species, a glimmer of understanding had emerged during their brief alliance.

As they ventured into the unknown, Gravakus and Stanley were propelled by personal quests, intertwined with the looming threat that had now become a global concern. The supernatural world, once hidden in the shadows, was now thrust into the spotlight, and the choices made by each protagonist would echo through the fate of their kind. The separation marked the beginning of a solitary journey for both, a journey fraught with danger, revelations, and the unrelenting pursuit of answers in the face of an impending supernatural storm.

As Gravakus swiftly disappeared from Stanley's immediate surroundings, the werewolf found himself standing at the crossroads of uncertainty. Feeling a tinge of disorientation and a pressing need for answers, Stanley attempted to contact Jeremia, only to be met with the frustrating silence of unanswered calls. With Nevada offering little solace, he made a crucial decision to return to Kain's house in Kansas, a place he believed might hold crucial clues and be less susceptible to tracking due to its secluded nature.

Navigating through the labyrinthine streets of Nevada, Stanley eventually left the opulence of the MGM behind, heading to a nearby car rental facility to set the wheels of his journey in motion. The road stretched before him, leading back to Kansas, where the echoes of the past and the mystery of the present awaited him.

As the miles rolled away beneath the tires of his rented vehicle, Stanley couldn't escape the realization that the war he had long foreseen was now looming on the horizon. His senses, heightened by his werewolf nature, became his compass through the turmoil of confusion and loss that marked this critical juncture in his life.

Driving out of Nevada, Stanley observed the people he passed, his keen eyes discerning a subtle glint in their eyes – the unmistakable shine that betrayed their vampiric nature. The realization struck him with a chilling truth: vampires were amassing in significant numbers, and the werewolf breed was likely doing the same. The world, unbeknownst to its human inhabitants, was becoming a battleground for supernatural forces, with unsuspecting souls navigating among the undead.

As the city lights faded in the rearview mirror, the road ahead became a solitary path winding through the vast expanse. The number of beings surrounding him dwindled, providing a momentary respite for Stanley's thoughts. Amidst the solitude of the open road, he grappled with the weight of his decisions, the gravity of the impending conflict, and the intricate dance between humanity and the supernatural. Each passing mile brought him closer to the heart of his quest, where the secrets of Kain's house in Kansas awaited, and the fate of his kind hung in the balance.

S.K. Ballinger

TROUBLE AWAITS

Stephen and his newly formed pack, comprised of werewolves like him, moved with determined agility through the rugged hilltops. Their destination was the Swanson plantation, a place that held significant meaning for Stephen, resonating with memories of the past. Little did they know, the world around them was shifting, and the events on the highway had sent ripples through the supernatural community.

Unaware of the news coverage detailing the tragic incident on the highway, the pack pressed on, focused on their journey and the nostalgia-laden destination. The tranquil hilltops, once a familiar landscape to Stephen, now harbored an unforeseen danger that lurked in the shadows.

As they moved stealthily, Stephen, the de facto leader of this newfound pack, recognized the potential threats looming in the supernatural realm. His instincts, honed by years of experience, warned him of the unseen eyes that observed their every move. However, the pack remained oblivious to the intricate web of alliances and conflicts unfolding around them.

"Be silent and lay low," Stephen whispered to his pack, a directive rooted in the primal survival instincts that governed their kind. The hilltops, usually echoing with the sounds of nature, now carried an eerie silence as the pack huddled together, their heightened senses attuned to the surrounding danger.

Little did they know that the vampires, dispatched by their powerful masters from various corners of the world, were already on the scent. Drakulis, vampires, and werewolves alike were mobilizing, responding to the unseen forces that guided their actions. The supernatural world was in flux, and Stephen's pack, in their quest to return to the Swanson plantation, unknowingly walked a path fraught with peril.

    The hilltops, once a serene backdrop to Stephen's life, now bore witness to a clandestine dance of predators and prey. As the pack moved cautiously, their fates intertwined with a global tapestry of supernatural intrigue, they remained unaware of the storm that loomed on the horizon, threatening to shatter the fragile peace they sought.

    As the group of werewolves, led by Stephen, navigated the hilltops with the precision of their remarkable senses, a troubling realization dawned upon them. The air carried an unmistakable scent, a pungent mix of vampire and, potentially, Drakulis. The supernatural beings had become more than mere myth; they were tangible threats, lurking in the shadows and closing in on Stephen's pack.

    Guided by the instincts ingrained in their very nature, the werewolves, including Stephen, moved stealthily through the terrain. Stephen, with his heightened senses, discerned the approaching danger and urged his pack to adopt a low profile. Crawling silently on the ground, they sought refuge from the unseen forces converging around them.

    Amid the tension and uncertainty, Sheree, a member of Stephen's pack, voiced the question that lingered in their minds.

    "Why all of a sudden are we in what appears a constant battle with the Drakulis?" The query hung in the air, echoing the confusion that enveloped the group.

    "I am not exactly sure, Sheree, but whatever the reason may be, we are in for a very large battle soon," Stephen responded, the weight of impending danger evident in his voice. The scent of vampires grew stronger, underscoring the urgency of their situation.

However, amidst the impending conflict, a sudden disappearance added to the complexity of the situation. Stephen turned back to his pack, only to find Sheree gone. The darkness of the approaching night intensified, and the realization that they were vastly outnumbered loomed over them. A sense of urgency enveloped the group as the inevitability of a fast-approaching battle took hold.

"Where in the hell did Sheree run off to?" Stephen questioned, a note of concern in his voice.

"She is smart, Stephen, no worries, friend. She is still around," reassured one of the pack members, attempting to alleviate the growing unease.

"I hope this is true," Stephen muttered, his focus shifting between the looming danger and the mystery of Sheree's sudden disappearance.

The hilltops, once a place of tranquility, now bore witness to a brewing storm of supernatural proportions, and the werewolves stood at the precipice, ready to face the unknown.

As the onslaught of vampires surrounded Stephen's pack, the werewolves wasted no time transitioning, their powerful forms emerging in the face of imminent danger. A swarm of vampires, numbering in the dozens if not hundreds, closed in from all directions, marking the beginning of a fierce battle.

The werewolves, standing back to back, fought with an

unparalleled ferocity. Clawing, biting, and using their immense strength, they held their ground against the relentless onslaught. Graphic scenes of bloodshed unfolded, and the sounds of combat echoed through the hilltops. In the midst of the chaos, a strategic move by Sheree showcased her cunning instincts. With relentless clawing, she targeted a massive tree, toppling it strategically to crush vampires beneath its weight.

Rejoining the pack, Sheree's maneuver bought them precious moments, allowing the werewolves to flex their collective might. The circle they formed, backs against each other, proved to be their only defense against the relentless assault. Vampires, one after another, lunged at them, only to be met with claws, bites, and powerful throws.

Despite their valiant efforts, exhaustion began to take its toll on the werewolves. The once-strong fighters now found themselves weakened, panting heavily as they continued to fend off their attackers. Then, an unexpected turn of events occurred. The vampires, sensing the pack's fatigue, stepped aside, creating a clearance for a figure to approach – Dimitris.

With a sinister smile, Dimitris walked swiftly up the hill towards the exhausted werewolves. His chilling words hung in the air as he addressed the pack, particularly recognizing Stephen's connection to Stanley.

"The war has begun, you sick beasts that remain. I assume you are Stanley's brother, as I can see the resemblance, no?"

Dimitris spoke with an air of superiority, heralding the ominous commencement of a war between werewolves and Drakulis. The hilltops, once a place of quiet beauty, were now transformed into a battleground where the fate of supernatural beings would be decided.

Stephen, still in his werewolf form, responded to Dimitris's taunts with a menacing growl. With his three pack members standing behind him, Stephen advanced towards Dimitris, his eyes filled with an intense determination. The muddy hill beneath their paws bore witness to the imminent confrontation.

Dimitris, seemingly unfazed, met Stephen's approach with a smile that betrayed his confidence. He spoke condescendingly, taunting Stephen about the apparent imbalance in numbers favoring the vampires.

"You, Stephen, I believe we have some unfinished business to attend to. That was nice and brave of your breed to come help you, but it would appear that this time you are outnumbered. Where is your help at now?" Dimitris said, cupping his ear as if mockingly searching for any signs of reinforcement, all the while maintaining his sinister grin.

Stephen, unable to speak in his werewolf form, responded by growling louder, a display of his strength and readiness to face Dimitris. However, the vampire continued his verbal assault, disparaging the werewolf as an "ignorant and putrid slave." Dimitris claimed knowledge of a new way to destroy werewolves, emphasizing the perceived weakness of the werewolf breed.

"Put your claws down, you hell hound. You stand no chance, you ignorant and putrid slave. You do not even know what I have learned of a new way of destroying your breed, but I assure you that it is very neat. When will you pathetic and once slaves of ours understand that you are the weak, as we will prevail!" Dimitris declared arrogantly.

Stanley Swanson – Breed of a Werewolf

Stephen, fueled by the indignation and the primal instincts of his werewolf form, struggled to contain his rage. The stage was set for a showdown between the ancient adversaries – werewolf and Drakulis – on the desolate hill, echoing with the distant sounds of the ongoing supernatural war.

The struggle between Stephen and Dimitris intensified as they tumbled down the muddy hill, their claws tearing at each other with primal ferocity. The three werewolves watched, ready to intervene if needed, while the vampires stood by, observing the unfolding battle.

Despite Stephen's formidable strength, Dimitris's speed proved a challenging adversary. The vampire delivered powerful strikes from various angles, leaving Stephen battered and bloodied. However, in a momentary lapse, Dimitris made a crucial mistake, moving in too fast for another attack. Seizing the opportunity, Stephen extended his right arm and clamped his hand around Dimitris's throat, the Drakulis's struggles evident as his eyes widened with the realization of being caught.

In the midst of their physical struggle, Dimitris managed to shout a command to his followers, his voice echoing across the hill.

"NOW!" he yelled, the signal for his followers to take action.

As if on cue, the sky began to transform, bathed in an eerie red hue as the late evening light gave way to darkness. Unbeknownst to Stephen, Dimitris had developed a new weapon – the red rose dust. The vampires had ground rose petals into a fine powder, creating a deadly substance that showered down like crimson snow. This was their experimental project, a method to

S.K. Ballinger

unleash death upon the werewolves.

With the sky now raining red dust, Stephen, still maintaining his grip on Dimitris's throat, bellowed commands to his pack.

"Clear the skyline and go seek all breeds of werewolves. Share what you are witnessing with all of them!"

The werewolf pack, understanding the urgency of Stephen's words, quickly dispersed, their agile forms blending into the night. The mission was clear – warn other werewolves of the deadly threat posed by the red rose dust. The sky, once a tranquil canvas, now bore witness to the ominous crimson fallout, signaling the beginning of a new and perilous chapter in the ongoing war between werewolves and Drakulis.

The red dust fell like a morbid snowfall, covering Stephen's weakened form. The transformation back to his human state left him vulnerable, and Dimitris, savoring the moment, stood triumphant above him. The once-powerful werewolf was now at the mercy of the Drakulis.

With a sinister grin, Dimitris gloated over his prey, relishing the opportunity to enact revenge upon the werewolf breed. "I have waited a long time for this," he taunted, his voice dripping with sadistic pleasure.

"The only way to kill your kind was with a silver bullet, which I find a joke. To know the suffering your breed takes in by a simple red rose is so much more fun. I hope you enjoy your death just as my brother did with, what was her name... Julie Swanson!"

Stanley Swanson – Breed of a Werewolf

The mention of Julie Swanson's name struck a chord with Stephen. The pain of losing her, compounded by the knowledge of Dimitris reveling in her demise, added to the torment he was already enduring. Dimitris continued his mockery, expressing disdain for the Swanson family and the werewolf breed.

"It seems that this Swanson family is not much to fear after all. Just look at yourselves as I have you now. One by one, your breed will no longer be able to sustain the Drakulis as we were meant to walk these grounds of this planet. This has now become an easy task."

Stephen, undeterred by Dimitris's arrogance, responded defiantly.

"You should know that our breed will never succumb to your ignorance. Legend in the code of Lycans will hold true that one breed of a werewolf will make right and see that we continue strong."

As Dimitris gloated on top of Stephen, the red dust began its insidious work. The burning sensation intensified as the first particles landed on Stephen's skin. Dimitris, reveling in the agony he inflicted, mocked Stephen with cruel words.

"Burn, you sickness to us all, as no one likes your disgrace, your features, or your nature of life. Hurts, does it not, you worthless slave?"

The red dust, a deadly weapon devised by Dimitris, had brought a new dimension to the conflict between werewolves and Drakulis, a weapon capable of causing excruciating pain and weakening the formidable Lycans. As the crimson fallout continued, the battle for survival reached a critical juncture for

S.K. Ballinger

Stephen and his kind.

Dimitris, reveling in the suffering he inflicted upon Stephen, forced the weakened werewolf to face him. Blistering burns marred Stephen's once-powerful features, and the pain intensified with every passing moment. The agony was unbearable, and Stephen, though defiant, felt the crushing weight of his helplessness.

"Look at me as you suffer, and know that you are soon to be free from slavery, hellhound," Dimitris taunted, his grip on Stephen's cheeks unrelenting.

"This legend of the code you speak of will not come to fruition as you think. I will make sure of that and will speak at the council of all that has taken place. The committee will pride themselves in my knowledge, and we will rise to the occasion of war."

Dimitris, confident in his victory, spoke of the impending council and the committee that would relish the information he'd gathered. The red dust continued to fall, creating an eerie backdrop to the unfolding tragedy. The once formidable werewolf was reduced to a battered, burned figure, a stark contrast to the imposing Lycan he had been moments before.

As Dimitris reveled in his perceived triumph, the realization of the dire circumstances weighed heavily on Stephen. The fate of his breed now hung in the balance, and the repercussions of Dimitris's actions were likely to reverberate throughout the werewolf community.

Stephen, in his weakened state, could only hope that those who managed to escape the encounter would spread word of the impending threat. The council, Dimitris's committee, and the Drakulis would undoubtedly use this information to escalate the conflict.

The battlefield, adorned with the red dust of the deadly rose, painted a grim picture of the escalating war between werewolves and Drakulis. As Stephen endured the torment, he clung to the hope that his sacrifice might serve a greater purpose, inspiring his kind to unite against the looming darkness.

In the aftermath of Stephen's gruesome demise, the red dust, once swirling with vitality, began to settle, creating an ominous atmosphere on the hill where the life of a werewolf hero had been extinguished. Dimitris reveled in the success of his experiment, a sinister weapon born from the crushed petals of the deadly rose. This new tool, capable of dispersing lethal dust, marked a turning point in the brewing war between Drakulis and werewolves.

As the remaining vampires bore witness to Stephen's internal combustion, Dimitris, consumed by thrill, watched with glee as the red glow erupted from the werewolf's stomach, signaling the inferno that consumed him. The experiment proved successful, providing the Drakulis with a potent advantage in the impending conflict. The small, disk-shaped objects designed by Dimitris promised a devastating impact on the werewolf population.

Seizing the opportunity, Dimitris ordered his followers to pursue the remaining werewolf pack, eager to test the new weapon's effectiveness in a live encounter. While the other vampires dutifully obeyed, a couple of them ventured after Sheree and her pack. In this chaos, Sheree, a lone werewolf, had a tactical advantage, strategically eliminating vampires who pursued her pack members and buying them precious time.

As the vampires closed in, Sheree successfully fended off almost ten of them, ensuring the escape of the remaining werewolf pack. Her quick thinking and lethal skills demonstrated the resilience of her kind in the face of the emerging threat. Dimitris, however, eventually called off the chase, recognizing the dominance of werewolves in wooded territories. The pursuit halted, and Sheree, undeterred, followed the scent of her pack.

Back at the hill, Dimitris, having satisfied his thirst for vengeance, ordered his followers to disperse. The red dust-covered ground became a chilling reminder of the deadly weapon they now possessed. Dimitris, realizing the significance of the moment, set a course for the temple in Santa Cruz, California, where the council convened. The committee, comprised of influential Drakulis, awaited his report on the successful use of the red dust weapon.

The war had officially begun, and as the news spread, tensions rose among both Drakulis and werewolf communities. The fate of the werewolf breed hung in the balance, and the council's decision on mass-producing the lethal weapon would determine the course of the conflict. Meanwhile, Sheree, unbeknownst to the events that unfolded, pursued her pack, unaware of the impending threat that loomed over their kind.

THE TRUTH BE TOLD

The desolation inside Kain's house mirrored the devastation Stanley felt as he confronted the grim reality of his friend's fate. The once-peaceful home now bore the unmistakable signs of a violent intrusion. Stanley's journey back to Stull, KS, had been fueled by hope, but as he surveyed the wreckage, dread seeped into every fiber of his being.

"Kain!" Stanley called out, the echoes of his desperate cries resonating through the shattered remnants of the house. His heart sank with each unanswered plea, a gnawing fear creeping in. The scent of vampires lingered lightly, confirming his suspicions – the malevolent Drakulis had been here.

Amid the wreckage, Stanley stumbled upon a large pool of blood, and his stomach tightened with anxiety. The telltale signs suggested a violent encounter, but the absence of the putrid odor of a newly turned vampire puzzled him. A faint glimmer of hope flickered within Stanley – perhaps Kain had managed to escape the clutches of Siluk and his followers.

Bracing himself, Stanley descended the staircase, his footsteps echoing in the hollow emptiness of the house. The air downstairs felt heavy with an unspoken tragedy, and as he approached, his worst fears materialized. There lay Kain, lifeless on the floor, a haunting stillness enveloping the room.

Stanley's hands trembled as he gently cradled Kain's motionless body, his mind grappling with a surge of grief and anger. The weight of the moment pressed down on him, and he hurriedly ascended the stairs, seeking the comfort of daylight to unravel the mystery of Kain's demise.

S.K. Ballinger

"What have they done to you, my friend?" Stanley's anguished question hung in the air, unanswered. He laid Kain in the light, a pool of sunlight casting a harsh contrast on the pallor of his friend's face. Stanley scanned Kain's lifeless form for clues, his eyes searching for signs of the torment inflicted upon him.

As the truth began to unfold, Stanley felt a burning determination to seek justice for Kain's untimely end. The road ahead was dark and treacherous, but Stanley vowed to uncover the sinister forces at play, to avenge his friend and protect the remaining members of his kind from the looming threat of the Drakulis.

Stanley gently laid Kain's lifeless body on the couch, his gaze lingering on the brutal injuries inflicted upon his friend. The visible marks on Kain's legs bore the unmistakable signature of Drakulis, igniting a flame of rage within Stanley. The loss of Kain, a trusted ally and confidant, cut deep, and he couldn't bring himself to scrutinize the extent of the brutal assault.

As the weight of grief pressed upon him, Stanley instinctively reached for Kain's head. In an unforeseen turn, an extraordinary connection unfolded. Despite Kain's demise, Stanley found himself tapping into fragmented glimpses of the past. The visions, though broken and incomplete, painted a poignant tapestry of Kain's cherished memories.

Stanley's mind swirled with fragments – a fleeting image of his late wife, Zea leaving the house, and pivotal moments witnessed through Kain's eyes. It was as if Kain, in his final moments, had bequeathed a precious part of himself to Stanley. The memories, carefully preserved by Kain, held the key to unraveling mysteries and secrets that now threatened to fall into the wrong hands.

Stanley Swanson – Breed of a Werewolf

Gratitude and curiosity intermingled within Stanley as he grappled with the unexpected gift Kain had granted him. The glimpses into the past were a testament to the trust and camaraderie they had shared. Stanley recognized the value of the information embedded in these memories and pondered how best to honor Kain's legacy.

Yet, the bittersweet revelation also cast shadows of regret upon Stanley. The visions unveiled the tragedy of missed opportunities – moments when timely intervention might have altered the course of events. A wave of sorrow and self-blame washed over him, fueled by the realization that, once again, his actions might have cost a dear friend his life.

The lingering scent of vampires in the air added another layer of torment. Stanley pieced together the puzzle, realizing that he had narrowly missed the confrontation with Kain's assailants. The faint traces of their presence only deepened his sense of remorse, amplifying the weight of responsibility that now rested on his shoulders.

As Stanley grappled with conflicting emotions, he resolved to safeguard the memories Kain had shared, to cherish and preserve them as a testament to the enduring bond between them. The journey ahead had become more perilous, yet fueled by grief and determination, Stanley vowed to confront the looming threat and ensure that Kain's sacrifice would not be in vain.

Stanley lingered in the aftermath of the past travel, the weight of newfound truths pressing upon him. His fingers ran through his hair as he closed his eyelids gently, ensuring they were sealed shut. The room, now dimly lit, held a somber atmosphere, encapsulating the gravity of the revelations that had unfolded.

S.K. Ballinger

Addressing the lifeless form of Kain, Stanley's voice resonated with a mixture of sorrow, gratitude, and self-pity. His right hand brushed back his own hair, a subconscious gesture that mirrored the countless times he had witnessed Kain do the same. The connection between them, a thread woven through shared experiences and unspoken camaraderie, now echoed in the quiet room.

"Thank you, friend, and may you rest in peace," Stanley whispered, the words carrying a heavy weight of loss. Kain, a unique and irreplaceable presence in Stanley's life, had left an indelible mark. The sincerity in Stanley's tone underscored the depth of their connection, emphasizing the profound impact Kain had on his journey.

A fleeting battle against tears played out on Stanley's face, emotions bubbling beneath the surface. The anguish of knowing that meeting Kain had set into motion a series of tragic events hung heavily in the air. Stanley grappled with the conflicting emotions of appreciation for the memories Kain had shared and the regret that their meeting had become a catalyst for so much pain.

In the solitude of the room, Stanley's words were both a farewell and an acknowledgment of the intricate role Kain had played. The room seemed to echo with the weight of unspoken conversations and shared moments now confined to memories. As Stanley confronted the reality of his choices and their consequences, he carried the burden of a friendship cut short by circumstances beyond his control.

The dim light cast shadows across the room, a visual metaphor for the complexities of life and the inevitable interplay of light and darkness. Stanley, left alone with his thoughts, would

Stanley Swanson – Breed of a Werewolf

need to find solace in the memories Kain had gifted him, navigating the path ahead with a heavy heart and a resolve to honor the legacy of a departed friend.

Amidst the melancholic atmosphere, Stanley's attention shifted to a crucial detail that could potentially tip the scales in this clandestine war. Kain's meticulously kept journal, a repository of invaluable information, was now encapsulated in a USB drive hanging from a necklace around his neck. Stanley's keen observation discerned the significance of this unassuming accessory.

In a moment of bitter realization, Stanley marveled at the irony that even Siluk, with his cunning intellect, had overlooked the simplicity of the necklace. The USB drive, containing the secrets and insights Kain had documented, hung inconspicuously around his neck, a hidden gem in the chaos that had unfolded.

With a swift and decisive movement, Stanley's right hand snatched the necklace from Kain's lifeless form, the USB drive glinting in the dim light. He adorned the necklace around his own neck, a symbolic gesture that interwove his fate with the revelations contained within. The weight of responsibility settled around Stanley's neck, laden not only with the secrets of Kain's journal but also with the tangible symbol of his wife's memory— the wedding band.

As the necklace rested against his chest, Stanley's mind swirled with a myriad of emotions. The USB drive, now a talisman of knowledge, became both a weapon and a burden. The intricacies of the journal held the potential to reshape the trajectory of the looming conflict, a power that ignited a flicker of hope in the darkness that enveloped him.

However, this newfound hope was quickly overshadowed by the raw surge of anger. Stanley, betrayed by Zea's actions, could no longer contain his frustration. The weight of the USB drive and the symbols it carried served as a stark reminder of the web of deceit that had entangled his life. The isolation of the room amplified his shouts as he vented his rage, the words reverberating against unseen walls.

"Zea, you fucking traitor!" Stanley's exclamation cut through the air, a guttural expression of betrayal that echoed the anguish of a man who had trusted only to be deceived. The room absorbed the intensity of his words, leaving Stanley to grapple with the harsh reality that those closest to him had become players in a sinister game.

With the necklace now a tangible link to the secrets held within Kain's journal, Stanley stood at the precipice of a revelation that could alter the course of the impending conflict. The journey ahead, fraught with peril and uncertainty, was now guided by the weight of both knowledge and the emotional scars of betrayal.

As Stanley left the scene in Stull, KS, a bittersweet farewell lingered in the air as he covered Kain's lifeless body and made the crucial call to the police. His voice carried a mixture of gratitude and grief as he whispered, "Goodbye, friend, and thank you," a final acknowledgment to the man who, in death, had bestowed upon him a legacy of knowledge and a quest for justice.

As he quickly departed from the small town, Stanley's thoughts were consumed by a singular goal – to find Zea and make him pay for the betrayal that had cost Kain his life. The determination in his heart fueled a burning resolve, overshadowing the grief that threatened to overwhelm him.

Stanley Swanson – Breed of a Werewolf

Positioning himself at a safe distance in the nearby cemetery, Stanley observed the unfolding scene, ensuring the authorities responded to his call. The distant wail of sirens pierced the quietude, heralding the arrival of police and paramedics. From his concealed vantage point, Stanley witnessed the macabre dance of professionals as they attended to the grim task of handling Kain's remains. The body bag on the gurney, a shroud for the departed, served as a stark reminder of the brutality that had unfolded within the walls of the once-quiet house.

Once satisfied that the authorities had taken control of the situation, Stanley resumed his journey. The road stretched ahead, winding through the desolate landscape, mirroring the twists and turns of his tumultuous life. His thoughts swirled with questions, uncertainties, and the weight of the revelations hidden within Kain's journal.

With each step, Stanley pondered the prospect of sharing this newfound knowledge with Gravakus. The bond between the two had evolved through a series of revelations, and now, faced with the urgency of the situation, Stanley grappled with the decision to confide in his unlikely ally.

As the miles passed beneath the wheels of his vehicle, Stanley persisted in calling his elusive brother, yearning for a connection that remained elusive. The unanswered calls were a poignant reminder of the fractures within his family, a theme that echoed in the void left by Kain's demise.

Amidst the uncertainty, a familiar voice pierced through the static of unanswered calls – Jeremia, responding at last. The weight of the world seemed to lift momentarily as Stanley seized the opportunity to communicate with one of his own.

"Jeremia," Stanley's voice betrayed a mix of relief and urgency, "we've got a lot to talk about."

The conversation between Stanley and Jeremia unfolded with a blend of relief, excitement, and a shared sense of urgency. As they delved into the details of all that had transpired, Jeremia expressed his thrill at learning of Stanley's survival, echoing the sentiments of the others who were undoubtedly overjoyed, especially Stanley's children.

In a heart-to-heart exchange, Stanley conveyed the unfortunate news of Kain's demise. Jeremia, though saddened by the loss of their comrade, focused on the crucial information Stanley had gained from Gravakus. The intricate details of their conversation formed a tapestry of shared knowledge, laying the foundation for their collaborative efforts against the looming threat.

"I'm on my way to meet all of you. Thanks for keeping my kids safe, and I'll be there tomorrow," Stanley assured Jeremia, his commitment to reunite with his family resolute.

"Just be careful. The war has begun, and small battles have already erupted in many areas from what we've gathered, my friend," Jeremia cautioned, a sober acknowledgment of the escalating conflict.

Stanley concurred, acknowledging the gravity of the situation.

"I will do all that I can to end this and this weaponry of a rose. Tell my kids I love them and will see them soon," he reassured Jeremia.

Stanley Swanson – Breed of a Werewolf

"Will do, Stanley. Be safe. Looking forward to seeing you as we can work together to solve this new death trap to our breed," Jeremia responded, the shared determination evident in his voice.

Before parting ways, Stanley sought information about his brother, Stephen, a missing piece in the intricate puzzle of their lives. Jeremia admitted that none had heard from Stephen but pledged to continue making calls, emphasizing the need for collective vigilance.

"Oh, you should change the name of the phone you're using. It shows that of a Drakulis. Just saying that perhaps that is why not many answer your calls," Jeremia advised, highlighting the importance of discretion in their perilous world.

As they concluded their conversation, the connection between Stanley and Jeremia became a lifeline in the face of adversity, reinforcing their bond and shared commitment to navigate the challenges that lay ahead.

As Stanley embarked on his journey, a light laughter escaped him as he considered Jeremia's advice about changing the name on his phone. It was a moment of levity, a brief respite from the grim reality that enveloped their lives. With a casual "goodbye," he disconnected from Jeremia and turned his attention to the task at hand—changing the identity on his phone.

Driving away from the desolate remnants of Kain's house in Stull, KS, Stanley couldn't contain the anger that simmered within him. The rear-view mirror reflected eyes ablaze with fury as his hands met the dashboard in a series of punches.

"This is going to end, and fast!" he declared aloud, his

words cutting through the tense silence within the car. The determination in his voice was unwavering, echoing the resolve that had fueled him throughout the challenges he'd faced.

As the miles stretched ahead, the urgency of the situation weighed heavily on Stanley's mind. Time was no longer a passive entity; it had transformed into a critical factor that demanded attention. The impending confrontation with the Drakulis, the rising tensions, and the sinister weaponization of roses underscored the need for swift and strategic action.

With every passing mile, Stanley felt the weight of responsibility settle on his shoulders. The impending war necessitated not just reaction but careful preparation for the unpredictable events that could unfold at any given moment. The road ahead was fraught with danger, but Stanley was prepared to meet it head-on, armed with the knowledge and determination to protect his family and the werewolf breed from the looming threats that cast shadows across their world.

THE IMPORTANT CALL

Stanley's drive took an unexpected turn as his phone rang, and Gravakus's name lit up the screen. An air of anticipation surrounded the call, and Gravakus wasted no time diving into the heart of the matter.

"On your drive to your friends and family, I would assume, and if so, I thought you might like to know the traitor to your breed known as 'Zea' is safely hanging out at a nice underground vampire pub."

The news struck a chord with Stanley, who felt a mix of anger and satisfaction. Gravakus's information confirmed what he suspected, and he acknowledged that Zea had indeed betrayed the werewolf breed.

"Zea is going to die painfully by my hands for what he has done, and I only ask that you keep a close eye on him. While he is very wise of our breed, he is going to get an unexpected visit from me soon. See to it that you keep him around and give me the address. Are you sure that it is him?"

The determination in Stanley's voice echoed through the phone, emphasizing the gravity of the situation. Gravakus, ever willing to assist, assured him of the accuracy of his information.

"I can do that, and yes, I am sure because I am at the pub as we speak. He seems to be very comfortable at the moment while in a pub full of vampires. Hell, I might even join him for a drink," Gravakus replied, his tone carrying a hint of satisfaction.

Stanley, appreciative of Gravakus's help, expressed his gratitude and emphasized the importance of keeping Zea within reach. The conversation concluded with a shared understanding of the impending confrontation that awaited Zea in the not-too-distant future. As Stanley continued his drive, thoughts of vengeance and justice fueled his determination to put an end to the traitor's actions once and for all. The road ahead seemed to twist with the promise of confrontation, and Stanley was ready to face whatever challenges lay in store.

Stanley's rage simmered as he processed the information Gravakus had shared about Zea's whereabouts. The abrupt halt on the side of the road was a release of frustration, a moment where the weight of betrayal settled heavily on his shoulders. Gravakus, understanding the gravity of the situation, provided not only a vivid description of Zea but also a photo, solidifying the truth that had eluded Stanley until now.

"Son of a bitch!" Stanley shouted, the echo of his anger bouncing off the car windows.

The realization struck him like a thunderbolt, and questions swirled in his mind. Why would Zea turn against his own kind? What dark alliance had he forged with the Drakulis?

Before resuming his journey, Stanley ensured Gravakus understood the urgency and the need to keep a watchful eye on Zea. Gravakus, committed to the cause, assured him that he would do his best, aware that the traitor might not linger at the pub for long.

"I do not know how long he can be entertained at this pub, but I will do my best," Gravakus reassured, providing an additional warning.

"Oh, by the way, you might have a little bit of a threat

Stanley Swanson – Breed of a Werewolf

upon your entrance to the pub as this is the first time I have ever seen or heard of a werewolf in such a place. Whatever Zea did, he seems as though he is safe, obviously which you and I can agree with."

"Nothing is going to get in my way of slaying this once-trusted breed of mine. Now, give me the directions," Stanley demanded, his voice laced with determination.

Gravakus complied, offering the necessary directions. As Stanley revved the engine and sped towards the vampire pub, he took a moment to call Jeremia. The conversation that followed was one of shared understanding and caution, with Jeremia acknowledging the dangers of confronting such a cunning adversary.

"That would explain his early retreat from the night of the transfer of Natalie. Also explains why he had taken Kain to a past travel. I cannot believe I did not notice," Jeremia confessed.

"That is what makes us wiser in time, Jeremia. Do not blame yourself," Stanley reassured, appreciating the support.

"Be careful, Stanley, as you know yourself that the wisest of our breed are ferocious fighters."

"I'll make it fast, Jeremia. He is responsible for my wife's death and sharing the new way of killing our breed off with something so small. I will ask a question to him as of why before I put him to rest. Now, send my kids love and be well as I will keep in touch with you."

The line went silent as Stanley, fueled by determination, embarked on the drive that would lead him to a confrontation with the traitor among their ranks. The road ahead was fraught with danger, but Stanley remained resolute, ready to face whatever challenges lay ahead in his quest for justice.

Zea, immersed in his revelry, was oblivious to the looming presence of Gravakus, who had decided to have some fun at the pub while keeping an eye on the traitor. As Gravakus moved closer to Zea's booth, the loud music played as a backdrop, providing the perfect cover for eavesdropping.

What he overheard was shocking – Zea seemed carefree, laughing and sharing the intricate details of the night he spent with Kain. He casually disclosed information about the red rose, the impending deaths of Julie and the others, displaying a newfound camaraderie with the vampires. The once-wise werewolf had become overconfident in his alliance with former slave owners.

Gravakus, relishing the opportunity to unsettle Zea, decided to play a little prank. He swiftly made his way to a nearby flower shop, purchasing a single rose. Plucking one petal from the flower, he discarded the rest on the ground before re-entering the pub. At the bar, he procured a bottle of the finest vodka available, mirroring Zea's choice of drink that night. Placing a single rose petal into the bottle, he sealed it tightly after giving it a swift swirl. With mischievous delight, Gravakus confidently approached Zea's table.

"You don't mind if I join you, do you?" Gravakus asked with a positive smile, feigning camaraderie.

Zea, unaware of Gravakus's true identity, welcomed him as just another vampire eager to hear his tales. The two shared laughs and stories as if they were old friends. Gravakus, seizing the moment, decided to make a bold move. He offered a round of shots to everyone at the table, presenting the bottle of vodka in hand.

"Cheers to ending all breeds, and let's thank this rare and wise old one sitting before us!" Gravakus proposed, toasting with a hint of irony in his voice. The atmosphere in the pub shifted subtly, setting the stage for what was to come.

The pub erupted into applause and cheers, the vampires celebrating the supposed end of a long-standing war between their kind and the werewolves. Gravakus, reveling in the dramatic atmosphere, directed his triumphant words predominantly at Zea.

"Thanks to this fine traitor to the breed of werewolf, we can finally bring an end to the long-lived war between us and them. I propose we continue this fine night with an offering of my new brand of Vodka to all, and especially to this wise man," Gravakus declared, holding the vodka bottle in his hands.

As Gravakus removed the cap from the bottle, Zea's eyes caught sight of the red rose petal within, causing a sudden shift in his demeanor. Uncertain of how to react, surrounded by a multitude of vampires, Zea grew increasingly disgruntled. Unfazed by Zea's discomfort, Gravakus proceeded to pour the vodka into shot glasses neatly arranged on the table. With the final glass poured, Gravakus lifted it high, proposing a toast.

"This one is for him, this brave breed of a werewolf! One of a kind and very wise to join our side. If not for him, we may have never known a more powerful secret to extinguish our enemy that was once our slaves," Gravakus exclaimed, his words dripping with both charm and malevolence as an evil grin played across his face. The atmosphere in the pub was charged with an eerie anticipation of what was unfolding.

As Zea grabbed the shot glass from Gravakus's hand, already feeling a bit sick, he threw it against the wall. The vampires in the pub, not fully aware of the power of a red rose or its petals on a werewolf, were taken aback by Zea's reaction. Despite Zea having shared this knowledge with a few at the table before Gravakus's interruption, it seemed far-fetched to the vampires present. Only Gravakus truly understood the potent effects of a red rose on his kind, and the room became slightly tense as Zea's actions unfolded.

Standing up and moving very close to Gravakus's face, Zea, with a slight snarl, questioned him, "Who are you to dare suggest something like that towards me?"

Gravakus, maintaining a calm and casual demeanor with a light chuckle, responded, "My friend, this is a new drink I wanted to share with all of us here. I like to call it Shairose Vodka, which simply means 'Share' and 'Beauty.' Was not the kind of response I was expecting, Mr. I do not know your name as of yet."

The well-played response from Gravakus brought amusement to him, but Zea found no humor in it.

"My name is Zea, thanks but no thanks to your bottle of Shairose. If you had listened, then you would have known that we are weak to a rose. Now, if you do not mind, leave us be."

Accepting this as confirmation of Zea's identity, Gravakus left the booth to sit back at a distance, patiently waiting for Stanley to arrive. Meanwhile, Zea reluctantly sat back down, resuming conversation with those he considered friends as part of the agreement he made with Siluk, ensuring his safety in

Stanley Swanson – Breed of a Werewolf

exchange for his allegiance in the upcoming war.

As Gravakus hung up the phone, Stanley, still many miles away, felt a surge of anticipation upon hearing the upbeat tone in Gravakus's voice. Gravakus enthusiastically recounted the encounter with Zea at the pub, describing how the wise werewolf wasted a shot of vodka by throwing the glass against the wall.

"I am a few hours out but am making good time. Keep him there, and I will show this wise breed of ours that his time of being so wise is over. I look forward to hearing in more detail of why you pissed him off," Stanley replied.

Focusing on the road and amplifying the radio volume to the song "Thunderstruck" by AC/DC, Stanley gripped the steering wheel tightly. The rhythm of the music matched the rhythm of his thoughts, fueling his anticipation as he raced toward the pub on his quest to confront Zea. The powerful beats of the song seemed to mirror the intensity building within Stanley as he approached the imminent confrontation.

S.K. Ballinger

CATCHING UP WITH THE PACK

Jeremia tried to reassure the anxious children, Sabe and Jade, who were under the protection of the pack. The news in the past few days had raised concerns about the secrecy of their existence.

"Is this true that we are now known to the world?" Sabe inquired, his eyes reflecting a mix of curiosity and anxiety.

"It would appear so, young Sabe, but let us not jump to conclusions just yet," Jeremia responded in a calm and soothing tone, attempting to ease their worries.

The uncertainty of their situation lingered in the air, and the pack, including Sabe and Jade, couldn't help but feel a sense of vulnerability.

As they waited for Stanley to arrive and provide guidance, the pack members discussed their plans and strategies to safeguard the young werewolves in this new, potentially perilous situation.

Meanwhile, Stanley continued his journey, thoughts swirling about the unfolding events. The atmosphere was charged with anticipation as the destiny of the werewolf breed seemed to hang in the balance.

The tension among the pack members grew as the revelation of Zea's betrayal and the newfound threat of roses permeated the air. Drennan, fueled by frustration and a sense of urgency, advocated for an immediate strike against the vampires. He felt that waiting around was a waste of time, especially considering the traitorous actions of one of their own.

Stanley Swanson – Breed of a Werewolf

"We have a traitor among us, and Stanley continues to lose those he loves. We are wasting our time in these phone conversations and this waiting game. Why should we remain here doing nothing? We need to make our own strike. Let us make our move on them as they have done on us," Drennan passionately argued.

Sabe and Jade, the younger members of the pack, were inclined to support the idea, eager to avenge the death of their mother. However, Francais voiced concerns about the safety of Natalie and the two young werewolves.

"What of my niece Natalie and these two young ones who are not ready? We have promised Stanley that we will take care of his kids," Francais pointed out, emphasizing the responsibility they had towards the younger members of the pack.

Jeremia acknowledged Francais's valid concern and added, "Like we were supposed to do for Julie, which we failed at."

Jade, displaying a determination beyond her years, chimed in, "I am ready! They killed our mother, and we are not like any of you. We are strong, like our father Stanley, and this is what he would wish."

The pack found themselves at a crossroads, torn between the desire for immediate retaliation and the responsibility to protect their younger members. The impending war demanded difficult decisions, and each member grappled with their own emotions and convictions.

The tension within the pack continued to escalate as different perspectives clashed regarding the next course of action. Francais, kneeling down to Jade's level, explained that she hadn't fully transitioned yet, only to be surprised as she effortlessly transformed, demonstrating her readiness to join the fight. The display astonished everyone, including Francais.

"We know not of Stephen's situation or that of Stanley's, but to sit and wait would be somewhat foolish," Jeremia stated, acknowledging the uncertainty surrounding the fate of their fellow pack members.

Drennan was eager to take immediate action, suggesting they contact werewolf breeds from around the world, particularly in Germany and England, to form a united front against the Drakulis. He believed striking first was crucial before the news of their existence became widespread.

Jeremia, more cautious and hesitant, tried to call Stanley to inform him of their plans, emphasizing the need to start in America before advancing to other countries. Drennan, however, was adamant about targeting England and Germany first, where he claimed to have strong alliances.

"I still think we should take flight to either of the two places I mentioned as I have a very good relationship with many breeds there. It would be a way to strike them off guard easier than here in the U.S. Go where we are more populated and push out from there, why do you not see this, Jeremia?" Drennan argued.

Jeremia, maintaining his cautious stance, was not willing to debate with Drennan and insisted on waiting for Stanley's arrival. He believed Stanley would prioritize the safety of his kids and disapprove of an overseas mission.

"No, Stanley would be proud of our breed for taking

action. Sabe and Jade will be kept in fine shape, and Natalie as well. If you wish to stay here and do nothing, that is fine. I will leave alone, as I am not going to sit here any longer with thoughts of wondering when we will be attacked with this new weaponry towards our breed," Drennan boldly declared, expressing his frustration and impatience.

The pack found itself divided on the best strategy, torn between immediate action and the prudence of waiting for Stanley. The impending decision weighed heavily on their shoulders as they grappled with the uncertainty of the unfolding war.

The decision to act swiftly and take the fight to the Drakulis resonated with the majority of the pack, especially with Drennan's persuasive arguments. Francais, acknowledging the consensus, took charge and laid out the plan.

"Who all can agree with this move he suggests?" Francais inquired, seeking affirmation from the members.

Without hesitation, and with unanimous agreement, they voiced their support for Drennan's proposal. Jade and Sabe, now fully clothed with Natalie standing close, were among those eagerly endorsing the idea.

"Then let us make our plans and prepare to fly. Drennan, call for a place to stay in England as that is where we should go first. We will take further actions from there. Jeremia, call Stanley to leave a voice message if nothing else about what we are doing and where his kids will be. Let us get our rest for this night and hope we all will be well," Francais declared, assuming a leadership role.

The pack aimed to head to England initially, recognizing the strength of the werewolf population there. Their strategy involved meeting other packs and subsequently splitting up to coordinate surprise attacks on multiple fronts. While the plan seemed straightforward, the unpredictability of warfare added an element of complexity.

Jade and Sabe, filled with a mix of anxiety and excitement, faced the prospect of their first flight. Natalie, after ensuring Jade had suitable clothes, felt a similar anticipation but sought comfort in staying close to her uncle Francais. He reassured her, promising to keep a watchful eye on her, regardless of the challenges that might unfold.

As preparations were set in motion, the pack braced themselves for the uncertain journey ahead, hoping to unite with other werewolf packs and face the Drakulis threat head-on. The night held a mix of tension, determination, and the anticipation of the battles that lay ahead.

The tickets were swiftly ordered, and the pack embarked on a flight to London, England. The urgency of the situation left no room for hesitation, and they understood that time was of the essence in facing the impending war. The vision Stanley once shared about werewolves and mortals coexisting was now being overshadowed by the stark reality of an imminent conflict.

The internet and news stations continued to buzz with the footage of the highway incident, showcasing the patrol officer's encounter with the werewolves. The video, captured by the campers whose vehicle Stanley had taken, went viral. It became a focal point of discussions, sparking debates about the existence of werewolves.

Stanley Swanson – Breed of a Werewolf

While panic had not yet set in, there was a collective curiosity and a growing realization that something extraordinary had been captured on film. The government, true to its nature, remained silent and discreetly planned its course of action, recognizing the need for a well-thought-out strategy.

During the eight-hour flight to London, the pack had a rare opportunity to relax and catch some much-needed sleep. The cabin provided a temporary respite from the escalating tensions and uncertainties awaiting them. The atmosphere on the plane oscillated between anticipation and weariness as each member contemplated the challenges that lay ahead. In the confined space of the aircraft, the werewolves took a momentary break, unaware of the intricate plans the government was weaving in response to the revelation of their existence.

S.K. Ballinger

THE PUB

Despite the intimidating presence of vampires both inside and outside the pub, Stanley was determined to confront Zea, the traitor to their werewolf breed. Gravakus, stationed inside as promised, provided a crucial advantage by keeping an eye on Zea and helping Stanley navigate the potentially volatile situation.

The pub, designed exclusively for vampires, emitted a strong and sickening scent that Stanley had to endure as he made his way inside. He understood the risks associated with his presence, considering that the news of the conflict had likely spread among the vampire community. However, fueled by frustration and a thirst for answers, Stanley pressed forward, his eyes ready to glow blue at a moment's notice, signaling his preparedness to transition.

As he moved through the pub, Stanley encountered some hostile stares and even engaged in a few stare-downs, but he remained steadfast. His determination to reach Gravakus, stationed at a table on the highest level, gave him the strength to endure the uncomfortable glares. The eyes of the patrons followed him, acknowledging the intrusion of an unfamiliar presence.

Shortly after entering, a vampire approached Stanley with a rude gesture, likely aware of the brewing tension. Stanley braced himself for potential confrontation, his focus unwavering on the task at hand—confronting Zea and seeking answers for the betrayal within their own kind.

As tensions escalated in the vampire pub, a confrontational vampire, angered by Stanley's presence, confronted him with aggressive language.

Stanley Swanson – Breed of a Werewolf

"What the fuck do you think you are doing in our place, you filthy piece of shit. Your kind should know better than to visit a place of ours. You have balls entering here, hellhound."

Stanley, maintaining his composure, responded firmly, "You say this to me when my intentions have no bearing with your kind. Another of my breed celebrates with yours over at that table. This is not a moment between us; I have come to settle an issue with another breed. Now, if you do not mind, and I will ask kindly, please remove yourself from me."

The vampire, seemingly unfazed, retorted, "Well, perhaps you should know that your fellow breed that sits at that table is protected by us. I advise you to leave these premises now while you still have an option to do so."

As the tension continued to escalate, Gravakus, observing the situation from the higher level, decided to intervene. He jumped down and approached the two parties in a swift motion, aiming to defuse the situation.

"Trust me when I say this is something you do not want to be a part of," Gravakus cautioned the confrontational vampire. However, the vampire remained defiant.

"Who the hell do you think you are to say that to me as a fellow vampire while another breed is in our sanction?" he challenged Gravakus. The atmosphere in the pub was becoming increasingly volatile, with the potential for conflict looming large.

With a triumphant smile on his face, Gravakus revealed his identity to the confrontational vampire who dared challenge him.

"Who the hell am I, you ask? My name is Gravakus, and yes, that Gravakus. I do not recommend you referring to me as a vampire follower, and it would be wise for you not to make a scene here. If you are willing to test me, then I can assure you that it will not turn out well. Let this creature sit with his breed, as I believe he wishes to have a little conversation with him. Trust me; this is going to be a show."

The vampire, now nervously aware of Gravakus's reputation, took a quick survey of Stanley from head to toe. Leaning in towards him, the vampire uttered with a hint of fear, "Count yourself lucky, hellhound."

Without any hesitation, Gravakus swiftly grabbed the vampire's wrist, effortlessly breaking it. "Not a way to treat someone looking for a drink with an old friend. I suggest you apologize."

The confrontation seemed to have de-escalated for the moment, with Gravakus asserting his dominance and making it clear that any further aggression would not be tolerated. Stanley, having witnessed Gravakus's swift action, nodded his appreciation for the assistance. The atmosphere in the pub became tense, with the patrons now watching the unfolding drama between two breeds.

The apology from the vampire came swiftly under Gravakus's firm grip, the broken wrist serving as a harsh reminder of the consequences of defiance. As Gravakus returned to his seat, he pointed Stanley in the direction of Zea before leaving, providing a clear indication of where the traitor could be found.

"There is your traitor named Zea, and he is very arrogant, I might add. I look forward to watching the two of you meet;

should be entertaining, to say the least. I will keep my eye out for sure," Gravakus remarked before taking his leave.

Stanley expressed his gratitude to Gravakus, acknowledging the challenge of dealing with aggressive vampires. Making his way towards the table where Zea sat, Stanley found Zea already on his feet, seemingly prepared for the confrontation.

"I am not sure how you made it in here, but please allow me to explain, Stanley, of what has happened," Zea hastily pleaded.

"You were once one of us, Zea, an elder and wise breed of a werewolf. How could you, of all, have had a hand in my wife's death and steal information from Kain, only to share what you know with them, the very ones who we were slaves to?" Stanley questioned with a mixture of anger and sorrow in his voice.

Stanley's anger surged as Zea attempted to justify his actions. The surrounding vampires wisely distanced themselves, creating an arena for the impending confrontation.

"Look around you, Stanley. I have safety here as promised by Siluk, a son of the highest Drakulis. The war you speak of is going to happen, and this was my way to keep our breed alive to ensure balance. I had no choice and a written promise of me not becoming a slave again. You do not even know what it is like to be a slave, as I once was, just as your mother had become," Zea defended himself, attempting to rationalize his betrayal.

"You will not speak of my mother or any breed of werewolf again. What you have sacrificed for yourself, you have killed many in a short time. You stayed at my place of stay only to know that a Drakulis was going to come and threaten my family, and they did, as they killed Julie and Kain. For that, I am here to take your life, as you are not worthy of any breed or life," Stanley retorted with seething anger, his eyes glowing with a fierce intensity.

The tension in the air was palpable as the two werewolves faced each other, each carrying the weight of their choices and the consequences that awaited them. The pub, now hushed in anticipation, awaited the outcome of this long-coming clash between former brethren.

As Stanley's anger boiled, fueled by the insincerity of Zea and the loss of his wife Julie, he couldn't contain the transformation any longer. The atmosphere in the pub shifted; a few vampires, sensing the impending confrontation, prepared to intervene on Zea's behalf. However, Gravakus, always the enigmatic instigator, swiftly arrived on the scene, signaling the onlookers to stay out of the impending clash.

With a dismissive shake of his pointer finger, Gravakus declared, "Let us not interfere in this. This is a battle I have only seen two other times in my illustrious life; do not ruin it for me. If any of you dare try to get in the middle of this fight between the two of them, then you will face me. With that said, would anyone care to make a wager on who wins?"

The vampires, initially poised to intervene, hesitated. Gravakus' warning carried weight, and the prospect of witnessing an unprecedented werewolf duel was too intriguing to disrupt. The pub fell into a hushed anticipation as Stanley and Zea, now both transformed, faced each other in a fierce confrontation.

Gravakus, ever the orchestrator of chaos, stood back,

Stanley Swanson – Breed of a Werewolf

ready to enjoy the spectacle unfolding before him. The tension in the air was palpable, and the pub's patrons were torn between the desire to witness the spectacle and the fear of Gravakus' wrath. It was a rare and riveting moment that would etch itself into the dark corners of the vampire pub's history.

Amidst the hushed anticipation, the pub witnessed a brutal and primal clash between Stanley and Zea, two werewolves locked in a deadly duel. The vampires wisely retreated, understanding the consequences of meddling with the impending confrontation and Gravakus' potential wrath. The atmosphere in the pub was charged with tension as the onlookers braced themselves for a display of raw savagery.

The battle unfolded with an intensity that shattered the pub's relative calm. Objects were flung aside as the combatants tore into each other with ferocity, biting, clawing, and leaving a trail of destruction in their wake. Stanley's stamina proved to be a decisive factor, a testament to his resilience and determination. As the struggle continued, Zea, despite his once-wise demeanor, found himself overpowered and fatigued.

In a pivotal moment, Stanley seized the opportunity to bring the confrontation to a brutal climax. With a swift and forceful motion, he pinned Zea's left arm to the ground, immobilizing him. The pub fell silent, save for Zea's anguished cries and heavy panting. The realization of his imminent defeat was etched across Zea's face.

In a final act of brutality, Stanley, now in human form, sank his teeth into Zea's exposed arm, gnawing at it with a savage determination. The gruesome scene unfolded with the visceral brutality characteristic of a werewolf duel. The pub, now a witness to the aftermath of Zea's demise, remained in a shocked

S.K. Ballinger

and somber silence.

Standing over Zea's prone form, Stanley, though victorious, bore the weight of the battle's brutality on his shoulders. The once-wise werewolf lay defeated, his severed arm a testament to the consequences of betrayal and treachery. The pub, marked by the echoes of the violent struggle, awaited the next development in this dark chapter, guided by the whims of the enigmatic Gravakus.

In the grim aftermath of the savage battle, Stanley stood triumphantly over the fallen and defeated Zea, whose arm lay severed on the blood-stained ground. The air was thick with tension and the echoes of Gravakus' provocative words, emphasizing the impending punishment for Zea's treacherous actions.

"You have taken my wife, threatened my family, shared secrets, and only helped to start a war that needed not be this soon," Stanley declared, his voice laced with a potent mixture of grief and rage.

The weight of loss and betrayal pressed heavily on his shoulders, manifesting in the brutal retribution he sought for the havoc wrought upon his life.

The ambiance of the pub seemed to freeze as Gravakus, with his characteristic flair, interjected with a suggestion that bordered on sadistic mockery.

"I believe he would like that shot now of my 'shairose vodka', see if he is willing to oblige," he announced, his tone holding a blend of amusement and malevolence.

Stanley Swanson – Breed of a Werewolf

In response, Gravakus tossed a bottle of Shairose vodka towards Stanley, who effortlessly caught it in mid-air.

As Stanley examined the bottle, his eyes fixated on the ominous red rose petal swirling at the bottom. A sinister revelation dawned upon him, and the connection between the contents of the bottle and the suffering of his late wife, Julie, became chillingly apparent. It was a cruel reminder of the pain and torment inflicted upon his family.

"You shall know what my wife had to endure as you will suffer the same fate as her. For one breed of ours that I would once look at for inspiration now falls before me as shame," Stanley declared with unyielding resolve, his words echoing through the pub.

The transformation of Zea from a revered elder to a fallen betrayer marked a tragic chapter in the saga of the werewolves.

Desperation gripped Zea as he pleaded for mercy, acknowledging his wrongs and vowing to destroy the written journal that held the secrets of their kind. However, Stanley, with a whispered revelation to Zea's ear, shattered any hope of salvation.

"I have the written journal, you fool," he disclosed, underscoring the futility of Zea's plea.

The pub, a silent witness to the unfolding tragedy, held its breath, awaiting the final act of justice and retribution as Stanley prepared to mete out the consequences of Zea's actions. The air was charged with a palpable sense of finality, and the echoes of Gravakus' sadistic amusement lingered in the somber atmosphere.

S.K. Ballinger

With the weight of justice and retribution upon his shoulders, Stanley invoked the ancient Lycan law, reciting the principles that defined their existence. As he spoke, each word resonated with the gravity of their sacred code, a testament to the profound connection werewolves held with their heritage.

"Live to what we are, not what others may perceive. Feed only what you will consume as you shed light for life. Adaptation of forming is a right to blend. To expand our territory, we must yield that of hate and not cause purpose of harm. Keep us from evil and live with trust. To stay as a breed of a werewolf is a mighty task but forever will be in the hands of us, as no boundaries will sever why we are created. You, Zea, have lost your conscience to what the code implies," Stanley proclaimed, his voice carrying the weight of centuries-old wisdom.

The shattered remains of the Shairose vodka bottle lay strewn next to Zea's head as a visual testament to the brutality of the impending judgment. Stanley, his eyes reflecting a blend of anger and sorrow, picked up the red rose petal from the bottle, a symbol of the torment and suffering inflicted upon his family. With meticulous care, he held the petal in his right hand, ensuring that Zea's desperate struggles would not thwart the imminent punishment.

"Open your mouth, or I will force it. Your choice, as I wish this to be fast. First time of killing a breed. Be wise, old man and once friend, as it is time for you to sample from what I hear is a painful death," Stanley declared, his words carrying an unyielding determination.

Zea, trapped in the vice grip of his impending demise, hesitated, torn between defiance and acceptance of his fate. The vampires surrounding them, witnessing the unfolding tragedy, held their collective breath, perhaps anticipating a last-minute intervention or an unforeseen twist. Zea, realizing the futility of resistance, acknowledged defeat, choosing the swift embrace of the inevitable over protracted suffering.

In a blur of motion, Stanley forcefully crammed the red rose petal into Zea's mouth, a symbolic enactment of the torment suffered by his wife. Gravakus, ever the dispassionate observer, shouted a caution to Stanley, "Now would be a good time to move away from him."

As the echoes of Gravakus' words lingered, the grim spectacle unfolded with eerie familiarity. Zea's body, writhing in agony, began the rapid transition back to its original form, mirroring the fate of Julie and Stephen before him. The air was thick with the stench of burning flesh as Zea's body succumbed to self-combustion, the flames erupting from within, consuming him from the inside out.

The onlookers, both werewolves and vampires alike, stood in astonished silence, witnessing the consequence of betrayal and the merciless application of justice. Stanley, his emotions hidden behind a mask of stoicism, turned away from the smoldering remains of Zea, leaving the pub without a backward glance, haunted by the shadows of the choices made in the name of preserving the honor of their kind.

Gravakus regarded Stanley with a sense of approval, acknowledging the swift resolution of their shared mission. "Well, that was much faster than I would have thought. I think it is time for both of us to go now. So what of you now, Stanley?" he inquired.

Stanley, with a determined gaze, replied, "Now I get to my family and try to stop this war to the best that I can. I have done what needed to be done and have no remorse in doing so."

Gravakus, considering the gravity of the situation, added, "This war, which has already begun, my friend, is about choosing sides now. I think I have already made my decision and will help to the best that I can, but know, I will not allow myself to fall victim to your kind."

As Stanley left, expressing his gratitude with a simple "Thanks Grav," he suddenly realized he was still without clothes. In a quick turn, he re-entered the pub, seeking one more favor from Gravakus.

"I need some clothes, and yes, I will be glad to be on your side, though not your kind. As for my breed and how they will take you in, I cannot give you an answer, friend."

Gravakus, appreciating Stanley's alliance, glanced at the vampire who had initially approached Stanley. "I think your clothes will fit him nicely," he declared.

The vampire, shocked by the request, protested, "Are you kidding me? You want me to give this hellhound my clothes?" Gravakus responded with a menacing demeanor, his right hand resting under the vampire's chin, "Do I look like I am just asking in regards to your suggestive opinions? You have belittled the breed for what they are worth, and yet this Stanley kills his own in this pub. Do I need to explain further to you?"

With no viable retort, the vampire, embarrassed and shamed, removed his clothes swiftly, handing them over to Gravakus, who tossed them to Stanley.

Stanley Swanson – Breed of a Werewolf

"Again, thanks Grav," Stanley expressed his gratitude.

As Stanley prepared to leave, those outside the pub refrained from confronting him further, aware of the events that had unfolded. However, one defiant vampire couldn't resist shouting, "You'll be slaves again, I can promise that."

Stanley, unfazed, smirked before driving off, leaving the vampire with a chilling response, "If what you say is true in what you believe, then know that if it were to come to that, you will be the first I seek. Keep on dreaming that the past will become again, as it is something that will never happen. Cross my path again, vampire, and you will never know what is going to happen now or later, as you yourself will die by the hands of me."

Stanley was well on his way with a very happy sensation that he had scratched one item off his chart and felt just a small justification towards his wife. Still knowing much more needed to be done; he was far from satisfied.

S.K. Ballinger

TWIN MEETING AT THE TEMPLE

Dimitris nodded, a grim expression on his face. "Gravakus has always been a slippery one," he replied.

"If he truly is the traitor, then we must eliminate him swiftly before he can cause further damage to our cause."

Siluk's eyes widened in surprise.

"You killed Stephen?" he asked, his voice filled with a mix of shock and admiration.

"You truly are ruthless, Dimitris. But tell me, what happened at the pub? Why was Zea left unprotected?"

Dimitris sighed, his gaze hardening.

"It seems that our plans were compromised. As I suspected, the Swanson brothers were in league with Gravakus. They had gone to meet him at the pub, and Stanley managed to succeed in his mission. Zea was left vulnerable, and I fear that Kain Edward might have taken advantage of the situation."

Siluk clenched his fists in anger.

"Damn it! I should have been there to protect him. How did this happen?"

Dimitris placed a hand on his brother's shoulder, offering him a reassuring squeeze.

"We cannot change what has already transpired, Siluk. What we can do now is gather all the information we have and present it to the council. Our father has already arranged a meeting for us."

Siluk nodded, his determination resurfacing.

"You're right, Dimitris. We must focus on the task at hand. We have valuable information and evidence against Gravakus and the Swanson brothers. It's time to expose them for the traitors they are."

Dimitris smiled, a glimmer of pride in his eyes.

"That's the spirit, Siluk. We will bring them down, and justice will be served. But first, we must gather our strength and prepare for the council meeting. It won't be an easy battle, but together, we can overcome any obstacle."

As the brothers made their way towards the council chambers, their minds were filled with thoughts of vengeance and justice. They knew that their actions would have far-reaching consequences, and they were prepared to face the challenges that lay ahead.

Little did they know that their journey was only beginning, and the battles they had fought with the werewolves were just a taste of the darkness that awaited them. But with their bond as brothers and their unwavering determination, they were ready to face whatever came their way. The fate of their family and their entire society hung in the balance, and they would stop at nothing to ensure a better future for all.

Siluk's expression grew somber as he listened to Dimitris's plans. The thought of Gravakus betraying their kind was deeply unsettling.

"I cannot fathom a Drakulis siding with a werewolf," he said, his voice filled with a mix of disbelief and disgust.

"If this accusation against Gravakus is true, it would be a betrayal of the highest order."

Dimitris nodded in agreement.

"That is why we must act swiftly, Siluk. I have taken matters into my own hands and started developing alternative methods to combat the werewolves. I have been working on creating weapons infused with the essence of roses, which I believe will be effective in eliminating the werewolf threat. I know it goes against the council's approval process, but I felt it was necessary under the circumstances."

Siluk's concern deepened.

"Dimitris, you must understand the consequences of your actions. Going against the council's trusted agreements can lead to severe punishment. We need their support and cooperation to tackle this war effectively."

Dimitris's eyes hardened with determination.

"I am aware of the risks, Siluk. But the safety of our kind and the eradication of the werewolves are my utmost priorities. I will continue my work on these weapons, regardless of the council's decision. We cannot afford to be complacent while our enemies grow stronger."

Before Siluk could respond, a chamber member approached them, informing them that the council meeting was about to commence and they needed to take their seats.

Stanley Swanson – Breed of a Werewolf

"We will join the council shortly," Siluk replied, acknowledging the chamber member's request.

Dimitris turned to his brother, a sense of urgency in his voice.

"Siluk, let me speak to the council and present my case for the approval of these weapons. You should remain silent during the meeting."

Siluk nodded reluctantly.

"Very well, Dimitris. But remember, the council's decision will have consequences. We must be prepared for any outcome."

Dimitris's eyes gleamed with determination.

"I understand, Siluk. Regardless of the council's decision, I will continue my research and development of these weapons. I have entrusted skilled scientists to explore the full potential of the rose, extracting its essence to create powders and liquids. The powder form weakens the werewolves, reducing them to their human state while impairing their abilities. The liquid form we are working on should be even more potent. My intention is to test these weapons on captured hellhounds."

Siluk took a deep breath, contemplating the gravity of their actions.

"May your studies yield success, Dimitris. If these weapons prove effective, it will be a great advantage for us. Stanley Swanson will stand no chance against us, especially after we have already eliminated his wife and brother. The next step will be to eliminate his children."

Their conversation was interrupted by the chamber member, reminding them once again of the council's waiting presence. Siluk and Dimitris exchanged a nod before making their way to the council chambers, knowing that the fate of their kind hung in the balance. They were aware that their actions would be met with scrutiny, but their determination to protect their people and avenge their losses remained unwavering.

As the council members settled into their seats, the atmosphere in the room became tense, anticipation lingering in the air like a storm waiting to break. The council area, adorned with intricate tapestries and ancient symbols, served as the backdrop for the impending discourse that would shape the fate of their kind.

Sirtimi, a venerable figure among the council, commanded attention as he rose to address the assembly. His voice echoed through the ornate chamber, carrying the weight of the issues at hand. The absence of Gravakus, a prominent council member, did not go unnoticed, casting a shadow over the gathering.

"It has become clear," Sirtimi began, his words measured and deliberate, "that movement has occurred, and our kind has engaged in battles against the werewolves. This conflict originated from information brought to my attention by a member of our kind, Stanley Swanson, who allegedly had a meeting with a mortal. We are not here to dwell on the source of this information, but rather to focus on the current state of affairs – a war between our two respective kinds."

The gravity of the situation hung heavy as Sirtimi emphasized the vulnerability that a video featuring werewolves had brought upon them. The revelation of their existence had exposed them to mortal scrutiny, leaving them susceptible to potential repercussions, whether the humans believed in the footage or not.

Sirtimi continued, his voice unwavering, "I will end my statement by declaring that Stanley Swanson has broken trust. His actions have led to a perilous situation for all of us, and he must be held accountable. I hereby order the council to seek out this fool and bring him back to face justice. His punishment shall be a painful death, a consequence of his betrayal."

The weight of Sirtimi's words settled on the council members, who exchanged glances that conveyed a mix of concern, determination, and, in some cases, reluctance. The absence of Gravakus lingered, raising questions about the unity of the council in this crucial moment.

The stage was set for a deliberation that would determine the course of their future, as each council member prepared to make their case and contribute to the decision that would shape the destiny of their kind in the face of this unforeseen conflict.

The council chamber was filled with a palpable tension as Malistaff's words hung in the air, prompting the assembled members to diligently take notes on the unfolding discussion. The gravity of the situation demanded a thorough examination of the facts before any decisions could be made.

Malistaff, a figure of wisdom and experience, spoke next, expressing skepticism about the credibility of the werewolf video. His voice resonated with a measured caution, emphasizing the need to ensure the accuracy of the information before declaring war.

"While I find it hard to believe that any breed of a

werewolf would present themselves like what took place, one of ours must have started it all," Malistaff pondered aloud, his eyes scanning the room, "and if this is war we are talking about, we must be certain to have all our facts."

However, before the conversation could progress, Siluk, unable to contain his frustration, impulsively stood up, violating the protocol of the council. His outburst was met with disapproving glances, but he was undeterred.

"Have you not listened to what started this, you incompetent fool?" Siluk retorted sharply.

"This Swanson breed that was ignorant to do what he did is the cause. I only followed what should have been done and made sure that I did so just as my brother Dimitris has. You play with the idea and try to justify their breed is unruly to our kind."

Malistaff's response was swift and authoritative.

"You will sit down!" he commanded, his eyes narrowing at Siluk's insolence, signaling a strict adherence to the decorum of the council.

Malistaff continued, addressing the larger issue at hand, "You ever speak to me or any member of this committee as you just did, I will see to it that you are removed!"

The sternness of Malistaff's warning reverberated in the chamber, setting the stage for the highest-ranking Drakulis, Sirtimi, to intervene. Rising from his seat with an air of authority, Sirtimi declared, "Enough! To try and remove either of my children from this committee would be doing of my own. It is true of what is happening, as you all can see that Gravakus is a traitor as he is not here. I will order attacks to find not just this Stanley Swanson but that of Gravakus as well. Any further information is welcomed at this point."

Sirtimi's proclamation marked a decisive shift in the proceedings, emphasizing the urgency of the situation and the need for collaborative action. The council members exchanged uneasy glances, their notes filled with the weight of the impending decisions that would shape the fate of their kind in the turbulent times ahead.

Dimitris, undeterred by his brother Siluk's insistence on silence, rose to address the council with an air of determination. The council members attentively turned their gaze toward him as he began to lay out his innovative plan to combat the werewolf threat using unconventional means.

"Father and committee," Dimitris began, his voice carrying a mix of conviction and urgency, "I, along with my brother, have knowledge of a new way to kill the werewolf breed using something as simple as a rose. I plan on conducting tests to explore various methods of using roses to defend ourselves from these hellhounds. We know for a fact that a single red rose petal placed in their mouth will result in their demise, and I have discovered that using rose powder in a specific form can weaken them. I implore you to allow me to continue developing new methods."

Dimitris's revelation captured the attention of the council, and a murmur of curiosity rippled through the chamber. The prospect of an unconventional weapon against the werewolves intrigued the assembly, but the atmosphere remained charged with the gravity of the ongoing conflict.

Siluk, who had been previously silenced by Malistaff, took the opportunity to support his brother's claims.

"It is true of what my brother says, as I have used the rose petal myself," Siluk admitted, his voice carrying a sense of conviction.

"Not only that, but surrounding werewolves with roses creates a fortress they cannot escape while simultaneously weakening them. I have tested this method on Stanley's wife."

The revelation of such a strategic advantage sparked a mix of reactions among the council members. Some exchanged approving nods, acknowledging the potential effectiveness of this newfound knowledge, while others wore expressions of skepticism, questioning the reliability of these unconventional methods.

Malistaff, maintaining a measured approach, addressed Dimitris, "Your discoveries are intriguing, and the potential for a natural defense against the werewolves is certainly noteworthy. However, we must proceed cautiously and ensure that these methods are thoroughly tested and proven effective before implementing them on a broader scale."

The council, now fully engaged in the discourse, awaited further details from Dimitris on the proposed experiments and the potential implications of utilizing roses as a means of defense against their formidable adversaries. The fate of their kind seemed to hinge on the delicate balance between tradition and innovation in the face of a relentless and unpredictable foe.

The council chamber buzzed with a mixture of anxiety and anticipation as members engaged in hushed conversations, exchanging thoughts and questions prompted by the revelations of Siluk and Dimitris. The unconventional approach to combating werewolves using roses had ignited a flurry of inquiries and speculations among the council members.

Amidst the discussions, an older member of the committee, known for his wisdom and measured judgment, rose to address the assembly. His voice carried authority as he expressed his approval for Dimitris to proceed with his groundbreaking discovery.

"I believe we should grant Dimitris the opportunity to continue his research and testing. This may very well be the key to our success in this war," he stated, his words resonating with a sense of sagacity.

The initial vote of approval from the seasoned council member paved the way for a cascade of agreements from others in attendance. One by one, the council members expressed their support for Dimitris's endeavors, recognizing the potential significance of the rose-based methods in the battle against the werewolf threat.

Sirtimi, the highest-ranking Drakulis and head of the council, seized the moment to bring the debate to a close. Rising with a commanding presence, he addressed the committee, emphasizing the urgency of the situation and the need for swift and decisive action.

"Tell all your followers to spread out and give them the order while letting them know of the movement of war," Sirtimi declared, his words cutting through the lingering tension in the room.

"We will have a mainstay in the United States, as well as Russia and China, as these territories belong to our kind in strength. We will diminish the hellhounds for good, as we need no slaves moving forward. If war is what this Stanley Swanson wanted, then we will bring it to him."

The decree from Sirtimi served as the catalyst for immediate action. The meeting quickly disbanded, and the council members dispersed to relay the orders to their respective followers. The world of supernatural beings, unbeknownst to humans, was about to be thrust into a covert conflict that had the potential to alter the course of history.

As Siluk and Dimitris prepared to part ways, Siluk shared a final piece of advice with his brother.

"Remember, Dimitris, that a small army is nothing when in separate locations; an army as a whole is what makes an impact. I trust you will curb your appetite for destruction, as for right now, we need not involve humans until we are set with ourselves."

"I will do my best to behave but promise nothing. Be safe, Siluk, and let the hunting begin," Dimitris replied, a glint of determination in his eyes as he embarked on the mission to test and perfect the deadly rose-based methods against the werewolf threat. The fate of their kind now rested on a delicate balance between innovation and tradition, as the supernatural world braced itself for the impending war that had been set in motion.

BREED OF WEREWOLVES MAKE THEIR ATTACKS

The six pack members, having landed in London, England, wasted no time in connecting with others of their breed. The atmosphere was a mix of camaraderie and shared purpose as they exchanged information about the ongoing war initiated by Stanley Swanson. Laughter and hugs masked the underlying tension of the daunting task that lay ahead.

The new pack, united in their mission, embarked on a strategic hunt for vampires, targeting their common haunts, whether it be a pub or an entire town. Three members, originally in charge of Sabe and Jade, took turns overseeing the surveillance, ensuring a meticulous approach to their operations.

Natalie, granted permission by her uncle Francais, eagerly participated in every surprise attack. From nightclubs to resorts, the pack executed well-calculated strikes, leaving no room for vampires to escape. The killings were swift, efficient, and devoid of hesitation. Drennan, the leader, spearheaded this well-coordinated offensive, catching fast vampires off guard.

The celebrations after each successful mission were a testament to the pack's prowess. Stories flowed among them, reinforcing the bond forged through shared victories. Francais expressed his pride in Natalie's performance but cautioned her against consuming vampire flesh in large quantities due to its toxicity to werewolves.

As the relentless fighting continued, Drennan recognized the need to extend their movement to Germany. The pack, along with newfound allies, swiftly made their way to the Harz

Mountains of Quedlinburg. Following the pattern established in England, they systematically targeted small towns, gathering more werewolves along the way.

However, the continuous surprise attacks began to leave a trail of unanswered questions among vampires. The disappearances and mass killings left shadows of death, becoming impossible to conceal. After almost a week and a half, thousands of vampires lost their lives, prompting a growing awareness among the vampire community.

Vampires, realizing the severity of the situation, started to communicate with each other, sharing information and preparing for potential werewolf invasions. The news reached the respective Drakulis masters, causing anger and frustration at being blindsided by werewolves.

As Drennan and his pack landed in Germany, they mirrored their actions in London, initiating a relentless slaughter in Quedlinburg and beyond. The vampires, caught off guard, started to prepare for the impending threat, setting traps and informing their masters.

The brutality of the war unfolded, with werewolves losing some of their own in the process. The escalating conflict prompted the Drakulis to mandate another meeting in Santa Cruz, where discussions focused on the ongoing battles in England and Germany. The widespread carnage hinted at the possibility of similar events unfolding in Japan and other strongholds of the breed.

The unprecedented bloodshed unleashed by the werewolves became a rallying cry for all breeds to come out from hiding and join the fight. Memories of past atrocities inflicted by

Stanley Swanson – Breed of a Werewolf

Drakulis and vampires fueled the werewolves' determination. The sheer numbers, combined with the element of surprise, allowed them to dominate, and satisfaction briefly eased their relentless pursuit.

As the werewolves momentarily eased off from the slaying, a lingering sense of fleeting satisfaction hung in the air. If only the respite could have lasted longer, but the echoes of war had set a tone that would resonate across generations, leaving an indelible mark on the supernatural world.

S.K. Ballinger

ANTIDOTE

Amidst the chaos of surprise attacks and escalating tensions in the supernatural world, Stanley Swanson found himself grappling with the newfound threat posed by the 'red rose' – a lethal weapon against his kind. Feeling the urgency of the situation, Stanley received a phone message from Jeremia detailing their journey to England. Recognizing the gravity of the threat, he decided to contact an old friend, Kevon, a scientist working for the government.

The decision to involve a government scientist, a clear violation of the supernatural code, reflected Stanley's desperation to find a solution to the werewolves' deadly discovery. With the location of Jeremia and the others uncertain, Stanley arranged a short-notice meeting with Kevon at an undisclosed facility in a neighboring state to Kansas.

Over the phone, Stanley conveyed the gravity of the situation to Kevon, emphasizing the need for a swift and effective antidote to neutralize the rose's lethal effects on their kind. The urgency in Stanley's voice mirrored the heightened stakes of the supernatural war.

"I need for you to invest as much time as necessary for an antidote to be made to prevent a rose from killing and harming our breed," Stanley urgently requested, aware that time was of the essence.

"I need you to do this as quickly as possible, as I believe time is not on our side."

Kevon, on the other end of the line, responded with a commitment to the task at hand.

Stanley Swanson – Breed of a Werewolf

"I will do my best, my friend, as I have never heard of anything like this before, so it may take some time."

Stanley, recognizing the challenges but also the importance of the mission, expressed understanding.

"I understand, and I only ask that you do your best, Kevon. This is very crucial to our existence."

The clandestine collaboration between Stanley and Kevon set in motion a covert operation to develop an antidote that could counteract the effects of the deadly rose. The secrecy surrounding the meeting and the involvement of a government scientist added an extra layer of complexity to the unfolding supernatural conflict, as both sides sought to gain any advantage in the high-stakes battle for survival.

Stanley Swanson, after conveying the urgency of the situation to his old friend Kevon, concluded the phone call by making a crucial request. Aware of the critical nature of the information they were seeking, Stanley implored Kevon to contact him immediately if he discovered anything that could serve as an advantage in defending against a red rose attack.

"Call me immediately if you find out anything, Kevon, anything that can give us an advantage against the red rose. We need every possible edge to protect our kind," Stanley urged, the gravity of the situation palpable in his voice. The commitment to staying informed reflected the dire circumstances the supernatural community faced.

Before hanging up, Stanley made a selfless offer that showcased his determination to find a solution, even at a personal cost. "I'm willing to be a test subject if it means saving our breed," he declared, underlining the depth of his commitment to the survival of their kind.

Kevon, on the other end of the line, acknowledged the weight of Stanley's sacrifice and responded with a solemn promise. "I will do all that I can. That is all I can promise you, friend."

The exchange encapsulated the sense of desperation and camaraderie among those who found themselves thrust into a supernatural war. Stanley, as a leader, was willing to put himself on the line for the greater good, while Kevon, a scientist bound by the pursuit of knowledge, vowed to exhaust every resource in the quest for an antidote.

As the phone call ended, the clandestine collaboration between Stanley and Kevon remained shrouded in secrecy, adding an intriguing layer to the unfolding narrative of a supernatural conflict. The fate of their breed hung in the balance, with each passing moment becoming more critical as the war against the werewolves intensified and the search for a solution reached a fevered pitch.

Upon receiving Stanley's urgent request, Kevon swiftly shifted his focus, temporarily setting aside all other projects to delve into the challenge at hand. Clad in a fully covered hazmat-type suit, he embarked on a meticulous and exhaustive exploration of the properties of roses and rose petals. Boiling, dissecting, crumbling, and liquefying, Kevon employed every conceivable scientific method to unravel the mysteries of the red rose's deadly effects.

As he meticulously worked through countless hours of experimentation, Kevon faced the formidable task of determining

Stanley Swanson – Breed of a Werewolf

how to test the potential antidote. The complexity of the challenge weighed heavily on his scientific mind, prompting him to think diligently about the most effective and ethical approach.

A week later, true to his promise to Stanley, Kevon contacted him with an update on his progress. The anticipation in Stanley's voice was evident as he answered the call.

"Well, I hope you are ready to check in, as I think I have an antidote in place to some degree, but nothing foolproof. I sincerely hope you reconsider being a test subject," Kevon cautiously conveyed.

Understanding the gravity of the situation but committed to the cause, Stanley replied with a mixture of nerves and determination, "Good work in such a short time, Kevon. What kind of pain might I be looking at if all fails?"

Kevon, candid about the potential risks, responded, "You will feel much pain, I would think, and if all else fails, then death looms around you. Prepare yourself is all I can recommend."

Stanley, perhaps trying to lighten the mood, responded with a touch of humor, "This sounds like fun, Kev. I will be there in an hour or so."

On the way to the facility where Kevon worked, Stanley's nerves heightened, a mix of hesitation and determination coursing through him. Entering the room where Kevon awaited, the sight of the scientist in a hazmat suit added an eerie air to the impending experiment.

"Good seeing you, Stanley, and I'm sorry for all the loss you have taken recently," Kevon greeted, expressing empathy for the challenges Stanley had faced.

"You as well, Kevon, and thank you. What is with the suit?" Stanley inquired, curiosity overcoming his apprehension.

"Precautionary is all. What you have told me of the rose, I really do not wish to experience such things upon myself," Kevon explained, his commitment to safety evident.

Stanley, ever the joker, responded with a touch of levity, "Well, at least you look the part, Kevon. So where do we begin?"

Kevon led Stanley to the lab area, where he began to explain the intricacies of the antidote and the potential ordeals that awaited him. The gravity of the situation became more tangible as Kevon detailed the various formulas derived from different types of roses, each administered in small doses. The uncertainty of the experiment loomed large, and Stanley prepared himself for what lay ahead, both for himself and the future of their kind.

In the sterile confines of the lab, Stanley stood, surrounded by individual rooms, each with its distinct setup, as Kevon had meticulously described. An air of apprehension hung over him, and Stanley found himself looking around, taking in the gravity of the moment. Clasping his wife's ring between his thumb and pointer finger, he couldn't shake the realization that this sacrifice was not just for the survival of their breed but also in memory of his beloved.

"This is not just for our breed but for you, my love," Stanley whispered, a quiet affirmation that resonated within the sterile walls of the lab.

Stanley Swanson – Breed of a Werewolf

Kevon, dressed in his safety suit, broke the momentary silence, his question hanging in the air like a solemn prelude to what was about to unfold. "Shall we begin, Stanley?"

"Ready when you are," Stanley responded, the gravity of the situation evident in his tone.

With a deep breath, Stanley shook off the nervous energy that clung to him. He stood there, wearing nothing but a pair of underwear, a deliberate choice to expose as much of his body as possible during the upcoming study. The vulnerability of the moment was palpable, as Stanley steeled himself for what lay ahead.

"We will begin with the first room, which consists of a simple full-stemmed red rose," Kevon explained, leading Stanley into the room, his own safety suit emphasizing the cautious nature of their experiment.

Inside the room, the atmosphere was clinical, with sterile surfaces and a sense of purpose that hung in the air. Kevon carefully directed Stanley, positioning him for the study. The simplicity of the first test – a full-stemmed red rose – belied the potential complexity and danger that lay within.

As Kevon initiated the first phase of the experiment, Stanley couldn't help but feel a mix of anticipation and anxiety. The weight of the moment was evident in the furrow of his brow, the tension in his posture. The room, now a stage for an unprecedented scientific exploration, bore witness to the sacrifice Stanley was willing to make for the greater good of their breed.

The scent of the red rose filled the room, a stark contrast to the clinical nature of their surroundings. In that moment,

S.K. Ballinger

Stanley stood at the intersection of science and sacrifice, embarking on a journey that held the promise of an antidote but also the potential for unimaginable pain and risk.

As Kevon continued to guide the experiment, Stanley's thoughts drifted to his wife, the love that fueled his determination, and the greater purpose that compelled him to take this perilous step. The lab, once a place of detached scientific pursuit, now bore witness to a profound act of courage and selflessness, as Stanley braced himself for whatever lay ahead in the pursuit of a solution to the werewolves' newfound threat.

As the lab room door closed behind them, Stanley, feeling a wave of sickness and nausea, approached the simple yet ominous full-stemmed red rose. Inches away from picking it up, he awaited guidance from Kevon, the scientist who was orchestrating this unprecedented experiment.

Sensing the opportune moment, Kevon gently suggested, "Transition if you can, Stanley, and do so with all your might. Think of your wife."

Stanley, focused on the task at hand and fueled by thoughts of his wife, attempted to transition. However, it proved to be a challenging endeavor, with only fleeting flashes of success and no full transition achieved. Kevon, diligently taking notes, recognized the struggle and then proposed a new approach – picking up the rose with his hands.

As Stanley grasped the rose with his left hand, a sudden onslaught of nausea overwhelmed him. He began to vomit profusely, hastily dropping the rose to the floor. The visceral reaction underscored the potency of the rose's effects on his werewolf physiology.

Stanley Swanson – Breed of a Werewolf

"Next test," Stanley declared to Kevon, determined to proceed despite the physical toll.

The next room revealed a simpler setup – a vial of water with a lone rose petal immersed in it. Stanley, still reeling from the effects of the previous room, voiced his unease.

"You were not joking with me about being a test subject. I still feel sick from the first room, Kevon," Stanley remarked, a hint of apprehension in his voice.

"If you wish to take a break for a moment, then perhaps that is best, Stanley," Kevon offered, acknowledging the toll the experiment was taking.

"No, we shall continue on with using me as that of a test monkey," Stanley resolved, his determination overriding the physical discomfort.

"Fair enough. Then do what you can to grab the glass of water and take a small sip of it if you can," Kevon instructed, preparing for the next phase of the experiment.

The resilience of Stanley in the face of adversity, coupled with the gravity of the situation, painted a picture of sacrifice and determination in the pursuit of an antidote for the werewolves' newfound vulnerability.

In the sterile confines of the lab, Stanley, having overcome the nauseating effects of the water with a rose petal, displayed signs of normalcy, a hopeful indicator in this perilous experiment. Holding the glass, he couldn't help but express his disdain for the taste, exclaiming, "That tasted like shit!"

S.K. Ballinger

Kevon, acknowledging Stanley's courage, spoke with a mix of admiration and concern, "Let us see what happens in the next room, Stanley. You're brave to do this. Remind me again of why you are willing to put yourself through this?"

"For our breed, and more so for my wife," Stanley replied, a resolute determination in his voice.

"Then focus on your wife as this next room will not be as kind to you as a sip of water was," Kevon cautioned, preparing Stanley for the challenges that lay ahead.

The next room presented an eerie emptiness, devoid of any visible roses. As Stanley entered, Kevon, even in his protective suit, left the room, creating an unsettling solitude for the impending test.

"Not staying with me on this one, Kevon?" Stanley questioned, a note of uncertainty in his voice.

"I'm afraid not, Stanley, and I suggest you prepare yourself," Kevon responded through a microphone, his voice resonating in the sterile air of the lab.

Alone in the room, Stanley felt a heightened sense of vulnerability, his determination to endure this trial for the greater good of his kind and the memory of his wife serving as his sole anchors. The isolation, coupled with the anticipation of the unknown, created a tense atmosphere, emphasizing the gravity of the sacrifice Stanley was making.

With bated breath, Stanley awaited the next phase of the experiment, a testament to his unwavering commitment to finding a solution to the werewolves' newfound vulnerability. In the silence of the lab, the experiment unfolded, with Stanley standing at the intersection of fear and determination, driven by a profound sense of purpose.

Standing resolutely in the center of the room, Stanley exhibited a facade of strength, his demeanor reflecting a mixture of readiness and determination. Despite the earlier bouts of vomiting induced by the rose and water experiments, he appeared physically unharmed. The anticipation in the room was palpable, a silent acknowledgment of the impending challenge.

With a quick push of a button from Kevon, the room's atmosphere changed dramatically. Fine particles resembling ash or snow began to fall from the vents above, filling the air with the crushed remnants of red roses. Almost immediately, Stanley's demeanor shifted from one of preparation to one of intense suffering.

In a matter of seconds, the werewolf leader collapsed to his knees, the weight of the experiment bearing down on him. The dust of crushed roses enveloped him, and Stanley soon found himself on his stomach, arms stretched out before him. Agony echoed in his voice as he cried out, "Enough!"

The room, once silent, now echoed with the sounds of Stanley's distress. The experiment, designed to expose him to the effects of crushed red roses, had taken a toll far beyond the physical. It was a stark reminder of the vulnerability of the werewolf breed and the sacrifices one was willing to make in the pursuit of a solution.

Kevon, monitoring the experiment from a distance, maintained a watchful eye on the unfolding scene. The decision to initiate such a test underscored the severity of the threat posed by the red rose and the urgency with which an antidote needed to be developed.

As Stanley lay in distress on the laboratory floor, the symbolism of his sacrifice for the greater good of their breed hung heavily in the air. The experiment, though agonizing, served as a testament to the lengths one was willing to go to protect those they cared about and preserve the existence of their kind.

As the lab doors quickly swung open, Kevon wasted no time administering an injection into Stanley's thigh, the culmination of his work and the antidote he had concocted. In mere seconds, the effects of the injection became evident as Stanley, once writhing in agony on the laboratory floor, now stood on his feet. The transformation into his natural form as a powerful werewolf unfolded seamlessly, leaving Stanley unaffected by the preceding ordeal. The resilience of his werewolf physiology seemed impervious to the earlier suffering.

After transitioning back to his human form, Stanley met Kevon's gaze with a look of confidence and gratitude. "I feel as though nothing happened to me, and I am not even nauseated. You, my friend, have done well with your work. Bring on the next example," Stanley proclaimed, the relief evident in his voice.

Buoyed by the success of the antidote, Stanley, now brimming with confidence, suggested to Kevon the idea of testing the antidote against the consumption of a red rose petal. However, Kevon, cautious and aware of the limitations of his current research, rejected the proposal.

"I have only had a few weeks of study, Stanley. I am aware that the rose or rose petal in the mouth of our breed cannot be consumed, as I have seen it destroy certain cells in my

Stanley Swanson – Breed of a Werewolf

research. Crushed form seems to lose its potency on that level, and the same with that of liquid. I do not even know how long the antidote, which just worked on you from the dust fall, will last, Stan," Kevon explained, emphasizing the need for further study and refinement of the antidote.

Though the night had proven eventful and successful, with tangible results validating Kevon's work, Stanley, eager to secure more of the antidote, expressed his gratitude and intention to stay in touch for future collaborations.

Before Stanley could take his leave, Kevon halted him with a proposition.

"One more thing I would like to try if you do not mind, Stanley." The anticipation lingered in the air as the scientist hinted at yet another experiment, leaving the outcome uncertain in the pursuit of further breakthroughs.

As Kevon returned Stanley's clothes, symbolizing the conclusion of the previous experiments, he presented a new suggestion to the werewolf leader.

"Go back to the first room that had the single rose placed on the floor," Kevon instructed.

"That room made me feel weak as it was, Kevon, so why again suggest I re-enter?" Stanley questioned, wary of revisiting a setting that had already induced discomfort.

"I am very curious as to what might happen if you are surrounded by roses. If it indeed creates some sort of force field for our breed. You accepted this study, and I am trying to explore as many possibilities as I can for vaccination or deterrent," Kevon explained, driven by the pursuit of knowledge.

"Kevon, I just put my damn clothes back on, and though I am feeling great after you covered me in the red dusting by giving me that injection, I really do not wish to get sick again," Stanley responded with a hint of reluctance.

"Which is what I like to refer to as experimenting, and this was the purpose, Stanley. Again, friend, suck it up, as I do not believe that it will cause you pain. Just as before, do it for your wife if not for our breed," Kevon urged, emphasizing the higher purpose behind the experimentation.

"I will do it, as I trust you, and I have heard briefly that this was a possibility of creating such a thing. From what I have gathered, it was what took place at my house the night I lost my wife, and my pack was extremely vulnerable. Let this be the last of the tests, Kevon, as I need to make my way," Stanley conceded, a mix of determination and weariness in his voice.

"Will be the last test, I promise. You should not feel any pain, but you will be weak nonetheless," assured Kevon, offering a reassurance that echoed through the sterile lab.

Returning to the first room, Stanley positioned himself in the center, where a single rose lay nearby. As Kevon entered, he surrounded Stanley with multiple roses, from bud to stem. The room, once again, became a stage for experimentation, and Stanley, feeling the effects of weakness and dizziness, dropped to his knees.

"Do what you can to fight it, Stanley. Do your best to crawl, if need be, outside of the roses," Kevon encouraged, his voice transmitted through the lab's speakers.

Stanley Swanson – Breed of a Werewolf

The atmosphere was charged with anticipation as the final test unfolded, a culmination of the night's experiments, with Stanley grappling against weakness in the pursuit of valuable insights.

With every ounce of strength and determination, fueled by memories of his late wife Julie, Stanley managed to rise to his feet. However, despite his efforts, he found himself unable to penetrate through the surrounding roses, no matter how hard he tried. Kevon, protected by the hazmat suit, observed the werewolf's struggle, a testament to the effectiveness of the experiment.

"Absolutely amazing!" Kevon exclaimed in genuine fascination before an idea sparked in his mind.

"One last test for now, and then we will end this session," Kevon proposed.

"You told me that was the last one, and I am done with this, Kevon," Stanley protested, the weariness evident in his voice.

"I did say that, you are correct, but allow me to do the same with only a few rose petals. I am very curious to see if, in a smaller size or amount, it has the same effect," Kevon explained, driven by scientific curiosity.

"Had I known you were going to keep trying more methods, I would not be here, but do as you must, Kevon," Stanley resigned, a sense of reluctance evident in his response.

Temporarily leaving the room, Kevon returned with a handful of rose petals. Placing them strategically around Stanley, just as he did with the full roses, Kevon observed the effects. As anticipated, the invisible force field manifested once more, trapping Stanley within its confines.

"I am done; please remove them, as I cannot do this any longer," Stanley pleaded, a plea that carried the weight of exhaustion and exasperation.

With a swift removal of the rose petals, the force field dissipated, granting Stanley the much-needed relief. The lab, once again, fell into a hushed stillness as the culmination of experiments unfolded before them.

Kevon, satisfied with the insights gained, couldn't help but marvel at the remarkable discoveries made throughout the night, pushing the boundaries of what was known about the werewolf breed and their vulnerabilities. The scientific endeavor, though demanding, had provided invaluable data, bringing them one step closer to understanding and combating the threats faced by their kind.

Feeling accomplished with the insights gained from the experiments and ensuring that Stanley was well after the rigorous tests, Kevon expressed gratitude to the werewolf leader for bringing the threat of red roses to his attention. The revelation that red roses were not only poison but deadly to werewolves was a significant breakthrough in understanding their vulnerabilities.

As they wrapped up the session, Kevon marveled at Stanley's resilience during the experiments, noting that even with the injected antidote, he displayed a remarkable ability to endure the challenges. It was a promising sign, one that hinted at the potential efficacy of the antidote.

Stanley Swanson – Breed of a Werewolf

Before departing the lab, Stanley, seeking answers about another potential threat, inquired about the effect of having a rose or rose petal placed in the mouth.

"I need to know what I have been told about having a rose or petal of a rose put in the mouth. Will the injections prevent death from that form?" Stanley questioned.

"I have not found a proven way to suggest that it would, Stanley. All from what I know or what you have told me is that it is a fast and painful death," Kevon responded honestly.

"I wish to find out, as my wife did. I know that when my time comes to face those that threatened my family and took the life of my wife, they will do the same when we confront one another in this war," Stanley explained, driven by a mixture of determination and vengeance.

"I cannot do that. Stay patient, Stanley, as I work on a way that is foolproof. Remember that I have only had a little time to work on what I have already made, and I still have more to do. I am not even sure of how long a single injection will last or to what degrees of weaponry they may or may not be making to kill us. You have given me a few weeks at best to make a serum; now, I ask you to give me just a few months more of study. I will not let you attempt something that may cause you immediate death at my lab and before me, friend," Kevon urged, displaying genuine concern for Stanley's well-being.

"I miss my wife dearly, Kevon," Stanley admitted, the pain of his loss evident in his voice.

"I know that you do, Stanley, but to suggest taking her fate as yours is not needed. Let me work and see what I can do. Take your sadness and love for Julie and channel your vengeance into the fight that looms against those who started this. I have a feeling that our breed is going to need you," Kevon counseled, acknowledging the emotional burden carried by Stanley.

"I understand, Kevon, and thank you for your concern. Perhaps you should have been a therapist," Stanley quipped, attempting to inject a touch of humor into the conversation.

"Not likely, friend. I am nothing more than a scientist of our breed hoping that we can prevail against the Drackulis and nothing more. I too knew a day would come when a war between our respective kinds would happen," Kevon reflected, emphasizing his commitment to the scientific pursuit of victory over their ancient adversaries.

Moments passed, the weight of the recent experiments and revelations lingering in the air. Before departing, Stanley extended his gratitude to Kevon, acknowledging the significant efforts put forth by his long-time friend.

"I have asked very much of you on such short notice, and I truly appreciate that, my long-time friend. You have done well. Now, if you do not mind, I am taking a few of these shots that seem to contain an antidote with me," Stanley expressed his gratitude and decision to take some of the antidote shots with him.

"I will try my best, and what you choose to do with the few shots is your own doing. I just warn you that further study has yet to be done, meaning that taking more than one dose is not recommended, Stanley. I wish you well in what is going to take place. You have my word that I will continue my work and inform you of any new methods as I come across any," Kevon cautioned, emphasizing the preliminary nature of the antidote and his commitment to ongoing research.

With a dozen antidote shots in hand, Stanley exited the lab, resolute and determined. The road awaited him, and with hopes of reuniting with his children and myriad emotions coursing through his body, he prepared for the challenges ahead.

The blame that threatened to consume him, Stanley sought to transform into a driving force for positive action. Images of his family before the influence of Kain flooded his mind—the joyous moments, the births of their children, the wedding, and the camaraderie with friends. Armed with memories of celebration, Stanley set his sights on the nearest airport, ready to embark on his journey to England and face the looming war.

S.K. Ballinger

MAKING WAY WHILE MEETING AN UNLIKELY COUPLE

The trio, feeling the weight of the recent chaos, cautiously made their way down the hill, eyes fixed on the controlled smoke rising from a distant cabin. As they approached, the smell of burning wood reached them, confirming the presence of a fire. The uncertainty of the situation compelled them to devise a plan that balanced the need for shelter and the potential threat they might pose to unsuspecting humans.

Caleb led the way, his keen senses alert to any potential dangers. The dense forest concealed them, allowing them to observe the cabin before revealing their presence. The flickering flames hinted at warmth and security, but the werewolves remained vigilant.

As they reached the outskirts of the cabin, hidden among the trees, Caleb spoke in hushed tones. "Let's shift back to human form. We don't want to alarm them. Remember, we're victims seeking help."

The trio transformed, their wolfish bodies shifting seamlessly into human forms. Naked, covered in dirt, and appearing vulnerable, they approached the cabin with caution. The night air was chilly, and the warmth emanating from the cabin's windows enticed them.

Sheree, with a convincing display of distress, knocked on the door. "Please help! If anyone is in there, please, I beg of you for help!"

Moments passed before an older man cautiously opened

the door. The werewolves, maintaining their act, displayed signs of desperation and fear. The man, identified as Michael, invited them in, offering warmth and blankets.

Inside the cabin, Anne, Michael's wife, joined them, expressing genuine concern for the apparent victims. The werewolves, still naked and wrapped in blankets, played their parts, fabricating a tale of abduction and escape.

As the kind couple offered tea and comfort, the werewolves grappled with the decision of revealing their true nature or adhering to the fabricated story. The potential for refuge versus the risks of exposure hung in the air, creating a tension that mirrored the looming conflicts in their supernatural world.

Little did they know that the choices made within the cozy confines of the cabin would set in motion a chain of events that could alter the course of their destinies and entwine their fates with those of the unsuspecting humans.

The werewolf trio, chilled by the night air and eager for warmth, found themselves at the doorstep of a seemingly welcoming cabin. The scent lingering in the air hinted at humans inside, and their vulnerability increased as they shifted back to their human forms. Naked and cold, they relied on their act as escaped kidnap victims to seek refuge.

Sheree, taking the lead, pounded on the cabin door with urgency. "Please help! If anyone is in there, please, I beg of you for help!" Her plea echoed through the quiet night, her performance convincing enough to stir empathy.

Despite the initial silence, an older man named Michael eventually opened the door, his expression a mix of concern and confusion. "What in the hell has happened to you young kids in these parts? Please come in from the cold and warm yourselves by the fire," he exclaimed, quickly calling to his wife, Anne, for assistance.

"Anne, grab some blankets, please!" Michael's urgency reflected genuine compassion as he ushered the trio inside. Sheree, Caleb, and Zanth were relieved that their fabricated distress seemed to have worked. Anne, responding to her husband's call, entered the room with blankets in hand, her eyes widening at the sight of the seemingly traumatized young visitors.

"Oh, my Lord, what has happened to you poor kids?" Anne's genuine concern filled the room.

"Let them warm themselves before we rush questions, Anne. It seems that they have been through a lot," Michael wisely advised, emphasizing empathy over interrogation.

"I will warm some tea for them, Michael," Anne volunteered, already taking steps to provide comfort for their unexpected guests.

As the werewolves wrapped themselves in the offered blankets, Michael addressed their immediate needs. "We have no phone here as we don't have any signal this far up in the hilltops, but once you are all warmed, I will be glad to provide you each with clothes, though they may not fit, coming from this old man or that of my tiny wife, and we will drive you to the police."

The trio, appreciative of the hospitality, continued their act, preparing for the next phase of their plan. Inside the cozy cabin, uncertainties loomed as the werewolves grappled with the consequences of revealing their supernatural nature or maintaining the facade for the sake of temporary refuge. Little did they know that the choices made within the warmth of the cabin would set the stage for unforeseen events that could alter the course of their destinies.

The old couple, Michael and Anne, continued to extend their hospitality to the supposed kidnapped and traumatized trio. Sheree, maintaining her act, expressed gratitude through tear-filled eyes as she spoke to Michael.

"Thank you for your help, Mister, as we have been missing for over two years, kidnapped while our parents were murdered." Sheree's performance was convincing, her tone reflecting the weight of the fabricated tragedy.

Michael, taking the role of a concerned guardian, reassured them, "As I said, warm yourselves, and I will drive you to the police. Hopefully, those that have done this to you all and your parents will be caught and served with the strictest of punishment."

While their initial plan seemed successful, a new challenge emerged. The trio, now wrapped in blankets and sipping tea offered by Anne, found themselves confronted with the prospect of facing the police. Panic flickered across their faces as they contemplated the next steps. The options were clear: they could either reveal the truth to the kind-hearted humans or resort to the drastic measure of transitioning and potentially harming them.

Anne, returning with the tea, played her part in comforting the distressed visitors. "This is just terrible. Drink up, kids, and know that you all are safe now." Her words were sincere, meant to offer solace to those who had supposedly endured a long and harrowing ordeal.

As the werewolves clutched their tea cups, uncertainty lingered in the air. The warmth of the cabin provided a stark contrast to the cold reality of their situation. To maintain the facade, they needed to navigate the delicate balance between trust and deceit. The decision to disclose their true nature or perpetuate the act weighed heavily on their minds, and the consequences of their choices would ripple through the unfolding narrative of their unpredictable journey.

The atmosphere inside the cabin grew tense as the werewolves grappled with their predicament. They cautiously sipped their tea, realizing that hasty decisions could jeopardize their chances of avoiding the police. The urgency of their situation prompted Caleb to voice a seemingly innocent suggestion.

"Well, I am warm now, and perhaps you could put the fire out as it is getting a little warm in here."

Caleb's ulterior motive was to avoid attracting attention from vampires who might see the cabin as a potential target. However, Michael adamantly rejected the idea.

"Well, seeing how you all have been through a lot and coming in from the cold as nightfall is coming soon, I wish to keep myself warm along with my wife. Trust me, this cabin needs a fire going at night."

Zanth, feeling the pressure of their hidden identity, couldn't contain himself. "Just put it out for the time being!" he shouted, startling the old couple.

"This is our place, and you are welcomed, but we need the heat and are only trying to help you kids," Anne responded, her husband echoing her sentiments.

Faced with the old couple's resistance and realizing the urgency of their situation, Sheree abandoned the act. Her tears ceased, and she spoke calmly, clinching her blanket close.

"We were never held captive, kidnapped, or such, Michael, nor were our parents murdered. While you may laugh at us, the truth is that we were running from vampires and a red sky."

The revelation hung in the air, the weight of truth replacing the fabricated tale. Michael and Anne, though startled by the sudden change, listened attentively. The werewolves had chosen transparency over deception, revealing the extraordinary reality they faced. The cabin, once a haven from potential danger, now housed an unfolding narrative that intertwined the lives of the werewolves and the unsuspecting humans. The choices made in this crucial moment would shape the path ahead, introducing uncertainty and perhaps forging unexpected alliances in the face of supernatural threats.

Before Michael or Anne could utter a few words, the oldest of the pack, attempting to salvage the situation, expressed his frustration with Sheree's revelation.

"Oh, Sheree, you are in need of much rest. I apologize to both of you for her tired mind saying what came from her lips. We have been through a lot, as we have told you. If you do not mind, those clothes now, so we can be on our way."

Yet, stern eyes from both Michael and Anne indicated that they were not buying the explanation. Anne, instead of reacting negatively, burst into laughter, her eyes locking onto Sheree's.

"Those damn vampires never seem to go away, do they, young lady?"

Sheree couldn't resist responding to Anne's remark, "Are you telling me that you believe in the myth of vampires?"

The atmosphere shifted from impatience to curiosity in the little sitting area of the cabin. Michael joined the conversation, his laughter audible as his wife left the room.

"You, as if her or even I, believe that vampires are real. Hell, we have been known to have killed some in our time, yet we have never seen a werewolf. We are well-equipped even at our own age, so what is it that you three are not sharing with us?"

Sheree, along with her pack, now wore dumbfounded expressions. Michael's suggestion that they share the truth, coupled with his acknowledgment that they might be werewolves, intrigued Sheree.

"So, tell me, Michael, if you don't mind. You claim to kill vampires or have killed vampires in your past. Why does it seem that you have an interest in seeing a werewolf?"

"Well, young lady, to be honest with you, I believe I see three in front of me."

Laughter ensued, and Sheree pressed on, "Obviously, you are suggesting that my two brothers and I are werewolves. Why would you entertain such a thought?"

Michael, unfazed, offered an explanation, "Very simple if

you don't mind me explaining."

"I cannot wait to hear this; please indulge us, old man," Zanth requested humbly.

"While we have in the past set out to extinguish that of vampires, we have also studied that of werewolves. I may very well be eighty-one years old, but I still have it in me. Your kind, that spawns from the Lycan like vampires have from the Drakulis, is not hard to figure out when paying close attention to details."

"What gives us away then, if what you say is true?" Sheree asked.

"Perhaps I should grab a mirror if you wish, so that you can see the very thin lining of your pupils, which are colored a light shade of blue. Or, if you prefer to look at your ears, even in human form as you all are, they have a slight point near the top. Last but not least, your facial expressions—your eyebrows nearest to each side of your nose all point lightly inward to your eyes and do so identically. Don't get me started with your mannerisms, which are often polite."

Anne returned to the room with a few photos and VHS tapes. Feeling no threat whatsoever, and in her characteristic humorous fashion, she jumped into the conversation of what she had overheard while away.

"About time we meet werewolves such as yourselves. You all seem very well with your respected ways. Lying can only get you so far, and I'm glad you were honest with us."

Caleb, curious to know more, asked, "So if we are, in fact, werewolves as you believe, are you not frightened at all?"

"My boy, if I was threatened, I can assure you that my husband would not have allowed you in our house, and I would not have offered you my tea in a silver cup."

Zanth, with a hint of arrogance, questioned, "So how can we know we are safe here, then, with those who claim to have killed vampires?"

"Because you are still here. I have brought some pictures of our past and even an old VHS tape of a vampire we killed well over twenty years ago, which was our last. This happened here, at our place of land that we thought we could retire at. How that vampire found us, one will never know. Then again, here sit three werewolves. Strange lives we have lived, Michael."

"That we have, dear."

Anne handed the pictures to Sheree and went to put the VHS tape in, eager to show evidence that what they had said was true. Sheree, examining the photos, saw nothing but snow on the ground backlit with many trees in their yard.

"What exactly is the proof you are showing me in these photos as there is nothing?"

"It is always easier to see motion and then look back at the pictures. I told you so, Anne. It is always best to watch the video first before looking at pictures."

"Yeah, yeah, now hush so they can see with their own eyes what she can't with the pictures."

As Anne pushed the play button, she explained to them that if they watched closely what she and her husband were shooting at in this video many years ago, it might be hard to see because the truth is hard to comprehend in the human mind.

"These vampires are essentially invisible to any recording device, just like having no reflection in a mirror. Just like the movies or what has been written, it all holds truth. Nothing but dead souls roaming freely to feed and do as they wish to."

In the video, it was evident that with a close eye, they could see branches moving, and the leaves on the ground shuffling towards them. Clearly, it held true that while a picture is worth a thousand words, a video shows much more in less amount of time. Michael, feeling almost as though he did that late evening when the footage was taken, could not help but narrate briefly.

"That was him or her for all we know that continued making its way towards us after you clearly hear both my wife and I ask this vampire to leave and let us be. I know the sound quality is a bit bad, but hell, this was taken well over twenty years ago. I learned long ago from both my father and grandfather to never take the old saying 'the little boy who cried wolf' lightly and to always take immediate action if need be. Glad we did so that day as we were well prepared, weren't we, Anne?"

"You were more than I was, Michael. I still would have been the one to shoot that son of a bitch had you just guided me where to aim."

"Yep, that's my wife. Was the last one we ever killed and have lived the last twenty years peacefully. After this video, I would love to know what actually took place with your kind."

As they continued to watch and listen to the narration of

Michael and Anne, the video showed that they were shooting this vampire with crossbows, each arrow tipped with wood. Playing the video back several times in slow motion and still frames, Sheree and the rest could see one arrow had come to a complete stop in mid-air before falling to the ground. It was clear, with a close eye on this video, that this vampire had caught the arrow just before it reached him/her, only to succumb to the next one that completed its course directly to the heart, leaving nothing more than a shadow—a common theme of death to a vampire.

Examining the photos afterward, it was easy to see not only the footsteps in the ground or the arrow that stopped mid-stride, but also the second arrow that stuck and slowly fell backward before standing straight up with nothing but a small spot of dark blood from where the arrow hit. All three were impressed with the old couple.

"That is just a great capture, and I applaud you, as all of our breed despise vampires, and even more, their masters. The Drakulis are ignorant in every possible way. Now, let me see those pictures, Sheree," Caleb asked with an upbeat, happy tone.

The conversations continued for almost an hour until Anne, with a gleam of interest in her eyes, asked Sheree, "So if the three of you are, in fact, werewolves, I would love to see it in person. As we share the same hate towards vampires and the research we have done in our youth, it would be great to witness such before we one day lay to rest."

Caleb, sensing the change in tone, interjected, "They are werewolves, Anne, and they should be on their way. I am more inclined to know why they made their way here with a silly lie, as the closest neighbor to us lives thirty miles away. It's very obvious to me that you all had not been kidnapped, but I could not let you all stand in the cold."

Sheree then explained, "As I mentioned, we were being attacked by vampires and this red dust that fell from the sky, which I witnessed with my own eyes killing another breed by the name of Stephen Swanson. His younger brother Stanley believes a war is to one day come, which will involve humans and wishes you mortals to join our side in case the war does unfold. Unfortunately, as it seems, the war has already begun between our two separate beings and has not yet shown signs of human interactivity."

Michael questioned, "So as powerful as a werewolf might be, you left this Stephen to die?"

"We did what he asked of us to do, which was to leave the battle and share this information about the falling dust and his death. You two should know that our breed is far outnumbered by those that you yourselves hate," Sheree explained, with both Caleb and Zanth listening attentively.

"I hear you clearly and am sorry for your loss and this war you speak of, or that of what this Stanley believes will happen with the idea that humans will join a side of either vampire or werewolf. I just don't see humans doing so, except with that of other humans, which will strike towards both your breed and those of vampires. Granted, if I were younger and could fight, I would do what I could to salvage your breed, but I feel that this Stanley Swanson is misleading in his thoughts. I think it is time for you all to go, and we wish you the best in the battles that have taken place. My only advice to you three would be to find this Stanley Swanson and try to end these battles between your two kinds as quickly as possible."

S.K. Ballinger

All agreeing that there wasn't much more to do, the pack expressed their gratitude for being allowed to stay for a short while, realizing that finding Stanley, as Michael had suggested, was the best course of action. The three werewolves removed their blankets to put on the clothes provided by Anne's husband.

As Sheree began to put her clothes on, she decided to show Michael and Anne what they had researched for so long by transitioning into her werewolf form. Anne, taken aback, exclaimed, "Oh my lord, not the prettiest of looking things I have ever seen," clasping her right hand over her heart while leaning back in her rocking chair.

Sheree, unfazed, was quick to change back to her human form while grabbing her clothes. She responded to Anne with a calm demeanor, "This is what you researched, and now you have seen. We thank you for your hospitality and kindness towards us. We may not be the prettiest of things, as you said, but we are not the ones that kill humans or change them to be like us."

The atmosphere in the room shifted from shock to a newfound understanding as the werewolves prepared to leave. Michael nodded approvingly, realizing that the creatures he had only read about were standing before him. With a mixture of respect and caution, Anne remarked, "You're right, dear. We've seen much in our time, and I believe these creatures mean us no harm."

The pack bid farewell to the old couple, expressing gratitude once again, and headed out into the cold night. The moon above cast an eerie glow on the landscape as they ventured back into the hills, contemplating the challenges that lay ahead in the impending war between werewolves and vampires.

Stanley Swanson – Breed of a Werewolf

Making their way out the door and thanking Michael and Anne once again, Zanth asked if they could use their car. Michael explained that they couldn't, as it was their only form of transportation. However, he allowed them to use his phone, cautioning them about the limited signal in the remote location.

Grateful for the offer, Sheree tried her best to make a call, but the phone displayed no bars, rendering it useless. Anne, showing her kindness once again, approached with a backpack filled with food, water, and other supplies suitable for humans. The pack expressed their gratitude, shouldered the backpack, and began their journey on foot down from the cabin into the deep valley.

As they walked away on the narrow path, Caleb turned one last time towards the old couple, expressing his appreciation, "One day, if I ever have children of my own, I will share about you two and our short visit this night."

"I hope you can share this moment one day with kids of your own. When they become old enough and you truly wish to share who we were, have them study Van Helsing," Michael responded with sincerity.

None of the werewolves understood the reference, and the future ahead remained unknown as they ventured into the night, grappling with the challenges and mysteries that lay ahead in the impending war between werewolves and vampires.

S.K. Ballinger

TO HOLD CAPTIVE IS TO TEST DEATH

Dimitris, fueled by a deep-seated hatred for werewolves and a desire to exploit any potential weakness in the treaty between the Drakulis and the Lycans, had long awaited an opportunity to further his cruel experiments with the rose's deadly effects on werewolves. Following a recent meeting at the temple where the treaty was discussed, Dimitris wasted no time in initiating his sinister plan.

Eager to continue his quest, he immediately issued orders to his followers and any who were not allied with the Lycans. Their mission was clear: track down and capture as many werewolves as possible. Dimitris emphasized the importance of keeping them alive, as he intended to test various weapons on them. Age was inconsequential to him; he sought a diverse group for experimentation.

Mirroring the Lycans' global campaign against vampires, Dimitris's followers, stationed near his underground facility, started their search. They strategically selected locations frequented by werewolves and keenly observed any reactions to their presence. Poisoned darts, laced with rose extract, were employed to incapacitate the werewolves – Dimitris's calculated gamble that paid off, as the darts proved to be as effective as silver.

In a matter of days, the vampire followers successfully captured seventeen werewolves of varying ages and genders. Satisfied with the count and fearing word spreading to the Lycans, Dimitris ordered an immediate halt to the search. The werewolves were swiftly transported to the underground facility, each held captive in separate chambers.

Inside the facility, Dimitris reveled in the diversity of the captured werewolves – elders, young ones, sons, and daughters. With a sadistic pleasure, he paced back and forth, anticipating the awakening of his captives. The facility displayed an array of weapons crafted from silver and red roses, symbolizing the twisted ingenuity behind his plan.

As time passed, the youngest captives were the first to emerge from their induced comas, crying and disoriented. Dimitris, though annoyed by their cries, remained patient, eagerly waiting for the others to awaken. The once-imprisoned werewolves, from the youngest to the oldest, gradually became aware of their grim surroundings, unaware of the impending horrors that awaited them.

Dimitris reveled in his sadistic anticipation, waiting for the youngest captive to awaken. However, he restrained himself, wanting the entire werewolf breed to witness each horrific test before their own ordeal. The underground facility had been meticulously designed, with separate chambers divided by thick glass walls to ensure that every werewolf could watch the torment inflicted upon their kindred.

Just before the testing commenced, Dimitris, driven by his twisted mind, bellowed loudly, echoing through the chambers.

"Shut up now, you worthless creatures, or I will release fire in each chamber you reside in, one by one."

The threat had the desired effect. The cries of the young children subsided into soft whimpers of fright. With their attention now focused on him, Dimitris continued his macabre announcement.

S.K. Ballinger

"It has been a long time waiting for a moment like this to do whatever I wish upon your breed without violating the treaty. I almost owe your breed a 'thank you' for allowing this to happen, especially a werewolf known as Stanley Swanson."

The werewolves, their faces etched with anguish, could only watch helplessly behind the glass walls. Adult males restrained their emotions, while a few of the oldest females attempted to console the children amidst tears. Two adjacent chambers showcased a heart-wrenching scene—a father and his daughter separated by the glass, their palms pressed against the barrier. Communication between the captives was limited to their eyes, laden with pain and desperation.

As the werewolves aged twelve and older stood on the brink of transition, Dimitris orchestrated another cruel act. With a simple push of a button, a dozen roses descended from the ceiling into each chamber. Almost immediately, the werewolves reverted to their human forms, writhing in agony. Dimitris, reveling in his malevolent joy, amplified his voice through the microphone.

"Let us begin, shall we, and end this noise of filthy and sad hellhounds."

Taking notice of the father and daughter embracing one another, he had one final mention to the father's chamber while approaching the glass of the chamber he was in.

"You hellhound, I am going to take great joy in seeing the love you share die."

The father looking his way pleaded to Dimitris to please not do this as he began to cry. His voice could not be heard to Dimitris which would not have mattered as he continued.

Stanley Swanson – Breed of a Werewolf

"My first test will be done to what I presume to be your daughter." He said with a smile.

As the mist filled the chamber, the cries of the little girl intensified. The werewolves, locked in their separate rooms, were forced to witness the horrifying spectacle unfolding before them. The father, unable to bear the sight, shouted desperately to his daughter, his voice echoing through the chamber.

"Take deep breaths, baby, and end it now, less suffering!"

The agonizing screams of the young werewolf echoed through the facility as the mist, infused with the deadly combination of rose extract and silver shavings, enveloped her. Her small form convulsed in pain, writhing as the poisonous concoction took its toll.

Dimitris, the architect of this sadistic display, observed with a twisted satisfaction. The mist continued to swirl, creating an ethereal yet deadly ambiance within the chamber. The father, his face pressed against the glass, continued to communicate silently with his daughter, offering words of love and encouragement amid his own heart-wrenching sobs.

The other werewolves, confined in their chambers, were paralyzed by the horror unfolding before them. The screams of the little girl seemed to pierce through the thick glass walls, amplifying the collective despair within the facility.

As the mist slowly dissipated, revealing the lifeless body of the young werewolf, the father's cries reached a crescendo of grief. His daughter's life had been extinguished in a manner that transcended the boundaries of cruelty. Dimitris reveled in the despair that now filled the air, savoring the success of his sadistic experiment.

The other werewolves, still locked in their chambers, were left to grapple with the trauma of witnessing such brutality. Dimitris, undeterred by the suffering he had inflicted, relished the psychological torment that lingered among the captives. The facility, now tainted by the echoes of a young life lost, became a haunting testament to Dimitris's malevolence and the fragile nature of the tenuous peace between the Drakulis and the Lycans.

The young werewolf, having heard her father's desperate plea, reacted with a poignant display of bravery. As the mist engulfed her and the torment intensified, she rolled onto her back, taking in a few deep breaths. Her small frame convulsed as she absorbed the lethal combination of rose extract and silver shavings.

Suddenly, her body transformed into a blazing ball of fire, a manifestation of intense agony and an unimaginable end. The flames consumed her entirely, leaving nothing but ashes behind. The father, still witnessing the tragic spectacle, was overcome with grief.

With the last remnants of strength, the weakened father staggered toward Dimitris, his eyes ablaze with fury and despair. Slamming his fists against the thick glass that separated them, he yelled at Dimitris, their faces almost nose to nose through the barrier.

"I hope to see you in hell!"

The father's voice reverberated with a mixture of anguish and rage. His words, fueled by the depths of his despair, echoed through the chamber. Dimitris, unfazed by the emotional outburst, met the father's gaze with a cold, unyielding stare. The display of defiance only seemed to amuse Dimitris further, as if the werewolf's pain and rage were nothing more than entertainment.

    The other captive werewolves, locked in their respective chambers, could only bear witness to this harrowing scene. The fiery demise of the young werewolf had left an indelible mark on their collective psyche. The atmosphere within the facility hung heavy with grief, anger, and the sinister satisfaction of the malevolent Drakulis leader.

    Dimitris, standing unscathed on the other side of the glass, reveled in the chaos he had orchestrated. The father, left alone with the ashes of his daughter, continued to seethe with a burning desire for vengeance. The facility, now tainted with the ashes of innocent life, became a chilling testament to the depths of cruelty orchestrated by Dimitris and the impending unraveling of the fragile treaty between the Drakulis and the Lycans.

    In the aftermath of the horrifying spectacle he orchestrated, Dimitris reveled in the twisted satisfaction that only the Drakulis leader could derive from such sadistic acts. As he uttered his chilling parting words to the father who had just witnessed his daughter's agonizing demise, each chamber housing different tests of weaponry went off simultaneously.

    The facility echoed with the anguished screams of werewolves subjected to various torment, each perishing with a unique and gruesome outcome. The air was thick with the scent of blood, fear, and burning flesh. The cacophony of suffering reached a crescendo before abruptly falling silent, leaving only the haunting residue of tragedy.

    Dimitris, unaffected by the horrors he had unleashed,

wasted no time in clearing the way to observe the aftermath. The once-soundproof glass walls of the chambers revealed the aftermath of his sadistic experiments, showcasing the effectiveness of his newly devised weapons. The satisfaction on Dimitris's face was palpable as he surveyed the lifeless forms within the chambers. Each test had served its purpose, and manufacturing of these lethal instruments of destruction would soon commence.

Seizing the opportunity for personal gratification, Dimitris relished the thrill of his newfound passion. His centuries-old existence had been void of such intense emotions, and the love for inflicting pain and suffering upon his enemies filled a void that time had failed to satisfy.

Ignoring the activities of his brother Siluk, who was engrossed in his own pursuits, Dimitris was eager to share the success of his sadistic experiments with the rest of the Drakulis council. His followers, obediently carrying out their leader's orders, swiftly began the grim task of cleaning up the aftermath and preparing for mass production of the gruesome weapons.

In his twisted satisfaction, Dimitris reveled in the chaos he had unleashed, savoring every moment of this dark chapter that would undoubtedly send ripples through the delicate balance of power between the Drakulis and the Lycans. The gruesome events within the underground facility were just the beginning of Dimitris's malevolent machinations, signaling an ominous shift in the dynamics of the age-old conflict between the two immortal breeds.

ORDERS OF SILUK

Siluk, having gathered the Drakulis and vampires in the stronghold of San Antonio, Texas, took his place at the center of the circle within the imposing building. With the signed consent form from the council in hand, he addressed the assembly of eighty-two, making it clear that they were bound by the decisions made.

"I have before me the signed consent form from the council, and you all will abide by it. The purpose of this meeting is that of war, which has started because a mindless breed of a werewolf has broken the treaty. If you have not yet heard or watched the news as of late, you will hear from me now."

However, one Drakulis in the assembly voiced his skepticism about Siluk's awareness of the ongoing events.

"It is not even that of a war in general. Where have you been as of late? Do you not have followers? If not, then it would appear that you pace this earth as lonely. We are very aware of the happenings of what has been taking place over the course of a month, Siluk."

Siluk responded, addressing the concerns raised.

"You know of the battles being taken place in other countries where the breed have killed many of us and the discovery of the red rose that kills them?"

"Yes, we are aware of all that, and we are also aware that weapons are being made to do so. While we honor the form and will do what you ask of us, we do not need human's involvement. While we need to act accordingly, we need to do so wisely," another Drakulis asserted.

Siluk acknowledged the validity of their concerns but emphasized the urgency of the situation.

"This is true of what you say, but it has quickly become that time. Gravakus, as most of you know, has joined sides, and in the form, we shall retain him to bring to the temple and present him to my father Sirtimi."

The tension in the room lingered as Siluk outlined the gravity of the situation and the necessity for decisive action. The shadows cast by the gathered Drakulis and vampires seemed to intensify as they contemplated the impending conflict that would shape the fate of both their kind and the werewolves they were poised to face."

As the discussion unfolded, another Drakulis rose to offer his perspective on the matter, acknowledging the importance of honoring the council's consent.

"My suggestion to you, as we will do our part while your brother is doing his, though he is not right-minded in his actions, would be to lure this Stanley Swanson in to us. Make fair grounds and kill him in front of all to see. End this nonsense and let both our respective beings be as we have been. In time, Gravakus will be retained and quickly punished accordingly as he is a fool."

Siluk, receptive to the proposal, questioned the urgency surrounding the potential war with humans.

"While I agree with you, we have not found the written journal that was shared between the mortal and Stanley. Why do you not sense the urgency of a war between not only our kind but that of humans?"

The Drakulis responded confidently, "Because we know that the mortal has died by your hands, and even though the journal was never found since you lacked that in your quest to find it, humans are naive to even consider battling against us, and that is why."

Despite the ongoing discussions, Siluk found himself challenged by the fact that he had no knowledge of the journal's whereabouts. The first Drakulis to speak up expressed his concern.

"The problem I have, Siluk, is that there is a journal that shares a lot or possibly all information about both our kinds, but you fail to have it?"

Siluk, visibly upset, retorted, "Tell me, what have you done as of late other than make more followers? Have you or any of you not been following the breed of werewolves, and if not for my brother Dimitris, I might be as foolish as yourselves on the occurring events."

The room fell into an uneasy silence, broken by the Drakulis who had questioned Siluk initially.

"You will not come in here and act as though we are all fools as you suggest! We follow the breeds, and as for your brother Dimitris, he is nothing more than a psychotic and ruthless killer. Do not speak of his name again while in this room!"

Siluk, maintaining his assertive demeanor, couldn't hide the disappointment in the current disagreement.

"I am ashamed of this argument we are having, and that you stand before me while taking all of this so lightly. We have more weapons now of this discovery that my brother has worked hard to build off, Kain is dead just as both Julie and Stephen Swanson are, and yet we have a traitor of ours working with Stanley. Do tell me that action is not needed?"

One of the Drakulis responded, acknowledging the need for action and expressing a willingness to follow Siluk's lead.

"Action is needed; that is why we are listening to you to begin with. Tell us what you wish for us to do, Siluk."

Siluk laid out a clear plan, emphasizing a decisive and aggressive approach.

"It is simple. Go to every small town and city of this state, seek out all breeds, and kill them. They broke the treaty, and this is now our time."

Another Drakulis, prepared to take charge, volunteered to form a large group and prepare for battle.

"I will form a large group and prepare for battle. What of you, Siluk?"

Siluk, unwavering in his commitment, outlined his broader strategy.

"I am taking this form from the council and sharing with all states that are strong in us to have them do just as you all are going to do. Then I will be meeting up with my brother to see how his new toys of destruction to the breed are coming along."

Stanley Swanson – Breed of a Werewolf

The room resonated with a renewed sense of purpose as the Drakulis pledged to follow Siluk's instructions and engage in a coordinated effort to eliminate the werewolves who had violated the treaty. The unfolding events hinted at a war on the horizon, with both the Drakulis and the Lycans preparing for a conflict that threatened the uneasy balance established over the centuries.

Siluk, having concluded the intense meeting with the Drakulis in Texas, carefully placed the consent form back into his jacket. His next destination was another state, where he planned to rally more followers and initiate a widespread offensive against the werewolves. Arizona, having already taken the initiative, was a clear sign that the Drakulis were mobilizing swiftly.

As Siluk moved forward with his plans, phone calls echoed through the dark corridors of the Drakulis' power structure. Leaders reached out to their followers in various parts of the world, coordinating their actions and sharing information. The reports that came in were mixed, revealing both successes and losses in battles against the werewolves. It became evident that the once-submissive creatures had grown into a formidable force.

Amid the discussions and updates, a Drakulis in particular drew attention by contacting a follower in England. The room fell into a hushed silence as he requested everyone to be quiet, preparing to share critical information. The footage from the follower's phone left the assembled Drakulis in shock. They witnessed the werewolves, once considered mere slaves, emerging as a significant and united threat. The realization struck them hard, dispelling any notions that the attacks were minor. Siluk seized the moment to reinforce the severity of the situation.

"Now you see how severe this has become," Siluk

declared as he left the room.

The movement initiated in Texas gained momentum rapidly. The war against all werewolf breeds was not taken lightly; it became a relentless pursuit with the sole purpose of eliminating every last werewolf. The Drakulis, fueled by a burning desire to reclaim dominance and erase the memory of werewolves once being their slaves, orchestrated a series of strategic attacks. The orders were clear: hunt down Stanley Swanson and Gravakus, the traitor among them. The hunt for both began, setting the stage for a brutal and escalating conflict between the Drakulis and the Lycans.

CHANGE OF PLAN

Stanley listened intently as Jeremia conveyed the recent successes the pack had achieved against the vampires. He felt a mixture of pride for his pack's resilience and anger at the escalating violence that was now engulfing the supernatural world. The mention of a Drakulis being obliterated in Germany piqued Stanley's interest, and he asked Jeremia to share more details.

"Jeremia, I get that we're hitting them hard, but this war, it's not going to be in our favor for long. We've got to be smart about this," Stanley urged, concern evident in his voice.

Jeremia, being the more aggressive and hot-headed member of the pack, responded with enthusiasm, "Stanley, we've got them on the run. We can't just back down now. We need to show them that we won't be pushed around anymore. Besides, we're making progress with the antidote. Once that's ready, we'll have an upper hand like never before."

Stanley sighed, understanding the pack's eagerness for revenge. "Jeremia, I know we're making strides, but we can't underestimate the Drakulis. They're ruthless, and they won't stop until they wipe us out. We've got to be strategic about our moves."

The conversation continued, with Jeremia advocating for continued attacks and Stanley insisting on a more cautious approach. The tension in the air was palpable as the pack leader tried to balance the desire for retaliation with the need for long-term survival. Stanley, having seen the horrors of the past, was wary of the consequences of an all-out war.

In the midst of their heated discussion, Stanley's mind

raced with thoughts of his children, Sabe and Jade. The fear for their safety intensified, and he couldn't shake the worry that they might get caught in the crossfire of the brewing conflict. Jeremia, sensing Stanley's internal struggle, finally relented, acknowledging the need for a careful strategy.

"Alright, Stanley. We'll ease off for now. But once we have that antidote ready, we're not holding back anymore. We'll show them what we're made of," Jeremia declared, the fire in his voice undeterred.

As the conversation concluded, Stanley couldn't shake the feeling that the calm before the storm was merely an illusion, and the pack's journey was about to take a more perilous turn.

Francais, the wise and thoughtful member of the pack, listened attentively as Stanley expressed his concerns about the escalating attacks. Stanley, aware of the potential consequences of the current strategy, emphasized the need for a more organized and strategic approach.

"   Please listen to me, Francais. The breed won't take my word for it, but you, being wise, must see that these ambushed attacks and slaughters need to end. We must form a better plan to counter their moves. These small attacks will only escalate into a full-blown war if we don't act now. I believe I can prevent that from happening," Stanley urged.

Francais, ever contemplative, acknowledged Stanley's concerns. "I understand what you're telling me, Stanley, but the damage has already been done. I think the best option is to wait until you land and arrive here to further discuss. Right now is not a good time to make any sudden moves and leave our current area."

Stanley Swanson – Breed of a Werewolf

Despite Stanley's initial plan to fly to England, he started to doubt the wisdom of that decision. He considered the possibility that England had already fallen under the control of the breed. Francais' caution and the uncertainty of the situation compelled Stanley to change his mind.

"You're right, Francais. I'll stay in the United States for now. We need to assess the situation and plan our next moves carefully. Let's prioritize the safety of the pack and avoid unnecessary risks," Stanley conceded.

Francais, sensing Stanley's unease, assured him, "We'll discuss this further when you arrive. For now, focus on getting back safely."

With that, the conversation ended, leaving Stanley with a mix of relief and concern. He knew that the challenges ahead required a united and strategic front, and he hoped that the pack could navigate the brewing storm with wisdom and resilience.

The following days were a hectic scramble for Francais as he worked diligently to contact every member of their pack and convince them to regroup. In a world where breeds followed the orders or suggestions of their wisest pack member, convincing them to change their approach required tact, persuasion, and a strong sense of leadership.

Francais spent hours on calls, patiently explaining Stanley's concerns and the urgent need for a change in strategy. Some members were resistant, having become accustomed to the thrill and success of their recent attacks. Others were skeptical about altering their course based on warnings from afar. It was a delicate dance of diplomacy, with Francais leveraging his wisdom and influence to bring the pack members on board.

One by one, Francais managed to get through to the various members of their global pack. He emphasized the importance of unity and strategic planning, painting a vivid picture of the potential consequences if they continued down the current path. As the wisest member of the pack, his words held weight, and gradually, the attacks began to dwindle.

The process was not without its challenges. Francais had to navigate different time zones, languages, and cultural nuances, making each conversation a unique negotiation. Some breeds were more receptive to his pleas, while others required more convincing. It was a testament to Francais' leadership skills that he could rally the diverse pack members under a unified cause.

Meanwhile, Stanley eagerly awaited the return of his pack. He had asked Francais to explain the situation to his children, emphasizing the necessity of regrouping and strategizing. Stanley understood the difficulty of Francais' task and appreciated the effort put into convincing the pack members scattered across the globe.

As the week progressed, Francais saw the fruits of his labor. The attacks that had once been relentless were now almost nonexistent. The pack members started to heed Francais' counsel, realizing the gravity of the situation and the need for a unified front.

Francais and his pack caught an early flight out of England, making their way back to the United States to join Stanley. Drennan, who was in Germany, also began preparations to reunite with the pack. The wheels were set in motion for a strategic and united response to the escalating conflict, thanks to Francais' dedicated efforts in steering the pack away from the brink of all-out war.

THE CAPTURE OF GRAVAKUS

As Gravakus addressed his followers in the dimly lit room, there was an air of tension and uncertainty. The loyal group that had stood by him for centuries now gathered around a large table, their eyes fixed on their leader, sensing the gravity of the situation.

"Friends of mine," Gravakus began, his voice resonating with a mixture of weariness and determination. "I think we need to prepare ourselves for what I would like to call a fight. You all have been so loyal to me, and some for as long as a few hundred years. I have made a choice that has put myself in this situation, and now I will face my fate."

His followers, a diverse mix of vampires from different backgrounds and eras, exchanged glances. There was a palpable tension in the room, as they grappled with the reality that their leader was openly acknowledging the consequences of his actions. The loyalty they felt toward Gravakus, forged over centuries, now faced a severe test.

Gravakus continued, his eyes scanning the faces of those gathered. "I have chosen to stand against the council, against my brethren, for a cause that I believe is just. The war that is brewing between our kind and the werewolves is inevitable, and I have chosen a side. The side that I believe will lead to a future that is more than just endless bloodshed."

He paused, allowing his words to sink in. The room remained silent, the weight of the impending conflict hanging heavily in the air.

"I want each of you to understand the risks we face,"

Gravakus continued. "The other Drakulis will come for me, and they will not be gentle. But I stand by my decision, and I stand by each of you. We will face whatever comes our way together."

The atmosphere in the room shifted, and some of the followers nodded in agreement, their expressions determined. Gravakus, despite his weariness, exuded a sense of conviction that resonated with his followers.

"Prepare yourselves, my friends. We may be on the brink of a war that will shape the future of our kind. But whatever happens, know that I appreciate your unwavering loyalty, and I am proud to call you my followers," Gravakus concluded, his gaze lingering on each face around the table.

The followers, now united in their resolve, began discussing strategies, fortifications, and contingencies. The impending conflict loomed large, but in the face of adversity, Gravakus and his followers prepared to stand together, ready to face the consequences of the choices they had made.

Gravakus stood firm, a lone figure in the dimly lit room, as his followers gathered behind him, forming an unspoken shield of protection. The atmosphere was charged with uncertainty, and the air seemed to thicken as the room became a battleground of conflicting loyalties.

"It has been a pleasure having you all by my side," Gravakus stated, his words carrying both gratitude and resignation. His followers, some of whom had stood by him for centuries, exchanged glances, grappling with the impending confrontation.

As the words lingered in the air, a subtle light fog began to seep under the door, a manifestation of the approaching Drakulis. Gravakus, recognizing the sign, turned his attention toward the front door. The fog subtly coalesced into the form of a Drakulis, a representation of the looming threat that had come to confront the disgraced vampire.

"You have seemed to have become a disgrace and traitor to us, Gravakus," the Drakulis declared, their tone accusatory and laced with disdain. The followers behind Gravakus tensed, ready to defend their leader, but Gravakus motioned for them to stand down.

"Do not waste your time, my friends, as this is my battle," Gravakus demanded, his voice carrying a sense of finality. His followers hesitated but ultimately complied, their gazes shifting between Gravakus and the Drakulis confronting him.

The room was enveloped in a tense silence, broken only by the subtle hiss of the fog dissipating. The Drakulis, still maintaining a formidable stance, eyed Gravakus with a mixture of disdain and anticipation.

Gravakus faced the Drakulis head-on, his expression unyielding. "I have made my choice, and I stand by it. The war that is unfolding between our kind and the werewolves is inevitable, and I have chosen the side that I believe holds a chance for a different future. If you must pass judgment, then let it be swift."

The Drakulis, clearly agitated by Gravakus's defiance, took a step forward, the tension in the room escalating. The followers, though prepared for conflict, remained at a standstill, waiting for the confrontation between their leader and the council representative to unfold.

Unfortunately for him, his friends who were extremely protective and loyal had been notified of the council of what he had done. Gravakus was blindsided as his once loyal followers and those that he called friends had ganged up on him. There was nothing he could in such short notice as he began to be beaten. Then the Drakulis let it be known to him of who he was.

As Mahlistaff revealed his identity and spoke with authority, Gravakus felt the weight of his betrayal sinking in. The room became heavy with an unspoken judgment, and his followers watched in solemn silence as the scene unfolded.

"I am Mahlistaff of the council, and I am sure you do not recognize me as you do not your righteous self, which is one with such gifted abilities. You think any of us would stay true to a traitor, little lone one that is helpful to a breed, a hellhound. You have failed miserably, Gravakus, and now you will be taken back to the temple to meet your fate as you may already know," Mahlistaff declared with disdain. "Such a shame to us for so many years to know now that you were never meant to be a powerful Drakulis. I hope you are proud of what you have done, fool, as your death will be that like never before."

Gravakus, overpowered and bleeding the signature black blood of his kind, could only lie on the floor, a defeated figure in the face of the council's judgment. The room echoed with the gravity of his actions, and his loyal followers, conflicted by their allegiance and the undeniable truth before them, could do little more than watch in silence.

"Get this pathetic and weak friend of the slaves off the ground. It is time to return to the temple where he will face his punishment," Mahlistaff commanded, his tone unforgiving. Gravakus's followers, torn between loyalty and the council's decree, moved forward reluctantly to lift their fallen leader.

The room, once filled with the anticipation of battle, now felt suffocating with the inevitability of Gravakus's fate. As the followers gathered around him, they exchanged glances, their expressions reflecting a mix of sorrow and anger. The path ahead was clear – a return to the temple and a confrontation with the consequences of Gravakus's choices awaited.

The journey to Santa Cruz with Gravakus in tow was a grim procession, marked by the echoes of his followers' desperate attempts to free him. A handful of loyal Drakulis made futile efforts to intervene, but Mahlistaff, swift and deadly, dismantled their resistance with chilling efficiency. Before they could launch a single strike, Mahlistaff moved with supernatural speed, tearing through them and leaving lifeless bodies in his wake. Eight loyal followers, devoted until the end, paid the ultimate price for their allegiance.

As the loyalists fell, the rest of Gravakus's followers, though saddened by the loss, seemed strangely satisfied. The mission had been accomplished, and their fallen comrades had fought for a cause they believed in. The air was thick with tension, the aftermath of a skirmish that pitted brother against brother, loyalist against defector.

The journey continued towards Santa Cruz, where the imposing temple awaited Gravakus's return. The council's judgment loomed, and with each passing moment, the inevitability of his fate became more apparent. The whispers among the followers spoke of uncertainty, fear, and the somber recognition that they had played a part in a betrayal that would not be easily forgiven.

Simultaneously, Stanley Swanson, unknowingly pursued by the Drakulis, navigated his own challenges. The vampires and Drakulis, eager for retribution, hoped that his capture would be swift and decisive, mirroring the ease with which Gravakus had been apprehended. The night, heavy with anticipation, held the promise of upheaval and consequences for both the traitor and the unwitting hero caught in the web of the brewing conflict.

THE CAPTURE OF STANLEY SWANSON

Stanley, in a secluded and shadowy spot, could feel the impending danger approaching. The air thickened with the scent of vampires, and his heightened senses confirmed the presence of Drakulis. It wasn't long before the figures materialized – two of them. To Stanley's dismay, one was none other than Siluk, a formidable adversary.

The father and son vampire trackers, relentless in their pursuit, had stayed on Stanley's trail since the highway battle. Their tenacity was unwavering, and now, with Siluk joining the hunt, the odds were stacked against the lone werewolf.

Realizing the imminent threat, Stanley wasted no time and swiftly placed a call to his pack. The urgency in his voice was palpable as he left a message on Francais' line.

"Take caution on your landing and travel to my home. I have heard of a breed named Sheree who was with my brother, and I suggest you do what you can to find contact with her. I am in danger, but I will find you in time. Send my love to Sabe and Jade."

The message conveyed both the urgency of the situation and the concern for his pack's safety. Stanley, isolated but resolute, prepared to confront the approaching Drackulis and vampires, aware that this encounter could alter the course of the ongoing conflict between the breeds.

In the confined space, the struggle intensified as Siluk led the charge, vampires pouring in behind him. Stanley, quick to respond, fought back with all his werewolf strength, using biting, clawing, and brute force to hold his ground against the overwhelming numbers. The small shelter became a battleground, echoing with the sounds of a fierce confrontation.

As the skirmish raged on, Siluk, seemingly unhurried, closed in on Stanley. The fear in Stanley's eyes grew as he noticed Siluk retrieving a bag of rose powder from his inside coat pocket. The threat of the lethal substance was imminent, and Stanley had to act swiftly to avoid falling victim to the deadly roses.

Two critical thoughts raced through Stanley's mind. Firstly, uncertainty lingered about the duration of the previous injection's effectiveness, leaving him in the dark about his current level of protection. Secondly, he realized that he needed to inject himself again, and time was of the essence. On the coffee table nearby, he spotted one of the few shots he had taken earlier.

With sheer determination, Stanley fought off the attacking vampires, creating a brief opening to reach the shot. As he injected himself, Siluk, with a sinister grin, released a cloud of rose powder into the air in Stanley's direction. Realizing the potential implications of the situation, Stanley, driven by instinct, sprinted to a nearby bag containing additional shots.

Wary of the vampires discovering the existence of the antidote, Stanley swiftly injected all the remaining shots into his legs. Uncertain of the outcome but knowing it was his only option, he braced himself for what lay ahead, surrounded by adversaries in the dimly lit space. The battle had taken a dire turn, and the fate of Stanley hung in the balance as the encounter unfolded.

Siluk, reveling in the triumph over Stanley, approached

him with sadistic pleasure evident in his eyes. Stanley, having injected himself with the antidote, played the part of a defeated werewolf, feigning the effects of the rose powder.

"Oh, how I love roses!" Siluk exclaimed with a twisted thrill, kneeling down beside Stanley as he continued his gloating monologue.

He marveled at the irony that something as beloved as a simple flower could be deadly to Stanley's breed. Siluk expressed his desire to inflict the same fiery fate on Stanley as he had on his wife but acknowledged the constraints placed by his father and the council. Despite his contentment with the prospect of Stanley's prolonged suffering, Siluk couldn't resist delivering a final ominous promise.

"Your death cannot come soon enough, you idiot. Your council, like that of your father, are ignorant. Let us not forget the written journal and to which hands it remains in. I will see to it myself that you will die slowly by my hands either now or later," Stanley retorted defiantly, shedding tears for his lost brother.

Siluk, angered by Stanley's words, momentarily set aside his father's wishes and produced a rose petal. He demanded that Stanley open his mouth, intent on initiating the fiery end for the werewolf. However, another vampire reminded Siluk of the council's directive to keep both Stanley and Gravakus alive.

With his immediate danger averted, Stanley seized the opportunity to deliver a final word, promising revenge and a slow demise for Siluk. Siluk, still harboring anger, expressed his wish to present a plea to the council to personally place the rose petal in Stanley's mouth after the impending torture at the temple.

As the ominous atmosphere lingered, Stanley prepared for the trials that awaited him at the temple, uncertain of the outcome but resolved to endure whatever suffering came his way. Siluk, fueled by vengeful delight, relished the prospect of witnessing Stanley's torment and eagerly anticipated the day he could contribute to the werewolf's final demise. The fate of the Swanson legacy hung in the balance, caught in the web of vampire machinations and werewolf resilience.

Stanley, feigning weakness, allowed himself to be captured, his thoughts consumed by the uncertainty of Gravakus's fate. A mixture of nervousness and fear lingered in his mind, but the realization that death wasn't imminent brought a certain degree of comfort. Exhausted from the relentless battles and losses, Stanley resigned himself to the grim circumstances, no longer finding strength in resisting.

In the midst of the despair, he clung to a few sources of hope. The necklace around his neck, holding his wife's ring and symbolizing the imminent reunion with his children, became a talisman of strength. The mere thought of embracing his kids in a day's time bolstered his resolve in the face of the unfolding tragedy.

"Drag this worthless hellhound on the ground to the vehicle and let us make our way," Siluk commanded, his tone dripping with disdain for the werewolf.

Without hesitation, the vampires seized Stanley's weakened form and callously threw him into the awaiting vehicle. As the engine roared to life, the group began their journey back to the Temple, the tension inside the vehicle palpable. Stanley, naked and vulnerable, braced himself for whatever awaited him at the heart of the vampire stronghold, contemplating the twists of fate that had led him to this dire moment. The wheels of destiny were set in motion, converging on the Temple where the stage was being set for the next chapter of Stanley Swanson's tragic saga.

S.K. Ballinger

TRIAL

Both Gravakus and Stanley, the captives with intertwined destinies, arrived at the imposing Temple within a day of each other. The Temple housed not only numerous Drackulis but also several hundred vampires, creating an environment ripe with tension and anticipation.

Sirtimi, the patriarch of the council, voiced his command. "Bring them both before me!"

The resonance of his authoritative voice echoed through the grand hallways of the Temple. The Drakulis and vampires swiftly obeyed, ushering the captured werewolf and traitorous Drakulis towards the central chamber where Sirtimi awaited.

As they approached, Stanley and Gravakus exchanged glances, their eyes filled with a mixture of weariness, defiance, and an unspoken acknowledgment of the tumultuous journey that had brought them here. The bond forged in the face of adversity was evident, a connection born from shared struggles and a realization that their fates were inextricably intertwined.

The Temple, adorned with ancient symbols and adorned with dark elegance, loomed large around them, adding an aura of foreboding to the impending confrontation. As the captives were brought closer to the heart of the Temple, the atmosphere crackled with an indescribable energy—a portent of the pivotal moments that were about to unfold.

The tension in the room was palpable, the air heavy with the weight of centuries-old conflicts and animosity. Gravakus, defiant and resolute, continued to voice his dissent, challenging the very core beliefs of the council.

"Balance is what we need; do you not see this, you fools!" Gravakus's voice echoed through the grand chamber.

Sirtimi, angered by the audacity of the traitor, responded with disdain. "You dare raise your voice to us in this temple, traitor."

The council, consisting of powerful Drackulis, watched the unfolding drama with a mix of curiosity and disdain. Sirtimi, the patriarch, continued his tirade against Gravakus, dismissing the notion of balance and asserting their superiority.

"Do you think that I or we do not know of the small war you started over three hundred years ago, as you sat back and watched when it was you that started it?" Sirtimi's words reverberated through the chamber. "You say before me it was for this 'balance' you claim. There is no balance as we are made to rule!"

Gravakus, undeterred by the condemnation, retorted with conviction. "You have grown blind to the truth, Sirtimi. The balance is fragile, and your insatiable desire for dominance will lead us to our demise."

The council members exchanged glances, some scoffing at Gravakus's words, while others contemplated the notion of a delicate equilibrium between species. The air in the room seemed charged, the clash of opposing ideologies creating an undercurrent of uncertainty.

Meanwhile, Stanley, weakened and distraught, stood silently beside Gravakus, his mind consumed by the loss of his wife, brother, and the looming threat to his children. The necklace, a poignant reminder of the family he once had, now rested in the hands of Sirtimi, a cruel trophy of the council's triumph.

Sirtimi, reveling in the perceived victory, addressed the council. "Let this be a lesson to all breeds. We are the rulers, the supreme beings. No one shall challenge our authority."

The fate of Stanley and Gravakus hung in the balance, their destinies uncertain in the face of a relentless and merciless council. The echoes of their pleas for mercy and justice reverberated through the hallowed halls of the Temple, unheard and ignored by those who deemed themselves the masters of night.

Stanley, weakened and defeated, could only nod in acknowledgment of Gravakus's words. The descent down the cold, dark staircase seemed to stretch into eternity as both vampires were led to their grim fate. Chains rattled with every step, a morose symphony accompanying their march towards the impending torture.

As they reached the dimly lit underground chamber, an atmosphere of malevolence hung heavy in the air. The room, adorned with ancient symbols and flickering torches, exuded an aura of dread that sent shivers down their spines. Sirtimi, Siluk, and the council members followed, eager to witness the torment they had orchestrated.

"Welcome to the final chapter of your existence," Sirtimi announced, his voice echoing off the stone walls.

The guards positioned Stanley and Gravakus side by side, their chains fastened to sturdy pillars, rendering any escape futile.

Siluk, fueled by vindictive fury, stood poised, ready to exact revenge upon Gravakus. The anticipation in the room was palpable, an unspoken understanding that this was a momentous occasion for the Drakulis hierarchy.

"Father, may I begin with Stanley?" Siluk requested, his eyes gleaming with malice.

"Proceed," Sirtimi granted with a nod.

Siluk approached Stanley, a cruel smile on his face. "Oh, how the mighty will fall. You'll get a taste of the torment you brought upon our kind."

Stanley, his gaze fixed on the ground, braced himself for the impending agony. The council members watched with indifferent expressions, reveling in the sadistic spectacle.

Gravakus, standing beside Stanley, whispered words of comfort. "Stay strong. We face this together."

Siluk, reveling in the torment, brought forth a vial containing a crimson liquid—rose extract. With deliberate slowness, he dipped a dagger into the vial and approached Stanley. The room fell into an eerie silence, interrupted only by the echoing footsteps of Siluk.

As the blade drew near, Stanley's mind raced. He knew the torment he was about to endure would be excruciating. But amidst the fear and despair, a spark of resilience flickered within him. He would not grant his captors the satisfaction of witnessing his complete submission.

Siluk, relishing the moment, lifted the dagger, ready to

inflict pain upon Stanley. The council members observed with sinister delight, eager to witness the suffering they had orchestrated. The underground chamber, steeped in darkness, became a stage for the unfolding tragedy of two beings ensnared by fate, awaiting the cruel hands of their oppressors.

Stanley's defiant words echoed through the cold, dimly lit chamber, challenging the executioner despite the excruciating pain from the silver knife embedded in his thigh. The atmosphere thickened with anticipation as the executioner, unfazed by the threat, considered his next move.

Sirtimi, observing from a distance, chuckled at Stanley's futile resistance. "Such spirit in the face of agony. We shall see how long that lasts."

The executioner, savoring the torment he was about to unleash, approached the table laden with instruments of suffering. He selected a rose, its crimson petals gleaming ominously under the flickering torchlight.

With deliberate intent, the executioner traced the rose along Stanley's exposed chest, the thorns leaving small trails of blood in their wake. Stanley winced, the pain intensifying with each prick of the thorns. The scent of the rose, once associated with love and beauty, now became a harbinger of despair.

"You may reconsider your threat, Mr. Swanson, for we have a limitless array of methods to extract your suffering," the executioner remarked, his tone dripping with sadistic glee.

Meanwhile, Gravakus endured the relentless onslaught of ocean mist. Each burst of saltwater brought searing pain, the constant healing preventing him from finding solace in death. The misters, like malevolent specters, continued their relentless assault on his immortal form.

Back in the glass room, Gravakus gazed through the transparent walls, witnessing Stanley's ordeal unfold. Despite their dire circumstances, a silent understanding passed between them. Their shared history and the bond forged through adversity bolstered their resilience.

Stanley, subjected to various forms of torture, refused to break. His body bore the scars of silver and thorns, yet his spirit remained unbroken. In the face of unrelenting agony, he found a sliver of strength within, drawing upon the memory of his wife and children for solace.

The council members, seated on ornate thrones, observed the scene with a detached fascination. Sirtimi reveled in the suffering, convinced that he held absolute dominion over these defiant creatures.

As the executioner continued his sadistic dance, the chamber resonated with the anguished cries of the tormented vampires. The once stone-cold walls bore witness to the brutality orchestrated by those who deemed themselves gods. Yet, in the shadows of despair, a flicker of resistance burned, refusing to be extinguished.

The voice startled Stanley as he slowly regained consciousness. Groggily, he looked around, trying to make sense of his surroundings. The night air was crisp, and the distant sounds of the temple were but a faint echo. Gravakus, still recovering, stirred beside him.

"We have to move," the voice urged again, and this time,

Stanley recognized it. It was Gravakus, speaking through their mental connection. The bond between them, forged in shared pain and adversity, allowed for communication beyond spoken words.

Cautiously, Stanley rose, his muscles protesting the exertion. Gravakus, though weakened, managed to stand beside him. They took a moment to assess their surroundings, and Stanley, guided by Gravakus's knowledge of the temple grounds, led them away from the imposing structure.

As they limped through the night, the weight of their injuries evident, Gravakus spoke to Stanley through their mental link. "We need to find shelter, somewhere hidden. They'll be looking for us, especially after what you did back there."

Stanley nodded in agreement, understanding the gravity of their situation. The bond they shared not only facilitated communication but also allowed them to sense each other's emotions and intentions. It was a connection that ran deeper than any physical wounds inflicted upon them.

Following Gravakus's guidance, they reached a secluded area obscured by dense foliage. The moonlight barely penetrated the thick canopy, providing them with a momentary respite. Gravakus, still weakened from the misters' relentless assault, leaned against a tree, his eyes reflecting a mixture of gratitude and pain.

"We can't stay here for long. They will send trackers," Gravakus warned, the urgency evident in his mental tone.

Stanley, catching his breath, agreed. "We need to keep moving, find a way to regroup with the pack. And we can't let them trace us back to the others."

Stanley Swanson – Breed of a Werewolf

As they ventured further into the shadows, Stanley couldn't shake the haunting images of the temple and the unspeakable cruelty that transpired within its walls. The taste of freedom, albeit fleeting, fueled their determination to escape the clutches of the Drakulis council.

The night unfolded in a series of painful steps, each one bringing them closer to a sanctuary that existed beyond the reach of their pursuers. The bond between Stanley and Gravakus, forged in the crucible of suffering, became their silent strength as they navigated the treacherous path of survival in a world where shadows concealed both allies and enemies.

Stanley and Gravakus, guided by the necessity of survival, found themselves on the run, seeking refuge from the relentless pursuit of the Drakulis council. Gravakus, fully recovered from the burns inflicted by the misters, took the lead, his knowledge of hidden sanctuaries proving invaluable.

As they moved through the shadows, Gravakus offered his jacket to Stanley, a simple yet meaningful gesture in the face of their shared adversity. The night air carried a sense of urgency, and Gravakus, the once-traitor to the council, now stood as a comrade forged in the crucible of escape.

"Take my jacket, but we must leave this area now. They are coming after us, Stanley, and are highly pissed off as no one has ever escaped the temple before. I thank you for saving my life, and one day will return the favor, I promise you," Gravakus urged, his voice a mixture of urgency and gratitude.

Stanley, still carrying the weight of his dreams, contemplated the idea of returning for his necklace. Gravakus, understanding the danger of such a venture, advised against it.

"Let us leave now, and I promise you, Stanley, I will get your necklace back for you."

With a mutual agreement, they pressed on, leaving the haunting grounds of the temple behind. Their path led them to the notion of finding a crowded place, a refuge where the masses would provide cover against potential attacks.

A cruise ship, Gravakus suggested, became their chosen sanctuary – a floating haven amid a sea of people. Stanley, cautious but intrigued, questioned the plan's feasibility. Gravakus reassured him, emphasizing the safety in numbers that the ship would provide.

"That would be mighty brave of you, Gravakus, and especially after you nearly died from ocean water. Are you sure about this, friend?" Stanley inquired, a term of camaraderie now woven into their shared journey.

"Ah, you finally referred to me as a friend, and yes, I think it is the safest option we have while everything around us unfolds," Gravakus replied with a confident yet weary smile.

The decision made, they sought out a phone to order their tickets, their escape plan unfolding against the backdrop of uncertainty and the relentless pursuit of the Drakulis council.

Siluk stormed into the cellar, his rage palpable as he discovered the lifeless body of the executioner, sprawled on the ground, his shadow lingering as a haunting reminder of the failed attempt to keep Stanley and Gravakus captive. A mix of anger and disbelief painted Siluk's expression as he took in the scene.

"They've escaped!" Siluk exclaimed, his voice echoing

through the dark, ominous corridors of the temple. In a swift and determined move, he rushed back to the council chamber to report the incident, his footsteps echoing the urgency of the situation.

The council, gathered in their imposing chamber, looked up with anticipation as Siluk entered, his face twisted with frustration and anger. Sirtimi, the head of the council and Siluk's father, noticed the distress in his son's eyes and gestured for him to speak.

"They're gone, Father. Stanley and Gravakus have escaped," Siluk announced, the weight of the revelation hanging heavy in the air. Murmurs of astonishment and disbelief reverberated through the chamber, the council members exchanging uneasy glances.

"How is this possible?" demanded Sirtimi, his imposing figure leaning forward as he absorbed the gravity of the news.

Siluk, catching his breath, recounted the escape, detailing the executioner's demise and the daring flight of the two fugitives. The council, once united in their pursuit of dominance, now faced an unexpected setback, their carefully constructed plans unraveling.

Sirtimi's eyes flickered with a mixture of anger and contemplation. "Find them. Bring them back. We cannot let this defiance go unpunished," he commanded, his authoritative tone resonating through the chamber.

The council members dispersed, each assigned a role in the relentless pursuit of Stanley and Gravakus. Siluk, his determination unyielding, took charge of the search, fueled by a personal vendetta against those who had dared to defy the council's grasp.

The temple, once a bastion of power and control, now echoed with the urgency of a manhunt. Siluk, fueled by a relentless desire for revenge, set out to reclaim the escaped prisoners and ensure that defiance against the Drakulis council would not go unanswered. The chase had begun, and the shadows of the night held the secrets of their pursuit.

THE TIME TO END ALL IS NOW

Siluk, standing at the forefront of the council chamber, faced a sea of concerned and agitated faces as he delivered the unsettling news. The air in the room thickened with tension as he began to recount the events that unfolded in the temple's cellar.

"Committee, I have bad news you should be aware of," Siluk started, his voice carrying an undertone of frustration and urgency. The gravity of the situation demanded their immediate attention.

"The executioner has died, and it appears to have been done by Stanley Swanson. His throat was ripped out, unmistakably a result of a single, vicious bite. I regret to inform you that both Gravakus and Swanson are nowhere to be found."

The council members, previously sitting in an air of authority, now erupted into a chaotic symphony of voices expressing disbelief, anger, and confusion. The very foundation of their carefully orchestrated plans seemed to crumble before them.

"I am afraid I do not understand how this could happen," interjected one member, his voice reflecting the incredulity shared by many. "Did the executioner not have weapons and the supposed theory of roses at hand, which is supposed to weaken the breed?"

Siluk, maintaining his composure, responded with a hint of frustration in his voice. "The executioner had weapons, and there were roses present. It seems their escape was calculated and executed with precision. We underestimated them, and now we must rectify this situation before it spirals out of control."

The council deliberated fervently, attempting to dissect the implications of the escape and the potential repercussions for their kind. Sirtimi, the head of the council and Siluk's father, remained stoic, his eyes narrowing in contemplation.

"What about the antidote? Have we made any progress?" Sirtimi inquired, shifting the focus to the ongoing efforts to counteract the red roses' deadly effects.

Siluk nodded, offering a semblance of reassurance. "We are working on the antidote, but it is a complex process. It will take time, and we must act swiftly to regain control of the situation before more unforeseen events occur."

The council, now faced with the urgent need to recalibrate their strategy, embarked on a renewed mission to track down Stanley and Gravakus. The shadows of the temple seemed to whisper secrets of their elusive prey, and the pursuit of the escaped fugitives intensified within the hallowed halls of the Drakulis council.

Sirtimi's rage echoed through the temple chambers as he demanded to inspect the scene where Stanley and Gravakus had been held captive. The chaos and urgency in the air intensified as the council responded to the unfolding crisis.

Once at the cellar, Sirtimi's eyes fixated on the lifeless body of the executioner, his features contorted with a mix of frustration and disdain. He ordered a few Drakulis to remove the body, his mind spinning with thoughts of how such a breach could occur.

"Forget this Stanley Swanson for now, I want his kids!" Sirtimi's command reverberated through the chamber, emphasizing the shift in priorities. The focus turned towards the vulnerability of Stanley's offspring, perceived as potential leverage against their elusive adversary.

A council member dared to question the fate of Gravakus, the erstwhile traitor. "What of Gravakus, what should we do about him as he is still a traitor that should have died?"

Sirtimi, resolute in his decisions, responded sternly, "If we find him, then death will be made immediately, just as if Stanley Swanson is noticed in our search for his kids. They both will be disposed of right away. We are no longer to take any further chances of their friendship."

The tension in the room thickened as the weight of the situation bore down on the council. However, Sirtimi's resolve remained unyielding.

"If they truly want war, then we shall bring it to them. We cannot afford for this to continue. I am asking all of you to return to your natural places of stay and gather as many followers as you can. The temple doors have been jeopardized now that two captives have fled from it. Share what we know with all. They have the right to prepare for war. Keep all sacred from the humans, as they, right now, pose no threat."

Sirtimi's proclamation set the stage for a response that echoed through the Drakulis community. The call for war was issued, and the council dispersed, each member tasked with rallying their forces and fortifying their positions. The temple, once a sanctuary, now resonated with the ominous preparations for the impending conflict.

The call to arms reverberated through the Drakulis

community as they responded to Sirtimi's directive. The atmosphere in the temple was charged with an electric excitement, as warriors prepared for an imminent war that would reshape the balance between Drakulis and Lycans. The applause and cheers of the assembled Drakulis echoed through the ancient halls, signaling their collective determination to face the impending conflict head-on.

Sirtimi, a formidable figure, left the temple, locking the doors behind him and leaving only two guards in place to watch over the sacred space. As he embarked on his mission to gather his own followers, the reality of the approaching war hung heavily in the air. The once-sacred treaty that maintained a delicate balance between Drakulis and Lycans now seemed like a relic of the past, rendered obsolete by the mounting tensions.

The war that loomed on the horizon posed an existential threat to both Drakulis and Werewolves, and the approach to be taken remained shrouded in uncertainty. The Drakulis, though not significantly outnumbered, recognized the need for careful strategy. The impending conflict forced them to confront a crucial decision: would humans be drawn into the chaos, forever altering the course of their history?

The question of involving humans added a layer of complexity to an already dire situation. It was a dilemma that both Drakulis and Lycans would have to grapple with, weighing the potential consequences of unleashing their supernatural war upon the unsuspecting human populace. The decision on this matter would not only shape the nature of the conflict but also determine the fate of both supernatural races.

As the Drakulis and Werewolves readied themselves for the impending war, the uncertainty surrounding their choices loomed large. The stage was set for an epic confrontation, one that had the potential to redefine the dynamics between the supernatural and the human world. Only time would unveil the path they chose and the consequences that would follow, as the shadow of war cast its long, foreboding reach over the supernatural realm.

S.K. Ballinger

THE CARNIVAL CRUISE

Stanley, understanding the discomfort Gravakus felt, didn't hesitate to offer his support. As they approached the cruise liner, the vast expanse of ocean surrounding it triggered an uneasiness in Gravakus. The prospect of being surrounded by sea water, a lethal substance to vampires, was undoubtedly unsettling for him.

"Of course, Gravakus. I've got you," Stanley replied reassuringly, placing a firm grip on Gravakus's arm. The camaraderie between them had grown during their shared trials, and Stanley was committed to offering whatever support he could to his newfound friend.

The cruise liner awaited them, a refuge where the sheer volume of humans would act as a protective shield against any potential threats from other supernatural beings. However, Gravakus couldn't shake the lingering fear of the ocean that coursed through his undead veins. Stanley, sensing this, tightened his grip on Gravakus's arm, silently conveying his understanding and solidarity.

As they approached the ramp, the transition onto the cruise liner represented a step into an environment significantly different from the dangers they had recently escaped. The ship's bustling activity, the laughter of humans, and the overall sense of normalcy offered a stark contrast to the darkness and turmoil left behind in the temple.

Once on board, Stanley and Gravakus would find a place among the crowds, attempting to blend in and remain unnoticed. The ship, a temporary sanctuary amidst the impending supernatural war, would be a place for them to gather their strength, regroup, and strategize for the challenges that lay ahead.

Stanley chuckled at Gravakus's request for a drink, understanding that even the undead could find solace in the familiarity of certain pleasures. As they reached their room on the cruise liner, Gravakus couldn't help but express his need for a strong drink to ease his uneasiness.

"I could really use a drink. I am not one to toy around with small ones either," Gravakus remarked, his tone carrying a hint of humor despite the underlying tension.

Stanley, still maintaining a good grip on Gravakus's arm, responded, "Why drink whiskey or such when it has no effect on you?"

Gravakus shot him a look, his expression turning serious. "Because I like the taste, damn it, and it calms my nerves!"

Stanley couldn't argue with that logic. Even for supernatural beings, habits and preferences persisted from their human lives. He nodded in agreement, understanding that sometimes it was about more than just the physical effects.

"Fair enough. Let's find the bar, then. A good drink might help both of us unwind a bit," Stanley suggested, leading the way as they navigated through the bustling cruise ship in search of a place to savor a momentary escape from the impending chaos that awaited them.

As they strolled around the cruise ship, Stanley couldn't help but feel a sense of camaraderie with Gravakus. The unusual circumstances that brought them together seemed to forge a bond that transcended their inherent differences. Gravakus, still feeling the effects of his unease, expressed his gratitude to Stanley for saving his life, a sentiment that touched Stanley in a way he hadn't expected.

"I would have liked to think you would have done the same for me, friend," Stanley replied, his words echoing the growing bond between them.

"I would have, Stanley. And let me just remind you that it will be me who returns your necklace that holds your wife's wedding band. I am truly thankful to have met you in such uncommon ways," Gravakus assured him.

Stanley nodded appreciatively, acknowledging the sincerity in Gravakus's words. "Well, let us see what this boat has to offer us, and let us get that drink you so badly need."

As they explored the amenities of the cruise ship, the two unlikely companions found themselves in a lively bar. The atmosphere was vibrant, with the sound of laughter and clinking glasses filling the air. Gravakus, despite not requiring sustenance, ordered a whiskey for the taste and tradition of it, while Stanley opted for a glass of red wine. They found a quiet corner to enjoy their drinks, looking out over the open sea.

"To new beginnings, unexpected friendships, and whatever awaits us," Stanley proposed, raising his glass in a toast. Gravakus, with a genuine smile, clinked his glass against Stanley's, appreciating the sentiment and the newfound companionship that fate had woven between them.

As Gravakus and Stanley prepared to leave the cruise ship, they found a secluded area on the upper deck, away from prying eyes, to discuss their plans. Stanley, relaxing on his bed, directed a question towards Gravakus.

"So what is your plan, Gravakus?" Stanley inquired, his gaze focused on the enigmatic figure.

Gravakus sighed, his eyes reflecting a complex mix of weariness and uncertainty. "I do not have much of one, but I think the next stop is where you should have your pack meet us. Even though your home was not a bad idea. Me, I have nothing outside of your breed. I no longer can even trust my followers now, it would seem."

As they shared the stories of their captures, Stanley reached out to Jeremia, his trusted ally. Jeremia promptly answered the call, concern evident in his voice.

"Meet us at Nasa Bay as I fear my home is being watched," Stanley instructed.

Jeremia, a hint of worry in his voice, responded, "Stanley, we have already landed and are only a few hours away from your plantation. What has been going on as of late?"

"Too much to tell you now, friend. Just make your way here. I will fill you all in upon your arrival. This is a very safe area for both of us, and where we will remain for the time being," Stanley assured.

Jeremia, now curious about the unexpected companion, inquired further, "Both of you. Who are you with, Stanley?"

"Just get here, and I will explain. I need to go, as our phone might be traced. Be safe, and look forward to seeing you all," Stanley urged, ending the call.

As the days passed, the bond between Stanley and Gravakus deepened, transcending the boundaries of their respective breeds. Gravakus, while still vigilant and cautious, found himself feeling apologetic for the actions he had taken in the past that inadvertently brought danger to Stanley's family.

"Stanley Swanson, you incredible being," Gravakus began, the weight of remorse apparent in his voice. "I am growing tired of my black heart and always wondering what is going to happen next. I have seen so much in my time as balance was my purpose; it is the key to all of our kind and humans alike. I was terribly wrong in doing what I did, and I am so sorry."

Stanley, ever the pragmatic one, responded with a touch of humor, "Maybe those drinks have got to you, Grav, after all."

"I could only wish, Stanley," Gravakus replied with a wistful tone. The acknowledgment of his mistakes and the genuine apology from Gravakus allowed a bridge to form between them, a bridge built on understanding and shared experiences.

As they awaited the arrival of Stanley's pack at Nasa Bay, the two mythological beings found solace in their companionship, each grappling with the complexities of their own existence. The looming war added an extra layer of uncertainty to their journey, but for the moment, they found comfort in the camaraderie that had unexpectedly blossomed between them.

Stanley, deep in thought about the impending war and the role their respective breeds would play, accepted Gravakus's apologies and emphasized the importance of addressing their current challenges. Despite their differences, he believed in finding a resolution before the war escalated into a catastrophic event.

"The past is past as we can only control the now," Stanley remarked. "We need to figure out how to settle all of this before the war of our kinds and humans becomes a reality. When and if that happens, it is going to be the end for mortals, as you know, and I cannot let that happen."

Curious about Stanley's affinity for humans, Gravakus questioned the nature of this sentiment, especially considering their roles as superior beings in the supernatural hierarchy.

"Why do you love or like these humans so much?" Gravakus inquired, sharing his perception that humans were merely a food supply or potential followers for their respective breeds.

Stanley paused for a moment before articulating his perspective. "The breed of werewolf, just as your kind, will always be seen as beasts or creatures of the night by humans. You know yourself that we are much more superior to them all. Why, you might ask? I will only speak for myself and others of my breed. I trust humans more than I like them, Grav, because, for one, we do not have to feed off them for survival. Secondly, they are, in reality, unconcerned with our breed as we remain hidden and so much more."

Stanley continued, reflecting on his interactions with Kain Edward, the human he could communicate and share with. "When I met Kain Edward and listened to his story while I shared mine with him, he was intrigued with both my breed and that of the Drakulis or vampires. He did not become afraid or scared easily from what I had shown him. He was the only human I was able to communicate with and share with. No burning of villages, tortures, or slavery. This is why I will show humans that we are not the ones to fear, but rather those that prey on them often."

Gravakus, acknowledging the dual nature of their breeds' interactions with humans, responded succinctly, "While we prey on humans, do not be fooled to think that others of your breed do not do the same, my friend." The complexity of their relationship with humans became more apparent, hinting at the multifaceted dynamics within their supernatural world.

The discussion between Stanley and Gravakus delved into the intricacies of their respective breeds and the challenges that came with their supernatural existence. Gravakus emphasized the inherent nature of all life forms to prey on each other, whether supernatural or not, and highlighted the difficulty of achieving harmony in their complex world. The example of Zea, a traitor to Gravakus's breed, served as a stark reminder that trust was a scarce commodity, even among their own kind.

"It's all too easy, and not all can be trusted," Gravakus remarked, reflecting the harsh reality of their existence. "This is what we call life, and this is how it works. The only problem remaining would be that of humans."

As Stanley settled into his bed, Gravakus couldn't help but express his concerns about the potential consequences of revealing their existence to humans. He questioned Stanley about how humans might prepare for the impending war between their species.

"Stanley, you don't think that if humans know of such war or become proven to our existence, they will not prepare for both species that we are?" Gravakus inquired, his tone filled with genuine concern.

Stanley Swanson – Breed of a Werewolf

Stanley, understanding the gravity of the situation, explained that his original intent was to gradually introduce humans to their breeds, emphasizing the importance of doing so on his own terms. However, Gravakus, sensing Stanley's fatigue, couldn't help but remark on his decision to go to sleep before concluding their conversation.

"Going to sleep before we finish our conversation?" Gravakus questioned.

"I am not you, friend. I get tired, and yes, I am going to sleep. I ask that you do not watch over me, as that would creep me out a bit," Stanley responded, emphasizing the normalcy of his need for rest.

"It has been so long since I had slept. I can only imagine what it must be like," Gravakus admitted, acknowledging the stark differences in their existence.

"It is just something needed for those that live, Gravakus," Stanley explained, highlighting the necessity of rest for beings like him.

As the night settled in, both supernatural creatures sought the solace of sleep, each carrying their own reflections and concerns into the realm of dreams. Moments later, with Stanley falling asleep, Gravakus pondered what to do in the quiet room, knowing he did not share the same need for rest.

Having an overwhelming feeling of being watched, Stanley cracked an eye open, discovering Gravakus just looking at him.

"Seriously, Grav?" Stanley questioned.

"What, I am bored," Gravakus responded casually.

"Go to the casino or something. Mingle with ladies, but do not turn them is all I ask. Plenty to do on this cruise rather than look at me while I try to sleep," Stanley suggested.

"Valid point, and I apologize. However, while I go about this boat and fall down because of the waves shaking it left and right, and you're not around to rescue me, do not fault me for my actions. Sleep well, Stanley," Gravakus declared, acknowledging the uniqueness of their nocturnal routines.

The cruise ship docked at Nasa Bay as the morning light painted the sky with hues of pink and orange. Gravakus, having spent the night exploring the various activities on the ship, returned to the room he shared with Stanley. The quiet corridors echoed his footsteps as he made his way back, and upon entering the room, he found Stanley still in peaceful slumber.

Watching over Stanley as he slept had become somewhat of a routine for Gravakus, a nocturnal being who did not require sleep himself. As he stood in the dimly lit room, Gravakus reflected on the events that had transpired, contemplating the newfound bond between them and the uncertainties that lay ahead.

The cruise had offered a brief respite from the turmoil they had faced, with Gravakus even trying his hand at the blackjack table, winning a few dollars in the process. However, beneath the surface of the serene ocean waves and the casual activities on the ship, the looming threat of war and the complexities of their existence lingered.

As the minutes ticked by, Gravakus observed the subtle

rise and fall of Stanley's chest, a testament to the vulnerability shared even by the supernatural. The room remained silent, save for the gentle hum of the ship's engines and the distant sounds of passengers beginning to stir.

Gravakus, still in his typical form as the night creature, felt a sense of tranquility in this quiet moment. The room's ambiance shifted as the first rays of sunlight began to filter through the curtains, casting a warm glow upon the surroundings. It was a stark contrast to Gravakus's usual nocturnal existence, and yet, there was a certain beauty in witnessing the sunrise, even for a creature of the night.

As the room gradually brightened, Gravakus decided to step out onto the balcony, allowing the morning sun to touch his skin. The crisp sea air filled his lungs as he contemplated the challenges that lay ahead. The war between their breeds was inevitable, and the consequences of revealing their existence to humans weighed heavily on his mind.

With a final glance back at Stanley, who continued to sleep soundly, Gravakus resolved to face whatever lay ahead. The cruise ship, now docked at Nasa Bay, marked the beginning of a new chapter—one that would unfold against the backdrop of war, secrecy, and the intricate dance between light and darkness.

S.K. Ballinger

NASA BAY

As Stanley embraced his long-awaited reunion with his children, the atmosphere at the bottom of the ramp was charged with a mix of emotions. The shouts of rejoice from the pack echoed through the air, blending with the powerful cries of happiness from Sabe and Jade, two voices that held immense significance to Stanley.

Gravakus, standing behind Stanley, offered a protective stance, ensuring the safety of the cherished family moment. Stanley, his knees weakened by both the emotion of the reunion and the fear of the narrow ramp leading to the ocean, held onto Gravakus for support.

Upon reaching solid ground, Stanley knelt down with open arms, inviting Sabe and Jade into a warm embrace. The air was filled with the sweet sounds of laughter, hugs, and the indescribable joy of being reunited with loved ones after a prolonged separation. Stanley's heart swelled with love and gratitude for the precious moments he was sharing with his children.

As Stanley and his children exchanged kisses, the weight of the time and the absence of their mother lingered in the air. With a tender expression, Stanley asked Sabe and Jade about their awareness of their mother's fate. Jade's tears flowed freely, and Stanley, using the gentle touch of his thumbs, wiped away the traces of sorrow from her face.

"Be strong, just as you have been, my love," Stanley whispered to Jade, his voice filled with both sympathy and determination. "They will suffer for their actions, and we will seek vengeance on those who have torn our family apart. Right now, Jade, I need you to stay strong, just as your mother would have wanted."

The pack, sensing the gravity of the situation, stood respectfully at a distance, giving the family the space they needed to reconnect and share their emotions. In the midst of joy and sorrow, a profound sense of unity and resilience formed the foundation of their bond—a bond that would be crucial in the challenging times that lay ahead.

As the reunion continued, Stanley's thoughts turned to the next steps. The war loomed, and the quest for justice for his wife's death was now entwined with the fate of their kind. The journey ahead would require strength, unity, and a determination to overcome the challenges that awaited them.

Standing tall after the emotional embrace with his children, Stanley expressed heartfelt gratitude to Jeremia, Francais, and Drennan for the care they provided to Sabe and Jade during their separation. However, the joyous reunion was swiftly interrupted by Drennan's vocal disapproval of Gravakus, who stood at a distance behind Stanley.

"What is this that you bring with you? Have you lost your mind?" Drennan exclaimed, his tone revealing deep displeasure.

Sabe, fueled by memories of the attack at their home, charged at Gravakus, prompting Stanley to intervene swiftly. "Son, he has no harm towards us any longer. There is much you all need to know, and Gravakus is going to be a part of it, as I will see to it," Stanley explained, attempting to quell the rising tension.

However, Francais voiced his own concerns, aligning with

Drennan's disapproval. "This is the very Drakulis that tried to harm your wife, Stanley. I cannot accept this notion you suggest."

Gravakus, sensing the palpable tension, offered a sincere apology. "If you do not mind, and you, young Sabe, I apologize for what I had done. You should know I only did what I did back then to prevent what is now taking place," Gravakus explained.

Sabe, unwilling to accept Gravakus's words at face value, expressed his distrust. "I do mind, Gravakus. What comes out of your mouth is nothing more than words of distrust. It is the Drakulis way."

Growing restless amidst the escalating argument, Stanley, aware of the public setting and the need for a resolution, demanded a halt to the discord. "Gravakus is staying, and if you will not accept it, then you are free to go. We have much to discuss, as I am sure you do with us. Now, we can stand here and argue, or we can be civil. I have said my piece, and I leave you, my pack, with your own choices moving forward."

The tension hung in the air, and the pack members were faced with a crucial decision—accept the presence of Gravakus and the circumstances surrounding him or choose a different path. The fate of their collective future rested on the choices made in that pivotal moment.

Reluctantly accepting Stanley's decision, the pack members displayed signs of frustration and displeasure, but they came to terms with it. Francais, still harboring reservations, voiced his concerns while expressing a measure of respect for Stanley's trust in Gravakus.

"Well, as I still do not like the idea, just as the rest of us do not, if you think you can trust him, then I will have to respect your decision. Just keep his distance from me is all I ask," Francais declared, setting a clear boundary.

Drennan, with an air of hostility, added a warning directed at Gravakus. "It would be wise to do as Francais says, or you could leave this Drakulis in a room with me for a moment," he said, making his feelings towards Gravakus unmistakably clear.

Sensing the tension and realizing the need to find a place to stay, Gravakus suggested, "It would seem that we should find a place to stay, and perhaps your pack will allow me the opportunity to give a further explanation of myself."

Turning his attention directly towards Stanley's kids, Gravakus addressed them with genuine remorse. "I truly am sorry for that night, and I know you may not believe me, but I am. If it matters, I am going to do everything I can to put those that caused fatal harm to your family to rest myself."

With Gravakus extending an olive branch, the atmosphere remained strained, but the pack acknowledged the need for unity and focused on the common goal of seeking justice for the harm inflicted upon their family. The journey ahead would demand trust, understanding, and a shared commitment to confronting the challenges that lay ahead.

Sabe, still harboring deep resentment towards Gravakus for the events at their home, couldn't contain his curiosity and anger. Standing at a short distance, he confronted Gravakus with a direct question, his eyes betraying a mix of suspicion and fury.

"Why did you do what took place at our home?"

Gravakus, sensing the sincerity of the moment, lost the somewhat playful demeanor on his face and replied with honesty and depth.

"You see, young child, I was not in popular favor of your father sharing information with this Kain Edward. You do not understand in full how critical it is for both our secrecy. I have been around for a very long time and even started a war myself, but did so in hopes of keeping balance among my kind, humans, and even your breed. This information that could easily be leaked out to the humans could or probably will have a very negative outcome for all those that choose a side one way or another. What the humans do have, which neither my kind nor yours does, is a military. They would be fast to substitute their weapons by simply exchanging regular bullets and making them silver, missiles made of rose ash, bombs that drop saltwater, etc. The list can go on. What I am trying to tell you, young boy, is that we have been kept secret from their race for a reason. I was looking for your father so that I could kill him. Your mother I truly had no intentions of harming. You are far too young to understand, I believe, but know that I will correct what I made wrong."

Gravakus, despite his history and past actions, presented a perspective that hinted at a complex struggle for balance and preservation of their supernatural world. Whether Sabe could comprehend the intricacies of such conflicts remained to be seen, but Gravakus vowed to make amends for the wrongs he had committed. The journey ahead would be one of understanding, forgiveness, and the pursuit of justice.

Gravakus, facing scrutiny from Sabe and the rest of the pack, found himself pressed for further explanation. Sabe, still grappling with the revelation of his mother being used as a means to get to his father, voiced his confusion and demanded more clarity.

"So you used my mother to get to my father. This balance you speak of, I do not understand. Why are you so afraid of the humans, as they know nothing of us?"

Gravakus, with a hint of regret in his eyes, delved into the intricacies of the supernatural world and the impending conflict.

"Balance was the key at one point, but I fear that your kind has been exposed, and a war is happening; in fact, it happens now as we speak. I have to make a choice on which side to stand for, and unfortunately, as I have seen it many times over, my kind is fast to 'change' humans to become vampires. If that were to happen, it could easily take just a little over a month before all would be consumed, either by death or making them followers, even to those in the military. While it may seem that mortals are not doing much right now, I believe they are already planning for your kind at this moment, along with my kind. This movement is going to happen in the near future, and for me, I wish to try and keep the balance I so believe in, just as your father believed in this war. Side note Sabe, I am not one who would like to continue walking this planet off eating rats, just saying."

Gravakus laid bare the complexities of his position, torn between preserving the supernatural balance and facing the threat posed by an escalating war. The impending conflict between the supernatural beings and humans loomed large, and the choices made by individuals like Gravakus could shape the fate of both worlds.

The room filled with a tense atmosphere as the pack deliberated on their next steps. Stanley, expressing the need for caution, suggested waiting for the antidote to be readily available before initiating any further confrontations with the Drakulis. He also proposed a personal quest to confront the Drakulis responsible for the loss of his family.

Jeremia, providing his insights, recommended setting traps in a concealed location to lure Drakulis and their followers, creating an opportunity to eliminate many adversaries at once. The pack members, including Drennan, Francais, and Natalie, nodded in agreement with the strategy.

As the discussions unfolded, Gravakus, reclined in the bedroom, made a light-hearted comment to break the tension, asking not to be sent the "big guy." His attempt at humor momentarily lightened the mood.

The decision to set traps and face the Drakulis head-on seemed unanimous among the pack. Stanley, however, couldn't help but glance at his children, Sabe and Jade, who were in the care of Natalie in the next room. A pang of sorrow struck him as he reached for where his necklace once hung, a poignant reminder of what had been taken from him.

Despite the emotional turmoil, Stanley remained resolute.

"They have no remorse for our breed; we shall not have any in return for them. I want to have a single fight between myself and the highest Drakulis so all can see. We will end this with me, as I am responsible for all of this to begin with."

The weight of responsibility hung in the air as the pack considered the challenges ahead, grappling with the complexities of vengeance and justice in the supernatural conflict that loomed on the horizon.

Stanley Swanson – Breed of a Werewolf

The room was filled with tension as Gravakus emerged from his boredom-induced isolation, offering his assistance in the upcoming battle. Drennan, unable to conceal his disdain for the Drakulis, expressed his distrust, warning Stanley against relying on Gravakus.

Stanley, however, vouched for Gravakus, highlighting the debt he owed the vampire for saving his life. The pack members, particularly Drennan, were visibly uneasy with the idea of trusting a Dra kulis, but Francais stepped in to mediate. He wrapped his arm around Drennan, guiding him away from the brewing conflict, attempting to diffuse the tension.

Sabe and Jade, fueled by a desire for vengeance and loyalty to their father, were ready to join the fight. However, Stanley, concerned for their safety, made it clear that they were to stay behind.

"Not going to happen, kids. I will need you two to stay behind on this fight. You both will be taken care of if something were to happen to me. I do not see failing as an option, so neither of you should worry," Stanley reassured his children.

The room buzzed with conflicting emotions, with the promise of impending conflict and the struggle to trust Gravakus casting a shadow over their plans. The night had only just begun, and the challenges that lay ahead were bound to test the bonds within the pack.

As Gravakus made his intentions clear to fly back to the Temple, Stanley expressed his concerns about the potential danger awaiting the vampire. However, Gravakus, confident in his plan, believed that the Temple might be deserted, with all Drakulis searching for their vendetta against the werewolves.

S.K. Ballinger

"To remind you a bit of my kind, I have a feeling in me that the Temple remains empty, as all Drakulis have left in search of killing your breed and even that of which you wish to have a showdown with. If I arrive, and that is the case, then you will not only have your necklace back, but I will gladly leave a trace of where it is you wish to fight, which I believe was at your plantation," Gravakus explained, outlining his strategy.

Stanley, trusting Gravakus despite the risks, agreed to his plan, appreciating the vampire's determination. He asked Gravakus to leave a trace to signify his desire for a one-on-one fight with the highest Drakulis at his plantation.

"I will not stop you as I trust in what you say, Gravakus. Your decision to do so, I can only appreciate. Yes, leave a trace to know that I am wanting to end this with the highest Drakulis, one on one with me. I hope we can keep in touch after all we have been through," Stanley said.

"We will, friend, and likewise to you," Gravakus assured, preparing to depart. The tension in the room lingered as plans were set into motion, and the impending confrontation between the werewolves and Drakulis grew closer.

As Gravakus swiftly left the resort, Stanley and the rest of the pack continued their discussions and calls to other breeds. Drennan, relieved to see Gravakus depart, expressed his satisfaction, but the night was far from over. Jeremia, with a sense of urgency, pleaded with Stanley to reconsider facing the longest-living Drakulis in a one-on-one confrontation. However, Stanley remained steadfast in his decision, acknowledging the risks but emphasizing the need to put an end to the conflict.

Debates ensued throughout the night among the four of

them, each member expressing their concerns and opinions on the matter. The stakes were high, and tensions ran deep. Natalie, having taken on the responsibility of watching over Sabe and Jade, kept a close eye on the unfolding discussions.

The atmosphere in the room became charged with conflicting emotions as they grappled with the decision to halt ongoing battles. Stanley, aware of the dangers, sought a peaceful resolution to the conflict, realizing that continued bloodshed would only worsen the situation. The discussions grew heated, reflecting the weight of the decisions that needed to be made in the face of an impending war.

S.K. Ballinger

BLOOD SHED & BATTLES STILL IN AFFECT

Sheree, Caleb, and Zanth, now facing the wreckage of their once-sacred home in the hills, were determined to take revenge on the vampires responsible for the destruction. The rooms were left in disarray, a clear sign of an ambush carried out by vampires. The fate of the elder Emery remained uncertain, adding to the urgency and anger that fueled their resolve.

Entering the front door, Sheree, with a heavy heart, informed Caleb and Zanth that the fight was far from over. The pack decided to take matters into their own hands, setting a trap in the valley below their home. Although nervous, they worked swiftly to prepare for the impending battle.

Sheree laid out the plan: leading the enemy to the open fields, they would dig trenches and place stakes made from trees, covering the trenches to catch their adversaries off guard. They needed to find oil to create walls of fire, while members of their pack stayed hidden in the tree lines. To stall the enemy, they planned to dig a canal to channel water from a nearby stream, eventually flooding the grounds when the time was right.

The urgency of their situation meant all work had to be done at night, ensuring their activities remained hidden from humans in the vicinity. The meticulous plan involved strategic elements, combining guerrilla tactics and environmental manipulation to gain an advantage over the vampires they sought to retaliate against.

As the trio worked tirelessly on their plan of revenge, the tension among them was palpable. The stakes were high, and the outcome of their efforts would determine the fate of their pack and the retaliation against the vampires who had wreaked havoc on their home. The night was filled with preparation, determination, and a sense of impending conflict as they readied themselves for the battle that lay ahead.

As Caleb initiated the calls to rally their werewolf brethren, Sheree and Zanth wasted no time and commenced the strenuous work needed for their intricate plan. Sheree, despite the uncertainty and Zanth's reservations, was resolute in her decision, urging them to embrace their lycanthropic nature and reclaim their strength.

"We were created for this, Zanth. Our strength, intelligence, and endurance—these qualities are meant for times like these. Look around you; the war has begun, and we cannot stand idle," Sheree proclaimed with conviction.

Zanth, though skeptical, acknowledged the urgency of their situation. "It seems like we're wasting time just talking. Let's start now. I'll make the calls and join in the physical efforts as well."

With Caleb coordinating the mobilization of their werewolf allies, Sheree and Zanth delved into the laborious tasks laid out in their plan. Trenches were dug, stakes were strategically placed, and oil was procured to create fiery barriers. The efficiency and agility of their werewolf breed allowed them to progress rapidly, mindful of the impending battle they were preparing for.

As the word spread among the werewolf community about the impending attack, a formidable force began to gather. Sheree's plan was gaining traction, with werewolves from various regions committing to the cause. However, a few cautious ones had decided to follow Stanley Swanson's directive to retreat, showcasing a division within the werewolf community.

The night echoed with the sounds of claws against the earth and the distant calls of werewolves, as the pack prepared to reclaim their home and exact revenge on the vampires responsible for the destruction. The air was charged with anticipation, each werewolf fueled by a shared determination to protect their own and respond to the call of war that echoed through their kind. The stage was set for a confrontation that would determine the fate of their pack and the ongoing supernatural conflict.

The fog thickened, concealing the werewolves waiting in the open field as the Drakulis and vampire forces approached. Sheree, standing with her two brothers and a select few pack members, maintained her composure, knowing that timing was crucial. In the treetops, the rest of the werewolf breed watched attentively, waiting for the signal.

As the fog dissipated, three Drakulis were revealed, leading the charge of hundreds of vampires. Sheree began counting down with her fingers, signaling the werewolves above. Just as she reached the fifth finger, the plan unfolded.

The first line of defense, a pit of stakes carefully prepared by the werewolves, claimed the lives of numerous vampires and even managed to injure one of the Drakulis. Anticipating the approaching enemies, the werewolves on the ground swiftly transitioned into their formidable wolf forms.

As the vampires jumped over the pit, Sheree's pack executed the next phase of their plan. The werewolves in the treetops, using their powerful claws, effortlessly felled trees, creating obstacles that tumbled down the hill toward the oncoming vampire horde. The chaos and confusion among the attackers played perfectly into the werewolves' hands.

The plan continued to unfold seamlessly. The Drakulis, standing back and assessing the situation, were bewildered by the unexpected resistance. The vampire forces, facing not just werewolves but also the falling trees, struggled to maintain their organized advance.

Amidst the turmoil, a glimmer of sunlight pierced through the smoke, revealing the true extent of the vampire army—more than three hundred strong. Sheree, recognizing the need to escalate the situation, arched her back and released a massive howl. Simultaneously, Zanth, positioned below, commenced the final phase of the plan by undoing the blocked trenches.

Water rushed through the canals, flooding the battleground. The vampires, now facing not only werewolves but also a rapidly rising stream, found themselves disoriented and vulnerable. The cunning strategy of Sheree's pack had created a battlefield advantage, utilizing the environment and werewolves' unique abilities to turn the tide against the vampires. The outcome of this supernatural clash hung in the balance, as the werewolves stood their ground, determined to protect their home and exact revenge for the devastation wrought upon it.

Sheree, still reveling in the victory against the vampires, made her way towards the approaching werewolf who carried an unexpected message. The atmosphere at Emery's property was filled with a mixture of relief and joy after the successful defense against the vampire onslaught.

"Which is the one who owns these grounds?" the

werewolf inquired as Sheree approached.

"It would be my brothers and I," Sheree responded, a sense of pride evident in her voice.

The werewolf handed Sheree a phone and mentioned, "I cannot believe it, but this phone is for you from Stanley Swanson."

Curious and intrigued, Sheree accepted the phone and brought it to her ear, "Hello?"

Stanley's voice echoed through the phone, "Sheree, it's Stanley Swanson. I heard about the remarkable defense you and your pack executed against the vampires. I've been trying to reach out to other breeds, and I believe it's time for us to unite against the common threat we face. Are you willing to join forces?"

Sheree, still processing the surreal nature of the call, replied, "Stanley, this is indeed a surprise. We've just fought off a vampire attack here. Your timing couldn't be more interesting. I'm open to discussion, but we need to meet in person to assess the situation properly."

Stanley agreed, "I understand. Let's arrange a meeting. There's much we need to discuss, and time is of the essence. I'll provide you with the details. Take care, Sheree."

The call ended, leaving Sheree with a mix of emotions. The alliance between werewolves and vampires, once thought impossible, seemed to be forming in the face of a greater threat. Sheree gathered her pack to share the news and discuss the upcoming meeting with Stanley Swanson. The night continued with both celebration and anticipation as they prepared for the challenges that lay ahead.

Sheree listened intently to Stanley's words, the chaos of the celebration outside providing a stark contrast to the gravity of their conversation. The mention of Stephen brought back memories of the past, and she couldn't help but feel a sense of responsibility in the unfolding events.

"I only call you because you were the last to be known around my brother Stephen, which gave him help. The friend we share of our breed, I only called, as I am doing what I can to inform all that it is going to be me who ends what I have started," Stanley explained. "He expressed to me what you and your brothers have done, which is astounding. I only ask that you do as what many others of our breed are doing, which is to retreat. If you wish to see the ending of all, then I welcome you and all those that are there at your place to join with no actions of fighting but to witness."

Sheree, puzzled by Stanley's request, questioned, "Why do you wish to stop what not only our breed has done because of you and what I have done this very night? I do not understand, Stanley. We are stronger now than ever before."

Stanley's response carried a weight of conviction, "Because this is not a meant war. I ask that you do your best to understand, Sheree, and not make it more than what it has already become."

Sheree paused, contemplating the implications of Stanley's words. The revelry outside continued, oblivious to the serious discussion taking place within. Finally, she responded, "Stanley, I will consider your request, but I need more information. We've faced challenges tonight, and your call adds another layer to the complexities. Let us meet in person to discuss this further. There is much we need to understand and clarify. I want to hear your side of the story directly."

Stanley agreed, "I anticipated this, Sheree. I'll send you the details for a meeting. Let's talk face to face. Until then, take care."

The call ended, leaving Sheree with a mix of thoughts and a sense of responsibility for the decisions that lay ahead. She gathered her pack once more, informing them of the unexpected turn of events and the upcoming meeting with Stanley Swanson. The night, which had started with celebration, now held an air of uncertainty as they prepared to face a new chapter in the unfolding saga.

Sheree, having absorbed the weight of Stanley's words, stepped into the midst of the celebration, the chaotic revelry pausing as she raised her voice to address the gathered werewolves.

"Listen, everyone!" she called out, her authoritative tone cutting through the cheers and laughter. The pack turned their attention toward her, curiosity etched on their faces. "I have received a message from Stanley Swanson, and he's urging us to retreat. He wants us to witness the end of what he started, but not to participate. This is his fight, not ours."

A murmur of uncertainty rippled through the pack, and Sheree continued, "I understand this may not sit well with some of you. We've fought hard tonight, and the victory is ours. But we need to consider the bigger picture. Stanley is asking for our understanding, and we owe it to ourselves and our brethren to hear him out."

She emphasized the importance of unity and cooperation, urging the pack to make an informed decision. "We have an opportunity to show respect to a fellow member of our breed. If you choose to retreat and witness, I respect your decision. If you want to continue the fight, remember what we achieved tonight and carry it with you. Whatever you decide, let it be a decision made in the spirit of wisdom and unity."

With that, Sheree left the pack with the choice, knowing that each member carried their own convictions and motivations. Some chose to accept Stanley's advice and retreated, understanding the need for a united front. Others, fueled by the recent victory, opted to return to their hiding places, acknowledging the complexity of the situation.

The celebration had transformed into a moment of reflection and decision. Sheree, as their leader, had set the tone for a measured response, emphasizing the importance of respecting Stanley's wishes while preserving the strength of their own pack. The night, once filled with exuberance, now held a sobering sense of contemplation as they prepared for the challenges that lay ahead.

S.K. Ballinger

PROMISE KEPT

Gravakus, with an air of nonchalance, casually swung his feet off the table and leaned forward, an unsettling smirk playing on his lips. Sirtimi's anger radiated through the room as he confronted the notorious traitor.

"Ah, Sirtimi, always the fiery one. How have you been, old friend?" Gravakus taunted, his tone dripping with sarcasm.

Sirtimi, seething with rage, retorted, "Save your pleasantries. You betrayed us once, and we were foolish enough to grant you clemency. Now you dare sit in our sacred chamber as if it were your own?"

Gravakus chuckled, unfazed by Sirtimi's fury. "Well, considering the circumstances, it seemed like the right place to be. Plus, I missed the ambience of this room. It's been a while, hasn't it?"

Sirtimi, barely containing his rage, demanded answers. "What game are you playing, Gravakus? Why have you returned?"

"Simple, really," Gravakus replied, his expression turning more serious. "I've grown tired of the chaos that your 'movement' has unleashed. It's getting out of hand, and it won't be long before the humans catch wind of our existence. I have my own plans, and I don't intend to let your misguided war ruin them."

Sirtimi, still suspicious, questioned Gravakus's motives. "And what makes you think we'll believe a word you say? You're a traitor, a pariah among us."

Gravakus leaned back, crossing his arms. "Believe what you want, Sirtimi. But consider this a warning. If you continue down this path, you won't just be dealing with your enemies; you'll be facing consequences beyond your imagination. I've seen it before, and I won't let history repeat itself."

The tension in the room escalated as Gravakus and Sirtimi engaged in a battle of words, each trying to assert their dominance over the other. The fate of the supernatural world hung in the balance, with Gravakus, the enigmatic traitor, once again playing a mysterious role in the unfolding drama.

The committee members stood frozen, caught between disbelief and fear as Gravakus calmly laid bare the intricacies of his cunning plan. Sirtimi, realizing the dire situation he was in, clenched his fists in frustration but remained defiant.

"You come here with threats, Gravakus, but you forget that you're still outnumbered. This temple is well-protected, and your petty revenge won't change that," Sirtimi declared, attempting to regain some semblance of control.

Gravakus chuckled, his eyes glinting with mischief. "Oh, I'm not seeking revenge, Sirtimi. I'm merely here to fulfill a promise. Now, about that necklace…"

Sirtimi hesitated for a moment before reluctantly revealing, "It's in my study, on the desk."

Without waiting for further approval, Gravakus casually walked past the committee members, making his way to Sirtimi's study. As he entered the room, his gaze fell upon the intricately carved wooden box that housed the coveted necklace. He picked it up delicately, inspecting the silver chain and pendant with a certain reverence.

"This, my friend, is more than just a piece of jewelry. It holds sentimental value," Gravakus remarked, a touch of nostalgia in his voice.

Sirtimi, growing increasingly agitated, demanded, "What is the meaning of all this? Why are you really here, Gravakus?"

Gravakus turned to face Sirtimi, the necklace dangling from his fingers. "I'm here to warn you, Sirtimi. The war you're pursuing, it's a fool's errand. The consequences will be dire, not just for us but for all supernatural beings. I've seen it happen before, and I won't let it happen again."

Sirtimi, unyielding in his convictions, snapped back, "I won't be lectured by a traitor like you. We will not back down."

Gravakus sighed, his patience waning. "So be it, Sirtimi. But remember, the path you've chosen may lead to your downfall. I've said my piece."

With that, Gravakus walked out of the study, leaving behind a perplexed and infuriated Sirtimi. The committee members, still unsure of the enigmatic Drakulis's true intentions, could only watch as he sauntered out of the temple, the necklace in hand, and disappeared into the night.

Gravakus smirked, his gaze fixed on Sirtimi as he absorbed the declaration. The tension in the room lingered, and the other Drakulis eyed their ancient leader, unsure of how this encounter with Stanley Swanson would unfold. Gravakus, still holding the controller, spoke with a touch of amusement.

Stanley Swanson – Breed of a Werewolf

"Very well, Sirtimi. Your determination is duly noted. Now, remember, this is no trap. Stanley Swanson seeks a fair fight, and you've just accepted. It seems the fate of your kind hangs in the balance of this encounter."

Sirtimi, despite his bravado, couldn't shake the unease settling within him. Gravakus, seemingly indifferent to the situation, gestured toward the door.

"Lead the way, old one. Take me to this meeting with Stanley Swanson, and we'll see what fate has in store for all of us."

The other Drakulis remained silent, their loyalty to Sirtimi wavering as they observed the unfolding events. Sirtimi, visibly frustrated, motioned for Gravakus to follow as they exited the committee room. The tension in the temple was palpable as the ancient Drakulis reluctantly led the way to the designated meeting place.

Outside the temple, the night air was thick with anticipation. The moon cast an eerie glow on the surroundings as the group made their way through the hidden passages. Gravakus walked casually, his hands in his pockets, exuding an air of confidence that irked Sirtimi.

"Do you truly believe this meeting will change anything, Gravakus?" Sirtimi sneered.

Gravakus chuckled, his voice carrying a cryptic tone. "Change is inevitable, Sirtimi. Whether for good or ill, that remains to be seen. But one thing is certain: the balance must be restored, and the sins of the past must not be repeated."

S.K. Ballinger

The journey to the meeting place continued, with the ancient adversaries locked in a silent exchange of glares. The fate of supernatural beings hung in the balance, and the impending encounter between Gravakus and Stanley Swanson would serve as a pivotal moment in the unfolding saga.

The chaos in the committee room ensued as the Drakulis desperately tried to shield themselves from the seemingly corrosive mist. Gravakus, having executed his plan with calculated precision, made a swift exit, leaving behind the agonized screams of his former comrades. The water from the misters, harmless to the undead, only intensified their confusion and panic.

Outside the temple, Gravakus strolled away, a satisfied smirk playing on his lips. He could hear the commotion behind him, and the realization that they had been deceived began to dawn on the Drakulis. Gravakus, still holding the necklace, hailed a passing car, commandeering it to facilitate his escape.

Back in the temple, Sirtimi, drenched and furious, barked orders to his remaining loyal followers. The humiliation burned within him, and the prospect of facing Stanley Swanson with such a setback loomed ominously. The committee members, now aware of Gravakus's betrayal, hurriedly made arrangements for their journey to California, as ordered by Sirtimi.

The mist dissipated, leaving the room in disarray. Broken phones and soaked vampires struggled to regain composure. Sirtimi, seething with rage, barked at his subordinates to regroup. The encounter with Gravakus had left them vulnerable and exposed.

As the temple descended into a frenzied state of

reorganization, Sirtimi's mind raced. The impending meeting with Stanley Swanson had taken an unexpected turn, and the once unshakable confidence of the Drakulis leader wavered. The balance between supernatural forces hung in the balance, and the consequences of their actions reverberated through the hidden corridors of the supernatural world.

Gravakus, having successfully deceived the Drakulis committee and retrieved Stanley Swanson's necklace, was determined to keep his promise. As he briskly made his way to a safe location, he pondered the best method to inform Stanley of the recent events at the temple.

Once he found a secure spot, Gravakus retrieved a concealed device, a communication tool tailored for supernatural beings. It was a relic from an ancient era, designed to transmit messages between creatures that existed beyond the comprehension of human technology.

With the device in hand, Gravakus began to transmit a message to Stanley. The encoded signal would reach him regardless of his location, bridging the gap between the undead and the supernatural. Gravakus, despite his infamous reputation, was a creature of his word, and he intended to uphold the promise he had made.

"Stanley Swanson, this is Gravakus. I hope this message finds you well and prepared. I've executed the plan we discussed. The Drakulis committee has been momentarily incapacitated, and your necklace is once again in your possession. The path to the highest Drakulis is clearer now, and our confrontation draws near.

I advise you to stay vigilant and gather your allies. The ime for our final showdown is approaching. The Drakulis will undoubtedly regroup, but the disruption has bought us a temporary advantage. We shall meet soon to settle this ancient vendetta once and for all.

Be prepared, for the battle that awaits will be unlike any other. The balance teeters on the edge, and the outcome will shape the destiny of our kind. Until we meet, Stanley Swanson."

With the message transmitted, Gravakus retreated into the shadows, blending seamlessly with the night. His actions had set the stage for the ultimate confrontation between the Drakulis and the werewolves. The supernatural world, caught in the throes of a brewing war, awaited the clash that would determine the fate of its inhabitants.

LEAVING THE BAY

The atmosphere grew tense as Gravakus approached the group, his words hanging in the air like a heavy fog. Francais, Drennan, and the others exchanged wary glances, unsure of what to make of Gravakus's unexpected return. Stanley, however, maintained his calm demeanor, trusting in the promise that Gravakus had made.

With an air of mystery, Gravakus produced Stanley's necklace, the very emblem that had been forcefully taken from him during the chaotic events at the temple. The glint of the pendant caught the moonlight, and Stanley's eyes widened in a mixture of surprise and gratitude.

"Gravakus, you've kept your word," Stanley acknowledged, extending his hand to accept the returned necklace.

Gravakus handed the necklace to Stanley with a nod, a subtle acknowledgment of the trust that had been built between them. The rest of the pack observed the exchange with a blend of skepticism and curiosity. Francais, still harboring reservations, couldn't help but voice his concerns.

"I appreciate the return of the necklace, Gravakus, but it doesn't erase the past. We need to stay focused on our goal and not be swayed by gestures," Francais cautioned, his tone stern.

Drennan, ever vigilant, added with a hint of suspicion, "This doesn't change the fact that he's a Drackulis. What's his game, Stanley?"

Stanley, however, chose to address the situation with a

level-headed approach, considering the larger picture. "Gravakus has played a crucial role in our plans, and for now, we need to move forward. We've got a battle ahead of us, and unity is key. Let's not forget why we're here."

The tension lingered, but the pack continued on their path toward the cruise liner. Gravakus fell into step with them, his presence stirring mixed emotions among the pack members. As they approached the boarding area, they couldn't help but wonder about the unfolding events and the significance of Gravakus's return.

The cruise liner loomed ahead, a vessel that would carry them to their next destination and the impending confrontation with the highest Drakulis. The air was charged with anticipation, and the pack, with Gravakus among them, embarked on a journey that would determine the fate of their kind.

The emotional reunion between Stanley and Gravakus marked a significant moment, a connection forged through shared struggles and a promise fulfilled. Gravakus, true to his word, had not only returned the stolen necklace but also engaged in a direct conversation with Sirtimi, leaving the temple with a satisfied smirk at the Drakulis leader's displeasure.

As the pack gathered around, Gravakus proposed a plan to expedite their return to California, emphasizing the urgency of securing their home before any potential threats materialized.

Francais, still grappling with reservations, voiced his concerns, "Stanley, are we sure we can trust Gravakus after everything that's happened? Flying back to the plantation might be risky."

Stanley Swanson – Breed of a Werewolf

Stanley, still clutching the returned necklace, offered a reassuring smile, "Gravakus has shown his commitment to our cause. Trust is earned, and he's earned mine. We need to be strategic, and if he's offering us a quicker way back, it might just be what we need."

Drennan, ever the cautious one, chimed in, "I agree with Francais. We shouldn't let our guard down, even with this gesture."

Gravakus interjected, addressing the concerns, "I understand your hesitation, but time is of the essence. We've disrupted their plans, and they'll be eager to retaliate. Flying back gives us the upper hand, a chance to prepare and safeguard your territory."

Stanley, considering the options, nodded in agreement, "Alright, Gravakus, we'll take your jet. But understand, we're doing this with caution, and any betrayal won't be taken lightly."

With the decision made, the pack spent the remainder of the day preparing for the journey back to California. Stanley, still emotional from the return of his necklace, couldn't shake the sense of impending confrontation with Sirtimi.

As the group boarded Gravakus's jet the next day, the atmosphere was a mix of anticipation and determination. The skies held the promise of both uncertainty and resolution, setting the stage for the battles that awaited them upon their return. The pack, accompanied by the once-disgraced Drakulis, soared towards their destiny, ready to face whatever challenges lay ahead.

Gravakus, surprised by Natalie's direct question, paused

for a moment before responding. The sincerity in her eyes prompted him to offer an honest answer.

"I've been around for a very long time, and over the years, you start to see the bigger picture. I've made mistakes, done things I'm not proud of, but there comes a time when you want to make amends. Stanley's cause aligns with my desire to maintain balance among our kind and protect the secrecy that's kept us hidden from humans."

Natalie, still intrigued, probed further, "But why help us? You were a Drakulis, part of a different faction."

Gravakus nodded, "True, I was. But in the grand scheme of things, we're all creatures trying to survive. There's a war brewing, not just between Drakulis and vampires, but against humans as well. The delicate balance is at risk, and if it tips too far, it could mean the end for all of us. I believe in Stanley's cause, and I want to ensure a future where our kind can coexist without revealing our existence to the world."

Natalie, absorbing his words, remarked, "It's a complex situation, Gravakus. Your actions may have consequences."

He nodded, "Indeed, they might. But sometimes, you have to choose the lesser of two evils. I've seen wars, both supernatural and human-made, and the devastation they bring. Helping Stanley is my way of trying to prevent another catastrophic conflict."

Natalie, though still cautious, seemed to understand the complexity of Gravakus's motives. As they stood in the hallway, the conversation shifted to discussions about the impending journey back to California and the challenges that awaited them.

Meanwhile, in their room, Sabe and Jade were excitedly planning activities for their extra day with their father, unaware of the conversations happening in the hallway. The night held the promise of both tension and camaraderie as the pack prepared for the challenges that lay ahead.

Natalie, touched by Gravakus's genuine empathy, smiled softly. "I don't see you as one of them, Gravakus. You're different, and your willingness to understand and acknowledge the pain is a testament to that. Not many would even care to look back and confront such darkness."

Gravakus nodded, grateful for her understanding. "Thank you, Natalie. I've done things I'm not proud of, but witnessing the aftermath of such cruelty is heartbreaking. It's a reminder of the consequences our actions can have on others."

As they continued to talk, the conversation shifted to lighter topics, with Gravakus expressing curiosity about the human experiences Natalie had enjoyed before her life took a tragic turn. She shared stories of her family, the joyous moments, and the dreams she had once harbored. The more they talked, the more they found common ground, transcending the boundaries of their respective species.

In the midst of these conversations, Sabe and Jade, who had been unaware of the detailed discussions happening between Gravakus and Natalie, knocked on the door. They entered the room, eager to spend more time with their father before their departure.

Stanley, sensing the change in atmosphere, asked, 'Everything okay here?"

Natalie, looking at Gravakus with a newfound appreciation, replied, "Everything's fine. Just getting to know each other a little better."

Gravakus nodded in agreement, and the evening unfolded with laughter, shared stories, and a growing sense of camaraderie among the unlikely group. The impending journey back to California seemed more than a mission – it was becoming a shared quest for understanding and perhaps even redemption.

Gravakus, though aware of Francais' anger and disdain, maintained a calm demeanor. "I understand your anger, Francais. The past is filled with pain, and I cannot change what has happened. But I assure you, I have no intention of causing harm or adding to the suffering that has already occurred."

Natalie, caught between the two, tried to mediate. "Uncle, please, we were just talking. Gravakus has been helping us, and he is not like the others. He saved my life, and I believe he is sincere in trying to make amends."

Francais, still fuming, retorted, "No Drakulis can be trusted. Their existence is a stain on our kind. I won't allow you to be deceived, Natalie."

Gravakus, with a hint of sadness in his eyes, responded, "I can't change what I am, Francais. But I can choose how I live. If my actions can help bring an end to the chaos and pain, then maybe there's a chance for a different future. I don't expect your trust, but I won't turn my back on those who need help."

Francais, frustrated and unconvinced, would reluctantly step back, allowing Gravakus and Natalie to continue their conversation. The others in the pack, still observing from a distance, could sense the tension but remained cautious.

Natalie, torn between her loyalty to her family and the undeniable sincerity she saw in Gravakus, was determined to find a middle ground. The night pressed on, and the complexities of their intertwined destinies unfolded, leaving an air of uncertainty and a glimmer of hope for understanding amidst the turmoil that surrounded them.

Gravakus, hearing Natalie's footsteps behind him, slowed down and turned to face her. Her tear-streaked face moved him, and he tried to offer some comfort.

"I didn't mean to cause you more pain, Natalie. Sometimes, the past is too heavy to carry."

Natalie, wiping away her tears, managed a faint smile. "You've done more for me than anyone else. I believe in second chances, Gravakus."

Meanwhile, Francais remained in the room, grappling with his emotions. Sabe and Jade, who had been silently witnessing the scene, exchanged glances, unsure of how to navigate the complexities unfolding before them.

Natalie continued walking with Gravakus, their conversation becoming a bridge between two worlds that seemed irreconcilable. She asked him about his past, his regrets, and what motivated him to change. Gravakus, with a heavy heart, shared snippets of his centuries-long existence – tales of betrayal, loss, and the struggle to find redemption.

As the night progressed, Francais, torn between his protective instincts and a niece who yearned for autonomy, would eventually find solace in the knowledge that change was inevitable. The past, though painful, could not shackle the future. In the distance, the moon illuminated the path ahead, casting shadows that held the promise of transformation.

The pack, observing from a distance, saw Natalie and Gravakus deep in conversation, and the air seemed pregnant with possibilities. The dynamics between werewolves and Drakulis were shifting, and the lines between friend and foe were becoming increasingly blurred.

Unbeknownst to them, the impending confrontation with Sirtimi loomed large, casting a shadow on the delicate threads of understanding being woven between individuals of different worlds.

Francais, caught in the grip of his own emotions, glared at Stanley. "I made her what she is, and I won't stand by and watch her willingly associate with those who would see us destroyed."

Stanley tightened his grip on Francais's shoulder. "You made her strong, Francais. But strength isn't just about physical power; it's about choices and the ability to rise above hatred. Gravakus has shown a different side. We're in the midst of a war, and alliances can shift."

Francais struggled for composure. "I can't forget what his kind did to my sister, Stanley. I can't forget the pain he might have caused."

Stanley nodded empathetically. "I understand your pain, Francais. We've all lost loved ones. But we can't let the past dictate our future. Natalie's making her choice, and if we force her to stay, it might only push her away. We need unity more than ever."

Francais, still conflicted, took a deep breath and nodded. "I can't promise to accept it easily, but I'll try."

Meanwhile, Natalie and Gravakus had reached a quiet spot outside, away from the tension in the room. Gravakus, sensing her distress, spoke softly, "I didn't mean to cause a rift in your family. Sometimes, the wounds of the past run too deep."

Natalie sighed, "It's not your fault. They just need time to understand."

Gravakus nodded, his eyes reflecting centuries of remorse. "Your strength, Natalie, it's inspiring. I've seen a lot, but rarely have I witnessed such resilience."

As they continued talking, their connection deepened, forming an unexpected alliance that hinted at a changing tide in the nocturnal conflict. The moon above witnessed the complexities of choices and the fragile threads that wove individuals from disparate worlds together.

Jeremia, still skeptical, responded, "I understand the urgency, but can we really trust Gravakus with this? What if it's a trap, Stanley?"

Stanley, having spent the night trying to console Francais, sighed. "I know it's a risk, Jeremia, but we don't have many options. Gravakus has proven himself trustworthy so far. If we're to face Sirtimi, we need to be strategic, and that means using every resource we have."

Drennan, who had been silently observing, added, "We

can't let personal feelings cloud our judgment. Gravakus might be our best chance at success in this fight. We need his jet to get back quickly."

Reluctantly, Jeremia nodded. "Fine, but I'm keeping my eye on him. If anything feels off, I won't hesitate to act."

With the decision made, the pack gathered their belongings and made their way to the private jet that Gravakus had left for them. The sun was rising, casting a golden hue over the resort, and tension lingered in the air.

As they boarded the jet, Stanley couldn't shake the uneasiness that lingered from the events of the past night. The intricate web of alliances and conflicts within the supernatural world was becoming increasingly complex, and every step forward felt like navigating a minefield.

Meanwhile, Gravakus, having distanced himself from the emotional turmoil, monitored the situation from afar. His commitment to fulfilling his promise to Stanley weighed heavily on him, and as the jet prepared for takeoff, he couldn't shake the feeling that the impending confrontation with Sirtimi would be a pivotal moment in the course of their intertwined destinies.

The private jet soared through the skies, leaving the picturesque scenery of Nasa Bay behind. Inside the cabin, the atmosphere was a mix of determination and uncertainty. Jeremia, though disappointed at being left behind once again, focused on the responsibility of guarding Sabe and Jade.

As the jet cut through the clouds, the remaining pack members engaged in conversations about the impending battle. Francais, still grappling with the recent events involving Natalie, kept mostly to himself. Drennan, deep in thought, pondered the complexities of their supernatural world, while Stanley sat quietly, staring out the window, contemplating the challenges that lay ahead.

Gravakus, who was not part of the cabin discussions, stood at the front of the jet, gazing out into the vastness of the sky. His thoughts were known only to him, but the weight of his promise to Stanley hung heavy on his undead shoulders.

The flight was relatively short, and soon, the jet began its descent towards the Swanson plantation. The lush greenery of the estate came into view, but the air was thick with tension. The pack prepared for what awaited them on the ground, each contemplating their role in the upcoming confrontation.

As they landed, the pilot bid them farewell, taking with him a substantial fee for his discretion and services. The pack disembarked, the air on the Swanson estate heavy with a sense of foreboding. The familiar sights of the home were both comforting and haunting, a stark reminder of the battles fought and the losses endured.

Stanley took a deep breath, addressing the group, "We don't know what awaits us, but we face it together. Let's secure the grounds and be ready for whatever Sirtimi has planned."

The pack, with varying degrees of apprehension and determination, set out to reclaim their territory and face the challenges that lay ahead. Jeremia, back at Nasa Bay, watched the departing jet disappear into the distance, wondering what fate awaited them all.

S.K. Ballinger

A LEGEND BORN

Sheree nodded in understanding, her eyes reflecting a mix of sympathy and determination. "We stand with you, Stanley. The battles have taken a toll on us all, but if there's a chance for peace, it's worth fighting for."

As they made their way towards the main building, Caleb and Zanth joined the group, their expressions reflecting a mix of relief and anxiety. The news of Gravakus returning with Stanley's necklace had already circulated among the werewolves, fostering a cautious hope.

Caleb spoke up, "We heard about Gravakus. Hard to believe, but if he's on our side now, it changes the game. What's the plan, Stanley?"

Stanley took a moment, his gaze sweeping over the assembled werewolves. "Our goal is to secure the grounds and ensure the safety of everyone here. The fight between Sirtimi and me is inevitable, but we need to protect our pack and this home."

The news of Sirtimi's impending challenge had spread, drawing werewolves from different areas. The atmosphere was charged with anticipation and anxiety, the air thick with the scent of supernatural beings preparing for a showdown.

As they approached the main hall, where Stanley had faced Sirtimi before, a somber silence fell over the group. The memories of the previous encounter lingered, a stark reminder of the stakes involved. Jeremia, Drennan, and Francais, who had been left behind at Nasa Bay, were missed in the moment.

Inside the hall, a makeshift war room was set up. Maps

were spread across tables, detailing the grounds, potential points of attack, and escape routes. Werewolves discussed strategies, ensuring that the defensive measures were in place. Sheree took charge, coordinating the efforts of the gathered pack members.

Meanwhile, Stanley and Gravakus retreated to a quiet corner. Gravakus spoke with a tone of sincerity, "Stanley, this is your fight, but I'll stand by your side. Whatever happens, let's ensure that this war ends tonight."

Stanley nodded, acknowledging the weight of the impending confrontation. The atmosphere in the hall was a mix of tension and determination, as the werewolves prepared for the culmination of a long and arduous war.

The gathered werewolves listened intently to Stanley's words, a palpable sense of respect emanating from the crowd. Sheree, Caleb, and Zanth stood by his side, a united front representing the Swanson breed. The weight of the impending battle hung in the air as Stanley continued addressing the diverse assembly.

"I've seen the toll this war has taken on our kind, and I'm responsible for sparking it," Stanley confessed, his voice carrying the burden of guilt. "I won't hide from the consequences, and tonight, I face Sirtimi to end this conflict. Win or lose, a new era begins. If I fall, I implore you all, let the cycle of vengeance end with me. The unity of our breed is more important than any single life."

The werewolves responded with nods of understanding and murmurs of agreement. Many understood the significance of this moment – a chance for reconciliation or a decisive end to the conflict. Stanley's humility and honesty resonated with them, and his call for unity struck a chord.

As the crowd dispersed, preparing for the upcoming battle, Gravakus approached Stanley. "You've earned their respect, Stanley. Facing your mistakes takes courage. Tonight, we'll end this."

Stanley nodded, grateful for Gravakus's support. The bond between them had evolved, and Gravakus had proven himself an ally in this quest for resolution.

The moon rose high in the sky, casting an ethereal glow over the Swanson plantation. The atmosphere was charged with anticipation as the werewolves made their final preparations. Sheree and her brothers ensured that defensive measures were in place, collaborating with the united werewolf pack.

Meanwhile, in a secluded area, Stanley donned his ancestral werewolf form. The transformation was a ritualistic process, symbolizing the gravity of the impending battle. Gravakus, standing nearby, offered a few encouraging words, "You're not alone in this, Stanley. We'll face it together."

As they approached the designated battleground, the tension was palpable. The werewolves stood at the ready, eyes fixed on the silhouette of Sirtimi, the highest of the Drakulis, approaching in the distance. The time had come for the final confrontation, a showdown that would determine the fate of their kind and the future of the supernatural world.

Stanley's departure from his home, accompanied by the rhythmic beat of raindrops, carried a weight of somberness. Sheree, Caleb, and Zanth watched him go, their hearts heavy with the knowledge that this might be a farewell.

As Stanley walked through the rain-soaked field towards the designated battleground, Gravakus joined him. The rain intensified, creating a dramatic backdrop for the impending confrontation. Gravakus spoke with conviction, "Stanley, we've come a long way. This battle is not just yours, but a culmination of our shared journey. Whatever happens, we face it together."

Stanley acknowledged Gravakus with a nod, appreciating the solidarity that had formed between them. The bond forged in the face of adversity was evident, and Stanley knew he wasn't alone in this fight.

Meanwhile, Sheree, Caleb, and Zanth returned to the gathering werewolves, ensuring the defensive measures were in place and preparing the pack for the uncertainty that lay ahead. The rain-soaked earth beneath them seemed to absorb the collective tension and anticipation.

As Stanley and Gravakus reached the open field, the rain intensified, turning the landscape into a watery battlefield. In the distance, the silhouette of Sirtimi emerged, a dark figure moving through the storm. The werewolf pack observed from a distance, their howls blending with the symphony of rain and thunder.

Sheree couldn't shake the feeling of unease. Turning to her brothers, she spoke, "We must be prepared for anything. The outcome of this battle will shape the future of our breed."

Caleb nodded, "Let's ensure that the defensive measures are intact. We don't know what Sirtimi might have planned."

As Stanley and Sirtimi closed the distance, the tension reached its peak. The werewolves held their breath, ready for the clash that would determine the fate of their kind. In the midst of the storm, a lone werewolf faced the highest of the Drakulis, each step echoing the gravity of the moment.

The exchange of words between Sirtimi and Stanley echoed across the rain-soaked field, adding a layer of intensity to an already charged atmosphere. The werewolf pack and the vampire horde watched in anticipation as the two adversaries closed the distance, ready to witness the outcome of this long-standing feud.

As Stanley and Sirtimi approached each other, their eyes locked in a fierce gaze, rain cascading down their forms. The tension hung thick in the air, and the werewolves, with bated breath, awaited the clash that would determine the future of their kind.

Sirtimi, his voice dripping with arrogance, continued, "You may have lost much, Stanley Swanson, but the true loss is yet to come. Your children, your legacy, will crumble, and their defeat will be a testament to the futility of your efforts. I will ensure that your bloodline ends with you, a failed protector of a dying breed."

Stanley, undeterred by Sirtimi's taunts, responded with a steely resolve, "You underestimate the strength of my children and the resilience of the werewolf breed. Even if I fall today, others will rise to take my place. Your reign of terror will come to an end, and the Drakulis will be remembered as creatures of the past, defeated by the unity of the supernatural world."

As they continued their verbal sparring, the tension reached its peak. The werewolves, led by Sheree, Caleb, and Zanth, braced themselves for the battle that would determine the fate of their kind. The vampires, though silent, observed with an eerie stillness, awaiting the outcome that could shift the power dynamic between the two ancient species.

The rain intensified, a torrential curtain veiling the impending clash. The field became a battleground where the destinies of werewolves and Drakulis converged. The moment had arrived for the final confrontation, a clash between the last of the Swansons and the highest of the Drakulis.

The atmosphere crackled with anticipation as the intense fight unfolded on the rain-soaked field. The clash between Stanley Swanson and Sirtimi, the highest of the Drakulis, was a spectacle that held the supernatural witnesses in awe.

As the combatants sprinted towards each other, the cheers of the vampires clashed with the resonating roars of the werewolves, creating a symphony of chaos. The ground quivered beneath the collective force of their excitement. The rain continued its relentless downpour, casting a veil over the battleground.

The meeting of claws and fangs created a gruesome dance of blood and violence. Dark blood mixed with Stanley's red oozed into the forming puddles, marking the field as a canvas of their brutal struggle. The combatants moved with astonishing speed, their bodies transitioning between wolf and Drackulis forms in a whirlwind of lethal strikes.

A critical moment arose when Sirtimi, in a momentary lapse, found himself momentarily vulnerable. Stanley capitalized on the opportunity, forcing the Drakulis onto his stomach. As Stanley prepared to deliver a decisive blow, the situation took an unexpected turn.

S.K. Ballinger

In a flash, Sirtimi transformed into a thick fog, causing Stanley to fall through him. The werewolves, witnessing this apparent shift in momentum, were on the verge of intervening. However, Drennan's voice echoed through their minds, reminding them of Stanley's wish to face this battle alone.

Francais reinforced this message, urging the werewolves to trust in Stanley's abilities and honor the breed's code. The vampires, too, held their ground, acknowledging the rules of engagement set by the two adversaries.

The onlookers held their collective breaths, torn between the desire to intervene and the respect they had for Stanley's wishes. The fight, though momentarily disrupted, continued to unfold with an air of uncertainty, leaving the fate of the supernatural world hanging in the balance. The rain persisted, bearing witness to a battle that would determine the future of werewolves and Drakulis alike.

The rain continued to fall relentlessly as Stanley Swanson lay on the rain-soaked field, weakened and wounded by the relentless assault of Sirtimi. The silver daggers, driven deep into his shoulder blades, inflicted excruciating pain on the hellhound, rendering him nearly motionless.

As Sirtimi leaned in, his words were like a venomous whisper, dripping with sadistic pleasure. The silver daggers gleamed in the dim light, each slash a testament to the ancient enmity between werewolves and Drakulis.

"I know Hellhound, it hurts, does it not," Sirtimi taunted. "You no longer have to worry, Swanson, as I wish to not stab you more. These wounds I have made will not heal for some time. It is what makes silver such a marvelous weapon, one we have used since the first treaty was signed. I have brought a rose with me to witness the magnificent power it has against the breed of werewolves. I have been waiting for this moment since I first heard of it."

Stanley, weakened and bleeding, could only listen to Sirtimi's sadistic monologue. The cuts inflicted by the silver daggers refused to heal, leaving Stanley in a vulnerable state. His once powerful growls had now diminished to slow, agonizing moans as he gazed at the gathered werewolves and Drakulis, realizing he had let down his breed.

The werewolves watched in helpless agony, torn between their desire to intervene and their commitment to honor Stanley's request. The vampires, witnessing the unfolding tragedy, observed with cold detachment, reveling in the defeat of their long-time adversary.

The rose, a symbol of the Drakulis' triumph, was brought forth by Sirtimi. Its mystical properties against werewolves were well-known, and Sirtimi seemed eager to witness its effectiveness firsthand. As the rain intensified, washing away the mixture of blood and rainwater, the fate of Stanley Swanson hung in the balance, a poignant moment in the ancient struggle between werewolves and Drakulis.

Stanley's world was a haze of pain, the wounds inflicted by the silver daggers throbbing with every beat of his weakened heart. As Sirtimi cruelly placed the rose in his mouth, the hellhound's acceptance of defeat was evident. The gathered werewolves and Drakulis watched with a mix of dread and fascination, knowing the dire significance of the rose's power.

With the daggers removed, Stanley rolled onto his back,

clutching his stomach in agony. As Sirtimi eagerly awaited the spectacle of the rose's combustion, a surreal moment unfolded before Stanley's eyes. A ghostly image of Julie, his lost wife, manifested beside him. Though her lips moved without producing sound, the message was clear: 'Fight it for your breed, Stanley.'

Julie's ethereal presence vanished, leaving behind a lingering sense of determination in Stanley's heart. Sirtimi, growing impatient, leaned in close to Stanley's face, taunting him with a condescending tone.

"You are here to try and prove something, are you not, beast? I do not have all day as my hunt for your kids is awaiting. Let it go, Stanley."

Stanley, fueled by the fleeting vision of Julie and the unwavering support of his breed, found a renewed surge of strength. With a sudden burst of defiance, he spat the rose out of his mouth, extinguishing its glow. The werewolves roared in support, and even some Drakulis were taken aback by the unexpected turn of events.

Stanley, though weakened, looked Sirtimi in the eyes and spoke with a raspy but resolute voice, "I'll never let it go, and I'll fight for my breed until my last breath."

Sirtimi, momentarily stunned, quickly composed himself and readied for the continuation of the battle, realizing that the war between werewolves and Drakulis was far from over.

The aftermath of Stanley's unexpected and triumphant counterattack left Sirtimi disfigured and incapacitated. The ball of fire, fueled by Stanley's determination and perhaps the lingering presence of Julie, had burned Sirtimi's face to a crisp. The blinded and agonized Drakulis screamed in pain, unable to comprehend the sudden turn of events.

With the injections or his sheer willpower overcoming the rose's effects, Stanley, though still wounded, rose to his feet and approached the suffering Sirtimi. The werewolves' roars of success echoed for miles around as Stanley, with a powerful bite, severed Sirtimi's head, putting an end to the reign of the highest Drakulis.

As the Drakulis and vampires quickly retreated, realizing the need for a new treaty, the werewolves celebrated their victory. Stanley stood amidst the cheers, weak from his injuries but surrounded by over three hundred of his breed, all shouting his name in triumph.

Sheree, pushing through the crowd, placed her head on Stanley's shoulder, conveying her joy and gratitude.

"Let this legend live, which is you. Let all who witness believe what they wish to. Never speak of an antidote that needs not to be mentioned. You have saved us, Stanley."

The werewolves continued to celebrate, embracing their newfound hope and the end of a long-standing conflict. Stanley, though weary, felt a profound sense of accomplishment and the support of his breed who hailed him as a savior. The legend of Stanley Swanson had taken a remarkable turn, and his legacy would be etched in the history of the werewolf lineage.

In the aftermath of the epic battle, Drennan emerged from the celebratory crowd, making his way to Stanley's side. Sheree, alongside Drennan, assisted Stanley back to his house to tend to his wounds. The days that followed were marked by a newfound peace, and the once tumultuous relationship between Drakulis, vampires, and werewolves seemed to shift.

Stanley's legend began to spread among the supernatural community. His unexpected victory over Sirtimi had become the stuff of legends, a tale that resonated across the realms of Drakulis, vampires, and werewolves alike. Whispers of Stanley Swanson echoed through the night, and his name became synonymous with triumph and the potential for unity among the supernatural creatures.

The battles that had plagued their existence for generations seemed to dissipate, replaced by a cautious optimism and a shared acknowledgment of the werewolf who had defied all odds. The once fierce adversaries now spoke of Stanley with a mix of reverence and awe, recognizing the power of his spirit and the symbol of hope he had become.

Stanley's home, once a site of tragedy, transformed into a hub for gatherings and discussions. Representatives from different supernatural factions visited, seeking a way to build a new understanding and forge a lasting peace. The legend of Stanley Swanson served as a catalyst for change, fostering an era where the old grudges and animosities began to dissolve.

Drennan, who had been by Stanley's side throughout the journey, played a crucial role in facilitating these discussions. The vampire's pragmatic approach and his connection with Stanley helped bridge the gap between the Drakulis, vampires, and werewolves. Together, they worked towards a future where the supernatural beings could coexist without the shadow of constant conflict.

As days turned into weeks and weeks into months,

Stanley's legacy endured. The tale of his victory spread far and wide, becoming a beacon of hope for supernatural beings grappling with their own internal conflicts. The legend of Stanley Swanson became a symbol of unity, reminding them that even in the darkest of times, unexpected heroes could emerge to change the course of history.

S.K. Ballinger

LET NOT FORGET

The atmosphere in the Oval Office tensed as the President's attention shifted from his hectic schedule to the urgency conveyed by his aide. Setting aside the stack of papers in front of him, he leaned forward, addressing the intelligence officer.

"What could possibly be so critical about a journal, even if it is from someone recently deceased?" the President inquired, a slight frown etching his face.

The intelligence officer, maintaining a composed demeanor, responded with a sense of gravity. "Mr. President, the contents of this journal detail confidential information about supernatural beings—werewolves, vampires, and Drakulis. It appears to be an eyewitness account of events involving these creatures and their interactions."

The President's eyes widened at the unexpected revelation. He knew the existence of these supernatural entities was a closely guarded secret, but the notion of a detailed journal exposing their activities raised concerns about potential fallout and the need for immediate action.

"I assume you have thoroughly verified the authenticity of this journal?" The President's voice conveyed a mix of skepticism and urgency.

"Yes, sir. Our experts have cross-referenced the information with existing classified data. It aligns with various incidents that have occurred over the years involving these supernatural beings. This journal could significantly impact the delicate balance that has been maintained."

The President took a deep breath, contemplating the implications of such a revelation. "Alright, let me see the journal. But, make sure this information doesn't leak, and have someone reschedule my meeting."

The intelligence officer handed over the carefully sealed package containing Kain Edward's journal. The President, with a sense of caution, opened it and began to read the detailed accounts of supernatural occurrences. As he delved into the pages, the weight of the information became evident, and he realized the potential repercussions on national security.

"This changes everything," the President muttered under his breath, a stern expression replacing his initial skepticism. "We need to assess the extent of this information and formulate a strategy to contain its impact."

The intelligence officer nodded, acknowledging the gravity of the situation. As they delved into discussions about the journal's contents, the President couldn't shake the feeling that this unexpected twist had the potential to alter the course of history, not only for the supernatural beings involved but also for the nation he led.

That is all that would need to be said to the President and the meeting was canceled indefinitely.

In the dimly lit room, shadows played across the worn walls, creating an atmosphere of mystery and secrecy. The only discernible feature was a wheelchair positioned in the center, waiting in quiet solitude. As the minutes ticked by, the room seemed to hold its breath, anticipating the arrival of an unseen presence.

S.K. Ballinger

From the depths of the darkness behind, a pair of hands emerged, confidently grasping the handles of the wheelchair. With a gentle pull, the wheelchair rolled forward, disappearing from the room's limited visibility. The movement was deliberate, suggesting a level of familiarity with the surroundings.

As the chair moved into a more illuminated area, subtle details became apparent. The upholstery was faded, bearing the scars of time, while the wheels creaked softly as they turned. The person in the wheelchair remained concealed, a mystery shrouded in the shadows.

The sound of a door creaking open echoed through the unseen space, allowing a thin stream of light to pierce the darkness. The hands manipulating the wheelchair navigated skillfully through the illuminated patch, revealing only fleeting glimpses of the occupant.

The anticipation grew as the wheelchair continued its journey, weaving through the unseen corridors. The person behind the hands remained hidden, their identity and purpose veiled in secrecy. The half-lit room served as a prelude to a narrative that unfolded in the uncharted territories beyond.

In this enigmatic setting, the wheelchair became a vessel, carrying with it the weight of untold stories and undisclosed intentions. The hands that guided it seemed to wield a certain authority, as if orchestrating a carefully choreographed dance within the shadows.

As the wheelchair moved further away from the dimly lit room, questions lingered in the air. Who was the occupant, and what motivations propelled them into the obscured recesses of this clandestine space? The answers remained elusive, obscured

Stanley Swanson – Breed of a Werewolf

by the deliberate play of light and shadow, leaving the imagination to craft its own narrative around the mysterious figure in the wheelchair.

The End...

Stay tuned for the third installment of the 'Swanson' series titled 'Swanson – The Uprising'

S.K. Ballinger

Please Leave a Review & Feed an Author

Other books by S.K. Ballinger

Sebastian Swanson – Rise of the Lycan
Sirtimi
Uncommon Lust
Mahlistaff
Journey of Kain Edward
Bloodline Chronicles Vol.1
Julie Swanson – Untold
Ainsley
Jade Swanson – A Legend in the Making
We, R Vol.1
We, R Vol.2
We, R Vol.3

DEDICATION

Dewey Fadler
9/13/24 – 8/15/88

Stephen Ballinger
1/3/46 – 10/24/12

Alexis Gingerich
(Lexi Lou)
2/21/02 – 8/27/10

Grandma Nina Fadler

&
Sophia & Amelia Ballinger
7/14/19 – 7/15/19

S.K. Ballinger